CARLY RIFON

The Stay

This book was professionally typeset on Reedsy.
Find out more at reedsy.com

The greatest thing about pain is that you're not dead; keep fighting.

Contents

1

Chapter 1

I've never really had anything good, anything nice in my life. I've had good times, but overall, my life's been pretty rough. I've done things that I didn't want to and I've gone places I didn't want to go. Most of the time this was for my family, but I figured if I could take away their pain, in any way possible, I wouldn't have to watch the people I love suffer.

My name is Iris Dallas Cooke and I was born and raised in Chicago, Illinois. I live with my mom, older brother, Colton and younger sister, Leannah. My dad cheated on my mom when I was seven and left us for her. I haven't heard from him since. Since then, my mom has had all kinds of boyfriends in and out of our lives. Some were good but most were bad. Most of the guys she's dated have been addicts, abusive, lowlifes, creeps, or all the above if we got lucky. She tried to be a good mom, and she loved us all very much but for a while, she just couldn't seem to break her addiction and be the mom she truly was.

There have been several nights where the cops have shown up at our house because Colton had gotten into fights with one of the asshole guys that my mom was dating. Rightfully so, but I hated that my mom kept dating these jerks and Colton kept getting in between them. He shouldn't have had to deal with that, especially at the ages he was. To say the least, it didn't bode well for a healthy mental development. He harbored a lot of rage…*a lot* of rage, he still does but my mom, Leannah, and I were the only ones he would never hurt. Believe me when I say Colton has always been *extremely* protective of us and he wasn't going to let anything happen to us, regardless of how old he was.

Even when my dad was around, we still were dirt poor. I'd always hear my mom and dad screaming and yelling, constantly getting into fights about money and bills. Even though what money we did have, they loved to waste on alcohol, drugs, and cigarettes. I guess I can't be too mad, that's what addiction does. But as a child, it used to make me so mad that my siblings and I would miss out on doing "normal" kid stuff like going on a school field trip due to it. But when my dad left, things only got harder. Some of the guys that my mom dated that weren't assholes would help us out a little bit with money, but the good ones always went quicker than the bad ones. I hated that, but I guess they didn't want to stick around to be a part of our fucked-up life…can't blame them. Sometimes I didn't even want to be a part of it.

Nothing changed when I got older and into my teenage years. We still struggled but I soon discovered The Stay program. The Stay program was something you could apply for if your income was a certain very low amount. From there, as many people in the household, age fourteen and up, could apply to get sent off to live with another family anywhere in the United States for a random amount of time. Only one person from the household would be selected at random to go and during this time, the government would cut that person out of your family's household expenses. The purpose was to help low-income families but also at the expense of having to move away from home for some time. I wanted to help my mom. I wanted to help my brother and my sister. It didn't matter to me where I went or who I lived with because that's just who I was. I was the type of person to go further than I ever should for people just to help. I knew this program could be risky, but I didn't care. All I wanted to do was help.

The day after I found The Stay program, I planned to tell Colton and Leannah. I knew Colton was *not* going to want either Leannah or myself to apply. Leannah was just fourteen, so technically she could, but I knew he was going to throw a fit that either one of us would even consider, and that's basically what happened.

I got Leannah and told her to come with me into Colton's room. I began to tell them about The Stay program and immediately Colton was not a fan of me applying for this, let alone our little sister. He started saying things like, "Iris, are you serious, there's no way I'm letting you go to some random creep's house across the country" and "Why would you even think about letting Leannah apply? She's just a kid, Iris. *You're* just a kid!"

I just kept saying, "Colton, I'm going to be fine. I did the math, and it would really help us out. Think about how much easier it would be on Mom."

"I think Mom much rather struggle with all of us than send one of us away to get kidnapped, raped, or killed!" he exclaimed.

Colton, as I mentioned before, has always been extremely protective of us. He worries about all three of us, but especially about Leannah and me.

"Colton, you can't worry about us forever. We may not even get selected. It's not like you apply and you're automatically going. I want to do this. Mom has struggled all our lives, it's time we do something to fix this. Let's just at least take the idea to her and see how it goes, okay?" I tried to convince.

He kind of gave me a defeated look and said, "Okay."

I asked Leannah how she felt about it, and she said she would go if she got selected. You could tell she was a bit nervous but didn't want to show that and wanted to be strong like we were. She always did that. She always was so brave and strong at times when we knew on the inside she actually was scared. That was just who Leannah was.

We took the idea to our mom, and you could tell she was immediately interested but didn't want to show it. She tried to act like she was concerned that it may be unsafe, and of course, she felt this, but I think she just really needed the extra help and didn't want to shoot down the idea to where we actually wouldn't apply. The look on her face told me everything I needed to know. It was the moment I knew I had to do this, the moment that it didn't matter if I wanted complete outs of this whole plan, I was doing this and there was no turning back.

She agreed hesitantly and Colton, Leannah, and I all filled out the paperwork that was required for the application process. We all put our paperwork in three separate envelopes and put them in the mailbox to be mailed to the appropriate address.

My mom hugged all three of us as she cried. "Thank you, thank you, thank you, I love you all so much," she said as a tear streamed down her cheek.

Colton kissed us all on the head with Leannah and my mom smiling. I smiled too but quickly pulled away from the hug telling them I was going to make us dinner.

I never told anyone, but each night, I prayed that I was the one that got selected to go, not Colton or Leannah. If this was going to happen, I much rather it happen to me than any of my family members.

My prayers must have worked because three weeks later Leannah came running in with the mail.

"Iris, Colton! Come here!" I heard her yell. "There's a letter from The Stay program!"

I was doing Laundry and Colton was in his room. Once we heard her yell, we both scurried into the kitchen where she was. Our mom wasn't home, but we ripped into the letter anyway.

Dear Iris, we are pleased to announce that after reviewing your financial history and required background check, you have been approved to partake in The Stay program.

The letter continued with dates, rules, and other forms to be filled out that were stapled to the back. I didn't see any of that until later because shock had already settled in from seeing my name on that paper saying I was approved. It was real now. Before I was just applying, I didn't think I'd *actually* be approved.

"Oh my God, Iris!" Leannah squealed as she grabbed the letter and kept reading.

"Iris, you okay?" Colton asked, noticing my shell shock.

He always noticed when my mood changed, but I snapped back into reality and tried to play it off. Colton was the last person I wanted to see me nervous because then he would just worry and rethink this entire plan. I mean, it already was hard enough to get him to let me apply in the first place.

"What? Yeah, I'm fine," I forced a smile as Leannah hugged me.

Just then, our mom walked in and before she could even get in the door, Leannah, still full of excitement, was at her feet yelling, "Iris got approved, Iris got approved!"

"What?" my mom asked in disbelief as she put down her bags. "Are you serious?" She walked over to the counter where the letter was resting and picked it up. "Oh my God, Iris, this is amazing!" She hugged me.

I gave a semi-sincere smile. I was excited to finally be able to help my family, I was. But I wasn't excited to leave them. They were *all* I had.

Later that night, I heard a knock on my bedroom door and then it slowly opened.

"Can I come in?" It was Colton.

"Yeah, of course," I said while sitting on my bed, book in hand. "What's up?"

"Are you okay?"

"Yeah, Colton. Why?" I closed my book.

He sat down next to me on my bed, "Because you looked a little shocked when you were reading the papers."

"Colton, I'm fine. I'm just gonna miss you guys, that's all."

Colton nodded his head, "We're gonna miss you too."

I gave a half-smile.

"I just don't want anything to happen to you," he said.

I sighed, moved my book from my lap, and crossed my room.

"What? You're my baby sister, can't a big brother be worried?" he said playfully, trying to enlighten the mood.

"You're always worried," I said coldly while I faced away from him, keeping my gaze fixed outside my window.

Colton sighed as he stood up and came over to me, "Look," he said, getting me to face him. "I promised myself I wouldn't let anything bad happen to you, Leannah, or Mom, and I mean it."

"I love you, Colton, but you can't promise that. You can't always protect us," I faced out my window again.

After a moment, I spoke. "Remember when I was ten years old and Mom's boyfriend punched me in the face for accidentally breaking his favorite whiskey glass while washing it?" I finally faced Colton.

His Adam's apple bobbed as he swallowed his fury. Colton wasn't home that night. Neither was Leannah. My mom was, though she'd taken enough Valium to put a bear down so her ass was out cold in the bathroom.

"There's things in this world that you just can't protect us from. I wish you could, Colton, but you can't."

He pulled his eyebrows together in a tight frown, "I'm gonna try my fucking hardest, Iris. I'll *always* try my hardest."

I looked at him then out the window, "I gotta pack, Colton."

He looked disappointed, "Just be safe, Sis. I love you," he kissed my head.

"Just take care of Leannah and Mom for me please, would you?" I asked.

"Of course." He began to make his way to my door.

"Hey, Colton?"

"Yeah?" He stopped in the doorway, turning around to face me.

"I love you too."

2

Chapter 2

Two days passed and it was now June Twelfth, the day I left. Those last two days that I had with my mom, brother, and sister felt like two minutes. It sucked but I signed up for this, and I was excited to finally lift some of the burdens and struggles off my mom.

The first house I was staying at was in Seattle, Washington. My sheet said there were nine other people scheduled to stay at that house with me. In The Stay program, you didn't just go to one house for your whole stay, you bounced between different houses at random times for random amounts of time. I think they said it's the government's way of monitoring the host and their benefits, something like that anyway.

Everyone was helping me get my couple of bags together and saying goodbye. I was scheduled to take a plane, that's another thing, you're assigned either a plane, bus, or a train to the home you're staying at from your current location. I'm glad they scheduled a plane for me because Chicago to Seattle is a thirty-hour drive; that's a pretty long bus ride.

We all waited by the door for my taxi to pick me up.

"I love you, Iris. Please be careful. I'm going to miss you so much.

Thank you so much for being so brave and considerate of your family," my mom said as she pulled me into a hug and kissed my head.

"I'll see you soon, Sis. I love you so much," Leannah said as she gave me a big hug as well.

"I love you too, Le," I said as I hugged her back. "Be good for Mom and Colton, okay?"

She looked up at me and smiled, "I will."

I smiled and we ended our embrace.

Just then my mom's phone rang. She went into the kitchen to take it, then called Leannah in. Colton and I stood there. I knew he still didn't like the idea of me doing this. Even though he knew I could take care of myself, he wouldn't ever let me.

"Everything is going to be fine," I assured. "Mom and Leannah need you here *way* more than they need me. I'll be home soon."

"Please be careful. Call me if you need anything or want to come home. I'll come get you. I don't care where you are, Iris. I love you," Colton said.

"I love you too, Colton…Thank you."

He pulled me in for a big, long hug. He tried to hide his worried expression, but I still saw it.

My mom and Leannah returned right as the taxi pulled onto our street.

"Okay, well, I guess this is goodbye," I said. "I'll call you guys when I land. I love you all so much."

I pulled them all in for a group hug. We said our final goodbyes and I got into the taxi; life was about to change so, so quickly.

$$3$$

Chapter 3

After I landed, a taxi picked me up and drove me to the house I was staying at. I arrived at the house, and it looked pretty nice on the outside. It was bigger than mine and in the suburban area of Seattle. I lived in a small two-story home but before that all I ever knew were apartment complexes and motels. Always in the worst parts of the city too. So, so far this house was something I wasn't used to.

After getting my bags out of the trunk, I walked up the steps to the door and rang the bell. Soon, a middle-aged, thin-lipped woman with long pink fingernails and blonde hair that was clipped up, appeared.

"Oh, hello, sweetie! You must be with The Stay program? I'm Susan! What is your name?"

Her personality bubbled as she flashed me a wide, straight-toothed smile.

"Yes, I'm with The Stay," I handed her my papers. "And my name is Iris," I said. "Iris Cooke."

"Iris, well that is just a beautiful name! Sweetheart, come on in."

"Thank you, ma'am."

She took my bags and walked me into her home.

"You can just have a seat on the couch as we wait for the rest of the group to arrive," she said.

"Alright," I smiled. "Thank you."

I walked into the living room where six other people were already seated. I gave a small smile and joined them.

No one said anything to one another. We all just watched people slowly, one by one, come into the living room. We waited about an hour for the final person to arrive and with her, followed Susan.

"Okay, hello, everyone! It is a pleasure to have you all," she gleamed.

She went on introducing herself, how it was only her that lived there, and so forth. We were all exhausted though from traveling so getting talked at wasn't something any of us were particularly in the mood for. She handed out the papers that had our room numbers on them and excused us to go unpack and make ourselves at home.

I unfolded the piece of paper and saw that I was in room number seven. I got my things and went to find the room. Once I did, I noticed there were two other girls already there.

"Hi," I said, flashing a smile. "I'm Iris, I guess your guys' roommate."

"Oh cool," the one girl said with a smile. "I'm Bianca."

She had shoulder-length dirty blonde hair and green eyes. She wore jean shorts, a tight low-cut tank-top with a lace bralette underneath, and white flip flops.

"Hey," the other girl said dryly, seeming uninterested in me. "I'm Melanie."

She had dark brown—basically black—hair, was about five-seven, and wore jean shorts and a T-shirt.

"Where are you guys from?" I asked as I walked in and parked my suitcase.

"I'm from Santa Ana, California," Bianca said as she had her suitcase sitting on the bed closest to the door, unpacking shirts and putting them into drawers.

"Oh, nice."

"How about you?" Bianca asked.

"I'm from Chicago."

"Oh, awesome," Bianca said.

I smiled, "How about you, Melanie?"

"I'm from Rhode Island," she answered as she sat on her bed that was farthest from the door, leaving the middle bed for me.

"Rhode Island? Wow, that's pretty far from Seattle," I said to her.

"Yeah," she responded, "I've been gone for a year and eight months now, so I've gotten used to being away from home."

Bianca chimed in, "Wow a year and eight months? Really? I've only been gone for five months."

Melanie then landed her gaze on me, "How about you?"

"Uh, this is actually my first night," I answered unsurely, not particularly wanting to disclose that.

"No way," Bianca said. "I haven't stayed with someone who this was their first night, that's really cool."

"Yeah," I answered dully.

"How old are you?" Melanie questioned in a cold way.

"Sixteen, you?"

"Twenty," she said. There were remnants of pride and smugness laced into her tone.

"Oh, cool," trying to ignore it. "How about you, Bianca?"

"I'm nineteen. Just turned nineteen two months ago actually," she flashed a large grin.

"Oh, well, happy belated birthday."

"Thanks," another large, egotistical grin spreading across her face.

I frowned slightly but turned to grab my suitcase and heave it onto the unclaimed remaining bed—my bed.

The rest of the night passed with us making simple small talk, somewhat getting to know each other better. Soon after, we all went off to bed.

4

Chapter 4

The next morning, Susan called us all downstairs to discuss the rules of the program. She began to tell us that we are free to roam around Seattle and to come and go as we please. She also stated that the program has a midnight curfew and to please not break that, as that is one of the strictest rules that the program instills. She carried on with typical rules of no fighting, no drama, no partying, and so forth. She warned us that if rules were to be broken, she has every right to contact the program and they can send us home. Where the program can revoke all the benefits our families have earned.

After she discussed all of this with us, she made a huge brunch. It was delicious to say the least. There were pancakes, eggs, French toast, hash browns, fruit, and so much more that I can't even remember it all. It wasn't until after I got my fair share of delectables that I wandered back to my room to call my family.

"Hey, everybody," I said on my beat-up, old iPhone four, that was given to me by my mom's ex-boyfriend. His name was Blake, and he was one of the decent ones. He actually bought all four of us iPhone fours.

"Iris! I miss you," I heard Leannah yell.

"I miss you, Le!"

"Hi, baby, how are you making out in Seattle?" my mom asked.

"I'm good, so far everything is going well. I have two roommates, Melanie and Bianca, and they seem okay," I said.

"That's awesome, baby. I'm glad it's going well so far."

"Hey, Sis, didn't forget about me, did you?" Colton asked playfully.

"No, no how could I forget about the best big brother ever?" I teased back.

Colton laughed only to be cut off by my sister's excitement.

"Iris! I got an A on my science final!"

"That's amazing, Sis. I'm so proud of you! When does school end?" I asked.

"June third."

"Oh, so not too much longer and you'll be in high school with Colton," I said.

"Yeah and you! Aren't you so excited?!" she asked joyfully

I was. I was really looking forward to us all being in high school together. That was before I applied for The Stay program. Now, without knowing how long I'd be away for, I wasn't sure if I'd make it back before Colton graduated, giving us the chance to do so. He was eighteen so he should have been a senior and graduating this year but since he started school late due to my parent's negligence and more importance of drugs, he was a year old for his grade. He didn't seem to mind it though. Colton may be short tempered but he tried to choose the hills he died on. I'll give him that much. Still the thought— the feeling of missing out on being with my siblings—turned on the faucet of sadness; taking me right down the drain.

"Hey, you still there?" Leannah asked after I hadn't said anything.

"Yeah, yeah, I'm still here. Sorry, there was someone outside," I lied.

"Oh, okay, no worries," she answered.

Colton remained quiet, probably not believing my bullshit.

"Well, I love you, baby…Thank you, again," my mom chimed in, sincerity weaved into her voice.

"Of course, Mom. There isn't anything I wouldn't do for you guys," weaving my own words the same. "I'll talk to you all soon?"

"Alright, baby," my mom said.

"Bye, Iris. I love you," Leannah said.

"I love you, Leannah. I love you, Colton."

"I love you more, Sis."

I hung up the phone letting out a sigh.

A couple of moments later, Melanie walked in.

"Hey Bianca and I are going to go take a drive and see what's around here, want to come?"

"Yeah, I'd love to…How do you have a car here?" I asked.

"I don't, it's Bianca's. She's been driving to all her homes. I don't know how she got away with that, but her car's here," she said.

"Damn, that's crazy. Is the program paying for her gas?" I asked.

"Fuck no, that's probably why they let her because they aren't paying for it."

"Hm, she must be doing something extra to be able to afford that much gas. I know back home, I share an old 1990 Honda Civic with my mom and brother, and we three-way split the hundred-dollar insurance. I can't imagine driving around the country and having to pay for gas, I'd never make it," I said.

"I guess the program gives you the option to either drive your own car at your own expense or get free transportation and have no car. But let's be real, most of us in this program don't even own a car," she said. "And I think we all know what that 'something extra' exactly is," she joked.

I frowned at her negative and insulting comment. Choosing to ignore it, I grabbed my purse. "You ready?"

"Yeah, let's go."

5

Chapter 5

We drove around Seattle for a few hours, seeing what our new, temporary home had to offer. After some time, we pulled off into the parking lot of a little diner as we were all pretty hungry.

Walking in, I saw two guys in their early thirties sitting at the bar top. You could tell they were bikers because of their all-black leather get-up and the most obvious fact, the two Harley-Davidsons parked out front. We sat down in a booth about twenty feet away from them. The waitress brought us menus and some water. Melanie and I began to look at the menus to decide what to eat, but Bianca was too busy twirling her hair and biting her lip at the biker guys. Melanie and I noticed this and exchanged equal facial expressions of *what the fuck*.

"Uh, Bianca? Can you stop the guy gawking for one minute and decide what you want to eat? I'm hungry," Melanie said with agitation.

I just sat there, observing the situation.

"You guys want our meals for free or what?" Bianca hissed back at Melanie.

"The fuck you talking about?" Melanie snapped.

"Look, I know you two girls just met me, but I guess there's something you both should know." Bianca went on, "I've been extremely poor my whole life. My dad died when I was an infant, so when I was a little girl, my mom constantly had men in and out of my house for a couple of hours at a time. Being young, I never understood what was happening until I got older. When I was fourteen, I figured out what she was doing and that's when I naturally followed in her footsteps. Ever since I've been sleeping around with people and prostituting myself to make ends meet. It's like second nature to me and doesn't bother me anymore. I know, it's truly a sickness, a disease, but this is what I've been doing for almost five years now. That's how I got my car. The only reason I'm here is because my mom *finally* started dating a guy that cares about us and when he found out what I've been doing, he thought making me apply for this program and shipping me away would fix me. But clearly, it's not. I just do what I do and that's all there is to it."

There was a pause.

"Bianca, you know you don't have to do that anymore. Your mom and her boyfriend are gonna receive benefits that will really help you guys," I said caringly.

Melanie scoffed after I said this. I looked at her with a frown, not knowing why she did that.

"Look, I didn't tell you guys this to try to go all "Doctor Phil" on me. I told you so you guys are aware. Just let me do my thing, and don't stand in my way and we won't have any issues. Now, if you excuse me, I'm going to go get our dinners for free." Bianca got up, walked over to the two men, and sat down with them.

Melanie rolled her eyes and shook her head in frustration, "She's pathetic."

I shot her a harsh look. Seconds later, we both watched Bianca string her arm over the one man and rub his back.

"It's sad," I said, staring at the broken and warped teenage girl.

I watched Bianca for a moment as I thought about Leannah. Leannah's fourteen. That's like her going out and sleeping with men twice her age to bring home money. That thought made me shiver.

"Uh, hello?" the waitress asked. "Do you know what you want to eat?"

"Oh, I'm sorry," I said, not realizing I had spaced out. "Uh, I'll just have a turkey club, please."

She scribbled on her notepad. "And for your uh, friend?" she asked in disgust as she looked over at Bianca who was now kissing on the grown man's neck while he laughed.

"Uh, she's okay. She's not, uh, hungry…thank you," I said as I embarrassingly closed the menu and handed it to her.

She scribbled some more, "Okay, that'll be out shortly." She grabbed the menus, closed her notepad, and popped a gum bubble.

Bianca soon came back over with the man. "Girls, this is Gordon. Gordon, this is Melanie and that's Iris."

"Hello," I muttered.

Melanie flashed an obvious fake smile.

"Iris…that's a cool name," Gordon said.

"Thanks."

"Gordon is going to take me on a ride really quick on his bike. Is that ok with you, guys?"

Like she was *really* asking our permission.

Melanie chimed in, full of bitter venom, "Sure, why not?"

Bianca frowned; part annoyance, part confusion. She then looked at me.

"Just don't be too long, okay? It's already starting to get dark. We should get back to Susan's soon."

A grin spread across her face, "I won't."

Hours of waiting were filled by an awkward silence and occasional slick remarks made by Melanie about Bianca. She was fuming that Bianca hadn't come back yet. We tried calling her, but we got a voicemail every time. I hoped everything was okay, but I figured she was just being inconsiderate of us. The waitress and two other employees that were working that night began cleaning the diner as it was about to close.

"She needs to get her ass back here, this is humiliating!" Melanie hissed. "We finished eating two hours ago, if she knew she was going to be this long, she should've left us the fucking keys so we could at least go wait for her in her car. I feel like a ten-year-old waiting for mommy to pick me up. Not to mention that the staff probably hates us."

"I know, I know," I sighed. "I'll just pay for everything so we can go wait outside. At least that way we won't be in anyone's way anymore."

As I was getting out my money, we heard the roar of a motorcycle and lights that soon broke the darkness that was surrounding the outside. All five of us—Melanie, the waitress, the two employees, and I—all watched as Bianca hopped off the bike and took off her helmet. She wrapped her hands around Gordon's neck for a final kiss then in she walked. All the employees were pissed.

"I'm so sorry," she said to everyone as she pulled out money from her bra and handed it to our waitress.

The waitress gave her a very cold and disgusted look.

"Let's just go," Melanie shot up from the booth and stormed towards the door, giving it a solid shove once she got to it.

"I'm so sorry," I mouthed to the waitress—who no longer wanted anything to do with us—as I trailed after Melanie.

After being at the diner for three hours and spending ninety-five percent of it waiting on Bianca, she unlocked the car door and we all got in. Melanie was so angry; if this were a cartoon, smoke would have come out of her ears.

"I'm so, so, sorry, guys. I am. I lost track of time, I never meant to make you both wait so long," Bianca said, seeming genuine.

Melanie was lethally silent.

I spoke up, "Let's just all go home, okay? It's almost past our curfew."

I tried not to seem too annoyed and keep the peace, but I was pretty aggravated.

We finally arrived back home right before curfew struck. The house was dead silent, and all lights were off, everyone must have been asleep. We all went straight to our rooms, without saying anything to one another. The tension that filled between Bianca and Melanie was unbelievable. We all got ready for bed, getting changed into our pajamas. Bianca, in just her bra and pajama pants, pulled out the remaining wade of cash that was in her bra and placed it on the dresser.

"What did you do, fuck his whole biker gang to get that much?" Melanie snapped. She was waiting to bark something at her.

"I may be a prostitute, but I'm not a cheap one," Bianca said in a snarky tone.

"Nice to know you have a *little* bit of self-respect," Melanie snapped back.

"Is there a problem?" Bianca asked in an agitated tone. "I said I'm sorry, can you just drop it now? I told you not to worry about what I do, just stay out of my business."

"Yeah, and I told you not to take long and you made us wait three fucking hours while you sucked off a stranger!" Melanie yelled at her.

"Come on guys, stop, it's late. Let's all just go to sleep now," I said, trying to mediate.

Being completely ignored, Bianca barked, "Yeah? Well, me sucking off a stranger got your dinner paid for, didn't it, sweetie?!"

"Oh please, I don't need you to pay for my fucking dinner," Melanie growled.

"Stop!" I yelled. "This is ridiculous! Yes, Bianca, you shouldn't have left us for that long, but Melanie, she said she's sorry. We all have to live together and it's not going to be very fun if we're at each other's throats all the time. Just drop it. For fucks sake it's only our first day here!"

They both stared at me defeated. They knew I was right but didn't want to admit it.

I continued, "Melanie, if this is what she does and wants to do, let her, she said she doesn't want us to meddle. And Bianca, if you're going to do this shit, keep us out of it. Alright, now can we just let it go, put it behind us, and call a truce?"

The two of them looked at each other, neither wanting to apologize.

"I'm sorry I made you wait so long," Bianca muttered.

"I'm sorry I blew up on you," Melanie mumbled.

Neither of them seemed genuine, but I was so tired that I really didn't care.

"See that wasn't so hard. Now just go to sleep," I added.

And that's what we all did.

6

Chapter 6

Surprisingly, the next morning there was no tension between the three of us. It's kind of, sort of, like the night never happened. The three of us simply got ready, then ate frozen waffles after we decided we'd go on a walk once we were done.

We exited Susan's house around nine a.m. We walked through Susan's neighborhood and onto the main road. The area wasn't anything special. It was the typical suburban area with grocery stores, gas stations, nail salons, and barber shops. Don't get me wrong, it still was really nice. It also was nice to have a break from the high crime area I lived in back home. There, my views were run down homes, shady characters on each street, and the constant blue and red lights whizzing by. But home's still home.

We had walked for quite some time, actually almost two hours, when I felt a drop hit my arm.

"I think it's starting to rain, guys," Bianca said as she looked up at the sky and held her hand out.

"Oh, yeah." I looked up, noticing the sky darkening, "Well, do you guys wanna go into that coffee shop and wait it out for a little?"

Melanie shrugged, "Sure."

"Yeah, let's do that. I don't want my feet to get all wet anyway," Bianca said.

Melanie exhaled sharply, "I told you to wear sneakers."

Bianca rolled her eyes, "I didn't know it'd rain while we were out."

"Come, let's just go," I said, rolling my eyes.

We crossed the street and entered Lush Coffee. The aesthetic was super naturecore. Vines lined chalkboard walls, stools were in the shape of tree trunks, and fairy lights twinkled above us like stars.

Melanie claimed a high-top against the window while Bianca and I got in line. After claiming our drinks, I noticed that the barista wrote his phone number on my cup. This, to say the least, thrilled Bianca. She wasn't too thrilled though when I told her I couldn't care less, and he wasn't my type.

"You're crazy, he's hot!" Bianca scoffed as we sat down on either side of Melanie.

"Who's hot?" Melanie asked.

"The barista!" Bianca exclaimed "But Iris doesn't think so, *even* after he gave her his number."

Melanie scoffed, "Why don't you call him then? If he's *so* hot."

"That's weird. He didn't give it to me," Bianca frowned.

"Maybe when he finds out what you do, he'll be interested," Melanie snickered.

"Melanie," I scowled with a look of disgust.

Bianca scoffed as she took a sip, focusing on the rain outside. I could tell she was trying her hardest not to snap back at Melanie for that unnecessary comment.

It got quiet for some time after that and we all just hung out for a little, watching the rain.

We arrived back home around noon. It was weird to call that house "home" because it wasn't home; it was a sojourn. Home was back in Chicago with my mom, Colton, and Leannah. I only ever had one "home."

We went to our rooms and began to do our separate things. Melanie laid on her bed and put her earbuds in, Bianca sat on her bed and scrolled through her phone, and I started to finish unpacking. The rest of the day was pretty uneventful, but definitely relaxing.

Around five o'clock, Susan knocked on our door.

"Hi, girls. Sorry to interrupt but are you ladies eating here tonight?" she asked. "I made chicken pot pie and a vegetable pot pie if anyone is vegetarian."

Although I had only met her a couple days ago at this point, I knew Susan was one of the greatest people I'd ever meet. It was just her aura. She was caring and empathetic and had so much love to give to everyone. Everything she did, she did it with all her heart and she went above and beyond to spread happiness and joy in this cold, dark world. She strived to teach us things that our parents, or lack of, never did. She valued manners, respect, and integrity. She was truly someone that I felt blessed to meet and that I'd remember for the rest of my days. She was simply doing this to help the ones that needed it the most, not just for the monthly check like other people I soon met.

"Yeah, I'm good with eating here. Melanie? Iris?" Bianca asked.

"Yeah, I'll have chicken pot pie, thank you," I said.

Melanie said the same.

"Okay great, I will let you know when it's ready!" Susan said happily as she closed the door to leave.

"That woman is too sweet," Bianca said.

"I know, it makes me have hope that there's still good people out there," I said.

"Right?" Bianca agreed.

Just then Bianca's phone rang.

"Shit, I gotta take this," she said as she got up and left our room.

Melanie watched her leave and when Bianca was gone, she scoffed, putting her earbuds back in.

I frowned, "What's your problem with her?"

She didn't hear me, so I spoke again. This time waving my hands. "Hello? Melanie?"

She then took her earbuds out, "What you say?"

"I said, what's your problem with her? Why are you always beating up on her ever since you found out she's a prostitute?"

Melanie scoffed, "It's kinda pathetic."

"You never know what someone is dealing with, Melanie," I said sternly. "And anyway, so is being miserable all the time," I looked at her coldly as I matched all my socks together and put them in the dresser.

Melanie rolled her eyes and put her earbuds back in.

Just then Bianca scurried back into the room. "Hey, can one of you tell Susan I'm not going to be eating here anymore? I'm gonna go out tonight instead."

"Where're you going?" I asked.

"Gordon from the other night just called and asked if I wanted to come to his place," Bianca said as she scrambled to get ready.

"Where's that?" I asked.

"I don't know, Ballard I think he said. It's like fifteen minutes from here. He sent me his address."

"I just want you to be safe, that's all."

"Iris, chill seriously," she said as she stopped right in front of me. "I know what I'm doing, okay?"

Silence as I held her gaze for a moment.

"Bye," she said, pushing past me and closing the door behind her.

Melanie snickered.

I flipped two socks into each other as I looked down. The thing is, Bianca may not have been my friend and I may not have agreed on her prostituting herself, but I still cared about her. I'll always care. It's a blessing and a curse to be this way.

After our amazing dinner, Melanie went back to our room while I decided to hang out in the living room for a little while. I watched TV with some of the other housemates, getting to know them a little. They all seemed decent enough, which was good considering I didn't see Bianca, Melanie, and I becoming BFFs.

Some time later, I headed back to my room to get my things to take a shower.

I turned the water on and let it warm up as my phone buzzed. I laughed to myself as the message was a picture from Colton. He was wearing one of Leannah's old dress-up blue wigs and making a goofy face.

Thinking this may be a new look for me. Does blue suit my skin tone?

I rolled my eyes playfully and texted back: *Looks great, you're destined to find a girlfriend now.*

He texted back three laughing emojis and: *Miss you.*

Miss you too. I'll call you guys tomorrow. I smiled as I put down my phone and stepped into the hot shower.

Once I was done, I headed back to my room. It was now about eight, so I put on my big, short-sleeved T-shirt and sat down on my bed. Melanie had been sitting on her bed too, earbuds in, preoccupied with her phone. The two of us really made no effort to talk. I didn't mind this though.

Around eleven-thirty, our bedroom doorknob turned, and in walked Bianca.

"Hey, guys," she slurred as she stumbled into our room. Clearly drunk.

"Hey," I said.

Melanie pulled out one earbud and stared at her. We watched her stagger to her dresser.

"You good?" I asked.

"Oh yeah, I'm cool. I'm a little fucked up, but I'm fine."

"Did you drive home?" I asked as I sat up on my bed.

She gave me a look like I was the dumbest person in the world. "Are you serious? I may be fucked up, but I know not to drink and drive."

Melanie scoffed. I guess she couldn't believe that she was capable of making responsible decisions.

I sighed and smiled at Bianca, "Alright good, well why don't you get ready for bed? It's late."

"Will you guys come with me to Gordon's tomorrow to get my car?" she slurred as she took one heel off.

"Yeah, sure," I said.

"Speak for yourself," Melanie mumbled as she put her earbud back in, rolling away from us.

Melanie's comment seemed to go unnoticed by Bianca. She smiled, "Thank you, you're like the best ever."

After Bianca got changed and into bed, I pulled the chain on our lamp, letting darkness surround us. As I laid there, staring up at the dark ceiling, I thought about all the nights my mom would come home obliterated. This was before she got hooked on pills. Colton and I, and sometimes Leannah, would have to take care of her and clean up the messes she made. Whether those messes were fixing the neighbor's flower bed because she was driving drunk and ran over them or cleaning up her facial wounds because she got into a fight at the bar or a party she was at. And having to get Bianca's car the next morning reminded me of all those little messes my mom would create that my siblings and I would have to fix. Of course, I was glad Bianca didn't drive drunk, I'd do anything to prevent that. But I guess when you deal with something for so long your mouth gets filled with a sour taste surrounding anything that has to do with it, and picking up this girl's car, that I barely knew, left my mouth feeling bitterly sour.

7

Chapter 7

In the morning, I woke up, had some coffee, and called my family. Mom had the morning shift, so only Colton and Leannah were around. I told them about Bianca and Melanie—how Bianca's an egotistical prostitute and Melanie's a miserable and pessimistic bitch. They were surprised to say the least. I told them how Bianca got drunk the night before so the three of us were going to get her car today. This led to Colton's rapid fire "Are you sure that's a good idea?" "He's how old?" "Iris, please be safe, okay?" I assured him everything would be and got off the phone. I took the granola bar Susan offered me and headed back upstairs.

"Where's my pink rhinestone hairbrush?" Bianca asked as she rifled through her drawers. "Iris, did you take it?"

I walked over to the trashcan and threw out my granola bar wrapper. "No Bianca, I didn't take your hairbrush."

"Watch out, she's already accused me of it," Melanie said, glaring at Bianca.

"Yeah, because you don't like me," Bianca fired back.

"Congrats, you pointed out the obvious! Step right up to pick out your prize!" Melanie sniped.

I rolled my eyes, "Melanie, shut up. Do you have another hairbrush, Bianca?"

"Yeah, I do. I'll find the pink one later," she said with a huff as she stood up, closing her drawers. "Are you gonna still come get my car with me?"

"Yeah, I gotta get ready first and all though," I said.

She smiled, "Thank you. Melanie? Are you coming?"

She frowned, ready to say something sarcastic but then quickly scoffed and changed her expression to a grin. "You know I might as well see where this dude lives. I got nothing else better to do anyway."

"Aw you can just admit you want to hang out with me so bad," Bianca mocked with a grin.

Melanie scoffed, "Yeah, you're right. It's not every day I get to see a prostitute's life up close and in person!"

"Stop," I interjected. "You both are seriously so annoying," I then grabbed my toothbrush and headed to the bathroom.

After I finished getting dressed and doing my makeup, the three of us made our way to the closest bus stop.

"Thank God we're here," Bianca sighed with relief as we approved the bus stop's bench.

"Oh my God," Melanie rolled her eyes. "It was like a two minute walk!"

I hit the *end* button on my phone's GPS and put my phone into my jeans pocket.

"And?" Bianca asked.

Melanie scoffed and pulled out her phone, putting her earbuds into her ears.

A moment later, Bianca said to me, "Thanks again, Iris."

I smiled slightly, "No problem."

She looked off into the street at all the cars passing by.

"So," I turned to her after a moment. "Why did you want us to come? It's not like you *needed* us to. Like, it's not like you needed one of us to give you a ride."

She shrugged, "I don't know. Company, I guess."

I nodded my head and looked at the cars in the street as well.

The bus pulled up ten minutes later. We got on, paid our fare, and took our seats.

The bus pulled away and we began traveling down the road. Ten minutes passed, then twenty minutes passed, then thirty minutes passed. I knew Ballard was not that far from Susan's, so I knew something was off. I looked at Melanie who was still on her phone, ignoring the world and Bianca had her eyes closed. I pulled out my phone and opened the map. It showed my little icon traveling down into South Seattle, way past Ballard at this point.

"Bianca," I shook her. "Did we miss our stop? We're past Ballard," I showed her my phone and a look came across her face, which told me everything I needed to know. Gordon didn't live in Ballard.

"Bianca, where are we going?" I asked sternly.

"Okay, fine! I'm sorry! Gordon doesn't live in Ballard. He lives in Beacon Hill."

"Beacon Hill?" I asked as I typed it into my phone to see where that was. Judging by the sound of her voice and the look on her face, I knew it wasn't close. "Bianca! That's another hour from here!"

"Oh my God," Melanie scoffed as she slumped back in her seat with her arms crossed.

"You told me last night he lives in Ballard," I said.

"I thought he did!" she exclaimed, trying to proclaim her innocence. "When I got in my car and clicked on the address he sent me, I realized it said Beacon Hill instead."

"How do you get Ballard and Beacon Hill mixed up?" Melanie hissed as she sat back up quickly, looking past me at Bianca.

I looked at Melanie then back at Bianca, "Why didn't you tell us this morning it was Beacon Hill that we needed to go to, not Ballard?"

"I don't know, I guess I thought you guys wouldn't come if you found out it was an hour and a half bus ride."

I sighed, "Bianca, you can't just lie to people," I said somewhat frustrated that she didn't tell us the correct place.

"Do you think we're stupid and wouldn't realize we'd been sitting on the bus for an hour and a half. I know we don't know the area, but we can tell fucking time," Melanie sniped.

Bianca sighed, "I'm sorry."

"Whatever," Melanie scoffed as she slammed back into her seat, replacing her earbuds.

"You know no one asked you to come!" Bianca barked, quickly changing her demeanor from upset to angry.

"Actually!" Melanie growled as she sat forward, one earbud in her ear, "*You* fucking asked!"

"Stop!" I yelled. "Are you too capable of getting along for five fucking minutes?! Seriously?! It's pathetic."

I slumped back into my seat and let out a huff.

"Iris, I'm—" Bianca started.

I put my hand up, "Stop. Let's just get to Beacon Hill and get your car," I said agitatedly.

Melanie huffed and sat back.

Bianca sat back softly and the three of us sat in silence for the rest of the bus ride.

8

Chapter 8

"Okay," I exhaled. "Where to from now?" I said as the bus doors closed and pulled away.

"He lives in this neighborhood," Bianca pointed to the street that was East Locust Street.

"Oh," I was taken by surprise because I figured with this girl, we'd have to walk another half an hour or something. "Okay, cool."

The three of us crossed the street and began walking down the road into the neighborhood.

"Here—turn here," Bianca said as we approached the first left we could take. It was a street called Landers Avenue.

We walked a couple more minutes down the road when I could see Bianca's car sitting in the driveway of a yellow painted house. The yard appeared to be in disarray.

"There's his house," Bianca pointed at the home.

We walked a couple more feet down the sidewalk, finally making it to his house. We climbed up the couple of concrete stairs and rang the doorbell.

"Oh hey, baby," Gordon said as he opened the door wearing only a pair of jeans. "Come on in."

Bianca flashed her large grin, though this time it seemed fake. Bianca entered the home, then Melanie, then me.

"I didn't know you were bringing your friends," Gordon said with a smile. He kind of disgusted me.

"Yeah well, they aren't really my friends but I came to get my keys. You have them right?"

Gordon stood up from the couch's arm he had been leaning on and went into the kitchen. He returned moments later but not with keys in his hand; rather a can of beer.

"Why the rush? Don't you guys want to hang out?" he smirked at me while he took a slug of the beer.

"No," I said sternly. "She wants her keys, and we want to go. We didn't know you lived this far away anyway."

"Oh, I'm sure it's not *that* far," he took another sip of his beer.

"Well, it doesn't matter. Just give Bianca her keys."

He then scoffed.

I looked at Melanie who was just standing there and then at Bianca, nudging her with my eyes to do something.

"I'll be back over soon, Gordon. We really do gotta go now," Bianca said, almost pleading.

"Hey, what's all the noise—" a man about five to ten years younger than Gordon came walking down the stairs. He cut himself off mid-sentence when he saw us three standing there. He then smiled, "Who are you pretty ladies?"

I rolled my eyes and exhaled sharply.

"Logan, this is my girl, Bianca and her two uh—" he didn't know what to call us since Bianca labeled us as "not her friends." "Iris and Maggie."

"Melanie!" Melanie growled.

"Oh, Melanie," Gordon said.

I snickered seeing how annoyed it made her.

"Nice to meet you two," he smiled creepily at us. I knew we had to leave at this point.

"Can we just have the keys?" Melanie asked, growing impatient.

"What keys?" Logan asked as he also got a beer from the refrigerator.

"Oh, just the keys to my girl's car. They wanna leave right now but I'm telling them to stay awhile and hang out with us," he then pushed Bianca's hair behind her ear.

Logan came walking back into the living room, "Yeah, why don't you guys stay a while, it'll be fun."

At this point, Gordon had his arm around Bianca who didn't seem like she liked it much and Melanie and I were standing next to each other by the staircase. I was closest to the railing.

"Look, we're not into 'fun.' We just came to get Bianca's car and to go back home," I said.

"Well sometimes plans change," Logan said as he came over to me and brushed my hair behind my ear.

"Don't touch me," I hissed as I shoved his chest.

He laughed as he took another sip from his beer.

"Alright look," Melanie said sternly with her hands out. "You guys either give us the keys right now or we're gonna call the cops."

They both laughed.

"Prostitution is illegal in the state of Washington, baby," Gordon said to Melanie. "You call the cops, your little "friend" or whatever the hell y'all are, goes to jail," he said as he held Bianca tighter. "And I know the little program y'all are in wouldn't like that either."

Melanie and I looked at each other with anger. We knew he was right, but we couldn't show him that.

"Yeah, well so is grand theft and kidnapping," I stated.

Logan choked on his beer from laughing at me.

"Grand theft and kidnapping, okay," they both mocked.

I frowned at them then looked past Logan into the kitchen. Something caught my eye. It was a big red, rhinestone heart. It was sitting on the counter that was furthest from us. I recognized the heart from two nights ago when we were in Bianca's car. I remember that big, obnoxious, heart dangling off her keys when they were in the ignition. There was no way I would be able to grab them without getting past Logan as he was standing in the door frame that led into the kitchen. So, I tried something else. Something I really, really didn't want to do, but knew I had to.

"You know what?" I turned my back on the two men and Bianca so that I was now only facing Melanie. I mouthed the words "the keys" to her and nudged my head to the right. She instantly knew what I was saying as I saw her look past me and spot the keys. I slowly turned back towards everyone else as I approached Logan, making it seem like I was just slyly walking over to him.

"You're right, we can stay and hang out a little," I rubbed Logan's chest forcing myself to be flirty instead of what I really was—repulsed.

A disgusting, large grin spread across his face as he set down his beer. I continued rubbing on his chest and giving him flirty looks. I looked over at Bianca who was staring at me like she had no clue as to what just possessed me. But with one right glare, she instantly knew my plan and began to do the same to Gordon.

"Yeah, you're right we can stay and hang out," Bianca smiled as she started kissing his neck.

I swallowed hard then began kissing on Logan's neck as I pushed him out of the doorframe and onto the couch. He took this opportunity to find my lips with his and when we began making out, it took every ounce in me to not gorge out his eyes. Bianca was still kissing on Gordon when I heard Melanie quietly scurry into the kitchen and grab the keys off the counter. I heard her come tiptoeing past us then once at the door she yelled, "Run!"

Bianca and I ripped away from the men and took off behind Melanie. The three of us bolted down the cracked concrete stairs and threw ourselves into Bianca's car.

The men came out, chasing us and almost catching us before we could close and lock our doors. Bianca threw it into drive, and we took off down the street. I looked back and saw the men run out into the street angrily as they wailed their arms and screamed vulgarly.

"Holy shit," Melanie exhaled. "Good thinking, Iris," she patted my arm from the back seat.

I rolled down Bianca's window and angrily spit out of it. I wiped my lips with my hands and spit again. I was trying to get the taste of that disgusting man off me.

"What the fuck was that?!" I yelled at Bianca, completely ignoring Melanie's compliment.

"I'm sorry!" Bianca shouted. "I've never seen Logan before in my life!"

"He wasn't the only one," I said coldly as I spit out the window again.

"I didn't know Gordon was going to act like that. I'm sorry, guys. I really, really am," Bianca pleaded.

"That's 'cause you don't fucking know him, Bianca!" I yelled.

"I-I—"

"Do you understand how bad that could have been?" I said. "It could have been *so* fucking bad," I spit out the window again.

"I'm sorry, I'm sorry, guys. I know, I keep messing shit up—"

"No!" I yelled, cutting her short. "You keep doing shit for yourself! You have been since we met you three days ago. It all started at that fucking diner and making us wait. Then today not telling us where we'd go 'cause you think we wouldn't want to go with you still. THEN, putting our lives at risk with those fucking perverts!"

I slammed back in my seat, taking a moment to breathe, "Don't lie and drag us into this shit ever again. You're already playing an away game with Melanie don't lose the one fucking person here that's on your side."

Silence so heavy you could feel it fell over the car. We traveled back to Susan's without saying a word to one another. That bitter taste flooded my mouth and I was so angry. It made me think of some of my mom's nauseating ex-boyfriends whose eyes linger on Leannah or me for too long. I felt disgusting and like a used prop. And I was nobody's fucking prop.

9

Chapter 9

The first thing I did when we got back to Susan's was storm up the stairs—ignoring everyone's stares— and went into the bathroom. I got in the shower and began to scrub myself from head to toe. I scrubbed my lips so hard I felt like there was no more skin left on them, but I didn't care. I wanted that forty-year-old freak off me. I still felt his hands on my butt and waist and the longer I thought about it, the sicker I grew.

Not wanting to spend time in our room after my shower as Bianca and Melanie were in there, I watched TV in the living room with two other housemates, Alisha and Tobey. Alisha was sky-scraper tall, had long ombre hair, and wore glasses. Tobey was quite tall as well with light brown hair and freckles. They both were twenty.

"Hey, guys, dinner is ready if you want to eat," Susan said to us after a couple hours. "I made pizza and salad!"

"You *made* pizza?" Tobey asked impressively.

"Yes! I made meat lover's, spinach and mushroom, pepperoni, and of course, cheese!" she exclaimed happily, per usual.

"That sounds amazing, Susan," Alisha said, standing up and towering over her.

"Yeah, it does, thank you!" I said as I stood up as well.

Susan smiled really big, "Well come on now!"

The three of us followed Susan's lead into the kitchen and began serving ourselves pizza and salad. The rest of the housemates trailed in, including Melanie, and after a beat, Bianca.

"This is really good, Susan," Tobey said as he took another bite of his meat lover's pizza.

"Thank you," she smiled.

"Yeah, it is, thank you," I said. I chose the spinach and mushroom kind, I didn't eat red meat, never have. I just didn't like it.

"I'm glad you all enjoy it."

We continued eating and once we were finished, we helped Susan clean up. Bianca, Melanie, and I then went back to our room.

It was a little past eight now. For the past two hours, we just hung around, somewhat doing our own things like typical when we heard a knock on the door.

"Come in," Bianca called from her bed.

The doorknob twisted and in Susan walked. "Hey, girls, how are you doing?"

"Good," Bianca and I said in unison.

I put my phone down, waiting to see what she had to say. I felt like this had something to do with how we acted coming into her house earlier.

"How do you guys like Seattle? Have you ever been here before?" she asked.

I shook my head. Melanie just now took one earbud out and acknowledged Susan.

"Nope never been," Bianca said.

"I like it so far though," I added.

"Oh well that's good," she smiled. "A lot different from Chicago, huh?"

I was caught off guard that she remembered where I was from. "Yeah, it is," I smiled.

"Good," Susan smiled, flashing her pearly white teeth.

She then walked over to Bianca's vanity and sat down in the chair. "So, earlier, I noticed when you three walked in you all looked very upset, very angry. Especially you, Iris," she met my eyes, but I quickly looked away. "I just wanted to come see what that was about, if you want to share of course, and if you guys are okay."

The three of us looked at one another, not really knowing what to say. Melanie looked away quickly.

"Uh, yeah. We're all fine," I said, taking the lead. "Just typical teenage girl things and being away from home, that's all."

Bianca looked at me and smiled, thanking me for not telling the truth. I smiled then looked away.

"Okay, I understand," Susan said.

I knew she was unconvinced that this was the truth but didn't want to push.

"You know you guys can talk to me about anything, anytime you need to," she smiled but spoke earnestly.

"Thanks, Susan, we know," I smiled.

Susan stood up from the chair. She walked to the door then stopped. "You know, some advice my mother gave me when I was a teenager that really stuck with me was about crazy eyes."

We all looked up at her.

"She told me, you can always tell if someone is crazy, meaning they have ill intentions, are bad people, malicious, and so forth, if they have crazy eyes. There's not a perfect description as to what "crazy eyes" really look like, but it's just something you know when you see them. Maybe they're big and wide-like or small like pinpoints. Maybe it's how they look at you, or maybe they're just simply piercing, in an evil or beautiful way. You've heard eyes are the window to the soul? Well, my mother fully believed this. She believed what you saw in someone's eyes is what their soul and their insides—what their personality encompassed. She always told me that the eyes will never lie to you and to really pay attention to what you see." She grabbed the doorknob, "Just something I wanted to share with you three," she smiled then exited the room.

I looked down as those words hit me like a ton of bricks. I looked over to Melanie, who couldn't care less about Susan's words as she put her earbud back in, then over to Bianca, who didn't understand a word of what she said. But I did, I understood it perfectly and as I laid down on my back, staring up at the ceiling, I thought about it over, and over, and over again. I had seen those very eyes she was talking about, before. And she was right, they *never* lied.

10

Chapter 10

Around noon the next day, the three of us sat in the Target parking lot while Bianca applied lip gloss. She wanted to go to get some beauty products. I was still irritated with her about what occurred the day before, but I think Bianca asking us to go to the store with her was her way of trying to apologize and make things normal again—whatever normal was for the three of us. Regardless, Susan needed dish soap and Cascade, so after she clamped a twenty in my hand, I told Bianca I'd go. Melanie came along too, for whatever reason.

We got into the store and immediately Bianca headed to the makeup section.

"I'm gonna go get Susan's things," I said to her as I passed by.

"Well, wait. Aren't you gonna look with me?"

I smiled mischievously, "Nope, that's what Melanie's for," I grabbed Melanie's arm and pulled her closer to Bianca. "Have fun!" I laughed to myself knowing they couldn't get along if their life depended on it as I walked off down the main aisle.

I found the Dawn and the Cascade then began to just wander around, window shopping at all the stuff they had. After some time,

I headed back to the makeup section in order to find Bianca and Melanie.

"Hey, there you are," Bianca said as she smelled a perfume. "Melanie hates this one, what do you think?" she extended the perfume out to me.

"Melanie hates everything, you can't trust her," I said, leaning down to smell the perfume. "No, this smells good," I leaned away. "See, you can't trust her."

"Whatever," Melanie said with agitation, "Did you get what Susan needs?"

"Yeah, I did. Are you ready, Bianca?"

"Yup," she said as she tossed the plastic perfume bottle into her basket of several other things.

We headed to the check-out line and Bianca put all her items on the belt. I added the Dawn and Cascade to them and then handed Bianca the twenty Susan gave me. The late twenties-year-old man started scanning the items and putting them in two bags. All of Bianca's items in one, and then the two cleaning products in another.

"I like your tattoos," Bianca said in a flirty way.

"Oh yeah?" he asked with a smile.

"Yeah, they're so cool," Bianca then twirled her hair. "My name's Bianca."

Melanie and I exchanged a look, knowing exactly what was going on. I sighed and Melanie rolled her eyes.

"Huh, Bianca, that's a pretty name. I'm Dalton."

"Nice to meet you, Dalton," she said, still twirling her hair.

"You as well," he said. He then pressed some buttons on the register, "Well, Miss Bianca, it's gonna be sixty-three, ninety-nine."

"Here you go," Bianca handed him Susan's twenty and then two twenties and a ten of her own.

He typed some things into the register. "Six 'o one is your change," he handed her the money, "And your receipt," he then handed her the paper.

She took both things without taking her eyes off his. "How about you take this receipt back and give it to me when your number's on it?"

He chuckled, "Okay," he took the receipt back, doing as she asked.

She smiled as she took it, "That's better," she picked up her bag of makeup.

I was already holding the other bag at this point. Melanie and I were at the end of the register waiting on her.

"You gonna call me?" he asked flirtatiously as he leaned closer to her.

"Duh and you better answer when I do. I *promise* you won't want to miss my call," she smirked at him then sashayed away. We followed behind, rolling our eyes.

"Can we go anywhere without you offering your vagina to someone?" Melanie asked Bianca.

"At least they want mine," Bianca said smugly.

"Mine's not up for offer," Melanie said as we walked into the parking lot. "Oh—I'm sorry, I mean for SALE."

"And thank *God*," Bianca said as she opened her car door, and got in.

Melanie scoffed as she got in as well.

"Okay question," I said as I got into the car, ignoring their bickering. "Don't prostitutes, I don't know, *not* meet their "clients" at Target?"

"It's not always pimps and abuse, Iris," she said as she put her seatbelt on. "And anyway, you'd be surprised how often the guys you meet in random places like this will be down to pay for sex. A lot of them either aren't looking for a relationship or they just want a one or two time thing."

"So, you meet people in Target, for example, call them, hang out with them, let them know you'll have sex with them for money, and they're down?"

"Are you kidding? Fuck yeah, most of them love it. Guys are pigs."

That comment made me frown. Yeah, a lot of guys were douchebags, a lot of them, but a lot of them weren't. A lot of guys were like Colton and didn't deserve to be inducted into that stereotype.

"Not all of them are," I said defensively.

Bianca laughed mockingly, "Okay, *most*."

I just rolled my eyes and looked out the window.

11

Chapter 11

Two weeks of unnoteworthy, typical, and boring-ish days passed and it was now June thirtieth. The three of us were in our rooms that night when Bianca began badgering us about going to a Fourth of July party.

"Come on, guys, please," Bianca pleaded. "It will be fun."

"What's fun about going to a hooker fest?" Melanie asked.

Bianca rolled her eyes, "Not a hooker fest. Just something to do and be *young*."

"I'm good," Melanie said as she slurped down the last of her milkshake.

I tried to ignore the conversation and focus on my book.

"Won't you tell her, Iris, it'll be fun! We could go to the mall tomorrow and get something cute to wear."

"Don't have money for a new outfit, sorry." I flipped a page in my book.

Melanie scoffed as she stood up to throw out her milkshake, "Yeah, no."

"Oh, come on, guys!" she begged again. "All we do is a bunch of nothing! Don't you guys want to have fun for once?"

"Who do you know here that's having a party anyway?" I questioned.

"Yeah, and that's not seventy years old?" Melanie asked as she walked back to her bed.

"I'll find one, trust me. And they won't be seventy," she rolled her eyes at Melanie.

"I gotta go pee—" I got up off my bed.

"Just think about it," Bianca said interjecting. "We'll go to the mall tomorrow, look around. *I'll* get something to wear, I'll find us a party, and we'll have fun this weekend."

I stared at her, unsure of how I could possibly have fun with Bodacious Bianca and Miserable Melanie. Yet as I thought about it, I figured what's the worst that could happen? After all, it was boring here, and this would at least give me something to do.

I sighed, "Okay," I said hesitantly.

"Oh great," Melanie sighed as she rolled her eyes.

Bianca's face lit up with a smile, "Yay! It's gonna be awesome."

I flashed a smile and walked out of the room.

We pulled into the parking lot of the Russell Brook Mall a few minutes after eleven. The three of us got out of the car and headed towards the entrance. We stopped at the directory sign and began to look at the stores. There were no more than twenty places in total, it was a pretty small mall.

"Welp, there's not shit here for your little outfit, Bianca," Melanie said as she turned away to toss her coffee out.

Bianca didn't say anything as she stared at the board. I could tell she knew there wasn't a store she wanted to go to.

Melanie walked back over, "Didn't you look to see if there's a store you wanted to go to before we came here?"

"Duh," Bianca said untruthfully. "There's stores here. Look, there's Zara, and Saks Fifth Avenue, Nordstrom Rack," she said.

"Would there be something you would want at those stores?" I asked, not believing so.

"Yeah, I think so. Let's try Zara first," she said.

"Alright," I said and took a step in the direction Zara was, Melanie followed.

"Well, wait," Bianca said interjecting. "What about you guys? Would you guys find something there?"

"I told you I don't have money for a new outfit," I said as we both turned around to face Bianca.

"And I don't care enough to buy a new one," Melanie said with a sarcastic smile.

"Oh, come on. I can't show up looking hot and you guys come in…well…like that," she pointed to our outfits in a disgusted manner.

Melanie scoffed, "Oh what? You think my fashion sense is gonna cock block you? Wait—*work*-block you."

I rolled my eyes.

"Well…yeah…kinda," Bianca said, crossing her arms.

"Okay then. Well, I would HATE to do that," Melanie said sarcastically. "So since you have ALL this money from these guys you fuck, buy me one. You know, since I don't want to get in the way of your work ethic," Melanie said once again with sarcasm and taking pleasure in it too.

Bianca grinned mischievously, not letting Melanie win. "Sure. I'll give you both thirty bucks," she dug in her purse. "How's that?"

"Oh, no. I don't want—" I jumped to say.

"Iris, you didn't have money to buy an outfit. Now you do. What's the problem?" Melanie asked mischievously.

"I don't want one, that's the problem," I said sternly.

"Aw come on. You're gonna put our girl out of work," she said with sarcastic puppy-dog eyes. "I mean LOOK at our outfits…we're *hideous!*" Melanie then glared at Bianca.

I sighed, rolling my eyes. "How do we even know what to wear? You don't even have an invite to any party yet."

"Iris," Bianca walked over to me. "That doesn't matter. You get something that you like and that's hot and you show up looking like the hottest bitch," she then held three tens out in front of me.

I looked down at it for a second. "I'll get something that I *like,*" I said as I snatched the money from her, shoved it down in my purse, then walked away towards Zara.

Several minutes later, we entered the store and began to look around. I went off by myself and within ten minutes I found a pair of jeans and a short sleeve cropped top.

"I'm checking out," I called to Bianca as I approached the register and saw her and Melanie looking at clothes.

"Whoa, whoa, whoa, whoa, whoa," Bianca said quickly as she scurried over to me, stopping me before I could reach the line.

"What?" I said, flicking my hands out in agitation.

"Jeans?" she questioned with a repulsed look. "No," she then took them from me.

I gave a *What the fuck?* face, "You said to get something I *like.*"

"Yeah, *and* something hot," she opened the jeans and looked at them with a twisted face. "These are hideous," she then tossed them onto a random rack.

I scoffed, "Well what would *you* like me to wear?"

"Something more like…this," she looked around for a second then pulled a hot pink velvet boxy dress off a rack.

My mouth hung open from how ugly it was, then I laughed, "You couldn't get me to wear that eyesore if you paid me."

"Well, it's better than those grandma jeans and this boring-ass top," she grabbed the crop top from my hands.

I scoffed as Melanie walked over.

"Okay, there's *nothing* in this store that I would even consider putting on my body."

"Thank you," I said, agreeing with her.

Bianca rolled her eyes, "Well whatever. We can go to Saks or Nordstrom."

"There's not gonna be anything there that we'll find that *you* want us to wear for thirty dollars," Melanie insisted. "We gotta go to like Charlotte Russe or Forever Twenty-One."

Bianca sighed knowing she was right, "Okay well we gotta hang around here first so I can find us a party to go to. While I do that, you guys wait at the food court and Google where those places are."

Melanie and I looked at each other, holding in our laughter at her.

"What?" she asked in total confusion.

"What do you mean, 'so you can find us a party to go to'?" I snickered.

She looked at us confused. "Why else did you guys think I chose to come to *this* mall?"

"For an outfit?" Melanie said in a tone like Bianca was stupid.

"Yeahhh?" she said, drawn out. "But why *this* mall?"

Melanie and I looked at one another then at her with confusion.

"Russell Brook Mall has about twenty colleges and universities within a mile and a half radius. I figured this place would be crawling with young guys. I know some of them *have* to be throwing July Fourth parties, so, I'll start talking to them, work my magic, and we'll have ourselves an in for this weekend," she said with confidence.

I actually thought it was quite smart for her. Melanie must have thought the same because we looked at each other and shrugged.

"Huh, there's a brain in there after all," Melanie said, knocking on Bianca's head.

I rolled my eyes, "Just meet us in the food court once you find one."

Bianca smiled, "I will. It won't take long," she said smugly.

We left the store and diverted paths. Bianca took a right and Melanie and I took a left. We found the only thing that resembled a food court. It was just a bunch of tables and chairs but no fast-food restaurant chains around it. There were like two, maybe three drink places but no food. Nevertheless, we found an empty table and sat down.

It didn't take Melanie long to find a mall nearby with a Forever 21 and Charlotte Russe in it. And about twenty minutes later, Bianca came up the hall, walking towards us. She was grinning from ear to ear.

"Thursday night, seven P.M., West Queen Anne," she said as she sat down.

Melanie looked at the time, "Twenty-five minutes. Not your best but you'll get 'em next time."

Bianca rolled her eyes playfully as she sipped a drink she had.

"So, what happened?" I asked.

"Well, I was on the third floor, walking down the hall, when I saw two guys, college aged. They were pretty good looking, so I walked up to them and played the whole, 'I'm not from here, I'm from California. Can you tell me where the smoothie place is?' card. Of course, I was flirting with them, and they were flirting back. I told them how my friends and I will be here for another week and want to do something fun for the Fourth of July and just like that, we got invited," she said in a self-satisfied manner as she sipped her smoothie.

"Ah, so *now* we're your friends," Melanie said.

I rolled my eyes and shook my head playfully. Bianca chuckled.

"The one guy told me it's supposed to storm pretty bad Friday though. Hopefully it doesn't rain Thursday and holds off," Bianca then added.

"Oh really?" I asked. "I didn't know."

"Did you even get their names?" Melanie asked with somewhat of an attitude.

Bianca rolled her eyes, "Of course I did, Melanie. It's Theo and Mason. They both go to Seattle University. So, I was right," she said with a smug grin as she sipped her drink once again.

"Okay and you think these college clowns are gonna pay you for sex?" Melanie asked.

"College guys have before, especially away from home in this program. But anyway, I'm not working that night, I just wanted to do something fun for the holiday."

Melanie smirked and sat back in her seat. I didn't say anything to that remark.

"Hey, isn't college done for the summer? Why wouldn't those guys go home?" I asked after a moment of thought.

"Ha!" Melanie laughed, thinking she found a flaw in Bianca's plan. "Didn't think of that now did you, Einstein?"

Bianca squinted her eyes and frowned at Melanie, "And you didn't think that there's *still* over twenty colleges and schools here. Not everyone goes home, dumb ass."

Melanie scoffed and rolled her eyes, having nothing to say as she couldn't prove Bianca wrong.

"Did you guys find the two stores?" Bianca asked, changing the topic after a second.

"Yeah, Melanie did. Some mall called Scatterfield, about ten minutes from here," I answered.

"Alright, cool. Well, let's go," Bianca stood up and pushed in her chair.

The two of us followed and we all exited the mall.

12

Chapter 12

We arrived at the Scatterfield Mall around twelve forty-five. Now, *this* mall was big, it was huge. Once we got inside, I saw how huge it really was. It was three stories, over two hundred stores, a bunch of restaurants, and even, an IMAX theater.

We entered Charlotte Russe and saw there were all kinds of cool, fashionable, and party-like clothes. Bianca took off towards the mini dresses while Melanie headed to the skirt section. I didn't know what to look for, so I just looked at everything. They had all kinds of clothes, shoes, accessories, bags, nail polishes, etc. it was actually quite amazing. After searching around by myself for some time, twenty minutes to be exact. I found Bianca outside the dressing room looking at herself in the mirror.

"Okay, how hot is this?" she asked with pure excitement as she turned towards me. She had on a very tight and very short dark red sparkly halter dress. It had a super deep V cut, so much so that it stopped like two inches from her belly button. The back was completely cut out as well.

"That's pretty, Bianca," I said somewhat lying. "I like the color."

"Thanks! Me too!" she exclaimed. "And it's only ten dollars. I might have to stock up on some things while I'm here at these prices."

"Good idea."

She turned towards the mirror and began admiring herself again. She then turned back around towards me, "Where's your stuff?" she asked in confusion.

"Uh, I haven't found anything yet."

"Irisssss," she said with disappointment. "Why not?"

"I don't know. I guess I haven't found anything that's caught my eye. I really don't know what I'm looking for," I said somewhat frustrated.

Her disappointed face went to a smile, "Come on, I'll help you."

She took my hand and began to show me some dresses that were close by.

"How about this?" she said as she pulled out a black strapless bodycon dress. It was plain and simple; I actually could see myself wearing it.

"Uh, yeah, that's not bad. How much?" I asked.

She looked at the tag, "Fifteen!"

"Oh great, what size is that?" I asked.

"Uh, large," she answered.

"I need an extra small probably," I was five-two and one hundred pounds, I was tiny. I began to rifle through the rack to find my size.

"Large, large, large, extra-large, medium. They don't have it in my size," I said.

"Well, that's okay, we'll find something else."

I followed her a couple more feet to another rack.

"How about this?" she asked as she held out a bright blue spaghetti strap bodycon dress with a cowl neck.

"Uh, that's okay...I guess. What size?"

"Large," Bianca said with disappointment.

We both began to search through the rack for my size.

"Extra-large, extra-extra small, medium, medium, large," I said as I filed through them.

"Small, extra-large, medium," Bianca said aloud. "They don't have your size either."

"They have every other size in the book but mine," I said, half with frustration, half with lightheartedness.

"I know, but it's fine, we'll find one," she protested. "What about this?" she said as she pulled out a dress from the rack right next to one that we were just looking through.

It was a black spaghetti strap bodycon dress. The sides, from top to bottom were completely cut out but strung back up. So, you were showing all the sides of your thighs, stomach, and boobs. The back was then three quarters cut out as well, stopping at like where your belly button would be if it were on your back.

I stared at it with a completely disinterested and an appalled face, "Absolutely not."

"Oh, why not, Iris? It's sexy! You'd look so good in it!" Bianca pleaded. "It's even an extra small!"

At this time, Melanie came up to us with some skirts and dresses in her hands.

"Whoa, what the fuck is that?" she asked invasively. "Bianca's whore style is rubbing off on you huh, Iris?"

"Melanie, shut up," I said. "No, I'm not getting that one, let's just keep looking around."

Bianca gave a defeated and disappointed look as she put it back on the rack.

Melanie went inside the dressing room Bianca was using and began to try on the things she had in her hands. Bianca and I then continued to look through all the dresses and found a problem with everyone. There were actually a lot of them I liked, they were just mostly all way too big. I tried to see if I could fit the extra-extra small as I sometimes did with other brands, but Charlotte Russe's was *tiny*. It probably wouldn't even fit a two-by-four.

"Alright, is this good enough?" Melanie asked as she walked out of the dressing room wearing a dark mauve long sleeve bodycon dress. It had a scoop neck, and the sleeves were completely made out of lace. It was actually one I looked at, but they only had mediums.

"Yes!" Bianca exclaimed. "I didn't know you could look *that* good!"

"Melanie rolled her eyes playfully, "Whatever, it's the only time you'll see me like this, so take it in."

I chuckled, "You do look pretty, Melanie."

"Thanks," she said. I could tell she wasn't used to compliments but it made her feel good. "Did you find anything?"

"No," I sighed in frustration. "They don't have my size in anything but that hooker dress...no offense," I said turning to Bianca.

She put her hands up like none was taken.

"Well, let's just go to Forever Twenty-One. I'm sure they have something there," Melanie said. "And anyway, it gives me an excuse to take this monkey suit off sooner."

"Alright," I said defeatedly, being frustrated by all the complications when I didn't even want to dress up in the first place.

"Don't waste your time going there," some random woman said to us. "They're closed. Something about a water leak from their break room? I don't know exactly but I just tried to go in there and the woman said their fridge was leaking and they were closed. She was pulling down the gate as she spoke."

I sighed in annoyance, "Alright, thanks."

"Soooo, now what?" Bianca asked as she and Melanie stared at me.

"Just get me the black one," I sighed.

I didn't want to wear that dress. Not an ounce of me did. But even *less* of me wanted to continue looking for one.

"Really?" Bianca said somewhat with excitement.

"Yeah, whatever."

"Okay!"

She got the dress and handed it to me. I started walking towards the checkout counter when she stopped me.

"You're not gonna try it on?" Bianca asked.

"No," I laughed. "Not at all. I'll be at the front of the store when you guys are done."

I proceeded to the counter while Bianca grabbed her stuff from the dressing room Melanie took over and went to the one right next to her.

They both closed their doors and got changed. I let out a huff, frustrated how I got dragged into this.

"Hello?" I said, answering my phone. I had just walked back into my room from finishing dinner.

"Hey, baby, how are you?" my mom asked.

I smiled, "I'm doing good, you?"

"I'm good, I miss you!"

"I miss you too, Mom," I smiled.

"On sec, let me get your brother and sister—Colton? Leannah? Iris!"

I heard them come and seconds later, Leannah spoke.

"Hey, Sis! I miss you," she said.

"I miss you too, Le," I smiled.

"How you doing, Sis?" Colton asked.

"I'm doing good, you?"

"We're all good over here. Same old same old," he said.

"I feel that."

"How're your roommates?" Leannah asked. "We caught Mom up."

"Yeah, they did," my mom said. "That's sad, that Bianca girl? And

Melanie too?"

"Yeah, they're fine, I guess."

Just then I heard a knock through the phone.

"Pizza!" Leannah gleamed like she was ten years old all over again. I already knew she took off towards the door. Leannah was a pizza *connoisseur*.

I chuckled.

"I got it, Mom," Colton said.

"It's alright, talk to your sister," Mom replied. "Honey, I'll talk to you soon, sorry it was short, I love you."

"No worries, I love you too, Mom. Enjoy your dinner."

"Thank you," she said.

"Love you, Iris!" Leannah shouted from far away.

"Love you too," I chuckled.

"So, is Seattle having any festivals or events for the Fourth of July?" Colton asked.

"I'm sure they are," I then sighed. "But Bianca is dragging me and Melanie to this party."

"Why don't you sound happy about that?" he asked.

"Because I wasn't crazy about it in the first place but reluctantly agreed, figuring it'll be fun and give us something to do. But she's just turned it into an ordeal."

"How so?"

I paused, not wanting to tell him the ordeal was making us dress up and being stuck with some stripper dress as an outfit.

"I don't know…she just is."

"Well, I'm sure you'll have fun. Who's party is it? Bianca's friend or something?" he asked.

"No, some random guys she met at the mall. She wanted to find a party so she took us to this mall that's near a bunch of schools, figuring young guys would be there. Well, leave it to her to find a guy having a party."

"Oh my God," Colton said with annoyance. "Iris, is that even a good idea?"

"It'll be fine. It's nothing serious, just something casual," I said monotonously, putting his worries at ease.

He sighed. "Be careful, please?"

"We will. Promise."

There was a brief moment of silence.

"Go enjoy your dinner, I'll talk to you soon. I love you."

"Alright," Colton said. "I love you too."

I hung up the phone and stared at my black dress that was hanging on the closet door. Bianca insisted I not leave it in the bag to prevent wrinkles. I didn't care, but she took it upon herself to hang it up anyway. I sighed, shaking my head. I should have known...Colton was *always* right.

13

Chapter 13

The day of the party and the Fourth of July was a Thursday. Susan had made a buffet-style breakfast, all American-themed. She had three large foil pans that contained pancakes and waffles, French toast, and scrambled eggs. She then had three medium foil pans full of sausage, bacon, and turkey bacon. Finally, there was a white ceramic container full of blueberries, strawberries, raspberries, and cherries. She also had out pitchers of orange juice and water, and of course a freshly brewed, hot pot of coffee at the machine. She even went as far as to decorate with little flags and red, white, and blue ribbons.

"Susan, this is beautiful!" I exclaimed as I stepped off the last stair into the kitchen. "You go above and beyond for all of us all the time. Thank you so much."

Susan smiled really big, "You are welcome! Happy Fourth of July!"

I smiled, "Happy Fourth of July, Susan."

Susan went on to tell me how her father fought in the Vietnam War for six years; from 1969 to when it ended in 1975. She said she always makes a big deal out of the memorial holidays in honor of all the men and women who served for us, had family that served for us, and or gave their lives for us. She thought it was important. And it is important. Most people my age didn't care about that stuff, they barely respected each other, let alone people in the military. But I always did. I thought it was important, too.

I enjoyed a delicious breakfast then found myself back in our bedroom. While making my bed, Bianca's phone binged. She paused her eyeshadow application and looked down at the screen.

"Theo texted me," she said. "'West Queen Anne party got busted already. New party in Steilacoom, same time.'"

"Steilacoom?" Melanie questioned as she had been listening with one earbud out.

"Yeah, he sent me the new address."

"Where even is that?" I asked. "I've never heard of that place before."

"I don't know. Who cares?" Bianca said as she set her phone down and proceeded with her eyeshadow.

Melanie sighed and rolled her eyes as she taped away on her phone.

"Oh my God," Melanie said moments later.

"What?" I questioned.

"Steilacoom is an hour and twenty minutes from here without traffic."

I scoffed, not surprised at all by this switch-up.

"Okay, so? We'll leave at like six," Bianca said in a confused tone.

"Oh right," Melanie said sarcastically, "Like the *time* was what I was concerned about."

I snickered and rolled my eyes playfully, pulling the sheets tight to the top of the bed.

"Okay, then what's the problem?" Bianca asked.

Melanie sighed out of frustration, "Never mind."

I looked at Melanie who was now rolling her eyes.

"Whatever, I guess it doesn't really matter," I said.

"See?" Bianca said to Melanie. "Iris doesn't care."

"Whatever," Melanie said as she put her earbud back in her ear.

Honestly, it's not that I *didn't* care, it was that I was becoming used to twists and turns with Bianca that something like this was expected. It's the *unexpected* that takes you down.

"Alright, well I'm gonna start getting ready," Bianca said around five o'clock as she plugged in her phone and got up from her bed.

"Yeah, I think I'm gonna go take a shower," I said as I got up from my bed as well.

I got my things, left our room, and started walking down the hall towards the bathroom. I tried to restore the somewhat excitement I had for this party before it turned into an ordeal but the idea of me wearing that stupid dress was making it hard. Regardless, I finished my shower, put on my pajamas, and went back into my room. Melanie was doing her makeup and Bianca was doing her hair.

I sat down on the floor in front of the closet's body-length mirror with my makeup bag.

"Can I use your hairdryer?" I asked Bianca as I unraveled my hair from the towel.

"Yeah, no problem," she said as she jumbled up the cord and handed me the hairdryer that was neon green cheetah print and decorated with rhinestones.

I snickered as I took it, that hairdryer was *so* her.

We all continued getting ready and talking for about fifteen more minutes.

"Okay, how's this?" Melanie said as turned to face us.

She was completely done getting ready, dressed and all.

"You look great!" I exclaimed.

I had never seen Melanie like that. Like, with that outfit on and that much makeup. She typically just wore casual clothes with mascara and foundation. But that night, she had on the whole works and she looked great. Melanie was actually a very pretty girl if you asked me. It was just her personality that made what she had on the outside, never be seen.

"Aww shit, girl!" Bianca squealed. "You look so hot!" she said as she grabbed her hands.

Melanie laughed and pulled away from Bianca playfully.

"Thanks, guys," she said, smiling at our compliments.

"All the guys are gonna want you!" Bianca teased.

"Shut up," Melanie said as she chuckled.

We all laughed, and Melanie began to clean up the small mess she created.

Several minutes later, Bianca finished her makeup and was now complete, just needing to get dressed. Which she did moments later, and it wasn't a big deal to her or us really because she wore this stuff all the time. I mean basically the entire closet that we shared was full of these types of dresses.

"You look pretty, Bianca," I said.

"Thanks, Iris," she said with a smile. "Come on, now you gotta get dressed!" she was *way* more excited for me to wear that dress than I was.

I crinkled my nose as I sat on the floor, where I had been procrastinating getting dressed for several minutes.

"Come on," she took my hands and ushered me up to my feet. "You're a beautiful girl with a beautiful little body. You should be happy you'll look good in a dress like this."

I forced a smile, "Thanks."

Melanie snickered. I guess she was enjoying the discomfort... figures.

"You're gonna look great," Bianca then took the dress down from the door and handed it to me.

I took the dress from her without saying anything and walked over to my bed. I laid the dress on my bed while I took my T-shirt off. I then slipped the dress on and turned to them.

"Yes! Oh my God, you look great!" Bianca said with much excitement.

"Yeah, it looks good, Iris," Melanie said.

I walked over to the mirror I previously used and looked at myself in that dress for the first time.

Sure, did I look attractive? Hell yes. I mean the dress was sexy, *very* sexy. But it just wasn't me. I didn't feel like *Iris*.

"Don't you love it?!" Bianca asked.

I stared at myself harder, "Not really—but it doesn't matter, it's fine," I said hastily as I grabbed my phone. "It's almost six, let's just go."

Bianca gave Melanie a pair of heels that were too big for her and gave me a pair of heels that were too small for her. The three of us then exited the room and headed outside. After a cigarette shared between the three of us, we pulled out of Susan's driveway and took off through the neighborhood, Steilacoom bound.

14

Chapter 14

"God damn it's dark out," I said as I leaned forward, looking through the windshield at the ominous clouds.

"Yeah, it is," Melanie said as she looked out her window as well. "They weren't lying when they said a storm was coming."

"When is it supposed to start raining?" Bianca asked.

"Well, let me just jump right on that," Melanie said with sarcasm as she pulled her phone out of her purse. "Not till three A.M."

"Okay, cool," I said.

"Yeah, that's not for a while, so we're good," Bianca added.

We continued the way the GPS told us to go for several miles when we hit some traffic in Central Seattle. I looked out of the window at the dark clouds that were taking over the sky. They were big and heavy and threatening. They almost were…alarming, like in some weird way, they were telling me to turn around and evade the storm. But…it wasn't talking about the storm *it* would be causing.

Fifty minutes had passed, and it was now around seven-thirty when we turned down Richard Street, the street the party house was on.

The home was the last one on the right, and it sat directly on the water. It was gorgeous. After this house, the street took a left bend and turned into a different street. Bianca parked next to the guardrail that guided that bend.

The three of us go out, and while Melanie began smoking a cigarette, and Bianca began to apply her lip gloss, I admired the water. It was beautiful.

"Iris? You ready?" Bianca called out, trying to gain my attention.

"Oh, yeah," I said as I turned around.

I caught up with them and the three of us walked the fifty feet to the front door.

The house was light blue with dark blue trim around the windows. There was a black iron gate that led to the front door that bent into a dome at the top of it. From here, a stone pathway led to the door, and above the pathway was a balcony that connected to an upstairs room. The balcony had a black iron fence as well and glass French doors. The house was expensive looking, to say the least.

We approached the door and Bianca rang the doorbell. We could hear music blaring from inside.

"Yeah, like anyone will hear that," Melanie said.

"Well?" Bianca said with agitation. "If he doesn't answer, I'll call him, calm down."

Melanie scoffed and stepped back.

Within no more than a minute, a tall, blonde hair, blue-eyed man wearing khakis and a Nike hoodie, holding a Coors beer can, opened the door.

"Bianca, you made it!" he said as he hugged her. "You look great."

Bianca smiled from ear to ear, "Oh stop it. Guys, this is Theo, Theo, this is Iris, and that's Melanie," she said as she stood there with his arm around her.

I smiled and gave a little wave, "Hi, nice to meet you."

"You too."

Just then another man, who was of average height with brown hair and brown eyes wearing khakis and a black T-shirt holding a Miller's Lite can came to the door.

He smiled, lookin at Bianca, "Look who it is!"

She once again smiled from ear to ear, "Mason! It's good to see you," she said as she gave him a big hug. "Mason, these are my friends, Iris and Melanie."

Melanie and I exchanged hellos and Mason complimented our outfits.

"Well, come on in, guys. Let the night begin!" Theo exclaimed as he ushered us inside.

Bianca entered first, then Melanie, then me.

The house was just as expensive looking on the inside as it was on the outside. There was a spiral staircase, a chandelier, high rise ceilings, the whole works. I'd never been in a house this nice. I looked around for a minute and took it all in as Bianca and Melanie followed Theo and Mason deeper into the house. Loud music was blaring, different color lights were flashing, and at least a hundred people were drinking, playing games, making out, and socializing. I looked around for another second then decided I'd get a drink. I walked over to a table that had several large coolers on it and all different types of alcohols, sodas, and mixers. I grabbed a red Solo cup, opened the cooler that had ice in it, filled my cup up then made my drink, which was just vodka and club soda.

I turned around, with one hand behind me on the table, and took a sip, looking out into the crowd. Just then, a tall attractive guy with light brown-hair and a beard that did not fit the frat boy stereotype at all (which was a good thing) came over to the table.

"Oh, sorry," I said as I moved to the right, trying to get out of his way of wanting to make a drink.

He moved the same way, "Oh, my bad."

We laughed as we both just got into each other's way.

"I'm sorry," he said with a smile, "I'm Montgomery," he extended his hand out for me to shake.

I shook it, "Iris."

"Iris, like the flower," he said.

"Montgomery, like the city," I smiled.

He laughed, "Yeah, like the city. You can call me Monty though, most people just call me that."

I smiled, "Okay, Monty it is. I like that."

"Well good," he smiled. "Are you one of Jordan's friends?" He grabbed a Solo cup and put ice in it.

"Uh no, my friend met these guys, Theo and Mason, at the mall and they invited us,"

"Theo and Mason?" he said as he thought to himself while he poured Jack Daniels into his cup. "I don't know them, but there's a lot of people here I don't know."

I inhaled and nodded my head, knowing how accurate that was for me, "Yeah, same. I don't know anyone."

"Well, why don't you get to know me?" he said flirtatiously as he opened a can of Coke.

I smiled, "Alright, that doesn't sound half bad."

He chuckled, "So do you live in Steilacoom or?"

"Uh no, I actually don't live in Washington at all."

"Oh really? Where are you from then?"

"I'm from Chicago."

"What?" he asked with a smile. "What are you doing here all the way from Chicago?"

I chuckled, "I'm just visiting a relative right now," I know, that was a lie, but I didn't *always* want to tell people the truth. It was mostly just easier to say that.

"Oh okay, I gotcha. That's awesome though," he said, taking a sip of his drink.

"Yeah," I smiled as I took a sip as well. "So where are you from?"

"I'm from here. I live about ten minutes, fifteen minutes down the road."

"Oh, nice. Have you been here your whole life?"

"Yup, whole life," he took a sip of his drink. "Well, now I'm going to college in Denver. It's pretty cool there."

"Oh yeah?" I took a sip of my drink. "What college?"

"University of Denver," he chuckled.

"Oh," I laughed. "I should have guessed that."

He laughed, "No, no, it's okay. There's a lot of colleges in Denver."

I smiled. "Yeah…so, if you're in college, how old are you?"

"I'm eighteen. It's my first year there. Are you not in college?"

I laughed, "No, I'm only sixteen."

He nearly spit out his drink, "Sixteen?"

"Yeah," I laughed.

"I thought you were at least eighteen or nineteen," he said in shock.

"I get that all the time," I took a sip of my drink.

"Well, that's cool though."

"It is now," I laughed. "It won't be when I'm fifty and look seventy."

"Aw no," he said. "Someone as pretty as you will always look good."

I blushed, "Thank you."

"You're welcome," he smiled.

Just then I saw Bianca, Melanie, Theo, and Mason approaching me.

"Oh, hey," Bianca said as she held a drink in one hand and Theo's hand in the other.

"Hey," I smiled. "Uh, Monty, these are my friends, Bianca and Melanie. And that's Theo and that's Mason.

"Hey, how are you guys?" Monty smiled at Bianca and Melanie.

They smiled and said hi back. Monty then shook Theo and Mason's hands.

"Nice to meet you, bro," Theo said.

"Yeah, nice to meet you, man," Mason said.

"Yeah, you too," Monty said.

"We were just about to play cornhole out back if you two wanted to join," Bianca said.

I crinkled my nose, "I don't like cornhole. How about we try our luck with the air hockey table in that room over there and we'll catch up with you guys later?" I asked, turning towards Monty.

"Yeah, that sounds great," he said.

"Alright, I'll see you two later then," Bianca said with a smile.

I smiled and she turned around, still holding Theo's hand, and walked away. Melanie playfully put up an "L" with her fingers on her forehead at me. She then turned around with Mason and the two followed Bianca and Theo out.

I chuckled and rolled my eyes, "Come on."

I led Monty through the glass doors and to the air hockey table. This room was surprisingly vacant of people and had a couch, a TV, the air hockey table of course, and a bunch of decorative books, vases, and other nick-nacks.

"Wow this is a nice ass hang-out room," I said as I set my drink down on the air hockey table and looked around.

"Yeah, it is pretty cool," he smiled. "God, I haven't played this in forever," he said as he set his drink down and examined the puck and pusher.

I laughed as I grabbed my pusher as well, "I know, me too."

"Well then this should be a pretty interesting game," he chuckled.

I laughed, "I think it will."

"Here, you go first," Monty said as he slid me the puck and turned the table on.

"Alright, let's see if I have any skills left in me," I said as I got ready to strike the puck.

He laughed and I hit it. It went down the table surprisingly with speed.

"Hey, there you go! That wasn't bad," he exclaimed as he hit it back.

"Yeah, touché," I said with surprise as we began to play, and his hits were even better.

He laughed, "Beginner's luck."

I made a *yeah right* face then laughed.

We continued playing and laughing when a little over an hour passed by when I had somehow reached ten points and won the game.

"Look at you!" Monty exclaimed, "I knew you were the *real* winner," he said with a flirty smirk.

I smiled and playfully rolled my eyes, "Thank you. I don't know how I did it, you were a lot to keep up with," I said as I sipped my drink and stepped away from the air hockey table, moving towards where he was.

"You're just naturally talented…Hey, I'm gonna go grab another drink. Do you want one?"

"Oh no, I'm good, thanks. Maybe in a little."

"Sounds good, I'll be back in a sec."

"Okay," I said with a smile.

He exited the room, and I sat down on the couch. I looked at my phone and saw it was now nine-ten. It didn't take him long to return.

"Hey," he said with a smile as he entered back into the room, "I saw your friends out there."

"Oh yeah?"

"Yeah, they're playing beer pong."

"Oh cool," I said with a smile as I sipped my drink. "I don't like beer."

"I'm not crazy about it either. It makes me feel all bloated and gross," he said with a repulsed face.

"Me too!" I exclaimed. "I much rather just drink liquor."

"Same," he smiled as he took a sip of his drink.

Monty then asked me how I knew Bianca and Melanie. I decided I should just tell him the truth and so I did. I told him that I didn't have a relative that I was staying with but rather I was in The Stay program. I explained to him what that was and how my family is poor and how I actually just met Bianca and Melanie. He was surprised as he never heard of anything like that before and apologized for my family struggles. I told him it was no big deal and the two of us carried on with getting to know each other better. I told him about my family, and he told me about his. He told me his plans for school and how he wanted to be a lawyer. Our small talk turned to flirting that only quickly grew.

"Yeah right, my muscles have nothing on your body," he laughed and sipped his drink. "By the way, that dress looks amazing on you."

I scoffed and rolled my eyes, taking the last sip of my drink, "Please, I didn't even want to wear this. Bianca made us dress up and it was the only thing in the store in my size. I kind of hate it."

"What?" he questioned in confusion. "I think it looks gorgeous."

I smiled, "Thanks, it's just not me, it's not really *Iris*. You know?"

"Well, whatever Iris I've been talking to all night, I like."

Feeling my cheeks turn red I said, "I like you too."

He then slid one hand into my hair, cradling my head as he kissed me.

We kissed for several long seconds then released. A big grin appeared across my face which made him smile. We both then slightly chuckled.

"I'm gonna go get another drink. Do you want one?" I asked as I stood up.

"Uh, yeah sure," he said. "Thank you."

"No problem," I smiled, then exited the room.

As I made my way through the crowd of people to the drink table, I saw Bianca and Melanie.

"Hey!" I yelled to them over the loud sounds of music and people socializing.

"Oh hey!" Bianca yelled.

"Hey!" Melanie shouted.

"Follow me," I grabbed each of their hands that didn't have a drink in them and ushered them to the drink table, which was in a slightly quieter area of the house.

"How're your guys' nights?" I asked as I filled up two new Solo cups with ice.

"It's good," Bianca said. "That Mason guy is really into Melanie," she laughed.

"Shut up!" Melanie said with annoyance but quickly laughed.

"Is he really?" I asked with a chuckle.

"Yeah," Melanie chuckled.

"Do you like him?!" I asked hastily with excitement.

"Yeah, 'cause *I* of all people would be *swoon* by some frat loser," she said sarcastically. "Please."

I laughed as I poured Jack into Monty's cup.

"And you talk about Mason liking me? You're *all over* Theo," Melanie said to Bianca.

Bianca shrugged, "It's not like that."

"Sure seems it," Melanie said smartly as she sipped her drink.

"I just have a flirty personality. You'd know if I was *really* into someone."

I snickered as I filled my cup with Vodka.

"And what about you and lover boy, *Monty*?" Melanie asked.

"Yeah, now *he's* hot!" Bianca exclaimed.

I laughed and rolled my eyes, "I know."

"Oooo!" Bianca exclaimed, "You like him!"

Melanie made a mischievous face.

"Stop," I laughed as I poured club soda into my cup. "I'm not even gonna talk to him again after tonight so there's no use making it a big deal."

Bianca rolled her eyes, "You keep saying that. Why can't you? You can keep hanging out with him until you leave."

"What good does that do? Then I'll just develop feelings and get hurt when I leave."

"So, what? Are you just gonna fuck him tonight then?" Melanie asked.

I rolled my eyes as I screwed the cap back on the bottle, "No, I may kiss him and stuff but I'm not gonna have sex with him."

"You already did kiss him!" Bianca exclaimed. "Didn't you?!"

I blushed and laughed.

"She did!" Melanie exclaimed.

"It was *one* kiss," I chuckled.

"About to be more," Melanie said with that mischievous grin.

"Maybe," I said with one back.

"Oooo!" Bianca exclaimed. "Now that's my girl!"

I laughed, "What are you guys drinking?" I asked as both of their drinks were bright blue.

"I don't know. Some Blue Curaçao drink Mason and Theo made for us," Melanie said.

"You wanna try it? It's pretty good," Bianca said as she held her cup out to me.

"No thanks, I'm good—they just randomly made that for you guys?" I asked.

"No, no, we wanted another drink and Theo recommended this. We watched them make these," Bianca said.

"Oh, okay, good," I said as I picked Monty and I's drink's up.

"Yeah, I'm not an idiot," Melanie teased.

I rolled my eyes and chuckled.

"Go back to Monty! You're making that hot man wait!" Bianca exclaimed.

I laughed, "Okay, okay,"

"Go!" she said again playfully.

"Okay, I am!" I exclaimed with a laugh.

"We'll catch up with you later, okay?" Bianca asked.

"Yeah, for sure."

Bianca smiled, "Have fun."

"I will," I smiled back.

"Not *too* much fun," Melanie smirked.

"Touché," I snickered back.

Melanie rolled her eyes playfully and I smirked as I walked away with the drinks in my hands.

"Here you go," I said to Monty as I made it back into the room and handed him his drink.

"Thank you," he smiled.

I smiled as I sat down next to him, "Hopefully it's how you like it."

He took a sip of it, "It's perfect," he said with a smile.

I chuckled, "Good," I took a sip of my drink.

We carried on our conversation of getting to know one another better, laughing and flirting for about forty-five minutes.

"So, wait," I laughed. "You're telling me you walked all the way back to your dorm in the pioneer's costume?" I laughed again as he was telling me the story about the time he was the mascot for the University of Denver's basketball team.

"I had to!" he exclaimed through a laugh. "I accidentally locked my keys in my locker along with my regular clothes and phone. By the time I was done saying goodbye to everyone and all that, I was the last one there, so there wasn't anyone to help me."

"That sucks!" I exclaimed with a chuckle. "Were you just carrying the mascot's head down the road?" I began to laugh harder at the mental picture of this.

"Yes!" he laughed hard as well.

"Oh my God."

"Yeah, it was awful," he chuckled.

"You're funny," I said as I took a sip of my drink.

He picked his drink up, took a sip of it, then set it back down, "And you're gorgeous."

"Oh yeah?" I said playfully as I set my drink down then shifted more towards him.

"Oh yeah," he said with conviction as he put his hand around my waist.

I chuckled, shifting onto his lap, facing him, in a straddle position.

He looked at me with bright eyes then smiled, "You're *so* gorgeous."

Just then he kissed me. I kissed him back and we began to make out. He was a really good kisser, and he wasn't instigating anything more as most guys did. We just made out and innocently touched one another's backs, legs, face, and neck. I really enjoyed it.

"You're a good kisser," I said bashfully, pulling away after some time.

"Oh yeah?" he said with a grin as he pushed my hair behind my ear. "Well, *you're* even better."

I laughed and rolled off him, now sitting next to him like before, as I picked up my drink and took the final decent-sized sip.

"I'm gonna go throw these cups out," I said as I picked up his empty cup and my phone. "Do you want another one or anything else while I'm out there?"

"Oh, nah. I'm good, thank you. Do you want me to throw them out? I don't mind."

"Oh no," I waved my hand as I stood up. "I can do it."

"Okay…don't take too long," he said with a flirty smile.

I chuckled, "I won't."

But I would. I would take long. I actually wouldn't even return at all. I walked through those French doors, leaving excitement, love, and fun behind. Only to enter a night filled with fear, urgency, and poison.

15

Chapter 15

I headed through the crowd of people to the back of the house, where the kitchen was. From the living room, where all the partygoers were, there was an open archway entrance into the kitchen and the sink was at the very back. There was a window above the sink that faced out in view of the lake.

As I made my way to the entrance, I saw Theo and Mason standing at the sink, pouring something down the drain. Bianca and Melanie were nowhere to be seen. I paused and moved behind the archway wall to not expose myself but still see what they were doing. As I glared for a couple seconds, I saw what they were pouring down the drain—it was the entire bottle of Blue Curaçao. My heart dropped and shivers ran down my spine.

"Yo, bro! Don't dump that shit out, let me get it!" some drunk guy slurred as he approached Theo, who was the one pouring the bottle out. I hadn't seen him before, but he was now in my view.

"No," Theo said harshly.

"Come on, bro! What's wrong with it? You're just pouring it out!" the drunk guy protested.

In an instant, Theo bursted with anger, "Back the fuck up!" he screamed as he slammed the bottle down and shoved the drunk guy very aggressively. "Get the fuck out of here!"

I was taken aback and somewhat rattled by the surprise of such anger. I watched as the drunk guy didn't say anything but looked shaken as Theo burned a hole into him. After another second, the drunk guy scoffed and walked away, towards the entrance I was hiding behind. I quickly turned around, putting my back to the wall, and taking a pretend sip from my empty cup as the drunk guy passed by me and into the crowd of people. Once he was gone, I turned back around and continued to spy on Theo and Mason.

"I told you to just put the drugs in their drinks!" Mason yelled. "You look suspect as fuck dumping that entire bottle down the drain."

My heart dropped when I heard him say that. It confirmed everything I was suspicious of from the beginning.

"No! What's suspect is trying to put drugs in someone's drink with them right in front of you and a hundred people around!" Theo growled at Mason as he got in his face.

"Half the people here are fucking drunk and they're two stupid bitches, they wouldn't even notice. Shit, isn't the one a hooker? Yeah, she'd have no idea." Mason mocked with a chuckle.

That line ignited a fire inside of me making my nostrils flare and my eye twitch.

"Whatever, dude," Theo continued pouring the rest of the Curaçao down the drain. "Let's just get rid of this shit, the drugs should be kicking in by now."

I couldn't listen anymore. Bianca and Melanie were off somewhere drugged. I needed to find them and I needed to find them fast.

I took off through the crowd of people and up the stairs. As I reached the second floor, I noticed there were about eight doors, all closed. I began to throw open each one and barge inside. I got through about five doors with no signs of Bianca or Melanie. I tried two more doors, and still no luck. The hall had curved, and I was now faced with the final door at the very end of the hall. I ran towards it and tried to open it—it was locked.

"Bianca?! Melanie?!" I yelled out as I tried to turn the knob several times. "Hello?!" I banged on the door.

I still heard nothing, I tried turning the knob and forcing the door open several more times but there was no use.

"Iris?" I heard in a faint voice on the other side of the door.

I froze.

"Bianca?!" I asked as I put my ear up to the door.

"Iris? Is that you?" I heard faintly again.

"Yes! Yes! It's me, open the door!" I tried twisting it again out of impatience.

Several seconds went by as I heard light scuffling on the other side. I started to hear the doorknob jingle and be messed with.

"Iris, you open it," she said in a dazed voice. "It's locked."

"It's locked on this side too," I said.

I quickly began to stretch up on my tippy-toes and feel the top of the doorframe. I tried the neighboring doors too in hopes to find the key but instead, I found nothing. I pulled up the runner that ran down the hall but again, I found nothing. I went back to the locked door and paused for a second while I pulled out the bobby pin that was holding back two pieces of my hair. Colton showed Leannah and me how to pick a lock with one of these when we were younger, it has come in handy a couple of times—and this was one of those times.

I flung the door open and saw Melanie unconscious on the floor with her purse next to her and Bianca fading in and out while sitting on the edge of the bed. I squeezed the bobby pin back together and stuck it on my dress while I closed the door almost completely.

"Bianca," I rushed over to her, kneeling to be at her level. "Are you okay?" I put my hand on Melanie's calf and checked on her.

"Iris?" Bianca asked.

"Yeah, it's me," I pleaded.

"Where am I?" she asked.

"You're at the party, but we need to leave, okay? We can't be here anymore, and we need to leave," I said in a hurried, gentle manner as I grabbed Melanie's purse and slung it over my shoulder.

"Why? Did I get in trouble? Are you mad at me?" she asked. She was so dazed and confused.

"No, no, you're not in trouble and I'm not mad at you. We just need to leave, okay?" I scrambled over to Melanie.

"Melanie, Melanie," I carefully rolled her over onto her back and lightly tapped her face.

"Iris, I think something went wrong with Melanie," she slurred as her eyes rolled around and she began to fade.

"Hey, hey, hey," I said, quickly scrambling back to her. "Stay with me, okay? I'm gonna need your help with Melanie. Please, you can do it, Bianca, just stay with me."

I went back to Melanie and slowly sat her up. She was completely passed out. A tornado could have ripped through that house, and she wouldn't have woken up. It disgusted me to see her in such a state. Once she was sitting up, I stood up and pulled her up to her feet. I struggled as her dead weight was nearly impossible for me to manage. I sat her down on the bed and crouched down so that her arm stayed slung around my neck.

"Okay, Bianca, come here and grab my neck," I said as I extended my other arm to her.

She didn't say anything, she just swayed back and forth. Her eyes would slam shut and seconds later she would try to force them open. I could see she was beginning to lose the fight to whatever those sick fucks put in their drinks.

I scooted on my knees closer to Bianca while Melanie was still around my neck. I grabbed Bianca by the waist and pulled her to me.

"Put your arm around my neck—put your arm around my neck," I said hurriedly.

I didn't have much time and I wanted to get out of there before Theo and Mason came in.

It took her a couple of seconds, but she slung her arm around my neck.

"Good. Okay," I said as I got myself ready to stand up.

"Now slide your legs off the bed and put your feet on the floor."

Her head fell.

"Bianca," I said as I reached up as best as I could with the hand that was supporting her and tapped her on the face. Her eyes opened. "Put your feet on the floor."

She slid one off, which I don't think she did because I was telling her to, I think it just naturally slipped off based on the position she was in at the very end of the bed.

I prepared myself and gathered all the physical strength I had to stand up with the dead weight of them and Melanie's purse. My adrenaline allowed me to though and naturally, Bianca's other leg dropped onto the floor.

"Okay," I said to myself as I stumbled slightly and breathed heavily. "Okay, Bianca we're gonna walk out of here and down the stairs," I said to her with my head cocked in her direction. "You can do it, Bianca, come on," I said encouragingly, trying to keep her conscious for just a little longer.

I walked towards the door, literally dragging Melanie. Bianca was stumbling over every step we took. "You're doing great. You can do it." I struggled to reach for the doorknob as I simultaneously held Bianca up, but I got it and pulled it open. I scurried down the hall as fast as I could with them and made it to the staircase.

At this point, Bianca was pretty much incoherent. So, I knew it would be no use and would only take longer to try to tell her to walk down the stairs. So, I once again mustered up all my strength and squeezed them to myself as hard as I could to ensure I had a good grip on them. I then slowly stepped down each stair.

As I descended the stairs and came into view of all the partygoers, some began to stop and stare. Others were so drunk they either didn't care, didn't realize, or both. I ignored all the looks and attention as my main goal was to get the hell out of that house and to Bianca's car.

As I reached the bottom stair, I looked out into the crowd and saw Monty. He was by the French doors that led to the room we had been hanging out in all night. His face was flushed with concern and desperation. We locked eyes and with my desperate, pleading face, I looked away and pushed through the crowd to the front door.

Once outside, I saw it was pouring. It was pouring badly. Thunder boomed aggressively through the sky and lightning struck the ground with startling flashes. I stepped off the landing and took off to the car. Rain soaked me instantly as *I* was now the one beginning to lose the fight. I fought off the demons of weakness, tiredness, and desperation for oxygen as I saw Bianca's car and moved even faster to it.

A minute later, I made it to her car and leaned Melanie against my body as I struggled to find Bianca's keys in Melanie's purse. The pouring rain and darkness made it incredibly hard. But soon enough, I felt that rhinestone heart that saved us once before and I pulled it out of the purse.

"Hey!" I heard a man scream.

I quickly turned around and saw Theo and Mason running towards me.

"No, no, no, no, no," I said to myself as I fumbled with her keys and began pressing buttons on it.

The car's lights went off and I flung open the backseat door, lowering Bianca and then Melanie inside the car. I slammed the door closed, locked it, and as I turned around, Theo, in an instant, grabbed me.

"There you are! We were looking for you!" he yelled in a caring tone over the loudness of Mother Nature.

"Get away from me!" I growled, pushing him off.

This startled the both of them and they stared at me.

"You drugged my fucking friends, you fucking sickos!" I yelled with wailing hands.

"No, no," Theo put his hands up. "We couldn't find them, and when you came down the stairs with them all drunk, we got worried—"

"No!" I screamed, interrupting them. "They weren't fucking drunk, you guys drugged them!" I then shoved them both with all my might as the rain crashed down. "I heard your conversation in the kitchen. I'm not fucking stupid—you did this to them!"

Their demeanor instantly changed.

"Yeah? And what are you gonna do about it? You're just as useless as those two," Mason shouted.

I stared up at them furiously as they both were much taller than I was, especially Theo, even in heels.

"Yeah, look at you," Theo laughed. "You're useless," he then shoved me away from him.

I stumbled and due to the pavement being wet and my five-inch heels, I tumbled to the ground. The two of them laughed but I just grabbed Melanie's purse, got to my feet, and tried to get in the driver's seat to leave.

"Where are you going?" Mason yelled as he pulled me away from getting in the car.

"Get off me!" I screamed over the claps of thunder as I tried to push him off, but he still held my arm.

Theo then closed the car door, "I don't think she's going anywhere, Mason."

"Oh, what? Are you gonna drug me too?!" I yelled angrily as I tried to shake Mason's clutch. "You gonna throw me in a room upstairs like a prop until your sick ass is ready to use me?! Huh?!" I screamed even louder as I shook again and freed myself from Mason.

Theo laughed, "You're a feisty little thing."

My nose twitched with enmity as I stared at them both with the utmost hatred.

Just then someone else came running towards us. With the two focusing on whoever was coming towards us, I tried to quickly open the driver's door and get in, but Theo grabbed me.

"No!" I screeched in a tone so ear-piercing that my voice cracked as I began to tussle with him, trying to get free. Mason jumped in the fight and held me still. I was now several feet from the car.

"Hey!" the person, who, by the sound of their voice, was a man, and Monty to be more specific, yelled angrily as he came running even faster toward us.

"Let her go!" he yelled as he shoved Theo down to the ground and then Mason.

I took that moment to grab Melanie's soaking wet purse and sprint to the car.

As I got to her car and unlocked it, I turned around and looked at Monty. I put my hands up in a praying formation and his disappointed face turned to a smile. He waved as I jumped into the car. I put the keys in the ignition, threw it in drive, and flew down the street, not *once* looking back.

As I got out of the neighborhood and onto the main roads, it seemed the storm had gotten worse. I tried to fumble with my phone to pull up directions on how to get back to Susan's, but the visibility was terrible, and it was too dangerous. I could barely see five feet in front of me even with the windshield wipers going as fast as they could. Roars of thunder broke through the sky and lightning bolts illuminated it, both causing me to jump from startlement. I just wanted to get us home but after ten minutes of aimlessly driving and the rain coming down even harder, I knew that wasn't going to happen. I knew if I wanted to get us home at *all*, I was going to have to pull over and wait Mother Nature out.

I pulled into a gas station and parked in the back corner under a poorly lit street lamp that was no match for the storm's darkness. I turned off the car and for the first time since I heard Theo and Mason's conversation, I could breathe. I exhaled deeply then turned around and looked at Bianca and Melanie. They both were unconscious. I squeezed my eyebrows together as my eyes filled up with tears. They were sad tears, angry tears, and happy tears. I was heartbroken to see them like this, I was furious that this happened to them, but I was happy because they both were okay, and I was able to get to them before something could happen.

I locked the doors, took off my heels, grabbed my hoodie, and climbed into the backseat with them. I sat in the middle and pulled them both close to me, resting their heads on my lap. I used my hoodie to dry them off as best as I could, then I draped it over the three of us.

"Everything's okay, you guys are safe now," I said to them as I pulled their wet hair from their necks and held them.

I kept an eye on them for a while, making sure they were okay as I listened to the claps of thunder in the pitch-black darkness that only lit up when the lightning said it was okay too.

I closed my eyes, holding both Bianca and Melanie as the rain continued to crash down, and drifted off to sleep.

16

Chapter 16

I slowly opened my eyes as I heard my phone's ringtone going off. I blinked a couple of times and squinted at the brightness of the fog. I leaned forward and grabbed my phone from the cup holder.

"Oh shit," I said, instantly waking up. It was Susan calling.

"Hello?" I answered frantically.

"Iris! Oh my God, you're okay. I've been worried all night! Where are you?" Susan pleaded on the phone. She really did sound distraught.

"Susan, I'm so, so, *so* sorry," I leaned back and looked down at Bianca and Melanie still sleeping on my lap. "Look, Susan, something happened last night where Bianca and Melanie really needed my help. I tried to make it home, but it was raining too hard and I couldn't make it."

Susan exhaled a sigh of relief, "Sweetheart, it's okay. I'm just so glad you're okay. Where are you guys?"

"Uh, we're in Steilacoom," I answered.

"Steilacoom? That's an hour away," she said in a worried tone.

"I know, I know. Look, I might be able to explain more when we get home, but everything's fine. We're all okay. I promise we'll be back before the afternoon."

"Alright, baby, please don't rush."

"Alright, thank you, Susan."

"You're welcome. Call me if you need anything, okay? A ride or money, anything."

I smiled softly, "Alright, I will. Thank you."

"Of course, bye, Iris," she said in a relieved tone.

"Bye."

I hung up the phone and saw I had about a dozen missed calls from her that started around twelve forty-five. I sighed as this made me feel really shitty. I didn't want to worry Susan. She actually was the *last* person I wanted to worry. Knowing I scared her the way I did, made me feel awful.

I was resting my eyes when I heard a noise. I opened them and saw Melanie was rubbing her eyes awake. I rubbed her arm, and she looked up at me extremely confused. She then looked around and looked even *more* confused.

"It's okay, Melanie. You're in Bianca's car," I said gently, trying to ease her disorientation.

It seemed to help a tiny bit as she sat up, "Why am I here? Wasn't I just at the party?" she rubbed her head as she asked this. Her voice was rough, and she was dazed looking.

I rubbed Melanie's arm then spoke, "Melanie, uh, Theo and Mason spiked your guys' drinks."

Melanie stopped rubbing her head as she looked at me with desperate, emotionless eyes. She swallowed hard, "What happened to me?" her tone was ice cold.

I smiled ruefully, "Nothing. I uh, I got to you guys before uh, they could."

"You did?" Melanie asked in a surprised tone. But not surprised like she didn't think *I'd* do that for someone. Surprised as in she couldn't believe someone would do that for *her*.

I nodded my head but before I could speak, Bianca rose from my lap, rubbing her eyes.

She stopped and began to blink repeatedly, trying to adjust to the light.

"Hey," I said kindly as I gently rubbed her arm.

She looked at me, then Melanie then around in her car in a dazed fog.

"Why am I in the backseat of my car?" she asked.

I swallowed as I put my hand back on her arm, "Uhm, Bianca, you and Melanie were uh…you were drugged."

She frowned as she looked very confused, "Theo and Mason?" she asked after a slight pause.

I exhaled, "Yeah."

She slumped back in her seat and started to rub her eyes again. This quickly turned into her head shaking from side to side and her lip turning in, I knew she was fighting back tears.

"Hey," I said as I pulled her into a hug. "You're okay," I rubbed her back. "You're okay."

She started to cry, and I held her tighter, Melanie surprisingly joined in and rubbed her back.

She let go of our embrace and sat forward as she wiped her eyes, "I'm sorry. This is like the fourth time this has happened," she said with her head hung low.

I felt awful. Absolutely terrible. I rubbed her back and pulled her in for another hug, "I'm so sorry, Bianca. None of this is your fault," I pulled away and looked at her deeply. "You know that right?"

She looked up at me with saddened eyes, "Yeah," she said in her frail, broken voice.

I looked at her for a moment full of sorrow, "I know this won't make it better, but they didn't do anything to you."

She looked up at me confused and whisked a tear off her cheek, "They didn't?"

I smiled softly and shook my head.

"Well, how do you know?" she asked in that frail, saddened voice.

"Because I uh, I got to you guys before they could," I smiled slightly.

"How?" she asked with great concern in her emotional state.

"Yeah, how?" Melanie asked as well, still in a dazed state.

I exhaled, "I went to throw out Monty and I's cups. When I got to the kitchen, I saw Theo and Mason pouring something down the drain. I didn't see you guys anywhere, so I stopped to see what they were pouring out…it was the Blue Curaçao. I knew something wasn't right and I *really* knew something wasn't right when some drunk guy that was in the kitchen asked why Theo was pouring that out and if he could have it and Theo exploded at him. When, uh, when the guy walked out, Mason uh, Mason said that they should have just put the drugs in your guys' drinks. That uh, that you guys wouldn't have noticed and all," I said that last line very reluctantly.

They both looked angry, disgusted, sad, and terrified for what more I had to say. I continued, reluctantly, but I continued. I told them everything. Everything. Everything up until the very moment of the three of us sitting in the back seat of Bianca's car.

After I finished, there was silence for a moment. They both didn't know what to say.

"You did all that for us?" Melanie finally said in a low tone.

My face twisted in confusion as I looked at her, "Well…of course…I would never leave you guys." I took a slight pause, "I know we all aren't the best of friends, and I know we're all three *extremely* different people with three *very* different lives. But…I would have never left you guys…ever. Even if you were my worst enemies, I would **never** leave you."

There was silence for another moment.

"Thank you," Melanie said with conviction as she met my eyes. It was the most genuine thing she ever said to me. I knew that for whatever reason, and I had my theories, that this meant more to her than I would ever truly know.

I smiled.

"Yeah, Iris, thank you," Bianca said. She shook her head in disbelief and sadness, "No one has ever done anything like that for me."

I squeezed my eyebrows together as pure sorrow came over me. I could see the pain she always hid away coming to light. I knew that feeling of not having anyone and it was truly daunting. Growing up, the only person I ever had in my life to look after me was Colton. He was the only one. My dad left; he didn't give a shit about me. My mom was strung out, she *couldn't* care. And Leannah was just a child. But Colton? Colton protected Leannah and I like hawks. I mean from day one, when he was just a child himself, he did everything in his power to protect us and to be there for us. He was the *one* person that would turn the world upside down, literally, if I needed him to. He was that *one* person that would do everything in his physical power to not let anything bad happen to us. He was the *one* person that just…cared. He was all I had. But it was enough. And I figured if I was that one person for someone…for Bianca and Melanie, then maybe it was enough, too.

I forced a smile as best I could through the sadness, "I'm just really, really happy you guys are okay."

Bianca smiled as her eyes welled up with tears, "Because of you," she said as she hugged me.

I hugged her back tightly and then Melanie joined in. She squeezed me so hard, and I just smiled as I forced my tears down.

17

Chapter 17

It was appropriately gloomy that morning. Not only from the storm the night before, but also, us. Everyone was dull, tired, and spooked. Somehow, the outside environment conveyed this as well. It was dark, quiet, and slightly chilly.

We changed into sweatpants, hoodies, and flip-flops that Bianca had in her trunk then headed home. Melanie had her head against the headrest with her eyes closed and Bianca was curled up on the door with her hands between it and her face. As I drove, my mind played thought after thought. I thought about how Melanie—before she fell asleep—told us she blamed herself for what happened. It shocked me that she was so vulnerable with us. I tried to tell her it *was not her fault* but I don't think my words reached her. I thought about Monty and how kind he was. I thought about Theo and Mason and how terrible they were. I thought about that doorknob that locked from both sides, making me think this wasn't the first or the *last* time they'd done this. I thought about all the things that could have gone wrong…if Bianca and Melanie didn't have me, if I didn't get up to throw those cups away, if I refused to go to the party, if I didn't care, if I got drugged…*all* these things my mind played over and over and

95

over and over…

I pulled into Susan's driveway and parked the car.

"We're home," I said as I looked over at Bianca.

She opened her eyes and looked around, "Okay," she said through a yawn.

"Melanie?" I asked as I shook her leg gently. "Mel, we're home."

She woke up and blinked a couple times to adjust her eyes. She didn't say anything, but she started to gather up her things.

"You guys need any help?" I asked.

Melanie shook her head, "No, I'm okay," she said as she rubbed her head.

"I'm okay too, thanks," Bianca said.

After we all gathered our dresses, heels, and purses, we met at the front of the car.

We smiled as we shared a hug that washed the feeling of *We made it home, it's all over* through us.

After a second of jamming our outfits and heels into our purses so Susan wouldn't see them, we all headed inside. Right when we got a couple feet into the house, Susan came scurrying towards us.

"Oh, you guys are okay! Thank the Lord!" she said as she pulled us all in for a hug. There were a couple of people in the living room that looked over, but they didn't seem to care too much.

"Are you guys okay?" Susan asked as she pulled away.

"Yeah, we're okay," I said.

"Susan, we're so, so, sorry we had you worried all night," Bianca said.

"Yeah, we're really sorry," Melanie added.

"Oh, don't worry about that. I'm just glad everything is okay. What happened?" Susan then asked.

They both looked at me blankly as they didn't know what to say. On the way home, Bianca and Melanie told me that not only did they not want to contact the police, they didn't want Susan to know the truth. This is what led Melanie to telling us how ashamed she felt for being drugged.

"Uh," I immediately jumped in. "Bianca and Melanie were driving around last night and ended up getting lost—which is why they were in Steilacoom. Uh, they got a flat and called me to help them. By the time the bus came, and I got down there, it was dark. I got the tire changed and thankfully Bianca had another actual tire and not a donut"—I said this in case Susan saw Bianca's car, she wouldn't wonder why there were four regular tires on it after I told her I changed one—"Because it started to rain really, really bad. It got so bad, Bianca couldn't drive, so we pulled over and tried to wait it out but ended up all falling asleep…I'm sorry."

"Oh, honey," she rubbed my arm. "You guys did the right thing by pulling over and not trying to drive all that way back up here. I'm glad you all are okay."

"Thanks, Susan," I said ruefully. I felt bad lying to her, but I wasn't going to tell her what really happened. Not only would that upset her immensely, but Bianca and especially Melanie didn't want me to, and there was no way I'd go against that.

"You're welcome. Why don't you guys go get settled back in and all?" she suggested.

"Alright," I said.

The three of us headed up the stairs and into our room. Once we entered, I closed the door and both Bianca and Melanie instantly plopped down their stuffed purses and took their flip-flops off.

"Hey," Melanie said to me in a low tone as she carefully perched on her bed. I looked over at her. "Thanks for not telling Susan."

I smiled softly, "Of course."

"Yeah, thank you," Bianca then added. "Pretty good lie too," she grinned.

I chuckled lightly, "Thanks."

The two of them then laid down on their beds, quickly drifting off to sleep. I was tired too but began to unpack my purse. I pulled out my scuffed heels and my dress which was still damp. I put my heels in my suitcase and then I pulled out Bianca and Melanie's dresses and heels. Their shoes were pretty much fine, and their dresses weren't nearly as wet as mine, they were practically dry. I gathered up the three dresses, along with some other random clothes that were on the floor and carried them downstairs to the laundry room.

I had just finished loading the washer and turning it on when my phone rang. It was Colton.

"Hello?" I said.

"Hey, Sis. How you doing?"

I exhaled, "Oh, I'm okay. How are you?"

"I'm good…why are you just okay?"

"Oh, uh, just a long night."

"What happened? Wait, wasn't that party last night?"

I sighed, "Yeah."

"How did that go?"

"Well," I exhaled. "It was good…before it turned bad."

Colton paused, "What happened?" he asked in a more serious tone.

I paused, "Uh, Bianca and Melanie got drugged by the guys who invited us."

There was silence.

"What?" he questioned with anger. "Where were you? Were you okay?"

"Yeah, Colton, I was fine. They didn't do it to me. I was hanging out with this really nice guy, Monty, that I met there. I overheard the two guys, Theo and Mason, talking about how they drugged them, and I ran off to find them. It's all okay now though. I got to them before something could happen."

"Jesus, fucking Christ, Iris," Colton exhaled. "Were they okay?"

"Yeah—well, no, not really. Bianca was barely conscious, and Melanie could have been mistaken for dead."

"Holy shit," Colton said. "That's awful."

"Yeah, it was."

"I'm proud of you for helping them," Colton said. "Not like I expected anything else though."

I smiled as I sat down on the wooden chair that was in the laundry room, "Thanks."

"So where are those punks now?" he asked with aggression.

"I'm assuming their house. They tried to stop me from leaving with them, but Monty shoved them down and I was able to get in Bianca's car and speed off."

Colton scoffed, "What fucking pieces of shit."

"I know, but don't get all mad, Colton. I don't need you to be angry and start worrying about me out here."

"You know I'm gonna worry," he said. "That could have easily been you."

"I know, I know—look it's been a long night, let's just talk about something else, okay?"

He sighed lightly, "Alright, yeah, fine…So, what are you doing now?" he asked after a beat.

"Just some laundry, you?"

"Nothing, gonna make a peanut butter and jelly in a sec."

"Oh yeah, isn't it like twelve-thirty or something there?" I asked as I pulled the phone away from my ear and looked at the time.

"Yeah, it's just about twelve thirty."

"I forget about the time difference sometimes," I said.

"Yeah, me too," Colton said lightheartedly.

"Where's Mom and Leannah?"

"They're at the Dollar Tree."

"Oh, okay. Well, I'll let you make your sandwich. Tell them I love and miss them," I said.

"I will. Be safe, Iris. I love you."

I smiled slightly, "I love you too, Colton."

After I got off the phone with Colton, I waited until the washer finished its cycle. I put our clothes in the dryer then headed back to our room. I opened the door quietly and saw both Bianca and Melanie were still asleep on their beds. I decided to finally lay down myself and soon, fell asleep.

18

Chapter 18

For the next two days, things were different. Understandably though. But by the time Monday came around, things were back to how they were before the party ever happened. Over the weekend, Bianca gave me her dress and heels. I didn't necessarily want either of them. Not only were they both too big but I wouldn't ever wear the dress she did. The only reason I obliged was because she said she didn't want to be reminded of such an awful night. From there though, a week and a half passed by that consisted of the same old same old. Bianca was out working again, and Melanie was still her rude, sarcastic, and bitter self. Although she was a *little* nicer, emphasis on "little," I was just glad everything and everyone was okay.

It was Friday, July nineteenth, around four-thirty when Bianca was out getting her nails done. I was vacuuming the room and Melanie was reading a magazine when Bianca called. She asked if we wanted to meet her at Papa Pizza, a pizza shop near the nail salon she was at. Melanie and I agreed and took the bus there.

We both crossed the street and headed inside of the pizza shop. We saw Bianca sitting at a booth, so we walked over to her then took a seat.

"Oh, hey," Bianca smiled as she set down her menu. "Look," she held out her hands, showing us her nails.

They were about an inch long, stiletto shaped, and were a bright orange with rhinestones and glitter.

"They're pretty," I said as I touched one of her fingers, examining it.

"They look like mini traffic cones," Melanie said as she stared at Bianca's nails.

Bianca rolled her eyes. She then stuck up her middle finger in Melanie's face as she picked back up her menu. We all chuckled and began to look at the menus.

"Do you guys want to just split a pizza?" Melanie asked.

"Yeah, I was just about to suggest that," I said.

"What kind do you guys want?" Bianca asked.

"Well, nothing with red meat on it for the princess over here," Melanie said sarcastically as she looked at me.

"Yeah, and nothing with optimism or happiness on it for the queen over here."

Melanie rolled her eyes playfully and I grinned.

Bianca laughed, "How about the Hurricane?"

I searched the menu for the name. It said it had mushrooms, green peppers, red onions, and mozzarella cheese.

"Yeah, that sounds pretty good actually," I said.

"Yeah, that's fine," Melanie added.

When our waitress, Jamie, came over, we ordered the pizza and three waters.

"I wanna go to the Space Needle," Melanie said as she slammed her straw down on the table a couple of times to get it to come out of its wrapper.

"Oh yeah! The Space Needle!" Bianca exclaimed. "I forgot that was here."

"Yeah, that'd be cool as hell. I wanna go to that too," I said with excitement. "When?"

Bianca and Melanie shrugged.

"Tomorrow?" Bianca asked.

"Well, why not. It's not like any of us are doing anything—or are *ever* doing anything," Melanie said as she put her straw in her drink and took a sip.

"I'm good with going tomorrow," I said. "How much are the tickets though?" I asked knowing I didn't have a lot of money.

"I'll look," Melanie said as she pulled out her phone. Moments later she said, "Their website says tickets are thirty-five dollars for ages thirteen to sixty-four."

"Yeah, I don't think I have forty bucks for a ticket," I said.

"Yeah, thirty-five is kinda steep for me too," Melanie locked her phone and put it down on the table.

"Well, I have a date tonight. I know I could get some good money from this guy too. I'll pay for you guys," Bianca said.

"No," I said immediately as I grabbed my glass of water and slumped back into my chair.

Melanie scoffed and looked away, confirming she didn't want Bianca to pay for her either.

"Come on," Bianca said, rolling her eyes.

"No, I don't want you paying for us. Especially with money you sell yourself to get," I said.

"Iris, I'm going on the date regardless. So, I'm gonna be selling myself regardless," Bianca paused then spoke again with a plea. "Come on guys. This is a once-in-a-lifetime thing for us. We're gonna leave Seattle one day and probably never return. But those hundred and five dollars are gonna come back to me. Money is replaceable, experiences aren't."

I looked at her pensively for a moment then looked at Melanie.

She shrugged like *why not.*

I sighed, "Are you sure?"

"Yes! Seriously, it's fine, guys," she smiled.

I smiled, "Alright. Thank you, Bianca."

She smiled, "You're welcome."

"Yeah, thanks, traffic cones," Melanie teased, grinning.

Bianca looked at her, "You're paying tonight."

I chuckled.

"'You're paying tonight,'" Melanie mocked with a twisted face.

We all started laughing and soon enough Jamie brought out our *huge* but delicious pizza.

"I still can't believe it was only seventeen minutes from here," Bianca said.

It was now the next day and the three of us walked up the round-a-bout driveway to the Space Needle Center.

"Yeah, you didn't know that?" Melanie asked. "Why do you think I said I wanted to go? I'm not like you, Bianca. I'm not gonna spring a ten-hour journey on everyone."

Bianca exhaled deeply and rolled her eyes, "You're literally the most annoying person I know."

"Ditto," Melanie said.

I rolled my eyes, "Well, I would have gone regardless of how far away it was."

"'Cause you're cool, Iris," Bianca said.

"Suck up," Melanie said under her breath.

I scoffed, "I don't need to suck up to anyone. Just stating facts."

"Yeah, whatever," Melanie said as she pulled out a cigarette.

"You can't smoke here," I said, taking the cigarette out of Melanie's mouth moments before she could light it.

Melanie threw up her arms, "Hey!"

"Oh, you'll survive," I said, putting the cigarette in my purse.

Melanie rolled her eyes.

We took pictures, then made our way inside of the center. We walked through the metal detectors, admired the place and *all* its moving parts, then got into line to get tickets to go up the Space Needle. The line wasn't too long. Maybe because it was early in the day but nevertheless, we got in line and soon enough had our tickets.

We walked through the hall that was decorated with both history of the area and the Space Needle. We made our way to a second line to wait our turn to go in the elevator to the top.

"This is so cool," I said as I looked around me.

I was amazed. It was beautiful. I was surrounded by glass windows that overlooked so much. So many people, so many little shops, and the busy, bustling city. I had never seen anything like it. It was amazing. I only wished Colton, Leannah, and my mom could have seen it, too.

"Alright everybody, we're going up at ten miles per hour up to five hundred and twenty feet in the air. We will reach the top in approximately forty-one seconds—" the tour guide said as the elevator carried the three of us and a few other strangers to the top. He carried on with more information, but I couldn't pay attention. I was too amazed.

Seconds later the elevator stopped, and the doors opened. We were now at the top. Everyone exited and the three of us walked a couple of feet to glass doors that lead out to the viewing area.

"Oh my God," Bianca exclaimed as we all walked through the doors and right up to the glass window. "This view is gorgeous!"

I looked out at all of Seattle and smiled, "Wow," I was speechless. "This is incredible!"

"You can see the whole city from here," Melanie said.

I continued to gaze in bewilderment. I felt like I was on top of the world. It was absolutely and truly stunning.

The three of us took in the incredible view, took turns taking pictures of one another, and enjoyed the beauty that was Seattle.

"Good idea, Melanie," Melanie said aloud in a smug tone, giving herself praise for the idea of coming here.

I rolled my eyes, "Yes, thank you, Melanie. What would we do without you?" I asked in a sarcastic, playful tone as I put my hands in a prayer formation.

Bianca laughed, "Yeah, whatever would we do!" She put her hands in prayer formation as well and made a desperate face.

Melanie rolled her eyes, play-shoved us, and laughed. The three of us laughed and carried on looking at the city beneath us.

After some time, a little after twelve-thirty, we headed back down and walked out onto the round-a-bout pavement that we entered from.

"That was so cool," I said.

"I know right," Melanie said.

"See, that experience was SO much more valuable than some hundred and five dollars," Bianca said.

I smiled, "Yeah, thanks again, Bianca. I appreciate it."

Bianca smirked, "Anytime."

<h1 style="text-align:center">19</h1>

Chapter 19

Another week of "normal" life passed by. I say, "normal" with quotes because nothing was normal about our lives—or any of the lives of the people who were in this program. But…it was as close to normal as our normal could get.

It was July twenty-seventh. It was a Saturday. I talked with my family that day, took a walk, then in the evening, Melanie and I relaxed in our room while Bianca was on a date. It was a quiet, simple day. That is, until night came around.

It was around one A.M. and the three of us were asleep in our beds. I jolted awake when I heard the sound of glass shattering downstairs.

"What was that?" Melanie asked as she sprung up.

Bianca frantically pulled the lamp's chain, turning it on, "I don't know."

The three of us went silent as we focused on listening to what the noise was downstairs.

"Where the fuck did you put it?!" We heard a girl scream from downstairs.

Melanie frowned to listen harder, "Is that Alisha?"

Bianca and I listened closer.

"Where did you put it, Susan?! Where did you put it?!" the girl—who definitely sounded like Alisha—cried.

We all looked at each other, now knowing that the girl downstairs *had* to be Alisha.

A split second later we heard things crash to the floor and the sound of yet again another glass object fracturing.

"Come on, let's go," I said swiftly as I threw the covers off me and hurried out of our room.

Bianca and Melanie quickly followed behind me and we all scurried down the stairs. Once we got to the bottom couple of steps and entered the kitchen, we saw the disaster Alisha created. She had opened all the cabinet doors and was throwing their contents of plates and bowls onto the floor. Susan was trying to physically restrain her and hold her back, but she struggled. Alisha was desperately trying to find something.

"Where the fuck did you put it, Susan?!" Alisha cried out in anguish, breaking from Susan's clutch.

"Girls, go back to your room," Susan said to the three of us. We, however, remained perched on the stairs.

I had *never* seen Alisha like that, ever.

"Alisha, you need to calm down, please," Susan pleaded as she backed away.

"Where did you put it? I know you have it!"

Then, in a split second her mood changed from crying and desperate to furious.

"Where the fuck did you put it?!" She yanked open another cabinet door and threw out a stack of plates onto the ground. The shattering sound echoed, and at this time, more housemates were coming onto the stairs to see what was going on.

Susan backed away further. She shook her head in despair as she held her hand to her mouth.

"Tell me where it's at! Please!" Alisha desperately rifled through more cabinets and closets. "Where's my fucking Percs, Susan?! Where the fuck are they?!" She threw the toaster across the room.

I had a feeling that this was about drugs. But I was shocked when I found out I was right. I had *no* idea she was addicted to opioids—like, at all. I somewhat knew Alisha. She was the complete opposite of someone that would be addicted to opioids. No. I take that back. I of all people know that addiction doesn't have a look and it sure as hell doesn't discriminate.

"Honey," Susan said as she cautiously approached Alisha, "they're gone."

Alisha's face dropped into despair, "Wha—wha—what do you mean they're gone?"

Tears streamed down Susan's face, "They're gone, honey"—Susan choked back her tears—"I flushed them."

"No you didn't. No, no, no, no, no." Alisha ran into the nearby bathroom.

Susan stayed put and began to cry.

"Why would you do that?!" Alisha screamed as we heard her tearing the bathroom apart. "Why would you fucking do that?!"

"Alisha!" I finally yelled as I hurried into the bathroom behind her. She was tearing through the medicine cabinet like a rabid animal.

"Get away from me!" she yelled as tears streamed down her face. "I need to find my fucking pills. I need to fucking find them, you don't understand."

She began throwing all the medicine cabinets contents onto the bathroom floor, "Where the fuck did you put them, Susan?!"

"Alisha!" I grabbed a hold of her arms with both of my hands and forced her to look at me. "They're gone. The pills are gone."

"No!" she bellowed, ripping herself out of my clutch and storming back into the kitchen. I followed swiftly behind her.

"Where the fuck are they?!" she screamed. "Please! Just fucking give them to me, Susan," she began to cry. "Just please. Im fucking begging you. Please. I need them."

She collapsed into the wall as she began to bang on it. She cried terribly hard.

Susan had tears streaming down her face from several feet away. She tried to approach her, and the instant Susan touched Alisha's back, all of Alisha's sadness and pain turned to pure rage and anger. She pushed Susan out of her way and began to destroy the kitchen again.

"You wish I wasn't like this, huh?!" she screamed as she took both her hands and cleared off all the remaining items that sat on the kitchen counter. "Well so do fucking I! I wish, I wish I could be someone else, anyone else but me but I fucking can't" she cried. "I can't! I fucking can't! I hate myself! Do you get that? I *hate* myself." She then—somehow—flipped over the kitchen table.

That's when Susan, Bianca, and I rushed over to her and began to restrain her. Melanie stayed watching from the steps…figures. Alisha kicked and screamed and just repeated over and over *I hate myself*. Her pain sunk into my bones like a frigid day. I knew she felt that. I knew it. Every single word, I knew she meant it. And that was the worst part. That she wasn't lying, or exaggerating, or being dramatic. She hated herself. She hated what opioids did to her and how they turned her into something she wasn't. I'm sure any addict could say the same. And *that* was the worst part.

"Do you hate me?" she asked Susan with a well full of tears in her eyes.

We were able to restrain her and at this point, Alisha stopped fighting. She had given up and was completely hopeless and desperate. She was laying on Susan's lap on the floor.

"Nobody hates you, baby," Susan said as a tear rolled down her face and she pushed Alisha's sweaty hair on her face. "Nobody hates you."

I never knew you could witness a heart shrivel up and die until I saw Susan that night.

A beat of silence washed over us.

"Why'd you flush the pills, Susan?" Alisha cried. "I needed them. I *needed* them."

My heart shattered into a million pieces while I stood there watching Alisha lay on her side, covered in sweat, holding her stomach, and crying. When I looked at Alisha and the state she was in, I saw my mom. I saw my mom a million times over, and what was left of my heart melted out of my body, onto the floorboards, and into the ground below.

There was nothing in this world that was more painful than to see someone addicted to drugs. *Nothing.*

20

Chapter 20

Morning finally came—well, afternoon I should say. It was twelve o'clock by the time I woke up. I didn't go to bed until five though due to the cops and paramedics coming, I guess the neighbors called them. Bianca and I also helped Susan by packing Alisha's things. The cops said they would take her to a rehab center. Melanie went back to bed soon after Alisha was restrained, so she helped with nothing. Figures.

"Good morning," I said to Bianca and Melanie as I rubbed my eyes, sitting up in bed.

"Morning," Bianca said as she put down her phone, she was still in bed as well.

"Hey," Melanie said, brushing her hair in the mirror.

I checked my phone—no notifications.

"That was really sad what happened last night," Bianca said as she got out of bed.

"Yeah, it was," Melanie added.

I frowned, "You weren't even there," I said coldly.

"You guys had it under control," she said.

I scoffed, "Oh, so *that's* an excuse to not help us?"

"What do you want from me? There doesn't need to be seven hundred people helping."

I scoffed. I could see Bianca was blown away by Melanie's lack of compassion as well but wasn't saying anything about it.

I agitatedly put my hand up, "You know what? Whatever."

Melanie rolled her eyes like *I* was in the wrong. She got up and walked towards the closet.

"Anyway, did either of you guys know she was taking pills?" Melanie asked.

"No, not at all," Bianca said with conviction as she sat down at her vanity. "Did you, Iris?"

I got out of bed, "No. Actually, I expected her the *least* to be doing something like that, or any drugs for that matter."

"Right," Bianca said with passion. "She was so well put together."

"I know." Disappointment washed over me as I began to get dressed.

We all got ready, not saying much to one another.

About fifteen minutes later, when I was just about to go downstairs to help clean up, there was a knock on the door.

"Come in," I said.

The door opened and I saw it was Susan.

"Hey, ladies. Can you all come downstairs for a few minutes?" she asked. "I just want to talk to everybody."

"Yeah, sure thing, Susan," I said, already knowing this was about Alisha.

She smiled, "Thank you. And thank you two personally for helping me last night," she looked at Bianca and I. "I really appreciate it."

The two of us smiled. Melanie didn't do anything.

"Of course, Susan…anytime," I said.

She smiled and closed the door.

"That's definitely about Alisha," Bianca said.

"Oh, of course," I said as we headed to the door.

We got downstairs and almost all our housemates were sitting in the living room. Minutes later, Susan came down the stairs with the rest of the housemates and they sat down.

"Alright…so I know you all either witnessed or heard the incident that took place last night. Well, I guess it was really this morning. Anyway, I'm not going to expose any of Alisha's private business, but I do think of you all as my family and I believe family should be honest with one another," she took a deep breath before carrying on. "Alisha had a substance abuse problem. It's a very sad thing. I'm sure some of you either know what that's like or know someone that deals with or *has* dealt with one. Well, I just want to say that all of you can come to me for anything at any time. Even after you all leave. You have my number, please use it when you need it."

From there, Susan gave each and every one of us big hugs. Her compassion and generosity were something I never forgot. She was hands down, the kindest woman I had ever met.

After the "meeting" was over. The three of us walked into the kitchen and looked around at the mess. The same mess that was there the night before, only it looked a lot worse in the daylight. The floor was still covered in shards of glass, ceramic pieces, forks, spoons and butter knives. All of Susan's cookbooks were on the floor, recipes skewed about, the cabinets were swung open, and their contents were all over the place. And that was only half of it.

"This is fucked up," Bianca said.

I felt horrible. I felt horrible for Alisha, and I felt horrible for Susan. I know Alisha didn't necessarily mean to do what she did. She had a disease. A disease that changes your mind, fogs your vision, and makes you burrow your way through anything to get to what you're addicted to. Just like a rat when it's under a hot lamp. I felt horrible for Susan because it was her house. It was her things that got ruined and all she ever wanted to do is help those that needed it the most. It was sad—for everyone.

I grabbed a broom from the kitchen closet, "I guess I'll start with this," I said as I began to sweep.

"I'll collect the books," Bianca said, then knelt to gather them.

I noticed Melanie walk away and back up the stairs. I scoffed to myself and shook my head. How inconsiderate? Whatever her deal was with "Alisha being a drug addict" she needed to get over it. This was no longer about Alisha; it was about Susan. That woman did *everything* for us, and Melanie couldn't even help pick up some fucking silverware? It was truly disgusting. I had *never* met someone shallower than her.

"Thank you so much, girls," Susan said as she walked into the kitchen from the living room. "You guys don't have to help, really."

I frowned and paused my sweeping once more, "Susan, stop. Of course we're going to help."

She smiled, "Thank you."

I smiled ruefully and continued sweeping.

Susan announced she was going to clean the bathroom up, leaving Bianca, me, and three other housemates cleaning the kitchen.

About an hour later, the living room, kitchen, and bathroom were put back together. The only difference now was the lack of several plates, bowls, and cups as they had been smashed.

"It looks great, guys. Thank you all so much," Susan said with a smile, although she still seemed sad inside.

"Anytime, Susan," Bianca said.

"Yeah, it was no problem. You do so much for us, it's the least we can do," I added.

Susan then smiled a more genuine smile, "Thank you."

We then heard the front door being jingled with and within another second, it opened.

"I'm back," Tobey said, grinning ear to ear as he carried four heavy bags.

Susan's face looked surprised, "What's all that?"

"It's for you," he said as he carried over the bags to the counter and set them down.

Susan, who still looked shocked, didn't know what to say. Tobey winked at us, gushing over the surprise.

"Go on, open it," Tobey urged.

The six of us, Bianca, Tobey, the three housemates, and I, all watched impatiently, trying to see what the gifts were.

Susan pulled down the bags and exposed what was inside of them. It was boxes of plates, bowls, and mug sets.

"Oh, Tobey, this is too sweet!"

I looked up at Tobey and smiled. It was a really nice thing he did.

"You didn't have to do this, sweetheart," Susan said as she placed her hand on his arm.

Tobey shot her a *Don't worry about it face*. "It's no big deal."

"Let me pay you back, please," Susan said.

"No, no, seriously it's fine. I wanted to do this," Tobey said.

Susan hugged Tobey. "Thank you so much."

"You're welcome."

For the next two hours, all seven of us unboxed the sets, washed them, and put them away. We ate lunch and overall, just had a nice afternoon. Who knew something so sad and destructive could turn into something so generous and beautiful.

21

Chapter 21

~ Chapter 21 ~

It was now Monday, August nineteenth. Almost a month had passed
by since the incident with Alisha. Nothing too eventful took place
during that time. I wasn't surprised by all this boring, down time
though. It's not like Bianca, Melanie, and I were best friends. We
weren't even friends. Well, I wouldn't consider them my friends
anyway. Sure, we had our moments that we got along and liked one
another, but the majority of the time, we were simply acquaintances.
We didn't do everything together and we didn't spend every waking
second together, but we still cared for one another. Well, at least I

know *I* cared for them.

"This looks cool!" Bianca exclaimed as she parked the car and the three of us stepped out.

We were at Hercules Park in Southeast Seattle. It was a gorgeous day; seventy-five degrees and not a cloud to be found.

"Look at the lake! It's gorgeous," I said. The parking lot basically sat directly on the water while a two-mile walking trail was directly adjacent to it.

"Yes, yes, nature is beautiful. Now let's go," Melanie said as she slipped her sunglasses down over her eyes.

I rolled my eyes and shook my head, "Can't you enjoy anything?"

"I enjoy not enjoying things," she said sarcastically. Although I'm sure she meant it.

"Oh, I can tell," I said.

Bianca chuckled, "Come on, let's start walking."

We hopped on the trail and started down the path. I led us next to the lake, through the woods, and past a playground and picnic area. I really enjoyed it. About three quarters of the way through, we had a perfect view of the lake.

"Oh, this is a great view of the lake. Let me take a picture," I said, stopping the other two.

"Yeah, same," Bianca said.

The two of us pulled out our phones and began to take some pictures of the gorgeous body of water.

"Don't you want to take a picture to remember this moment?" Bianca turned and asked Melanie.

"Why? Do you plan on performing brain surgery or some shit on me so I can't make memories in my head?" Melanie asked as she got up from the bench she was sitting on. She simultaneously pulled out her phone and joined us.

Bianca made a face like *That was a stupid comeback.*

I chuckled at Bianca's face.

"Whatever," Melanie said as she pointed her phone at the lake and took some photos.

I knew she wanted to take some but didn't want to seem impressed by the lake…that was Melanie for you.

After we got all the shots we wanted, we sat down on the bench and took a break.

"All this riveting nature makes me need a cigarette," Melanie said as she took one and lighter out of her bag.

I exhaled. She was a *true* piece of work.

"Let me get some," Bianca said as she grabbed the cigarette out of Melanie's hand just as she got it to light, barely giving Melanie any chance to puff on it.

"Hey—" Melanie said with her hands up.

Bianca laughed and pulled on the cigarette.

"Very cute," Melanie flashed a smile and snatched the cigarette from Bianca's fingers, puffing on it.

Bianca and I chuckled.

Just then, a young man, probably mid-twenties, wearing basketball shorts and a short sleeve shirt approached us. He had brown hair that was cut short, brown eyes and didn't have quite a full beard, but he had facial hair.

"Hey," he said to Bianca with a smile.

"Hey," she said, eyes lighting up.

"I hope you don't think this is weird, but I just was over there playing basketball and I saw you and thought you're really beautiful."

Melanie and I made an *oooooo* face at one another.

Bianca smiled and sat forward, "Oh yeah? Well, thank you. You're quite handsome yourself."

The man smiled, "I'm Steven," he put out his hand to shake hers.

"Bianca," she said, shaking his hand.

"Hey," Steven said with a slight wave as he looked at Melanie and me.

"Hi, I'm Iris."

"Melanie."

"Nice to meet you guys," he said.

"You too," we both said.

"Yeah, so I just wanted to tell you that," Steven said bashfully. "Have a good day."

"Wait," Bianca said. "Why don't we get to know one another?"

He chuckled as he looked down, "Alright, yeah. I'd like that."

Bianca smiled, "Me too."

She then handed him her phone. He took it and then handed his phone to her.

"I'll call you for sure. Maybe if you're not doing anything tonight, we can do something," Steven said.

"No doubt," Bianca said with her signature flirty smile.

"Alright, I'll talk to you later then."

Bianca smiled and Steven gave Melanie and I a goodbye wave before jogging back to the basketball court.

"Look at youuuu," I said in a boosting kind of way.

"They must smell the hooker," Melanie added sarcastically as she pulled on her cigarette.

I smacked her arm.

"Well, whatever it is they smell, they definitely don't smell it on you," Bianca said.

"Thank God," Melanie said with her hands in a prayer formation, looking up to the sky.

I rolled my eyes, "You're so annoying, Melanie."

"Let her have her only moment of joy," Bianca said.

I chuckled and Melanie rolled her eyes, taking another puff.

"So, you gonna bang him or what?" Melanie asked as she blew out smoke.

Bianca scoffed, "I gotta see if he's even down to."

"Oh, come on," she pulled on her cigarette. "Why wouldn't he?" she exhaled. "All he has to do is pay you and besides you're the one that said, 'you'd be surprised how many guys will have sex with you for money,'" Melanie said inconsiderately.

Bianca looked at her with disgust, "Yeah. But not all guys want to. Truly, it's not really your business." She said this with an attitude as Melanie had just pissed her off. Melanie really had a way of starting something from nothing and annoying people quicker than anybody else I had ever met.

"Alright, well, Bianca, you can do what you want, and Melanie, you can just shut the fuck up sometimes," I said, now growing a little agitated myself.

Melanie widened her eyes and put up her hands up defensively before she took another puff of her cigarette.

"Whatever, let's just go enjoy the rest of the walk before you somehow ruin it," I said to Melanie as I stood up.

Melanie threw her cigarette on the ground, standing up as well, "Yeah, we better."

Bianca rolled her eyes so hard I thought they'd fall out of her head. All conveying that Melanie was annoying. Yeah—you don't say, Bianca.

22

Chapter 22

"Alright, I'm gonna head out," Bianca said to me as she grabbed her purse from the floor.

After we got back to Susan's, Steven called Bianca and they talked for like an hour and a half. She was so giddy and excited. It seemed like they really hit it off and she liked him in a way that wasn't transactional.

"Be safe," I said, peering up from my book. "Hey, where does he live?"

"In Pinehurst."

"Oh, okay," I said, somewhat surprised as Pinehurst was literally like five minutes away. "Cool, well, have fun."

She smiled, "Thanks, Iris."

Just then, Melanie opened the door to walk into our room. They both stared coldly at each other as Melanie walked past her. Bianca then turned away and exited our room.

Melanie plopped down on her bed, took her phone out of her back pocket, and began going through it without saying anything to me. I looked over at her for a second then continued reading my book.

About an hour went by, it was eight-thirty-ish and I was ready to do something else. I didn't care to hang out with Melanie on a good day, so that night, a night where she was so far under my skin, that was the last thing I wanted to do. So, I headed downstairs and into the living room where Tobey, Tim, and two other housemates, Gwen and Demetrius, were watching TV.

"Hey, Iris," Tobey said as I approached the couch.

"Hey," I smiled as I sat down and looked at the TV. "What are you guys watching?" I asked with a confused face as I saw a grown man trying to make a stranger hide something in the park for him.

Tim laughed, "It's called *Impractical Jokers*. You've never heard of it?"

I shook my head.

"Oh my God," the three boys let out in playful despair.

Gwen laughed at their reaction as did I.

"What?" I laughed. "What's *Impractical Jokers?*"

"I can't believe you've never heard of it before!" Tobey said.

"What is it?" I asked again.

"It's about four dudes that have been friends for, like, ever and they compete to embarrass one another. They have to do challenges and whoever loses, at the end of the episode, they get punished," Demetrious said.

"Yeah, and the punishments are always super cringey and embarrassing and they can't refuse a punishment like they can a challenge," Tobey added.

"Ohhhh," I said with interest as I readjusted myself to be more comfortable on the couch.

"This episode just came out two nights ago. It's called *Film Fail*," Demetrious said.

"So, what are they doing now?" I asked.

"They're trying to get strangers to hide random objects in the park for them," Gwen said. "Whoever can't get the stranger to hide it for them, loses."

"Okay," I laughed. "Sounds interesting."

"Oh, it is," Tobey said, "Trust me. This show will make you laugh your ass off. Those guys are hilarious."

And Tobey was exactly right. For the next two and a half hours we all watched reruns of old episodes and laughed our asses off. It was a great night, until it wasn't. I guess all good things do come to an end.

It was now a little after eleven and the four all said goodnight and that they were headed up for bed. There was still no sign of Bianca though. I knew curfew wasn't until twelve, but…she was typically home way before twelve. Like, ten-thirty, ten-forty-five-ish. She also hadn't answered any of my numerous texts I sent her. I was a little concerned, but I tried to ignore it. I figured she was just having a good time. She *did* seem to really be interested in him considering she talked with him on the phone for almost two hours.

But after some time, around eleven thirty-five, I still couldn't shake the feeling that something wasn't right with her. So, I opened my contact book on my phone and clicked on Bianca's name. I clicked on the phone icon and put my phone up to my ear.

"Please leave your message for seven, one, four—" the automated message played instantly.

I knew this meant her phone was off because it didn't even ring out. Now, I *knew* something was wrong.

"Have you heard from Bianca?" I asked Melanie as I opened our bedroom door.

"Nope." She didn't even lift her eyes from her phone's screen.

"Well, I'm worried about her," I crossed my arms. "It's almost eleven-forty and she's still not back."

Melanie shrugged, "So?"

"So?" I said somewhat aggressively. "She's *never* out this late."

"Iris, relax. It's not even midnight yet," dismissing my concern.

"And? Bianca's home before eleven each time she goes out."

Melanie shrugged again, "Call her if you're so worried."

"I did," I said harshly like I wouldn't have already thought of that. "It went straight to voicemail. Her phone's off."

"Well, I don't know, Iris but she's probably fucking that guy right now as we speak, and she just isn't paying attention to her phone."

I scoffed at her uncaring attitude.

"You're the one that said, 'maybe she likes him in a non-transactional way and is a decent guy.' I mean Christ, she spent two hours talking to him on the phone," Melanie added.

I scoffed, "No, you don't get it. Something's wrong. She *never* is out this late, she *never* ignores my texts, and she *never* has her phone off."

"Well, I don't know what to tell you," she picked her phone back up.

"What's your fucking problem?" I snapped.

"Me?" Melanie shot up from her bed. "You're the one freaking out over this chick who's a PROS-TI-TUTE and isn't home tucked away in bed before midnight."

"Are you fucking deaf?!" I yelled. "She's NEVER home this late and she NEVER has her phone off."

"Well, what do you wanna do, Iris? Huh?!" she snapped.

"Let's go look for her!"

Melanie scoffed and leaned against her headboard, "Yeah okay, Iris. What are we gonna do? Get on the bus and go looking for her someplace in all of Seattle? Or who knows, she may not even be in Seattle."

"She's in Pinehurst," I said coldly. "It's four minutes from here."

Another scoff, "That's great," she looked at her phone again.

"So, come on!" I yelled. "I need your help. Something's not right."

"I'm not going to look for her. You go if you're so desperate."

I couldn't believe how selfish, callous, and heartless she was being. Guess, I shouldn't have been surprised.

"Are you serious?!" I yelled. "You're being a fucking bitch."

"I'm being a bitch because I don't want to help someone that DOESN'T—NEED—HELP?!" She shot up again. "Why should I help her anyway? She's not my friend," she said coldly as she slumped back down against her headboard.

Her words were a slap to the face. How could she be so evil? I was absolutely and utterly appalled.

"Fine," I said, just as cold and stern. "Don't help me, but just remember when I helped you that night of the party, you weren't my fucking friend either."

I gave her a disgusted and ire face then took off down the stairs. I was so angry with her, but I couldn't focus on that now. I had to focus on helping Bianca, because I *knew* she needed it.

23

Chapter 23

I ran out of Susan's house and began to run down the street towards the stop sign. I didn't really know how I would find Bianca, but I knew that I had to do something. It ended up not mattering though because that's when I saw it. A girl whimpering and walking down the street came towards me. It was too dark out to tell who it was, but I could tell it was a girl and the silhouette resembled Bianca's.

"Bianca?" I yelled out to the girl.

The girl stopped walking, "Iris?" I heard her say in a weak cry.

"Bianca!" I yelled again and started running towards her.

Bianca started running towards me, although her run was not nearly as strong or as fast as mine. She looked weak. Seconds later we met, and she fell onto me for support. Bianca was crying hysterically. I had never seen her cry like that, or well, cry at all.

"What happened?!" Concern lacing my voice as I looked down at her, holding her upright.

She pulled away and it was with the nearby streetlamp that I could finally see her clearly. It was bad. It was really bad. She had a busted, bloody lip, blood running down the side of her face from a wound on the side of her forehead, bruises on her arms, and worst of all, a big black and blue bruise strung around her neck.

"Oh my fucking God, Bianca. What the fuck happened to you?!" I cried.

"He, he"—she struggled to speak from being out of breath and crying—"he hit me." She cried harder, "He beat me up."

"What do you mean he beat you up?" I asked gently. "Come here, sit down," I ushered her to the grassy area on the side of the street.

We sat down and she began to calm down.

"Okay, tell me what happened."

"Okay," she took a breath. "I got to Steven's house, and everything was fine for the first couple hours. He was nice and talkative, and we were just getting to know one another. After some time, we started kissing. He did that stupid thing that guys do, asking how you're so good at it. Well, I told him I'm a prostitute, thinking it was sexy but it was not at all to him." She took a pause as she got somewhat choked up but forced it down.

"He freaked out on me, Iris," she started to cry, not being able to hold her emotions down. "He said, 'What do you mean you're a prostitute?' I said, 'What do you mean, what do I mean? I'm a prostitute' and he completely freaked out. He yanked me off the couch and threw me down to the floor. He started screaming at me saying I'm a whore and that I'm disgusting and why would I even come here. I stammered to my feet, and he kept violently shoving me and saying such awful things, Iris," her eyes welled up with tears as she looked at me.

"He said how dare I kiss him with such disgusting lips and that I probably have herpes and AIDS and all these other nasty diseases. I yelled at him and said I didn't have any of that and that he was being an asshole and that's when he punched me in the mouth. I fell down but got to my feet and tried to run to the door. When I grabbed the handle, he grabbed me and punched me again in the face. I fell and hit my head on the coffee table. That's when he picked me up and started *screaming* in my face," she paused to cry again. I hugged her from the side and squeezed her tight. After a moment of her crying, she spoke.

"He said he should kill me for even coming over here and that I was a waste of a life. I had my phone in my hand and when he saw it, he grabbed it and threw it against the wall with all his strength. I watched the glass shatter, and the frame fall off the back. He started screaming saying I'm not going anywhere and that now I can't call anybody. He was completely and utterly freaking out, Iris. He then grabbed my purse and dumped everything out, threw my purse, and then grabbed my keys and threw them outside into the backyard. That's when he started to choke me. He was still screaming all kinds of things at me, but right before I felt myself about to pass out, I was able to knee him in the dick hard enough to make him let me go. I dropped to the floor and started coughing violently. I didn't waste any time though. I got up, stumbled towards the door, swung it open, and began to run. I ran as fast as I could and when I knew he wasn't following me, I hid behind some trash cans and just cried," Bianca began to get emotional again.

I held her as she cried.

"Bianca, I'm so sorry," I whispered to her as she cried. "This isn't your fault."

She smiled ruefully as she pulled away from our hug and dried her eyes. "I just want to get my car."

"We'll get it, I promise. But let's get you home and cleaned up first, okay?"

"Okay," she said quietly.

I helped Bianca to our room, opened the door, and found the lights were off. Melanie was asleep in her bed. I couldn't fucking believe her. Animosity boiled inside of me.

"Wake the fuck up," I barked as I flicked on the light with my hand that wasn't supporting Bianca. "This is what was wrong. This is what I was trying to fucking tell you," I said bluntly as Bianca and I hobbled in.

Melanie squinted at the light and blinked to adjust her eyes, trying to look at us. "Oh shit, what happened?" Not an ounce of true sympathy linger in her voice.

"What happened?" Bianca growled. Melanie's lack of sympathy wasn't lost on Bianca either. "What the fuck happened? I got beat the fuck up, that's what happened. Are you fucking serious? You didn't even care to see if I was alright? I always answer my phone when I'm out and you *know* I always come home before eleven."

Melanie sat up in bed, "Didn't think there was anything to check on," she said monotonously with a cold, blank expression.

That line ignited a fire inside of Bianca. "Didn't think there was anything to check on?!" Bianca yelled. "Didn't think there was anything to fucking check on?!" She stormed towards her.

I followed behind concerningly. Bianca was MAD.

"Does my fucking face look like there was 'nothing to check on'?!" She barked again, pointing at her face. She was now face to face with Melanie who hadn't moved a muscle and still displayed a look of disgust. "How about my fucking neck? Huh?" she asked as she swung her hair to the side to expose the entire bruise.

Melanie still was just staring at Bianca with hate.

"You're a fucking bitch," Bianca said as she lightly pushed on Melanie's shoulders. She then turned to walk back towards me.

"You know, it ever dawn on you that maybe if you didn't fuck everything in sight, this kinda shit wouldn't happen?" Melanie hissed.

I watched the look on Bianca's face turn from angry to enraged faster than the speed of light. In an instant, Bianca shot around and charged towards Melanie. Before Melanie could react, Bianca shoved her violently and Melanie jolted back, Melanie now got out of the bed and stood up right in Bianca's face.

"If I didn't fuck everything in sight, huh?!" Bianca screamed. "I didn't fuck him! You wanna know why he beat me up?! Huh?! It's 'cause I told him I'm a prostitute," Bianca laughed out of anger. "Yeah"—she laughed again—"he's just like you! A piece of fucking shit that somehow, the fucking shit I do affects you all so bad for some fucking reason!"

"Well, he's fucking right!" Melanie finally yelled back.

"Go to fucking hell, Melanie!" I barked.

"You're just a dirty fucking slut that wants everyone to feel bad for her. Oh no, you got beat up when you told a guy you fuck people for money. Big fucking surprise!" Melanie yelled callously. "You act like this shit isn't supposed to happen or some shit. You walk around here like you're top shit and every dude wants you. But you wanna know something?" Melanie stepped closer to Bianca, and they were now inches apart. "Nobody wants someone like you. Nobody wants a used, ran through, fucking whore."

Bianca's breathing grew heavier and heavier and within a split second, she pulled back and punched Melanie in the face.

"Bianca!" I yelled as I grabbed her. As much as I wanted to see Melanie get her ass beat, I wasn't going to let Bianca do that.

Melanie stumbled back and held her face. A grin then grew onto her face and she laughed.

"I'd hit you back, but it seems your little friend already did that for me," she said with a smirk.

Bianca lunged for her, but I held her still and pulled her away.

"You're a fucking bitch! You're a fucking bitch!" she yelled as I restrained her.

After a moment she broke out of my clutch and got right back into Melanie's face. She breathed heavily and put her finger up in her face.

After seconds of exchanged ire glares and Bianca's heavy breathing, Bianca spoke extremely calm but full of hate.

"You're dead to me. You're fucking dead."

24

Chapter 24

I woke to the sound of Bianca rifling through her suitcase. I blinked my eyes a couple of times, adjusting them to the light when I saw the clock in our room said seven a.m. I noticed Melanie wasn't in her bed.

"Sorry," Bianca said, pausing her hunt. "Did I wake you?"

"No." She kind of did but it was okay. "What are you looking for?" I asked after I sat up.

"A hoodie or some shit to cover my neck. There's no way I'm walking around with this gigantic bruise on my throat," she said bitterly.

I looked down ruefully. "What if you covered it with makeup?"

"Already tried," she said bluntly then lifted her hair up to show me how awful it turned out. It almost made it look worse.

I winced, "Oh." I didn't know what else to say.

"Yeah," she said bitterly.

I got up and walked to the corner of the room where my suitcase was. I laid it down, unzipped it, and began to dig through all my winter clothes.

"Here," I said as I walked towards her and handed her a thin gray scarf. "You can probably match it with your outfit to make it look like it's part of what you're wearing. Not like something that is being used to hide something."

She looked ruefully as she took the scarf, "Thanks, Iris."

I nodded, "I'm gonna make some coffee, you want some?"

"Yeah, I'll take one," she then stood up. "Hey, Iris?"

"Yeah?" I turned around to face her.

"Once you come back up, will you come with me to get my car?"

She seemed nervous to ask me, like she felt like a burden.

"Course," I said with a smile as I grabbed my phone and exited our room.

I wasn't going to make her feel bad or like it was a problem because, in reality, it wasn't. And I never was the type of person to abandon someone when they needed me the most. Also, there wasn't a chance in hell I'd let her attempt to get her car back alone from the guy who used her as a punching bag the night before. That was just me. I cared. Even if it were a time where I shouldn't, I still did. I always tried to fix things and help people even if they weren't worthy of it. But, I figured, I rather make others feel like someone cares and has their back, then how Melanie makes people feel, any day.

I got downstairs, where I saw no one. Not even Melanie. I wasn't sure where she could have gone but I didn't care. I knew she was just evading Bianca and me. I made our coffees, went back upstairs, threw on some clothes, and was ready to go to this asshole's house.

"Ready?" I asked Bianca.

"Yeah, I'm ready," she said as she took one last look at herself in the mirror and adjusted her scarf.

She had on jean shorts, a loose racerback tank top, the scarf, and sneakers.

"There you go," I smiled, trying to boost her confidence. "You look like one of those boho-grunge-hipsters."

She forced a smile, "Thanks. I don't feel like one though," she said as she fixed her hair to cover the bandage.

"Well, that's the thing about confidence; nobody knows if it's real or not," I smiled, still trying to encourage her.

She smiled genuinely this time, "Thanks, Iris. Let's just go and get this shit over with."

"Alright, let's go," I said.

We took the bus and soon enough, arrived at Steven's house. Facing it from the street, it was a big brick duplex that had symmetrical garages and big glass windows over top of the garage doors. I could see that the windows had old, dirty curtains covering them. On each side of the split house, there was a flight of concrete stairs that wrapped around to the front door. Next to these stairs were shrubs and other greenery that hadn't been taken care of.

"Okay, which one?" I asked as we stood in front of the house.

"That one," Bianca pointed to the left side of the duplex with anger in her voice.

I looked over at her after hearing the sudden change in her voice, but she was just staring at the left side of the duplex with an ire face and a clenched jaw.

"Come on," she said aggressively as she stormed over to the concrete stairs and went up them.

I followed behind.

Bianca viciously began searching around for her keys. I began to also look around the poorly kempt small yard but in a calm manner. I didn't blame Bianca for being mad at all though. I was too, but I knew one of us had to be the sane one.

"Where are they?!" she yelled.

"Bianca!" I said in a stern hushed voice. "You're gonna wake him!"

"I don't give a fuck," she said. "Where are my fucking keys, asshole?!" she shouted again. She then knocked over a potted plant that sat on the sidewalk. The sidewalk trailed from the stairs to the front door. It broke into a few large pieces and soil spilled out. I kind of grinned at her doing this. It was satisfying to see her break something that belonged to this piece of shit.

"Where the fuck are the keys?!" I then yelled as I pushed a flowerpot over onto the sidewalk. It broke and soil spilled out like the previous one.

Bianca looked at me, surprised I did that and surprised I yelled. I smiled mischievously and once she understood I was now on the same page as her, she returned the same smile.

She grabbed one of the plastic chairs that was randomly sitting in the yard and threw it, "Give me my fucking keys, Steven!"

I laughed as I took a bucket that was filled up with rainwater and splashed it all over the front door and siding of the house.

We went back and forth yelling for him to give us the keys and destroying things in his yard. We flipped over a junky metal and glass table and watched the glass shatter, we kicked at his barely living flowers, and threw dirt at his house and windows. As we were dying from laughter from destroying Steven's house, Steven flung the door open and stared at us. He was still protected by his storm door, however.

"What the hell are you two doing?!" he screamed in disbelief through the storm door.

"Where's her fucking keys?!" I growled.

"Look what you guys did!" Ignoring my question. "I should kick both your asses," he then looked at Bianca. "AGAIN!"

"Where's her fucking keys?!" I barked again, not showing any sign of fear.

"The hell if I know or care," he scoffed, trying to bolster his masculinity.

I grabbed a nearby shovel and approached the door.

"Okay, okay" he put his hands up. "There, there. They're right over there," he pointed to the corner of the yard where the shed sat.

I turned my head to look. Bianca had scurried over to where he was pointing. I looked back at Steven, who still had his hands up and now had a worried look on his face.

"I got them!" Bianca yelled seconds later.

I turned my head again and saw her holding them. I was blinded for a second as the sun reflected off that damn rhinestone heart.

I looked back at Steven, "What kind of "man" beats up a chick?!" I yelled as I moved towards him with the shovel.

He still had his hands up but quickly locked the storm door.

Bianca laughed, "You're such a bitch. What? You're afraid of two girls but not one?" She then picked up a piece of the broken flower vase and walked next to me, "Give me my fucking purse and all my other shit you dumped out of it too!"

"No!" Steven said with a frown, putting his hands down.

Bianca then threw the broken piece of vase at the shed's caged light. She hit the bulb's cage and it rattled violently back and forth. She then kicked the bottom of the storm door with all her might, "Give me my *fucking* purse and *all* the shit you dumped out of it!"

Steven had his hands back up now, "Okay, okay," he scurried into the living room which we could see through the window. We watched as he grabbed her purse and then gathered up the pile of stuff that was on the floor, putting it back into her bag. "Here!" he yelled as he opened the storm door just wide enough to fit his hand through.

Bianca snatched it from him. She took a quick look inside to make sure all her valuables were in there like her ID and the little amount of cash she kept in it. "Alright," she said as she slung the bag over her arm.

I then walked up to the storm door, now face to face with Steven through the glass, "You're a piece of fucking shit, you know that?"

He glared at me with a hatful look on his face but didn't say anything. I stared at him for a couple more seconds then backed away.

"Come on," Bianca said as we both stared at him with loathe.

I didn't say anything and kept eye contact with him up until the last minute.

As I walked down the path, I aggressively threw the shovel at another small glass table. It broke and the glass and everything that was on top of it, crashed to the ground.

"Hey!" Steven yelled out as he held the storm door halfway open. "I'm gonna call the fucking cops!"

I stormed back over to him, and he quickly shut the door like the pussy he was. I violently smacked my hand against the glass part of it. "You're gonna call the fucking cops, huh?!" I barked. "While you have them on the phone, make sure you mention the part where you beat up a nineteen-year-old girl, broke her phone, and stole her car keys!"

"Oh, and also!" Bianca yelled as she simultaneously ripped my scarf off her neck and stormed over to me, "tell them how you said you'd kill me and then proceeded to strangle me to almost unconsciousness!" She held her hair back and lifted her head up so he could see the gruesome bruise he left on her throat.

Steven's face fell into a look like he knew he couldn't call the police.

"So go ahead," I said with hatred, "call the fucking police. But if you do, make sure you include all that shit too."

I stared at him harshly with disgust and he glared back at me with the same hatred. After a moment, I said, "Come on, Bianca."

She glared at him one final time and then followed me down the path and to the stairs. We descended the stairs and got into Bianca's car, once we did, all we could do was burst into laughter.

25

Chapter 25

"Oh! There you are, girls," Susan said as we walked in. She was pouring pancake batter onto the griddle. "Oh, Bianca!" she exclaimed. "What happened to your face?"

"Oh," Bianca said quietly, "nothing, just tripped and fell down some concrete stairs last night."

Susan came closer to examine her face, "Oh, honey, are you okay?"

"Yeah, yeah, I'm fine," Bianca said, trying to move away from Susan so that she could evade any further questions.

"Alright," Susan said unsurely, not really believing her lie but not wanting to push any further. I guess she picked up on Bianca's evading attitude. "Well, if you need anything, let me know."

"I will, thanks," Bianca said blandly, forcing a smile.

"Are you girls hungry?" Susan asked. "I'm making pancakes now and French toast, scrambled eggs, and turkey bacon afterwards."

I looked at Bianca, "Yeah, that sounds great, thank you," I then said to Susan.

"Yeah, I'd be fine with pancakes," Bianca said.

"Sounds good," Susan smiled and walked back over to the griddle.

I got myself some water then sat down next to Bianca at the table.

A couple minutes later, Tobey and Demetrious came down the stairs. Susan of course asked if they wanted breakfast and they of course said they did.

"Bianca, are you okay?" Demetrious asked, nodding towards her face after a minute of small talk. "What happened?"

"Just fell down some stairs, that's all." Bianca said in an annoyed and short tone.

"Oh, okay," Demetrious said, a little surprised she answered him that way.

"So," I said, changing the topic for her, "what are you guys doing today?"

"Uh, probably nothing," Tobey laughed. "You?"

I chuckled, "Same."

"Such fascinating lives we have, guys," Demetrious said jokingly.

Bianca and I laughed.

"I know right," Bianca said.

Just then Melanie came walking down the stairs. Her face looked a little red from where Bianca punched her. It wasn't bruised or bloody, and it *especially* wasn't like Bianca's. Instantly, Bianca's face turned from happy and smiling to angry and twisted. Melanie looked at her blandly.

"Good morning, Melanie," Susan smiled. "Would you like some breakfast?"

"Nah, I'm good…thanks," she replied.

"You sure? Breakfast is important," she smiled.

"Yeah, I'm sure," Melanie said as she grabbed the front door handle. "Thanks, Susan."

"Oh, well, okay. Well, be safe wherever you're going, honey."

"Will do," Melanie then closed the door behind her.

Bianca rolled her eyes to herself in disgust. I had never seen Bianca so mad. Like I said before, I don't blame her. Not only did Melanie say some really fucked up shit to her the night before, but she's also been a complete bitch to her these past two months.

The four of us continued talking and then ate our breakfast once it was ready. After we finished, I took a shower, did my makeup, and got dressed. Bianca left in the middle of this process to go get a new phone. So, I decided to call my family. I grabbed my phone and headed outside into the gorgeous weather Seattle was having that day.

"Hey, Sis!" Leannah exclaimed.

"Hey, Le!" I said back. "How are you? I miss you."

"Aw, I miss you too. I'm good, how are you?" she asked.

"I'm good too. What are you up to?"

"Nothing really, I was gonna eat a popsicle," she laughed. "It's pretty hot today."

I laughed, "Oh yeah? It's gorgeous in Seattle. It's like seventy-two."

"Lucky, it's eighty-five and humid as hell."

"Oh yeah, that's the worst," I said. "Better get that popsicle then," I joked.

She laughed, "Yeah, I will.

"Where's Mom and Colton?" I asked.

"Colton's here, Mom's at work."

"Oh, okay, can I talk to Colton?"

"Yeah, one sec…Colton!"—I heard her yell—then a beat later, "Here take the phone. It's Iris."

"Hey, Sis," Colton said a second later. "What's up?"

"Hey, nothing, what are you up to?"

"I was just doing some laundry. Did Leannah tell you it's fucking hot out today?"

I laughed, "Yeah she did."

"It's really just the humidity that's the problem," he said. "If that wasn't so bad, it'd be fine."

"Yeah, that humidity sucks," I said.

"You're telling me," he replied.

I chuckled.

"Hey, so I gotta tell you something," I said, changing the tone of the conversation from lighthearted to more serious. I wanted to tell him about Bianca and what we did to Steven's property.

"What's up?" he asked.

"So, you know my roommate, Bianca?"

"Yeah," he said in a confused tone.

"Well yesterday she met this guy, Steven, at a park that she, Melanie and I went to. She went over to his house later in the evening. Well, she ended up telling him she was a prostitute, and he freaked the fuck out on her, like, bad, Colton. He broke her phone, threw her keys outside, threatened to kill her, strangled her, punched her in the mouth, threw her to the ground, busted her forehead, I mean the list goes on—"

"Holy shit," Colton interrupted. "Is she okay? What a fucking doucebag!"

"Yeah, she's fine," I said. "Well, she obviously needed to get her car back and she asked me last night to come with her today to get it. So, we went and entered his backyard looking for the keys. Well"—I smiled unsurely—"we ended up destroying his backyard. We threw his flowerpots around and broke them, we threw dirt at his house, broke his table, threw his chairs, and just tore it up—"

"Iris, what the fu—"

"Let me finish!" I said loudly, already knowing he would be annoyed. "Eventually, Steven heard us and came running down to see what was going on. He stood behind the storm door and tried to be all big and masculine at first but once I came at him with a shovel—"

"A shovel?!" Colton interjected once again in disbelief.

"Hold on!" I said loudly again. "Let me tell the story."

I heard Colton slightly huff but I continued, and I told him everything. Once I finished, there was a pause. I knew Colton would be annoyed because I put myself in danger. But…I was a fearless person, even if I shouldn't have been at times.

"I don't even know what to say," he said. "Do you know how stupid that was, Sis? For real. He could have had a fucking gun. He could have killed y'all."

"Okay, but he didn't," I said.

"Oh my God," he said now annoyed. "I get he *didn't* have one but the next person you do this shit to, could. And if this dude beat the shit out of Bianca what makes you think he couldn't beat the shit out of you?"

"What was I supposed to do, Colton? Huh? Let Bianca go over there by herself? He'd *really* kill her then."

"I get it," he said monotonously. "Why didn't Melanie go?"

I scoffed.

"What?"

"Melanie is dead to Bianca, and I really mean *dead* to her."

"Why? What the fuck happened?" he asked.

I sighed knowing I'd have to tell the entire story. But once again, I continued.

"Jesus fucking Christ," Colton said with repulsion and anger after I told him all Melanie said. "That Melanie is a fucking bitch. How could she say that to her?!"

I shook my head, "I know. That's what I'm saying. So, Bianca and Melanie, well, Bianca and *I*, and Melanie are done. I didn't like her to begin with, but this really sent me over the edge."

"I can't fucking believe that," Colton said, still in shock. "And didn't you help them *both* that night of the Fourth of July party?!"

"Oh!" I exclaimed, realizing I forgot an important part of the story.

"When I asked Melanie to help me find Bianca and help her, she said 'Why? We're not friends.'"

Colton scoffed, "Did she really? What a fucking bitch."

"I know!" I exclaimed. "I told her we weren't fucking friends when she got drugged but I *still* helped her," I paused and scoffed. "Absolutely disgusting."

"Seriously," Colton said bitterly. "Well, I see why she didn't come this morning then," he somewhat joked.

I chuckled somewhat, "Yeah." I paused for a minute then spoke again. "Look, I know we should've just found the keys without causing any trouble and went on our way. But it felt good to mess his shit up. It felt good to pay back someone that did you wrong. I mean she's told me stories, Colton, that we're awful. And she's never told anyone, like, police wise. It just makes me sick."

"I get it, Sis," he said in a kinder tone.

"It's like, those fucking frat assholes that drugged her and Melanie, are still out there. They still have a "clean" reputation, they aren't in legal trouble, nothing happened to them. But yet, Bianca and Melanie have to deal with the aftermath. It just isn't fucking right, Colton. And there's so many more people and stories out there where someone that did them wrong is still walking the streets, it's sick," I said repugnantly. "And you would have done the same thing or probably worse if that happened to Mom, Leannah, or me," I added coldly.

Colton sighed, "Iris, I get it. Trust me—I get it. Growing up, being the oldest out of you and Le, I saw a lot of shit. A *lot* of shit I shouldn't have. It's infuriating. You want people to pay, you want people to suffer the way you did, but you can't always do that. I know I probably haven't been the best example of that…you know, I lash out and snap at anyone that tries to do you, Mom, or Leannah wrong. I get angry quickly and don't think about the things I'm doing. I know I can't be like that. And I've been trying really hard to be more level headed because, I think to myself, would I rather be able to help you, Mom, and Le, if God forbid something *did* happen but suffer from it being that way, or be locked up in jail or prison where I *can't* help you guys? Or better yet, if I'm dead and there's *nothing* I can do and I've left you three the grief of not having me? I know it's hard, trust me, it's hard. I battle with it every—single—time some shit happens. I mean, shit, I even got angry just from you telling me about what happened to Bianca, and I don't even know her. I gotta control it, at least a little bit, and so do you. And you're not even the crazy one!"—he laughed, then did I—"That's me! You're supposed to be the sane one. We can't have two crazies," he joked again trying to make the conversation lighthearted.

I chuckled again.

"What I'm trying to say, Sis, is I need you to just think rationally about what you're doing—and think about *who* you're doing it for. I know you want to help everyone and go to bat for everyone, but some people don't deserve that. They deserve a strike," he exhaled as he paused. "And I worry because you're a girl, and a small one at that. People take advantage of that and look at you as an easy target. I just can't get a phone call one day that you're missing, or they found your body in a ditch somewhere."

Colton's words meant a lot to me. I mean yeah, he was a hot head. He did lash out and get mad at anything that tried to hurt Mom, Leannah, or I. And he did make decisions out of anger. But to hear he was trying to fix that and how much more of a mess it makes than good it does, showed me that he really *does* want to change that part of him. And not only for himself, but for Leannah and me too. He wanted to show us that how he acted wasn't really okay and that there's other ways to go about things. Typically, I never acted the way I did at Steven's. Like Colton said, I was the "sane" one. Colton will always have that protective, defensive, big brother attitude, but now, hopefully, in a way that is healthier. I was proud of him and really loved him.

"Thank you, Colton," I smiled. "I appreciate it and I'm proud of you for wanting to change that part of you. I couldn't imagine anything happening to you, either."

"And nothing ever will. I love you, Sis."

I smiled, "I love you too, Colton."

There was a pause.

"But, you're pretty badass for that shit," Colton said in an impressed manner.

I chuckled and rolled my eyes playfully.

"You came at this guy with a shovel after he choked Bianca out?!" he exclaimed.

I chuckled again, "Yeah."

There was a pause, like Colton was thinking about it, "My fucking sister, man."

I laughed, "Didn't you just get done telling me violence and vengeance isn't the answer?"

"Oh, right. Yeah, no violence, no vengeance, no throwing flower-pots and kicking in storm doors."

"Hey, that wasn't me. That was Bianca," I teased.

"Oh right, you broke his table."

"Two of them, and threw mud at his doors and windows," I said playfully.

He laughed, "Now *that's* my sister."

26

Chapter 26

Bianca returned with a new iPhone Four which she said was pretty cheap since it was a few years old. She headed out and I made my way to the kitchen. Susan was stirring something in a pot and the smell of roasted chicken filled the air. A few housemates lingered in the living room, watching TV.

"Mhmm, it smells delicious in here, Susan," I said as I began washing my hands.

"Thank you, honey," she smiled. "I made chicken, mashed potatoes, asparagus, and cornbread."

"Ooo, I love cornbread," I said, drying my hands.

Susan laughed, "Well"—she opened the oven door, exposing the ginormous pan of cornbread inside—"I made a lot!"

"Oh my God!" I exclaimed as I looked inside the oven. "You *did* make a lot."

"Everybody loves cornbread," she said with a grin.

"That's true," I smiled back. "Can I help you with anything?"

"Oh, well if you wanted to set the table, that would be great. Thank you!"

"Okay," I smiled and proceeded to do so. As I finished, the front door opened and in walked Melanie. We made eye contact, but our faces were blank. Susan said hi to her, but Melanie mumbled out a hello and kept going up the stairs. An ire expression grew across my face but was soon interrupted by Susan saying dinner was ready.

Melanie now came down the stairs and sat at the other end of the table from me. She didn't really look at or talk to me, but I didn't care. I had animosity towards her. Regardless of everything she did to Bianca, how could she leave me hanging when I needed her help? Even after I helped her when she was drugged and stopped those guys from doing God knows what to her. It was infuriating, to say the least.

Everyone was done eating about twenty, thirty minutes later. It was now just about seven o'clock. I saw Melanie go upstairs and I couldn't shake the feeling of disgust I felt for her. I needed to say something to her. So, once the kitchen was all cleaned up, I went upstairs to confront her.

"What makes me different from her? Huh?" I asked, swinging open our bedroom door.

She was laying on her bed listening to music.

"What?" she asked as she pulled out one earbud.

"I said"—I closed the door behind me—"what makes me different from her?"

She looked at me, "What are you talking about?"

"I'm talking about you being a fucking bitch to Bianca since the first day we all met. And she never did anything to you to make you be that way," I said shortly. "So why haven't you been as rude to me as you have to her? Huh? Is it 'cause I'm not a prostitute and she is? Is that the main reason why you hate her so much? Because we've both treated you the same so I don't see any other reason why you would be so cruel to her."

She looked at me blankly, "I don't have to explain shit to you."

I scoffed, "So there is a reason why you're such a bitch to her."

"Look," Melanie said aggressively as she took out her other earbud and stood up from her bed, "I know that's your *best* friend and everything—"

"She's *not* my best friend," I interrupted coldly.

"Then why do you do all this shit for her?" she asked coldly as well. "You stick up for her, you don't care that she's a walking infection, you come to her rescue—"

"Oh what? You mean like a decent fucking person would?!" I snapped, now getting angry. "You treat her like fucking shit and thinks she deserves it or some shit."

"You know she takes on *all* the problems she has!" Melanie barked. "She puts herself in dumb situations and gets herself hurt, or makes other people mad, or gets in trouble, or gets herself BEAT—UP."

"How can you say that?!" I shouted. "How can you stand there and say she *deserves* that shit?!"

"Are you fucking stupid, Iris?!" she yelled. "She's a PRO-STI-TUTE. She's asking for it. She meets guys, goes over to their place the same night, and then gets mad or upset when something bad happens. Like no fucking shit. She CHOOSES to do that shit."

I scoffed repulsively, "You really think she chooses to do that shit? Do you seriously fucking think she WANTS to be a prostitute?"

"You think she *doesn't*?!" Melanie questioned. "She acts like she can pull any guy she wants and is *obsessed* with herself. She LOVES being a prostitute."

I laughed. "You're a fucking idiot, Melanie. A fucking idiot. I can't even argue with you about her anymore. What pisses me off, besides you being a total cunt, is how when I asked you to help me, you didn't."

Melanie looked at me.

"I fucking helped you!" I screamed. "Did you forget I got both

Bianca *and* you out of that fucking creep's house? Huh?! Do you know how fucking hard it was to get your lifeless ass body up as well as Bianca's and practically carry you out of the room, down the stairs, and to the car?! You were out fucking cold, Melanie!" I yelled. "Do you know how easy it would have been for them to do whatever it is they wanted to do to you?!"

Melanie slightly frowned.

"Really fucking easy! I was the one that helped you! I was the one that wasn't gonna go down without a fight to protect you! *I* was the one that found where you were. *I* was the one that picked the lock. *I* was the one that dragged you out of that house. *I* was the one that brought you to the car and put you in there safely. *I* was the one who went face to face with those assholes. *I* was the one that drove you to safety. *I* was the one that held you all night. *I* was the one that did it fucking all!" I yelled. "And I NEVER said you deserved it. I *never* threw it in your face, or used it against you, or made you feel like you owed me something. I fucking helped you because you needed it! And that's what people do, Melanie!"

Melanie continued to stare at me with that frown that locked away her emotions.

"Bianca's a prostitute, *you* drank! She got beat up, *you* got drugged! It's the same—fucking—thing!" I yelled in her face. "But nobody's telling you it's YOUR fault that you drank. Nobody's telling you it's YOUR fault you got yourself drugged! Because it's not! And it's *not* Bianca's fault she got beat up by some asshole that's just like you," I said coldly.

There was a moment of silence while I stared at her intently. Then I spoke.

"You know," I chuckled. "After the party, after I told you all I did for you, I thought you were starting to change. Yeah, you were being nice to Bianca, and you were being less miserable, and I thought, maybe in some *fucking* way, you getting drugged was a good thing. I thought, maybe it just took one really bad night, one really bad fucking night to make you realize, you're a fucking cunt. Maybe it just took one thing to happen to you like it always happens to Bianca and so many other people for you to get off your miserable—heartless—*disgusting* high horse and realize how shitty you are to others. But I guess not," I said, taking a step back. "Because you're the same fucking bitch you were before the party ever even happened."

Melanie stared at me with a tight frown. This was the first time I saw emotion in her. I could tell she realized how awful she had been to everyone.

I scoffed, turning away from her for a split second. I then returned to facing her.

"I never told Susan what really happened because you didn't want her to know because you were embarrassed. You were *ashamed*. Well, you know that feeling you felt? That humiliated, mortified, *ashamed* feeling? That's *exactly* how Bianca feels right now," I stared at her momentarily in disgust.

"And it doesn't matter if we're fucking friends or not," I said sternly. "You help people. You fucking help people—I didn't have to help you. I could have said it was your fault that you drank, and you deserved anything and everything that comes after. I could have left you there, walked to the bus stop, and went home. But I didn't—because then I would be just like you. And I'm fucking *nothing* like you."

Ice laced my words as I stared at Melanie with disgust. She stared back at me desperately although she tried to mask her facial expression with a bitter stare.

"You're mean, Melanie. You're fucking heartless and you don't even care. Not only did you leave the *one* person hanging who gave a fuck about you, you told the only other person that could stand you, and still liked you even after constantly beating down on her, that she deserved to get beat up for being a prostitute," I stepped back and shook my head. "How can you do that?" I paused. "Bianca's not the disgusting one here, you are."

I walked out of the room and slammed the door behind me. I hope Melanie felt bad. I hope she knew how evil she was. I hope she knew all the damage she was causing. And I hope she knew that she pushed away the one person that saw and understood why she was the way she was and didn't hold it against her. I hope she knew that there would *never* be someone like me in her life again.

27

Chapter 27

"Tucson, Arizona," Bianca read blandly off her sheet of paper.

It was the night of Wednesday, September eleventh. It had been weeks since the fight. And the days were nothing like they were before it. Although there wasn't anger anymore between the three of us, there still wasn't harmony. There simply was nothing.

All the guests were in Susan's living room. I was sitting with Tobey on the two-person couch and Bianca was sitting in the single chair that sat a couple feet away. Susan had just called us down and handed us our papers. She told us we were leaving that Friday, the thirteenth, to go to our new homes.

"That's a twenty-three-and-a-half-hour drive from here," Bianca said as she looked down at her phone.

Tobey chuckled, "Where are you going, Iris?" he asked, shifting his attention from Bianca to me.

"Uh," I opened up my packet, "New Haven, Wyoming, it says."

Tobey made a surprised face, "I never heard of there before."

I chuckled, "Neither have I. Where are you going?"

"Greensboro, North Carolina," he said as he read off the piece of paper.

I nodded my head, "Sounds nice. It'll be a warm winter."

"Yeah, it will," he said with a smile. "Well, a warm*er* winter," he added.

I laughed, "True."

Susan began to tell us that our papers will tell us what time our taxis will be picking us up, the routes our transportations will be taking, all the station names, street names, and any other identifying factors we may need to get from place to place.

"I leave at eleven Friday. What time do you leave?" I asked Tobey once Susan was finished.

"Oh same," Tobey responded.

"Nice," I smiled then began to look through the part of my packet that had the routes I would be taking.

"Holy shit," I said in shock.

"What?" Tobey asked as he looked down at the page I was staring at.

"I have five different routes I have to take to get to this New Haven place. There's like ten different buses and trains I'll be taking."

"Damn really?" he asked as he looked closer. "Oh, shit you do. Yeah, Seattle to Yakima, Yakima to Spokane, Spokane to Billings, Billings to Gillette, Gillette to New Haven; that's five." He then pulled out his phone and pressed the screen a couple of times. "Well, no wonder, Iris," he said in a now understanding manner, "New Haven, Wyoming is in the middle of nowhere. Look," he turned his phone towards me, and I took it.

"Oh shit, it is," I picked my packet up, read a part of it really quick, then looked back at the map on Tobey's phone. "No wonder I have an hour and forty-minute taxi ride from Gillette to New Haven," I handed Tobey back his phone and sighed.

"Hey, if it makes you feel any better, your total travel time is twenty-four hours. Mine is"—he picked up his packet—"Seventy-one hours."

"Is it really?!" I asked in shock as I took his packet and read it. "Damn…Hey, you're going to the Chicago Union Station. That's like twenty minutes from my house."

"Oh yeah?" he asked with a smile. "I'll make sure to say hi to your family," he teased.

I chuckled and rolled my eyes, "Thanks. They'll appreciate it."

Friday the thirteenth, the day I would be leaving Seattle and making my way to New Haven. Yesterday, I spent the day packing. I called my family too and told them I'd be leaving Seattle for New Haven and they were excited for me. Susan also threw us a big going-away party. She cooked a ton of food and even decorated her living room. It was really nice of her.

I woke up around eight on the thirteenth. Once I was up, I took a shower, did my makeup, and packed the rest of my things into my suitcase and duffle bag. Bianca and Melanie were also up doing the same thing. After I was ready and my bags were packed, I took all the sheets off my bed and remade it with clean ones. Bianca and Melanie began taking their bags downstairs as I strapped my duffle bag to the top of my suitcase. Now that I was done everything and was alone in my room for one final time, I paused for a moment to breathe. As I exhaled and stared at the freshly made bed in front of me, I heard a knock at the door then it opened.

"Hey," Tobey said with a smile. "Need some help taking your bags downstairs?"

I smiled, "Uh, yeah, actually that'd be great."

He came into my room and extended the handle of my suitcase.

"Thank you," I said.

"Anytime," he smiled.

We got downstairs and Tobey set my bags in the living room where everyone else had congregated. The two of us stood with Bianca.

It was now ten-forty-five and cabs were pulling in and out of Susan's driveway. As people left with their bags, Susan gave each person a hug and wished them the best. I knew it wouldn't be too much longer until my cab arrived.

"Melanie! Your cab's here," Susan yelled.

Bianca and I looked over at Melanie who was sitting alone on the couch with her earbuds in. We watched her get up and wheel her bags over to the door.

"It was a pleasure having you, sweetheart," Susan smiled. "Take good care of yourself and good luck with everything in your future," she then hugged Melanie.

As she opened the front door, suitcase in hand, she looked back at us with a somewhat sorrowful expression. Bianca and I looked back at her somewhat the same.

Melanie then smiled lightly, "See you, guys."

Bianca waved and pursed her lips.

I pursed mine as well, "See you."

She gave one final look of disappointment then walked out of the front door. Bianca and I looked at each other then looked down.

"Well, I guess this is goodbye. I'm gonna head out too," Bianca said, reaching for her suitcase. She extended the handle then threw her duffle bag on top, strapping it all together.

She wrapped me into a hug. "Thank you for everything, Iris. It really, really, means a lot," she said into my ear.

I smiled, squeezing her just a little bit tighter, "Just don't forget to be that way with others."

"I won't."

We let go, looked at each other, and smiled. Bianca grabbed the handle of her suitcase and wheeled it to the door. Susan and her hugged goodbye and I watched as she walked out the front door as well.

"And then there were two," Tobey said, enlightening the mood.

I chuckled, "And then there were two," I repeated.

Within five minutes, though, his cab pulled up.

"Alright, well I gotta go," he said, giving me a brief hug before slinging his two large duffle bags over his shoulder. "Have a safe trip."

"You too," I smiled.

Not too long after, Susan called out that my cab was here. I got up and wheeled my bags to the front door.

"Goodbye, sweetheart," she gave me a big hug. "You're a wonderful young lady with a great heart. Never forget that."

I smiled and we let go of our embrace, "Thank you, Susan, that means a lot to me. I can't thank you enough for everything you have done for not only me, but all the other housemates these past couple months. You go above and beyond, and the world truly needs more people like you."

"Oh, honey," Susan smiled with glassy eyes, "The best thing you can be in this world, is a person that the world needs."

I thought about that line a lot after I left Seattle. I had never thought of something like that, in that way, but it stuck with me to this day. I think it always will.

I walked to the backdoor of the cab. I looked back at Susan who was waiting in the door frame with a smile on her face. She waved to me, and I gave a small wave back before getting into the cab. Who knew this day would be so sad.

28

Chapter 28

After being dropped off at the train station, I took my bags and wheeled them to the escalator where I went up to the second floor. I followed the signs that were guiding me to where I needed to be. Within a couple minutes, I was waiting at the train's platform with my luggage.

After the train ride, I stood at the Greyhound bus stop in Seattle. This is where the first haul would take place as I'd be traveling three hours to Yakima. When I saw the Greyhound bus arrive, I stood up and grabbed my luggage then proceeded towards the bus. Other people began to board as well and we all filed up the couple stairs, showed our bus tickets, and took our seats. I made my way towards the back of the middle section. Since I was one of the first people to board, I was able to pick the seat I wanted. I stored my luggage in the overhead compartment then sat down with my purse beside me. I watched as the bus began to fill up with all different types of riders. Old and young, men and women, black and white, all types of various people filled the bus. They stored their bags then took their seats. Thankfully, the bus wasn't so crowded that someone had to sit next to me. So, for the trip I had both seats to myself, which I definitely was happy about.

Twenty minutes later, the bus started to pull away. *On the bus to Yakima, I should be there in three hours.* I texted to my family group chat. I locked my phone, closed my eyes, put my head back, and exhaled. Just then my phone buzzed. I opened my eyes and looked down at my phone. *Alright be safe, I love you!* my mom texted back. I smiled then my phone buzzed again. As I looked down it buzzed once more. *Be safe, Sis. Love you,* Colton said. *Love you, Sis!* Leannah wrote. I smiled, *I will, love you all more,* I texted back. I locked my phone once more then rested my head and eyes as I felt the bus head onto the main road and start the trip to Yakima.

I unintentionally fell asleep and when I woke it was one-fifty. I yawned and looked around. Once my eyes adjusted and I was fully awake, I looked out the window. I looked up at the big, green, beautiful pine trees. The highway we were driving on was surrounded by them. I always thought those trees were unique. They didn't lose their leaves once winter came around (although they didn't have leaves to lose) and they were always that beautiful hunter green, no matter the weather.

"Pretty cool, huh?" asked the middle aged rugged looking White man that sat across the aisle from me.

I looked at him and smiled, "Yeah they are."

I watched the trees and passing cars for miles. I actually ended up doing this for the rest of the ride, it made the time go by pretty quick. Around three-thirty, we arrived at the Yakima Train Station, where my first journey awaited me.

Just about thirty hours later, I finally arrived at the home in New Haven. In those thirty hours, I sat next to a chatty box alcoholic that was visiting her baby brother in Canada, saw someone get sick off the

Chinese food, or supposed Chinese food, in a seedy Greyhound bus station—which caused another person to vomit, listened to the same ten songs over and over again, saw about nine trillion pine trees, ate McDonald's at midnight at a super futuristic looking McDonald's in Montana, got hit on by some man in a rundown gas station with a southern accent that was more than likely fake, then applauded by a fellow passenger for rejecting said man in a, and I quote, "badass way," spent the night in another seedy Greyhound bus station, got a flat tire on Route eighty-seven in Wyoming and had to wait two hours for someone to get there and finally fix it, then waited about an hour for my cab driver at a gas station in Gillett to take me to New Haven as he got stuck in a huge traffic jam due to a tractor trailer overturning on the highway. It was an exhausting thirty hours to say the least. Being done with all the traveling was something I was thrilled about.

It was five-twenty p.m. when I walked up the two porch steps and knocked on the front door. A middle-aged man, wearing a ripped, white tank top, answered the door.

"Hi, are you with Stay?" the man asked unwelcomely.

"Yes, I am. My name is Iris, it's nice to meet you," I said, trying to ignore his hostility.

"Alright, alright," he groaned as he lit a cigarette and ushered me inside. "Come on in, set your bags down here, and have a seat at the dining room table."

"Thank you," I said.

He cleared some of the junk that laid on the kitchen table while the cigarette hung out of his mouth. I was the first person there.

"Where you from?" he asked.

"Chicago."

"I've been there a couple of times," he took a big puff of his cigarette. "Dirty place, got good deep-dish pizza though."

Confused, I just nodded my head and gave a slight smile.

Just then, a woman about the same age as the man, walked in from the back door with a trash can.

"God dammit, John. I told you to take the trash out and clean up the kitchen before people get here"—she cut herself off once she saw me—"oh, Christ, people are already here!" she yelled in a frustrated tone.

"Nice to meet you, ma'am," I said, trying to be respectful, even though these people seemed like a handful.

She flashed a fake smile, "Ginger."

It was then quiet for a minute.

"Well, uh, I can show you to your room if you like, or you can wait here," John said, trying to break the silence. "It says there's only supposed to be six other people staying here," he then read off a piece of paper.

"Uh, well if you don't mind, I guess I'll go unpack my things."

"Alright," Ginger said abruptly.

I began to gather my suitcase and purse as I picked up the vibe that I was unwanted by her.

"And, John, clean up the damn table, would you! Before anyone else gets here!" she ordered.

"Worry about your damn self!" he hollered back.

She grunted and rolled her eyes, "Come on, this way."

She led me up the steps and into a bedroom.

"You know how men are, don't you?" she snickered.

"Uh yeah, sure, I guess," I said blandly.

"Well, don't your dad act like that?" She had terrible grammar.

"I don't live with my dad, just my mom, sister, and brother."

"Ohhh," she smiled and laughed. "Well, I know your brother does that then. How old is he?"

"Eighteen. He'll be nineteen in November," I said, growing

annoyed.

"Oh, yeah, he *definitely* acts like that," she laughed.

I gave the same fake, insincere half-smile I gave John. Colton was nothing like that, and he never was. She just wanted someone else to be as much of an asshole as her shithole husband was.

29

Chapter 29

As time passed by and I was unpacking, I heard more people coming into the house from downstairs. Soon, around six, a much older guy opened the already cracked door and came in.

"Uh, hi," he smiled. "I'm Campbell."

The man was very tall. Standing at about six-four with a nice, muscular build. He had lots of tattoos and brunette hair. His eyes were a shade of green that could only be described as intense.

"Iris," introducing myself, I smiled.

"Room ninety-three?" he asked.

"Yeah...you're my roommate?" I asked in confusion, considering he was a guy. I didn't think they would pair boys and girls together, but they did. I also soon found out, I, besides Ginger, was the only girl in the house.

"Yeah, guess so," he replied.

I just smiled as I continued unpacking. I didn't know how I felt. To tell the truth, he was attractive, but he had to be at least twenty-five, at least.

"So," he said, trying to break the silence that I had just created, "where're you from?"

"I'm from Chicago, you?" I asked, sitting down on my bed next to my suitcase.

"Redmond, Oregon. It's basically dead center in the middle of the state."

"That's cool, I just came from Seattle, so that's not too far away, I guess."

"No, no it's not," he smiled as he sat down next to me. "So how old are you?"

"I'll actually be seventeen in two weeks, on the twenty-ninth. You?"

"Seventeen, wow," he was blown away in shock. "I thought you were at least twenty. You look old for your age."

I smiled bashfully and looked down, "I get that a lot. But no, no, I'm only seventeen…almost anyway."

"Close enough," he said with a smile. "But to answer your question, I'm twenty-nine, I'll be thirty in December."

"Oh, wow," I said as I sunk back into unease.

Twenty-nine, I thought to myself. What was the age cap on this program? I don't know how much sense it made to put a young, teenage girl with a grown man in the same room. But that was only the tip of the iceberg of the many things I learned that didn't make sense in this program.

Just then, I heard John and Ginger screaming at each other.

"Can you ever be the one to fucking cook dinner?" Ginger yelled. "Why do I always have to do this shit?"

"You're the woman! That's your job, ain't it?" John's misogyny seeped through.

"Oh, go fuck yourself! I'm out of here, you feed these damn people!" she barked as the front door slammed shut.

"What a bitch!" John growled. "Everyone! Get down here!" he then added.

We both got up and went downstairs into the kitchen where he was.

"Alright, y'all, I don't know how to cook, I don't," he confessed. "So whatever y'all find, y'all can eat. But don't eat my vanilla pudding pie, I mean it."

The other housemates and I had bewilderment written all over our faces. He stared back at us, knowing he embarrassed himself.

"Alright…I'm going out back to smoke," he said, evading the humiliation.

A couple of people went upstairs, and the rest scrounged the cabinets and fridge for food. I wasn't hungry but I guess that was a good thing considering it didn't look like anyone was having any luck.

While Campbell stayed downstairs and ate, I trailed back upstairs and called my family, letting them know I was there. Afterwards, I started unpacking once more. Soon enough, Campbell came in.

"Those people are nuts," he laughed as he sat down on his bed.

"Yeah, they are," I said. "I guess we got the winning hosts of the program," I added sarcastically.

He laughed, "Yeah, I guess so. You know, my folks used to fight like cats and dogs all the damn time too."

"Oh yeah? Over what?" I asked.

"Just typical bullshit. Money, bills, who's cheated on who this week. Just about everything. What about you, did your parents fight?" he asked.

"Yeah, when I was younger. My dad left my siblings and I when I was seven so after that, it was my mom and her various boyfriends that would argue. But yeah no, they argued about the same things as yours," I said looking down at a shirt in my hands.

"It's a shame, ain't it?"

I smiled softly.

"I'm sorry to hear about your dad leaving you. My dad hates me, so I feel the same way."

"Why does he hate you?" I asked curiously.

"He just doesn't like me. He thinks I'm a waste of space. We never agree on anything and all we do is fight. I don't know, we're just toxic together, I guess," he said.

I stood there and tried to be sympathetic but the whole time I wondered how a grown man was in this program and why. Of course, I know you can be grown and still struggle but I just really wondered how he ended up here.

"I'm sorry to hear all that, no one should be considered a waste of space...Uhm so, you're twenty-nine, can I ask why you're in this program? Do you know the age limit?" I finally asked.

"Well, I'm here because my dad kicked me out," he said. "I had a hard time getting a job, so I didn't have a lot of money and no place to go. My stepmom is the one who found this program. She thought I could go here, have a place to live, and they wouldn't have to deal with me financially. It was kind of selfish of her, but I'd be homeless if not, so here I am. Oh, and the age limit is thirty-two. So, once I'm that old, if I'm still here that is, they'll send me back home."

"Oh, okay," I didn't know what to say. "I'm surprised the age limit is so high. I thought it stopped at like twenty-five."

"Nope, thirty-two."

I smiled slightly and walked over to my bed, "Well, it's nice to meet you. I'm pretty tired from all the traveling, so I think I'm just gonna lay down and go to sleep. I'll talk to you in the morning."

"Alright, well it was nice meeting you too," he smiled. "Have a nice sleep."

He got up from his bed and walked out of the room, closing the door behind him.

I laid there thinking to myself for quite some time before I fell asleep. I thought about how I'm sleeping in the same room as a grown man. A man who's *thirteen* years older than me. How stupid were the program directors? I guess they didn't care because *they're* helping *you* out. I thought about how he was attractive though, he really was. Oh, how he soon became the little white rabbit that I followed right down the dark and ugly rabbit hole.

30

Chapter 30

It was six in the morning when I was awoken by the sound of breaking glass followed by Ginger screaming at John.

"Why haven't you paid the damn hot water bill yet, John?!" she barked.

"I told you! I'm not paying that shit until the guy changes our bill's price from last month!" John exclaimed.

"He already told you he couldn't do that! Stop being so damn cheap!" Ginger yelled inconsiderately. "These people don't wanna take cold showers every day! Hell with them, I don't wanna take cold showers every day!"

I rolled my eyes and sat up in frustration as I knew I wasn't going to be getting any more sleep. Somehow, the commotion didn't affect Campbell, as he was still sound asleep.

"Oh, stop being a big, old baby! Cold showers ain't that bad!" John yelled.

"You drive me fucking nuts!" Ginger yelled then the sound of more glass breaking followed.

"Jesus, Ginger! You're going to slice my fucking face off! Watch yourself!"

"Maybe that's my goal!"

Just then, the front door slammed and a car's ignition started.

"This place is so toxic," I said to myself under my breath. I let out a deep sigh and threw the covers off me. Off to the cold showers I went.

Once I was done and dressed, I simultaneously was drying my hair with the towel as I opened the bathroom door to walk down the hall back to my room.

"Jesus, God!" I plowed into Campbell's wall of a body as I opened the door. "You scared the shit out of me."

"Oh, I'm sorry, I didn't mean to," he said.

I scrunched my hair with the towel then laughed, "I'm sorry, I should've been paying attention."

He laughed too, "No, no it's fine, no worries."

After a beat, "You just shower?" a smile spreading across his face.

"Yeah."

"You smell good."

I smiled but rolled my eyes playfully.

"I like your necklace," he then added.

"Thank you," I smiled.

"Did a boyfriend give it to you?"

"No, no," I looked down. "My brother did. I don't have a boyfriend."

"That's hard to believe," he said flirtatiously.

"What? That I don't have a boyfriend or that my brother gave me it?" I asked playfully, knowing what he meant.

He chuckled, "That you don't have a boyfriend."

"Oh," I smirked.

"But your brother? You two must be pretty close."

"Yeah, yeah, we are."

"That's nice," he said. "But it's even nicer that you don't have a boyfriend."

"Is that right?" I played along, even though I knew I shouldn't.

"Yeah, it is," he then got closer to me and grabbed the necklace, admiring it as he rubbed it.

I chuckled out of awkwardness, "I'm going to finish getting ready." I smiled as I pushed through him and walked down the hall back to our room.

I sat down on my bed and exhaled. Just then my phone rang, it was Colton. "Hey," I said.

"Hey, Sis!" he gleamed. "Sorry I wasn't home when you called yesterday."

"It's fine," I said. "How was work?"

"It was good. Same old same old, you know?"

"Yeah, I know," I said.

"Well, how are you? How's the home in Wyoming?" he then asked.

"It's alright, I mean the hosts are a married couple and all they've been doing is screaming at one another. They don't have hot water because they're arguing about that too, but it isn't that bad so far."

"Shit, really? That's not right. That's not fair to you guys."

"Yeah, I know. It's whatever though, nothing much I can do about it," I responded.

"Well, how's your roommate? What's she like?" he asked. "Is she better than Melanie and Bianca?" he laughed.

I didn't laugh. I went silent for a moment. I didn't want to tell Colton that my roommate was a man. A twenty-nine-year-old man at that. But I also couldn't lie to him.

"Uhm," I said with hesitation, knowing he wouldn't like what I was about to say, "actually, my uh roommate isn't a girl."

"What do you mean your roommate isn't a girl?"

"I'm the only girl here, besides Ginger, our host. So, my roommate is uhm, actually a guy."

"What? Why the fuck would they do that, Iris?" he said with agitation in his voice. "I don't like that at all. What's this motherfucker's name?"

"Colton," I said, trying to disperse his hostility. "It's Campbell."

"How old is he?" he then asked.

I went silent. I *really* didn't want to tell him his age.

"Iris, how old is he?" he asked again.

I sighed, "Twenty-nine."

"Wait, wait, you're telling me your roommate is a twenty-nine-year-old man?"

"Yeah," I said reluctantly.

Colton sighed in annoyance.

"Well, what do you want me to do about it, Colton? Make a random girl magically appear and ask her to be my roommate instead?" I asked, somewhat hostile.

"Iris, I know you can't control it, and it's not your fault. I just don't like the fact some random ass grown man is staying in the same room as you."

"I know, Colton."

"Like, why would the program directors, or coordinators—whoever the fuck makes up the roommates—do that?"

"I don't know," I said monotonously. "Not their problem I guess."

Colton scoffed, "Figures."

A short moment of silence fell over us.

"Just please be careful, Sis. Please?"

"I will, Colton. You don't have to tell me that all the time, you know I can handle myself."

"Iris, I don't know why you constantly say that. It's not about what you can and can't handle. Just be careful, okay?"

"Yeah, okay," I said dully.

"Thank you."

Colton tried to enlighten the mood by changing the subject to our birthdays coming up. Mine was in two weeks and his was November twelfth. It didn't really work though. All it did was make me think about how I wouldn't get to be with him on his birthday. It would be the first time ever that we weren't together for our birthdays…Not wanting to get too down, I told Colton I had to go.

Soon, Campbell came back into our room with a cigarette and lighter in his hand. He smiled at me and walked over to his suitcase. He pulled out a black, V-neck shirt, took off the shirt he was wearing, and put on the fresh one. I watched him in the mirror as he did this. I didn't want to admit it, but I was attracted to him. He was just the type of guy I liked. But I didn't want to like Campbell though. He was too old, and the circumstances weren't normal. Just so many things that weren't right. But I couldn't help how I felt.

"Anything you want to do today?" he asked as he put the cigarette in his mouth and walked over to the window. "I have my car here—oh, do you mind if I smoke in here?"

"No, no, it's fine."

"Cool," he smiled and opened the window.

"You have your car here you said?" I asked.

"Yeah," he blew out smoke. "So, we can go anywhere you want to go."

I exhaled and shrugged, "I don't know anything around here, or anything to do,"

"Neither do I," he said as he pulled on his cigarette. "But that's the beauty of it," he smiled.

A smile unwillingly spread across my face.

"We can go drive around, see what's around here, and just explore the area," he said as he blew out more smoke.

"I'm down with that," I smiled. "Let me just finish my makeup and I'll be ready."

He inhaled his cigarette then blew out the smoke with a frown,

"For someone as pretty as you, you don't need makeup."

I looked at him with a weary smile. Like I said, I wanted to keep myself from liking him—yeah that didn't work.

"Thank you," I simply said.

He smiled and took one final pull on his cigarette. I watched him as he twisted the glowing orange, lit end of the cigarette, down onto the edge of the window frame, putting it out. The orange glow was immediately snuffed out and turned charcoal black.. I watched as he threw the butt out of the window and to the ground below.

"You're welcome," he grinned.

31

Chapter 31

"Where you kids going?" John asked in an unfriendly tone as we made our way downstairs. He sat in the recliner chair in the living room, smoking a cigarette.

"Nowhere," Campbell said coldly.

It struck me as odd because of how friendly and charming he was with me. But I just figured Campbell just came off as dismissive and didn't *actually* mean for it to be that way.

"Just on a ride," I said, pausing and flashing a smile at John.

He didn't say anything and just continued smoking his cigarette.

"Come on," Campbell said.

I followed next to Campbell, and he escorted me to his car. It was an old, black, Lincoln Continental.

"I'll get that for you," he said, stopping me before I could open the passenger door.

I smiled, "Thank you."

"Of course. I'm a gentleman, you know?" he said playfully.

"I can tell," I said with a smile as I got into his car.

He walked around the other side and got in.

"I already know the radio won't work out here," he said as he buckled his seat belt.

I chuckled, "Yeah, not a chance."

"At least I can sing…I CAME IN LIKE A WRECKING BALL!" he screamed playfully.

I laughed, "No way you listen to Miley Cyrus."

He laughed and then frowned, "Not at all. That song just played about nine hundred times on the way here. I was ECSTATIC when I lost connection."

I laughed, "Yeah, I'm not really a fan either."

For the next couple hours, we drove around. We got to know one another more, we laughed, and we just overall had a great day.

Back at John and Ginger's, we began to find something to eat for lunch.

"What do you want to eat, Iris?" Campbell asked as he opened the fridge.

I turned around as I washed my hands, "Uh, I'm fine with anything." I then dried my hands and walked over to him, "I just don't eat red meat."

"No?" he asked, turning towards me.

I shook my head with pursed lips.

"Any reason?" he asked.

"Not really, other than I just don't like it."

He shook his head, "I'm a *big* red meat eater," he said as he looked back into the fridge.

"Hey! Bonnie and Clyde!" John yelled out. He was in the same spot as he was when we left him. "Either get something to eat or close the fridge. Last time I checked you two don't pay my electric bill."

"Why would we? We're broke," Campbell said, looking at John bitterly.

John huffed and went back to reading his magazine.

Campbell turned back around and looked into the fridge, "There's ham. Want me to make you a ham and cheese?"

I frowned slightly, "You don't have to do that. I can make it myself," I said kindly.

"No, no. I want to," he said as he grabbed the ham and cheese and then closed the fridge.

"Okay, thank you."

"You're welcome," he smiled and we made eye contact that lasted a couple seconds.

I broke it and turned towards the cabinet, "Uh, do you want something to drink?"

"I'll take a black coffee actually, thank you."

"Okay," I smiled as I opened a couple cabinet doors, searching for the mugs. "Uh, John," I turned around towards him as I couldn't find the right cabinet, "where are the mugs?"

John exhaled deeply as he still had his eyes fixated on his magazine, "Top cabinet, to your left."

"I already looked. They're not there," I said.

John let out a deeper huff and now looked at me, "Well, there's no other place they'd be. Top cabinet, to the left," he repeated then looked back at his magazine.

I stood there for a split second until Campbell jumped in.

"I'll get it for you, Iris," he said with annoyance in his voice towards John.

Before I could say anything he quickly came over to where I was and opened the left cabinet, the mugs of course weren't in there as I already looked. He then opened the cabinet to the right and there they were.

"Thank you," I said quietly to Campbell.

He smiled then looked at John who was looking at us. Campbell's smile disappeared.

"They were in the cabinet to the *right*," he said with agitation.

John groaned, "Left, right, same thing."

I rolled my eyes and dug out a mug. I then poured the coffee that was in the pot into the mug and put it in the microwave. Campbell began to make our lunch. Soon enough, we ate and afterwards, we spent the rest of the day watching TV, flirting at times, even though I tried not to, and just hanging around with some of the other housemates. It actually was a nice start to my stay in New Haven.

32

Chapter 32

A couple days passed, and it was now Wednesday, the eighteenth. In those three days, Campbell only got flirtier. But also in those three days, I got worse at ignoring it and even instigated it.

That Wednesday was beautiful in New Haven. I woke up around nine, but Campbell was still asleep. I got myself all ready and decided I'd take a walk on the long trail that was in the woods behind John and Ginger's house. It was gorgeous. The woods were made up of big, tall pine trees that muffled any unwanted nearby sounds. The only thing I could hear was the sounds of birds chirping and water from a nearby creek. It was serene and quiet and peaceful.

I walked around for quite some time, enjoying the tranquility that the soon-to-be autumn air brought. I sat on the bank next to the creek and enjoyed the beauty that nature provided. After some time, a good amount of time actually—as my phone now said it was two—I decided I'd go home.

I walked in through the front door and found Ginger and John in the kitchen pouring shots of tequila.

"Want some?" Ginger asked, holding the shot glass out to me.

I frowned, "No thanks. You know I'm only sixteen, right?"

"Honey," Ginger said. "I been drinking since I was twelve. Sixteen's plenty old enough."

I frowned again but nodded my head, "Well, I'm good…thanks."

Her and John both shrugged as they washed down the tequila. I simply walked away and up the stairs to my room.

As I opened the door, I saw Campbell standing there with a pair of sweatpants on and no shirt. He had his back to me as he was putting away some of his clothes. The window was open, and a cigarette laid in an ashtray that sat on the windowsill.

"Hey, Iris," he said as he turned around with a smile.

"Hey," I smiled. I tried to not focus on how good he looked, but the truth is, he looked really good. *Really*, really, good. His chest and arm muscles were displayed perfectly behind several tattoos that clothed his upper body. Each fold he made of his T-shirts, showed off his strong arms. I tried not to stare, but my eyes traced over every vein, freckle, and hair that resided on his strong, defined body.

"How was your day?" he asked, breaking my trance. He picked up his cigarette and pulled on it.

"It was good," I said as I watched him, feeling my heart speed up as he exhaled a cloud of gray smoke through the window. "I took a long walk," I sat down on my bed, containing myself. "What did you do?"

"I just stayed in," he said, exhaling more smoke out of the window. "Did some laundry, cleaned the room up a bit."

"I see," I looked around. "It looks good."

"Thanks," he said with a smile.

"Today was pretty productive for you then, huh?" I asked playfully.

"Yeah," he smiled. "I tried to be at least. You should have stayed here, you missed a fun day of cleaning," he teased.

"Oh, did I?"

"Yeah, we could have cleaned together," he said as he walked over towards me. "We could have cleaned the carpet, the sheets…each other."

He then pushed his hand into my hair, holding my face.

I swallowed hard, "Seems like I missed out."

"You did," he said as he stroked my face and stared into my eyes.

Not wanting to, I broke his clutch, "Well maybe another time," I said, trying to suppress the drama we created.

"Maybe," he grinned, going back to the window to pick up his cigarette again and puff on it.

I swallowed again as I watched him, feeling my heart pick back up speed.

Yeah, that was it. I was into him.

Around six o'clock, John yelled up to everyone to come eat. Campbell and I got up from my bed where we were laying and talking and headed downstairs.

In the kitchen, Ginger was putting dinner on the table. At this point, mostly all of the housemates were already seated around the table. Campbell and I sat down next to each other and a minute later, Ginger put a plate of burgers on the table then sat down. I felt like a deer in headlights. I didn't know what to do. All the housemates started serving themselves and there was nothing else to eat except some poorly cooked fries. But I also didn't want to tell them I wouldn't eat this because they weren't exactly the kindest and most understanding of people.

"Eat. It's dinner time," Ginger said, shooting me daggers.

Campbell looked at me then at the food. I saw the pieces click together in his mind.

"What's the matter with you? Don't you eat, girl?" John asked while he had a mouth full of food.

"Uh, no I'm fine actually, it's just uh, I don't eat red meat. But it's fine…thank you anyway." I tried to be unproblematic and deflect the attention away from me.

"Well, Jesus Christ, Iris," Ginger barked. "You could have been a little bit more considerate and told me you weren't going to fucking eat this shit! I don't have to cook for your ass."

"Uh, I'm really sorry, I didn't mean to cause an issue."

"Ungrateful little white bitch. I swear every one of them has an issue in some way or another," John growled. "Aw, are you sad for the cows? Is that why you don't want to eat it?" John laughed as he mocked me.

"I just don't like it," I said coldly.

Ginger scoffed, "So stupid."

"If she doesn't want to eat it, she doesn't have to eat it," Campbell said, venom lacing his words.

John laughed, "Who the fuck are you? Prince Charming or some shit? Oh, that's right, you two are Bonnie and Clyde!" he mocked.

Ginger filled the room with her ugly cackle.

"And who the fuck are you? An old bastard who has nothing else better to do than pick on a woman? Low life piece of shit."

John was taken aback by Campbell's remark. So was I. Everyone had already stopped eating minutes early at the start of the drama.

"The fuck did you just say to me, boy?" John growled.

"I *said*, you're a low-life piece of shit."

John laughed, "Uh-huh, well I'll show you who's a piece of shit, boy."

John quickly got to his feet and gripped Campbell up by his shirt, pulling him out of his chair, and pinning him to the wall.

"Stop!" I yelled, getting up from my chair.

Campbell aggressively shoved John off him and laughed, "I've lived with my dad my whole life, I'm not scared of assholes like you."

"I ain't nothing like your dad, baby boy. I'll fuck you up in a heartbeat," John threatened.

"I'm standing right the fuck here!" Campbell yelled with his large arms flailed out.

John grabbed Campbell by the throat and pushed him up against the wall. Campbell—who was six foot four and John—who was about five foot nine, was taller and much stronger than John. Campbell threw John against the wall and began choking him. John started to turn purple, but Campbell wasn't stopping.

"Campbell! Stop, stop!" I screamed as I got in between the two, trying to break up the fight. Although my small stature had no impact.

"I'll fucking kill you, bitch," John struggled to say to Campbell as he was losing oxygen.

I finally somehow managed to pull Campbell off him and John gasped for air.

"Fuck you!" Campbell screamed at John as I held him back.

John leaned on the chair, gasping for breath. He coughed and coughed and coughed, struggling to recover.

No one said anything. Everyone was in shock. Even Ginger's big mouth was quiet for once.

"Come on," I pushed Campbell towards the stairs to get him away from trouble. He shot John daggers while I forced him up the stairs and to our room.

"What was that?" I asked concerningly with somewhat aggression as I closed the door behind us.

"I don't like them, Iris. And they're not gonna treat you that way."

"I can handle myself," I said respectfully.

"No!" Campbell quickly yelled. "*I'll* protect you and keep you safe!"

I was taken aback by how upset he was.

"Campbell, I appreciate it, but I'm okay…really."

"No!" he yelled, still furious. "No one's gonna treat you that way. I'm tired of this shit. I'm tired of these people, I'm tired of—"

"Hey, hey, hey," I interjected. "Don't get upset, it's okay," I pulled him in for a hug. "Let's just lay down."

And that's exactly what we did. We laid down on my bed and soon after, Campbell fell asleep on me, and I drifted off. But before I did go to sleep, I thought about what happened and how I couldn't believe it did. He could have *killed* John. That should have been a red flag, but I guess I was caught up in someone sticking up for me. No guy ever did. Besides Colton, anyway.

$$33$$

Chapter 33

The next morning, Campbell and I sat in his car as we decided to go to a (somewhat) nearby diner for a late breakfast.

"How do you know about this place?" I asked as Campbell put the directions into his phone.

"I stopped there on the way from Destin," he replied. Campbell had just stayed in Destin, Florida for five months.

"Oh, okay."

"Yeah, they have really good home fries," he said as he hit the start button.

"I'll have to try some," I smiled as I poked him playfully.

We started down the dirt driveway and got onto the main road. I began to think to myself how Colton or maybe, really anyone, would kill me if they found out about what Campbell and I were starting to be. But as I thought, I figured *maybe* it wasn't such a bad thing after all. I mean plenty of couples are years apart…I just happen to be a minor and he just happens to be thirteen years older than me. But— I would only be a minor for one more year…basically…basically. I knew it was wrong, but I wanted to convince myself otherwise because I liked him, and I liked this. Oh, how *I* now was the warped teenage girl.

We pulled into the diner's parking lot and got out of the car. Campbell finished his cigarette while I looked at the squat, nondescript building that was the diner. Campbell threw the cigarette butt to the ground and snuffed it out with his shoe. He then stuck his hand out for me to grab. I laced my fingers through his with a smile on my face and heat on my cheeks.

We walked into the cafe and were escorted to a table by the hostess. I ordered a ham and cheese spinach omelet and Campbell ordered a meat lover's omelet. Of course, we both ordered the home fries Campbell raved about. About fifteen minutes later the food came out.

I picked up my fork and looked at the "home fries." I then chuckled.

"What?" Campbell asked as he put ketchup on his plate.

"These are hash browns, not home fries," I teased.

Campbell made a confused face, "What do you mean?"

"Home fries are cubed potatoes, hash browns are shredded ones like these."

"No way," he said playfully. "They're home fries!"

I shook my head and laughed, "No, Campbell."

He laughed, "Are you serious? I thought hash browns were like the ones from McDonald's?"

"The patty formed ones?!" I exclaimed through a chuckle.

"Yeah!"

I laughed, "No, that's just McDonald's being McDonald's. Home fries are cubed, hash browns are shredded."

"Ma, whoever thought I'd be getting schooled on home fries."

"Look, someone had to break it to you," I teased.

We both laughed but soon enough began to eat our food.

"Okay, hash brown and home fry drama aside, these *hash browns* are really good. You were right."

"I told you," he smiled. "I wouldn't bring you to a place with bad food."

"How kind of you," I joked.

"Told you I'm a gentleman."

I chuckled, shook my head, and smiled.

Once we were "home," it started to pour. Campbell jokingly rushed over to my side of the car, swung open the door, and picked me up, carrying style.

"I will save you from the dreaded raindrops, my dear!" he exclaimed.

"Why, thank you!"

I laughed so hard with him as the rain flooded down on us. He rushed me to the porch stairs and set me down under the small awning. We continued laughing but soon sobered up when our eyes met. Pieces of his wet hair stuck to the side of his face and his captivating green eyes glimmered behind his dark eyelashes—also wet from the rain. I swallowed dark as I stared up at him.

"Iris, I really like you," he said as he touched my face; thumb on my cheek, fingers cradling my neck.

"I"—I dropped my eyes to his chest—"I, like you too." I flashed my eyes back up to his, meeting his gaze again.

Just then, Campbell leaned down and kissed me. He cupped my face with both his hands as mine held him at his torso.

The world began to spin then went dark. For those few seconds that we kissed, I felt like we were the only two people in the world. The way he held my face, the way he kissed me so deeply, I felt out of my body. I felt myself drift away from myself, off the porch, and into the sky. I only came back to earth when we pulled apart and smiled.

Later, I decided to try the new FaceTime feature with my family. FaceTime was a video call feature where any two iPhone users could use. Apple had just released it, and I had been wanting to try it out.

"Hey, Iris!" Colton exclaimed.

"Can you see me?" I asked. I wasn't very tech savvy and new technology was *definitely* not my strong suit.

"Yeah, I can see you! Can you see us?" he asked.

"Yeah, I can!" I exclaimed. "Oh my God, it's so good to *actually* see all of your faces!"

"I know!" Leannah exclaimed.

"Still gorgeous as ever, my love," my mom said with a smile on her face.

I smiled, "Same to you, Mama. "You *all* look so great!"

"You too!" Colton said.

"How is everyone?" I asked.

"We're good," my mom said. "Your sister and I are just getting lunch together."

I then saw my mom and Leannah wander into the kitchen a few feet behind my brother, who had the phone propped up on the coffee table.

"Oh yeah?" I asked as I sat down on the floor. I leaned my back up against the footboard of my bed. "What are you guys making?"

"Tuna fish," Colton said with a disgusted face. Colton always hated tuna fish. Same thing with me and red meat; no rhyme or reason, just didn't like it.

"Shut up, Colton," Leannah said playfully as she began to cut up celery. "Tuna fish is good."

I snickered.

"Yeah sure, if you have no taste buds," he said.

My mom laughed, "Your sister is the only one that'll eat anything," she was talking about Leannah. "You and Iris with your tuna fish and red meat."

Leannah laughed.

"Hey, at least that's the *only* thing we won't eat," I said in a playfully defensive manner.

"Right!" Colton exclaimed in allegiance. "Be happy it's not something you make all the time."

"*You* better be happy 'cause you'd be the one hungry," our mom joked.

Colton, Leannah, and I all snickered.

"You're right," Colton laughed, knowing his place.

"I know," my mom teased.

We continued talking and messing around until Leannah playfully threw a piece of celery at Colton, hitting him in the head.

"Hey, I'm gonna get you!" Colton got up and chased after Leannah.

"No!" she screamed playfully as she ran away from him.

I laughed as I watched them mess around.

"Would y'all knock that off?" my mom laughed as she playfully hit them with the oven mitt.

I laughed and after a moment, Colton came running back into the frame. "Hey, Iris!" he picked up the phone, taking off down the hallway, "Do you know where I can find your—"

He was interrupted by Campbell coming into the room. He had on only a pair of boxers and was still wet from his shower. He also had an unlit cigarette dangling out of his mouth.

I turned to look at Campbell then quickly tried to move my phone so that Colton wouldn't see him, but he did.

"Uh," Colton said, "who is that?" he asked.

"Who's that?" Campbell asked as he looked over at my phone, unaware I was on FaceTime.

"Uh, Campbell, this is Colton, my brother. And uh, Colton this is uh, Campbell, my roommate," I faltered.

"Hey, Colton, nice to meet you," Campbell said with a smile, peering over my shoulder into the camera.

Colton didn't say anything. His face, however, said a thousand words and none of them were ones I wanted to hear.

"Why doesn't he have any clothes on, Iris?" Colton asked without caring that Campbell could hear everything.

Campbell looked at me.

"Colton, stop," I said sternly.

"Uh, I'll give y'all a minute," Campbell said awkwardly as he grabbed his lighter and a pair of shorts, walking out of the room.

"Great, thanks a lot, Colton. Now you made me look like a freak."

"Me? He's the grown man without any clothes on, walking into my sister's room. Talk about a freak," he said. "And why is he smoking inside?"

"It's his room too. You walk around in your boxers all the time, why is it different?"

"Why is it different?" Colton asked in disbelief. "Hm, I don't know, maybe for one, I'm not, A: a stranger, B: thirteen years older than you, and hmm C: I SHARE THE SAME DNA AS YOU," Colton said sternly. "Why are you sticking up for him anyway?"

"I'm not, you just always overreact about the smallest shit! Like, calm down a bit! Whatever happened to, 'I need to choose my battles' and 'I can't freak out over every little thing'" I snapped back. "Gosh! Why did you have to say something? If you cared so much you could have at least asked me in private," I said upsettingly.

There was a pause as disappointment came across Colton's face.

"Look, you're right. I didn't mean to embarrass you. I'm sorry," Colton said.

I sighed, "It's fine, Colton. Don't worry about it." I was slightly annoyed, but I hated fighting with my family, they were all I had. "I think I should go."

"Sis," he gave me a defeated look.

"It's fine. But you know, I'm sure Campbell wants to come back into *his* room."

He sighed, "Alright, I get it. I'm sorry, Sis. I love you. I'll talk to you soon."

"It's alright," I said, and it was. "I love you too."

I then hung up the phone. I sat there on the floor for a second, pushing my hands into my hair shaking my head. Minutes later, Campbell knocked on the door and slowly opened it.

"Everything alright?" he asked. "I'm sorry, I didn't know you were on the phone."

"Hey...yeah, everything's okay. Don't be sorry," I said as I stood up. "*I'm* sorry. My brother is just super protective of me, well my mom and sister too, but—" I shook my head.

"It's all good, no worries. I'd be kind of upset if I saw some guy with no clothes on, walking into my little sister's room too."

I forced a smile. Moments later, I frowned, "Hey, if you would have a problem with it if it were your sister, why are you into me? I mean, you know I'm only sixteen. Why are you always flirting with me and stuff?"

He seemed confused. "It doesn't seem like you *don't* like it. You seem into me too."

"Well," I paused, "well, I am into you. But doesn't that contradict what you just said?"

"Look, Iris, age is only a number, right? I like you and you like me. Why does there have to be anything else to it?" Campbell asked. "Sure, I wouldn't be over the moon if it was *my* sister, but at the end of the day, that's just how I feel. We all make our own decisions, don't we?"

"But there's like laws and stuff Campbell. It's not like I'm twenty-two and am an adult. I'm still considered a minor."

"Well, if anyone asks, you just say you're eighteen. Nobody has to know," he said convincingly.

"That doesn't seem wrong to you?" I asked.

"Iris, I like you and you like me? Why can't we just forget age and just feel how we feel?" He came over to me and cupped my face. "Nobody needs to know our ages, it doesn't matter. How we feel matters."

Convinced, although I should have known this was the mentality of a pervert, I agreed.

"Okay," I said as I smiled at him.

He kissed my head then my lips, "That's my girl."

34

Chapter 34

Eight days went by, and it was now Friday the twenty-seventh. There was nothing special that took place that week. Ginger and John were still terrible people. So much so, that they made *Melanie* look like a superstar. Campbell and I were even more of whatever we already were, and I wasn't second guessing it. Life was…good. It was also nice because that day, John and Ginger were out at the casino all day, so we didn't have to deal with them being home.

When night finally came around, we all ordered pizza for dinner. I showed all the guy's *Impractical Jokers* and they loved it. The episode we were watching was called, "Joe Needs Toilet Paper." It was when Joe had a challenge of going into a coffee shop, sitting on the toilet, then opening the door, and begging the patrons for toilet paper. It was hilarious.

When it got later into the night, and we all were done watching TV, Campbell and I headed back to our room. I sat on my bed brushing my hair in my oversized T-shirt while Campbell walked back and forth in the room, brushing his teeth. When he finished, he got into bed with me. For almost a week, we had been sleeping together each night.

"Do you know how gorgeous you are, Iris?" he asked as he laid on his side and looked at me.

I smiled, "Do you know how handsome you are, Campbell?"

"Not nearly as good looking as you."

I playfully rolled my eyes.

"I mean it," he said seriously as he took the hand that wasn't suspending himself and began to caress my cheek. "And not only are you beautiful, you're funny, and kind, and someone that brings out the best version of myself."

"Really?" I frowned, not believing that to be true.

"No doubt," he said. "You make me see the bright side of things and you make me happy."

I smiled as I turned over more on my side to see him better, "You make me happy, too."

He smiled and then kissed me. We began to kiss more and more and soon, he shifted himself on top of me. We started to really make out and one thing led to the next. He took my shirt off, I took off his, and then eventually, we had sex. I can't lie, it was great. And no, this wasn't my first time. I lost my virginity when I was fourteen. I know, it's kinda young. I've had like one other person I've slept with in between my first time and now, but this was the best. *Campbell* was the best. If only I could say that now without feeling *disgusted*.

35

Chapter 35

Two days passed and it was now Sunday, September twenty-ninth, my birthday. Campbell wasn't in bed when I woke up. He wasn't even in our room. I didn't know where he could have gone, but I got up and took a shower. When I returned, there was a teddy bear and a bouquet of flowers laying on my bed. I smiled at them, knowing they were from Campbell.

A moment later, he came up behind me, wrapping his hands around my waist, and kissing me on the cheek, "Happy birthday, Iris!"

"Thank youuuuu," I said, turning around, grabbing his face, and kissing him.

"I know it's not much, but—"

"No, no, it's perfect. I love it," I interjected, picking up the roses to smell them. "Thank you."

"Of course," he said, hugging me.

Just then my phone rang.

"It's my family, they're probably calling to wish me happy birthday," I said looking down at the screen.

"Of course, right, right. I'll give y'all a minute," he said. He kissed me, smiled, then left the room.

"HAPPY BIRTHDAY TO YOU! HAPPY BIRTHDAY TO YOU! HAPPY BIRTHDAY DEAR, IRIS! HAPPY BIRTHDAY TO YOU!!" Colton, Leannah, and my mom yelled after I said hello.

I smiled, "Thank you, guys."

"How's my big seventeen-er doing?" my mom asked joyfully.

"I'm good, Mom, thank you."

"What are you doing today? Any fun plans?" Colton asked.

"Uh, I'm not sure yet. Probably just hang around here. There isn't much to do."

"I'm sure you'll find something, baby," my mom chimed in.

"Iris, I made you something and I want to show you! Turn on your FaceTime!"

"Okay, okay," I said, clicking the FaceTime button on my barely surviving iPhone Four.

"Look!" Leannah exclaimed.

It was a poster covered with pictures of Mom, Colton, Leannah, and I. It said, "Happy Birthday" in huge letters across the top and "We love you" at the bottom. It was super colorful and topped with tons of glitter, which was Leannah's signature touch to everything.

"Oh my God, Leannah, that's beautiful! I love it so much! Thank you! I wish I could have it now so I could hang it up and look at each day."

"Aw yay!" she said in pure joy. "I'm so glad you love it! Don't worry, I'll make sure to keep it safe while you're gone so when you get home you can have it!"

"Perfect," I smiled.

"Baby, this is for you too," my mom said. "It's not much, but we all chipped in to get you it."

"Oh stop, you guys didn't have to get me anything. You all do enough for me."

"Yeah, like we wouldn't get you something for your birthday,"

Colton said.

I smiled and watched as my mom put the item into view. It was a silver chain bracelet that had one charm hanging from it, reading, *B, C, I, L.*

"That's all our initials in order, Sis. Now wherever you go, we'll always be with you," Colton said.

I was speechless, I loved it.

"Thank you all so much. These are the best gifts I've ever received," I said.

"You're welcome, baby," my mom said. "We're going to send it to the program's mail station in Wyoming and they'll deliver it to you. You should get it in a couple of days."

I had no words, I just smiled from ear to ear. They had no idea how much those two gifts truly meant to me. I was eternally grateful. I *truly* loved my family.

36

Chapter 36

On the night after my birthday, Campbell made our relationship official by asking me to be his girlfriend. Now, however, it was about nine in the morning on October third when Campbell and I were in the kitchen making ourselves breakfast. There were other housemates eating and watching TV as well. Soon enough Ginger's voice broke the tranquility as a classic fight was about to ensue.

"How many times does it take to get through your *thick* fucking skull that this isn't the right toothpaste?!" Ginger screamed as she wailed the tube of toothpaste around, following John down the stairs.

"Oh, Jesus, Ginger. Does it fucking matter?!" John barked.

"If it didn't, I wouldn't be screaming about it!"

"You scream about everything! And anyway, it don't matter what toothpaste you're using, your breath still stinks!"

Campbell and I both snickered under our breath at John's comment.

Just then, Ginger picked up the vase of flowers that sat on the countertop and threw it at

John. She missed him by inches and the flower vase hit the wall right next to where Campbell and I were standing. The vase shattered into hundreds of pieces.

Campbell pulled me into him, sheltering me from the shrapnel. "Yo, calm the fuck down!" he screamed at Ginger.

"I hate you!!" Ginger yelled at John, ignoring Campbell. "Why do you have to be so fucking annoying?!"

She then stormed off and I watched her go by.

"What are you looking at?" she hissed at me.

I didn't say anything.

Ginger slammed the door and got into her car and left. She always left when they fought.

No one said anything for a minute. Everyone in the kitchen and living room kind of turned and looked at John. You could tell he was humiliated. Without saying anything, John turned around and headed up the stairs.

I shook my head in disgust as I turned back towards the stove to continue cooking, "These people are ridiculous."

"Yep," Campbell said in agreement as he kissed my cheek, comforting me. "You okay?"

"Oh yeah, I'm fine."

"Better be," he smiled then walked over to the fridge.

We ate our breakfast and once we were done, we headed back up to our room to get ready for the day. Campbell suggested going to Devil's Tower, which I instantly agreed to as it sounded like a great idea. It was only forty-five minutes away, so around ten-thirty we got into Campbell's car and started the trip.

It was a beautiful fall day. It was mostly sunny and fifty degrees. We traveled down dirt roads that were lined with both pine trees and open fields of dry grass. It all was so perfect. I wasn't used to seeing so much nature.

Around eleven-twenty, we pulled up to the entrance station.

Campbell paid the twenty-five-dollar entrance fee and disputed all attempts of me putting any money in. We drove down the long, paved road until we reached the visitor center lot. The paved parking lot to the left was filled so we turned right into the gravel parking lot.

"Is this okay, babe?" Campbell asked as he parked his car.

"Yep, this is fine," I smiled.

I picked up my bag and began to get myself ready when Campbell stopped me.

"Give me a kiss, gorgeous," he smiled.

I rolled my eyes playfully then kissed him.

After he pulled away, Campbell said, "Alright, now we can go."

I laughed and rolled my eyes once more as I got out of his car. He took my hand as we began to walk towards the hiking trail.

We took the Tower Trail which looped around Devil's Tower and began hiking. It was absolutely gorgeous. The trees were tall and thick, we saw Native American prayer cloths, which represent the tribe's spiritual connection to Devil's Tower, we saw prairie dogs (which I had never seen before), and of course, we saw Devil's Tower.

"This is amazing," I said passionately as we stood in clear view of the huge rock.

"Yeah, it is," Campbell smiled as he swung his arm around me.

I smiled as I took out my phone and took pictures of the astonishing creation in front of me.

"This was such a good idea, Campbell," I looked up at him and smiled.

He kissed my forehead, "I knew you'd love it."

After some time of walking and admiration, we completed hiking the trail, and made it back to Campbell's car.

"That was stunning," I said as Campbell closed his car door.

"I know right," he smiled as he took out a cigarette from his pack and picked up his lighter.

"It's really cool I get to see all this stuff. I don't think I'd ever be able to witness things like this if it wasn't for this program," I said.

"I totally get that. I think the same thing, especially living in the middle-of-nowhere, Oregon," he chuckled.

"Yeah. My roommates and I in Seattle went to see the Space Needle. That was really cool."

"Oh yeah?" he asked. "Yeah, the Space Needle is pretty cool," he said as he put the cigarette in his mouth, cupped his hands, and lit it.

"You've been there?"

"Oh yeah," he exhaled smoke out of the car window. "It's only like five, six, hours from Redmond, so one year I took a road trip up there with an old buddy of mine."

"Oh, that's pretty cool," I said.

"Yeah, it was fun," he exhaled more smoke.

We made it back to John and Ginger's around three p.m. We walked in and saw the two of them once again, taking shots of tequila.

"Where you kids been all day?" Ginger asked as she made a sour face from the tequila she just washed down.

Campbell looked annoyed by simply the sound of her speaking to us.

"We went to Devil's Tower," I answered monotonously.

"Devil's Tower?" John asked in a slur. I could tell he was already drunk.

"Yeah, Devil's Tower," Campbell repeated with agitation.

"What for?" John then asked.

"For the experience," I said.

"What experience? All it is is a big rock…whoopty-doo," Ginger mocked.

"Come on, let's go," Campbell said, still annoyed as he took my hand and led me to the stairs.

"Where you guys going now?" John asked.

"Jesus Christ, why are you always asking us what are we doing, where are we going? Like, you don't give a shit so stop being so fucking nosey," Campbell then barked.

"Campbell, stop. Come on, they're drunk," I said as I tried to usher him by his waist up the stairs.

"I'll be as nosey as I fucking want to be, boy. This is my fucking house," John slurred.

"Campbell," I said sternly. "Come on." I pushed him once more to go towards the stairs.

He glared at John harshly. I could tell he wanted to say something really bad to him. But, thankfully, he didn't. He just gave him an ire look then headed up the stairs in front of me.

We got into our room, and I closed the door behind us.

"Thank you," I said, looking up at him as I held him by the waist in a front-facing hug.

He sighed then smiled, "You're welcome."

"They're drunk. They're just going to say stupid shit that's gonna piss you off."

"They always piss me off," he added, then walked over to the bed and sat down.

"I know," I sighed and sat down next to him. "Just ignore them."

"Yeah," he said blankly.

Silence then fell for a moment.

"I'm gonna go take a shower," he stood up then kissed my head.

I didn't say anything but watched him grab his towel. He then grabbed a cigarette and lighter then headed out of our room.

Before he exited, he turned around with a smile, "Wanna come?"

A grin spread across my face. I nodded my head then got up and grabbed my towel. I took his hand, and we proceeded down the hall to the bathroom.

37

Chapter 37

The weekend went by, and the days were just like all the other days with Campbell. They were happy, full of love, and joyful. That is, until Monday, October seventh came around. That day, things forever changed.

The seventh was a typical day at first. Nothing was out of the ordinary. Around seven, Campbell and I were downstairs playing cards with some of the housemates. After about an hour, my head began to pound. I decided I'd go upstairs and just lay down. I told Campbell then headed up to our room.

Not too long after, I heard the door creek open and saw light break through.

"Hey, you okay, Iris?" Campbell asked as he closed the door behind him.

"Yeah, I'm fine," I said, laying on my side with my eyes closed and my back towards him.

He got into our bed, under the covers, in a spooning position. "I know something that will make you feel better," he began to rub my thigh.

I chuckled as I pushed his hand off, "Maybe tomorrow, babe. I just want to sleep now."

"Come on, baby," he shifted on top of me, in a straddle position. "Let's just do it, it'll be fun. I promise it'll make you feel better."

I sighed, "I don't think so."

He began kissing my neck.

"Come on, Campbell, stop. My head hurts and I just want to sleep," I said playfully as I began to try to push him away.

He continued to ignore me and kissed my neck.

"Campbell," I said. "Come on, stop."

He didn't.

"Stop, Campbell," I said, now aggravated as I pushed harder at him.

"Iris!" he yelled in a tone he had never used with me before.

Fear washed over me as I stared at him while every ounce of blood in my body turned to ice. I swallowed the rising lump in my throat, "I-I just don't want to tonight, Campbell. I don't feel well."

"Well, *I* want to," he said seriously and with conviction.

He was beginning to scare me. Campbell never acted like this. Never. At least with me, anyway.

I swallowed again as I laid still and looked at him, "Well...I don't want to, not tonight."

"I'm your boyfriend. You're supposed to have sex with me."

I frowned, "Let's just do it tomorrow, please, babe?"

"No, come on, Iris, you never act this way."

"Neither do you," I faltered.

There was a split second of silence, so I used that opportunity to try to push past Campbell and get out of the bed.

"Iris!" he snapped as he pushed me back down. "It's not that fucking serious. You're making this such a big deal."

"No, no, I'm not—" I tried to sit up again but he pushed me back down. We began to tussle as I tried to free myself from him. "Campbell," I cried in fear.

"Iris, calm down," he said in an annoyed tone as he pinned me still. "We do it all the time. Don't make this harder than it needs to be."

Just then, he pushed up my oversized T-shirt and tried to pull off my underwear.

"Stop, Campbell!" I shoved his hand away. "What are you doing?"

"You stop!" he shoved my hand. "What do you mean what am I doing? You're the one acting like a bitch."

Fear, anger, and sadness flooded into me, "No, I'm not."

He lowered his face to mine, cold and stern, "Then cooperate."

I swallowed as I stared into his harsh green eyes. They had never looked so cruel.

He then continued taking off my underwear.

"No, no, stop, Campbell, stop!" I collected all the courage I owned and forced it to the surface. I began to fight. Punching and kicking, pushing and shoving the best I could but it had no effect. He was so much stronger than I was. He held me to where I was immobile and did exactly what he wanted. I never had a chance.

38

Chapter 38

The next morning when I woke up, Campbell wasn't in the room. I looked around, confirming what happened last night was in fact reality, not some horrible nightmare. I pulled my knees to my chest as I began to cry. I cried hard. I should have known. I should have gone with my gut. I hated Campbell. I even hated myself a little bit.

Eventually, Campbell walked in.

"Hey, baby," he smiled, grabbing my face to kiss me.

"Don't touch me," I said monotonously as I turned my head away.

He frowned, taken aback, "Dang, what's wrong with you?"

I coldly met his eyes, "I didn't want that last night."

Campbell scoffed as he picked up his pack of cigarettes, "Oh please, you're still on that?"

I frowned, "Yes, Campbell. I'm still on that."

He took out a cigarette, not yet lighting it, "You're my girlfriend, we do it all the time. What's the big deal?"

"The big deal is I didn't *want* to last night. And I told you that."

"But *I* wanted to, Iris," he said, staring harshly into my eyes.

I looked at him pensively for a moment. "I'm done, we're over. I told you to stop and you didn't." I pushed past him, trying to walk away, but he grabbed my wrist and pulled me back.

"Hey!" he scolded. I tensed up. "And where exactly do you think you're gonna go? Huh? You live here, Iris, remember? You live with *me*." I stared at him coldly. "You gonna tell John or Ginger?" he snickered. "They don't give a shit about you." He then leveled his eyes with me, "no matter what you do, no one will ever believe you."

I continued to look at him as sorrow rushed into all my cells. I tried to walk away but Campbell still held my wrist.

"Hey!" I looked at him coldly. "I'm talking to you. Do you really think anything is going to change between us, Iris?"

I held my gaze and said nothing. Maybe Campbell did what he did next because he was mad I wasn't speaking or maybe because he wanted to scare me. Either way, he instantly, catching me off guard, slammed me against the wall. His large hand wrapped tight around my shoulder.

"Nothing's changing between you and I, Iris," he growled face to face. "Got it?"

I swallowed. Fear spread through me like a disease. This was not the Campbell I was gushing over for the past three weeks. I simply nodded my head.

"Good," he let go of me without care and left the room.

I stood there with my back up against the wall wanting to cry or vomit, or maybe both. A million things played through my mind. I felt like Alice when she fell down the rabbit hole. Only, my story didn't have a cute white rabbit that carries a pocket watch, or a disappearing cat, or even body altering food. My story had bruises, blood, and tears. I didn't fall down a rabbit hole and find Wonderland. No. I fell down a rabbit hole and found hell.

39

Chapter 39

"Hey, pretty little Iris," Campbell said as he walked into our room with a lit cigarette in his hand. It was two days later and I was putting clothes away in their respective drawers.

I didn't say anything but forced a smile as I pulled open the closet door to put jeans away.

"Did you hear me?" he asked in an annoyed tone. "I said hello."

"Yeah, no, I heard you, I was just—"

"Just what?" he grabbed my arm and then he pushed me against the wall, "If you heard me, why can't you say hi?"

My eyes locked on to his cigarette burning in between his two fingers, smoke dancing off it, "I-I-I was just—"

"Just what? Ignoring me?" he began to squeeze my arm.

"No, I was just—owe, Campbell stop, you're hurting me," I pleaded.

"Oh, I'm hurting you, huh? I'm hurting you?" he mocked. The flame began to swim down his cigarette and create a trail of dark ash behind it. "I'm not hurting you, you're full of shit."

"You are! Stop, Campbell, please!"

More and more ash grew on his cigarette, eventually forcing some to fall to the floor.

"Get the fuck off me!" I blurted out as I tried to push him off.

I guess yelling at him made him angry because just then, he let go of my arm to pull back and smack me dead across my face.

I clutched my cheek as it began to throb, "Campbell—" I faltered.

He put his cigarette in his mouth, "I told you, Iris, nothing is changing."

I looked up at him as tears welled in my eyes, still holding my cheek. Gray smoke billowed and kissed the ceiling.

Almost three weeks went by of the same thing, and I was scared. Scared of Campbell. Scared of what he could do. He hadn't hit me since that day in our bedroom, but I was still afraid. Because he could. And he would.

I finished dinner and got back into my room when I felt my phone buzzing in my back pocket. It had been a normal Wednesday that day. Well—as normal as a day could have been. I sat down on my bed as Campbell just left to take a shower.

Colton, my phone read as it continued to buzz in my hand.

I sighed, not because I didn't want to talk to him, or my family but because every time I did since Campbell assaulted me, it sucked the energy out of me from faking that I was happy. I wasn't the kind of person that could hide my emotions well. I could, if I had to, but it took all my power and it was extremely draining. So, with reluctance, I answered the phone.

"Hello?"

"Hey, Sis," Colton gleamed. "How are you?"

"I'm fine," I forced happiness into my voice. "How are you?"

"I'm good! I miss you."

I smiled slightly, "I miss you too."

"Whatcha been up to?" he asked.

I sighed, "Oh, nothing. Not much to do around here."

"Well taking it easy is always nice," he said. "You doing anything for tomorrow?"

"Tomorrow?" I questioned. "What's tomorrow?"

"Halloween?" he questioned in a confused manner. "You love Halloween."

"Oh," I said.

To be honest, I hadn't even realized it was the day before Halloween. Colton was right, I did love Halloween, well—New Year's Eve was my favorite holiday, but Halloween came second. I guess I just wasn't paying attention to the days anymore…they were all the same, anyway.

"Right," I said. "I completely forgot. It's so boring here, all the days are just blending together," I lied and forced a chuckle, trying to seem believable.

"Right," I could hear in Colton's voice that he didn't believe me. I could never pull anything over on him.

"Well…*are* you doing anything?" he asked again.

"Oh…probably not," I said. "You know the hosts are assholes and wouldn't want a party or anything."

"I gotcha," he said in a different tone than before, knowing something was off with me.

"Uh, are you doing anything?" I asked, trying to make the conversation normal.

"Uh, you know, probably just pass out candy to the neighborhood kids," he said.

"What's Leannah doing?" I asked.

"She's going to some costume party a girl in her grade is throwing."

I made a surprised face, "Huh, that's nice," Leanna didn't usually do that stuff.

"Yeah, she seems excited," he said.

"What's she dressing up as?" I asked.

"Uh Bella? Belle? That Disney Princess?" he asked in a confused tone.

That made me chuckle, "Belle, yeah," I smiled.

He chuckled, "Yeah her. A group of girls she's going with thought it'd be funny to all dress up as the princesses."

I smiled again, "Yeah."

"So how are you?" he asked.

I tried to fake a smile, but it didn't work, "I'm okay."

"Just okay?" he questioned.

"Yeah, I'm okay, like I'm fine, everything is normal," I lied.

Colton paused, "You don't sound fine. Is something wrong, Iris?"

I pulled my eyebrows together as I felt my eyes welling up with tears, "No, nothing's wrong. I'm all good."

"You sure?" he asked.

"Yeah, I'm sure."

After a beat, "Is it Campbell?"

I clenched my jaw, swallowed the rising lump in my throat, and blinked away my tears, "No."

Another pause, a longer one this time. "Alright. Well, call me if you need anything, at any time, okay?" he said.

"I will, thank you."

Again, a pause. "I love you," he said seriously.

"I love you too, Colton."

I took the phone away from my ear and ended the call. I began to cry. I rolled over on my side and cried and cried and cried. I just wanted to go home. I wanted to leave, I wanted to go someplace that wasn't here, but I couldn't. I couldn't leave, I couldn't see my family, I couldn't tell Colton, I couldn't do anything. And that lonely fucking feeling I felt, that lonesome, having absolute no one, feeling, was something I wouldn't wish on anyone in this entire world.

40

Chapter 40

It was Halloween day when Campbell walked into the kitchen—where I was making a sandwich—with two Walmart bags. "Hey, baby."

I looked at him, "Hey."

"What's up?" he nodded to the two housemates that looked over at him. They nodded back.

"What's in the bags?" I asked as I put the top piece of bread on my sandwich.

Campbell set down the bags on the counter beside me, "Our Halloween costume."

"What do you mean, 'Our Halloween costume'?" I asked monotonously.

"The housemates and I are having a costume party tonight," he said.

"Oh," I said dully. "You guys are?"

"Yeah, of course," he said in a confused manner.

"Well, what about John and Ginger?" I asked.

He frowned, "They're already talking about some "masquerade"" they're going to in a couple hours. And you know they won't be back until like tomorrow, or Saturday morning."

I smiled, "Oh, okay."

"Wanna see what I got you?" he grinned.

"Sure," I tried to sound enthusiastic, but I wasn't at all.

He put his hand into the plastic bag and pulled out a pair of black cat ears, a matching black tail, and a stick of cheap black eyeliner. The quintessential, ever-girl-ever cat halloween costume.

"What's this?" I asked, trying to hold back my disgust.

"It's a cat costume," he smiled.

"Oh," I said dully. "Yeah, that's…cute," I lied.

"I was going through your suitcase—"

"You were going through my suitcase?" I frowned.

"Yeah, is that a problem?" he questioned with somewhat aggression. "Are you hiding something?"

I looked down to the floor, "Oh, no. I'm not, it's fine."

He looked at me with a frown for a moment then continued. "Anyway, I was going through your suitcase and found two raunchy ass dresses. When I saw the black one, I figured it'd make a hot ass cat costume."

I sighed, "Campbell, I hate those dresses."

"Why?" he looked shocked. "They're hot. Especially that red one."

"That was my roommates back in Seattle. She didn't want it anymore."

"Lucky you," he grinned. "So, I figured you'd wear the black one for the costume."

I sighed, "I really don't want to. I have black leggings and a black shirt I can wear?" I tried to suggest.

Campbell frowned in confusion, "That's not hot."

"Well, why do I have to look hot? We're only going to be here."

"Just wear the black dress, Iris," I could hear the agitation growing in his voice.

"Alright," I said monotonously to avoid trouble. "What are you wearing?" I asked to deflect his growing hostility.

He dug his hand into the other plastic Walmart bag and pulled out a blue Superman T-shirt, a white button-down dress shirt, and a red tie.

"This," he said as he held the pieces up. "Clark Kent," he said in a clarifying way.

"You like Superman?"

He shrugged. "Maybe when I was younger, but Walmart didn't have shit." He shoved the items back into the bag. "And I already drove an hour and a half there, so I had to find something."

I frowned out of confusion, "Why did you drive an hour and a half to Walmart?"

"That was the closest one," he then put his arms around my neck, "And I had to get something for my baby."

I looked at him blankly. I then forced a smile onto my face as best as I could, "Thank you."

"You're welcome," he smiled then kissed me.

"Alright you eat, I'm gonna put this stuff upstairs really quick then we'll go to the liquor store."

"Aren't they gonna card me though?" I asked.

He frowned, "Probably not. And if so, you just say you must have left it in the car and you'll go look for it. Say your birthday is September twenty-ninth, nineteen ninety-two in a confident and quick manner to make it seem believable. Got it?"

Campbell's plan didn't sit right with me, but having no other choice, I obliged. "Alright."

Campbell went upstairs and I looked down at my sandwich. I wasn't even hungry anymore.

41

Chapter 41

We went to the liquor store but since it was an hour away, we got back to John and Ginger's around two thirty. The cashier did end up asking me for my ID as well. I did as Campbell told me too and the man believed it. Campbell told me I was a "Good girl" for following as he said, which made me want to peel my skin off and step outside of it.

We headed inside the house, leaving the alcohol behind as we would get it once John and Ginger left for their party.

"Yo, you get the alcohol?" our housemate, Nate asked as we walked down the hall to our room. "Hey, Iris," he grinned at me.

"Hi," I said quietly as I looked down at my feet.

"Yeah," Campbell huffed after looking at me. "It's in my car."

"Sweet, thanks, bro," he patted Campbell on the back. "How much do I owe you?"

"You wanted the handle of Fireball, right?" Campbell asked.

"Yeah."

"Twenty-five."

"Bet," Nate said, then dug into his pocket, pulling out the cash.

"Thanks," Campbell said as he took the money from him.

"No problem, bro. Thank *you*," he said. "I'm hyped for tonight!"

Campbell chuckled but it seemed forced, "Same, man."

"I'll see you later, bro," Nate said then patted Campbell on the back once more and then walked away.

We walked into our room, "That kid's annoying," Campbell said.

"How old is he?" I asked.

"I don't know, like twenty-three or some shit," Campbell said as he laid down on the bed.

"Oh, okay."

"Come here," he grinned as he reached his arm out to me.

I forced a smile, went over, and sat next to him. He motioned me to lay down with him, so I did. He started rubbing my arms and then kissing me, which unfortunately only led to more.

It was six o'clock when we heard John and Ginger go down the stairs, out the front door, and start their car.

"Let the party begin," Campbell grinned as he got up from the bed.

He began taking his "costume" out of the Walmart bag as I remained lying down. He pulled off the white long-sleeve shirt he was wearing and tossed it on the bed. He then ripped off the tags that were on the Superman shirt and pulled that over his head.

"Start getting dressed," he said to me.

"Alright."

I got up from the bed and lifelessly walked over to the closet door where Campbell had hung my black dress. I sighed, not a single fiber of my being wanted to put that dress back on. And even *more* of me didn't want to put it on to look "hot" for Campbell.

"It's just a dress, Iris. Don't make it a big deal," he said with agitation from behind me. "You're gonna look hot," he then grinned.

I ignored him for a moment as I stared at the dress. After a second,

I turned around and forced a smile onto my face, "Thanks."

He came over to me, lifted my head up by my chin and kissed me, "I'll be back up soon. I'm gonna go get things set up then I'll be back to finish getting ready."

I nodded my head, "Alright."

He exited the room and I turned to look at myself in the mirror. I felt nothing.

I walked away from the mirror so that I could get changed without having to look at what souvenirs Campbell left me. I stepped into that black dress once again. I wiggled it up my body and put my arms into the straps. I sighed. I felt the same way when I put it on back in Seattle. Only this time, I felt a *hell* of a lot worse. I dug out the cat ears and tail and put them on unwillingly. I then pulled out the black eyeliner and began to draw whiskers and a nose on my face.

Once I was finished, I tossed the eyeliner onto the dresser. I began to stare at myself intently in the mirror.

"You look so fucking stupid," I said aloud. I kept staring and the longer I did, the more I hated myself. I exhaled deeply and shook my head. "And cats are supposed to be your favorite animal," I scoffed.

My negative self-thoughts were interrupted by Campbell coming back in.

"Damn, baby," he said with a big grin, "you look sexy as hell," putting his hands on my waist.

I smiled although I felt disgusted, "Thank you."

"Can't wait to take it off of you though," he said with an even bigger grin.

I forced myself to chuckle.

"So," he said as he put on his white button up, "why do you have that black dress anyway?"

I looked at him, then down at the floor, then back up at him, "My roommate made me and my other roommate go to this party back in Seattle. Well—I guess the party was technically in Steilacoom, but yeah."

"Made you?" he questioned. "You didn't want to go?"

"Uh, no not really."

"Why?"

"I don't know, I just didn't really want to."

He looked at me for a moment while he continued buttoning up his shirt. I gazed down to the floor.

"Did you fuck any guys there?" he asked coldly.

I looked at him and frowned, "No."

He snickered, "Right. A girl as hot as you, wearing a dress like that, and you didn't fuck anyone, okay."

I frowned again, "I didn't sleep with anyone, Campbell."

He didn't say anything but just gave me a harsh look. I broke his gaze and continued touching up my makeup. I could still see him staring at me out of the corner of my eye. He looked somewhat disgusted.

"Make sure you cover those hickeys," he said as buttoned his last button. "I don't want people seeing that shit."

I looked at him then down to the floor as tears welled into my eyes. I felt like absolute garbage. "Alright."

He didn't say anything. He just put the red tie around his neck as I felt a tear roll down my cheek.

"I'll be back," he said blandly then left the room.

I put both my hands on the dresser for suspension as I began to cry. I felt worthless. I felt like a toy, I felt disposable, I felt like I meant nothing. And maybe I did. Maybe I did mean nothing. At least that's exactly how I was beginning to feel.

Downstairs I saw all the housemates were dressed up in various costumes and making themselves drinks. The bass of the music playing was thumping. The typical kitchen and living room lights were off and replaced by a randomized loop of the rainbow courtesy of LED lights that were strung up.

"What's up, man?" Brandon asked Campbell. He was dressed up as a lumberjack.

"Hey, what's up?"

"You guys look great," he said as he looked at the both of us, spending more time on me. I looked down feeling insecure.

"Thanks," Campbell said.

"You guys wanna make a drink?" he asked.

"Yeah sure," Campbell replied. "What do you want, Iris?"

"Uh"—I really didn't want anything—"club and Tito's?"

"Sure," he said, then the two of them walked off.

I wandered over to the snack table and started eating some of the pre-packaged vegetables and dip that were set out.

"Hey, Iris," Nate said as he approached me with the same grin as earlier. He was dressed as a firefighter and already reeked of alcohol.

"Hey, Nate," I said, trying not to look repulsed by the smell of him.

"You look really good," he said.

I forced a smile, "Thanks. Uh, you do too."

He laughed, "Thanks. I had to put some shit together."

I chuckled, "Yeah."

"Where's your boyfriend?"

I felt abhorred when Nate said this. I hated that people considered us as one.

"Oh, Campbell?" I asked blandly. "He's making us a drink with Brandon."

"Oh, cool. Yeah actually, I'm about to go get another one too," he said.

"Okay."

"I'll see you later," he grinned.

"I'll see you."

He stared at my body for a second before he somewhat stumbled away. I looked down. Here I was, the only girl, the only minor, in a house full of strange, grown, men. And to top it all off, I was dressed exactly how the prey wanted. How vulnerable and defenseless I felt. Thanks a lot, Campbell.

Just then, Brandon and Campbell walked towards me.

"Here," Campbell said as he handed me a red Solo cup.

"Thank you," I said. I took a sip but quickly stopped drinking, "This is tonic water, not club."

Campbell shrugged as he sipped his drink, "Same thing. Just drink it, it's not a big deal."

I looked at him blankly while I took another sip and he stared at me.

The party went on and the night consisted of perverted stares, forced smiles, and unwanted mingling. It wasn't until nine-thirty when things went really, *really* bad.

I went upstairs to use the bathroom. Once I was finished, I opened the door and standing right in the door frame was Nate. This time, however, he was ten times drunker than when I spoke to him at the beginning of the night.

"Shit!" I jumped. "You scared me."

"My bad," he slurred. "I just—I just really gotta pee."

I frowned, "Well, it's all yours," I tried to pass by him.

He grabbed my forearm and stopped me.

"Wait," he said very close to my face, "why don't we talk for a minute?" grinning again.

"Uh," I said nervously, "I can't."

"Why?" he asked as he brushed my hair behind my ear.

I tried to move away but he grabbed my arm again and held me still, "What's the rush?"

I stared at him nervously, "I should get back to Campbell."

"Oh please," he scoffed lightly. "You're always with him. Why don't you spend some time with me for a change?"

I swallowed my nerves, "Well, Campbell's my boyfriend."

"He doesn't have to be," he said as he ran his hand down from my face to my arm.

"I—I—I really gotta go," I said as I tried to push past him.

He then quickly put his hand down on the banister and then his other hand on the wall. I was blocked from going anywhere and was cornered in with the bathroom behind me.

"You don't have to go. Come on, stay with me. I'm more fun than Campbell," he grinned through his drunken state.

"No, I really have go," I said as I pushed on his chest to get by.

Smirking, he grabbed my wrist, pushing me into the bathroom.

"Stop!" I then yelled.

As I was pushed backwards, I tripped on the lip of the entrance and fell. I landed on my back on the bathroom floor. Nate stumbled down on top of me. I tried to quickly push him off and get up, but he pushed me back down. He then straddled on top of me with a grin and kissed me.

"Get off me!" I yelled with the last bit of confidence I had in me. I pushed him to the side and jumped up.

As I did, Campbell was standing there with a look of pure hatred and vengeance.

"Campbell," I pleaded, hands up, already knowing it looked completely different than what it was.

"What the fuck is this?!" he screamed as he stormed towards me.

Just then Nate stumbled to his feet. He turned around laughing with a smug grin, "Your chick *so* wants me, bro."

Just then, an expression crossed Campbell's face that I had never seen before. I felt like a boulder plummeted into the pit of my stomach. All my blood officially drained from my body.

Campbell slammed Nate into the bathroom wall and began to repeatedly punch him in the face, over, and over, and over again.

"Campbell, stop!" I screamed as I yanked at his arm that was throwing the punches.

He stopped punching for a split second only to shove me down hard with his bloody hand. I once again fell backwards but now onto the hallway floor.

I scrambled to my feet and rushed towards Campbell again. I then saw Nate's face and began to bawl, almost vomiting. Campbell was disfiguring it with each blow. He just kept punching him over, and over, and over again. And I wasn't crying because Nate was a good person and didn't deserve it or something like that. No, not at all. But because of the fear I had of Campbell that was so deeply embedded in me that I truly believed he could kill someone, and that someone could even be me.

"Stop!" I yelled through tears. "Stop!" I tried to pull him away.

Only when Nate passed out did Campbell swing around, viciously grab my upper arm, and drag me down the hall to our room. He shoved me down on our bedroom floor and slammed the door shut, locking it.

I jumped up quickly, "Campbell," I said, pleading with my hands up as tears streamed down my face, "it's not what you—"

Bam!

He punched me hard across my face. I held it with one hand and put my other one up defensively. I could already feel the wetness of my blood run onto my hand.

"I was using the bathroom and when I came out, he tried to hit on me. He pushed me down and kissed me!" I tried to protest.

Campbell grabbed me violently by the side of my neck, "You're a fucking liar!" he screamed.

"No!" I yelled. "No, I'm not. I promise, Campbell, I promise."

He yanked me closer to him, "You're a fucking whore!" he screamed in my face. "You probably fucked him in there, didn't you?!"

"No, I—"

"Didn't you?!" he screamed again as he shook me.

"I didn't, Campbell! I didn't! I'm telling you the truth!" I pleaded as tears streamed down and my face throbbed. I was the most scared I had ever been in my entire life.

"What did you do?!" he screamed inches away from my face.

"Nothing!" I pleaded. "Nothing!"

"Yes, you did!" he screamed as he shoved me away then punched me hard in the face yet again.

This time, I fell onto the floor. He grabbed me by my hair and pulled me back to my feet.

"You fucked him, didn't you?! Didn't you?!"

"No!" The iron taste of blood filled my mouth.

"I bet you liked it!" he yelled. "Did he fuck you better than me?!"

I weakly shoved him away as more tears streamed down, "I didn't do that, Campbell."

He grabbed me hard and pulled me towards him, "Don't fucking shove me!" Spit flew from his mouth. "You're a dirty fucking bitch! You're a fucking slut! Who the fuck fucks random guys in a bathroom? You fucking bitch!"

I tried to keep from crying, "I didn't—" I said desperately, not being able to hold down my emotions. "He pushed me down and kissed me, Campbell. I swear. I swear," I hiccuped. "I pushed him off me and that's when you came up."

He shoved me down on the bed, "Yeah right. You expect me to believe that shit?! Just like you expect me to believe you about that party in Seattle?!"

"What are you talking about?!" I crawled back in fear.

"I know you fucked someone there and you won't tell me! You think you can just keep things from me and get away with shit?! Just like right now, you think I wouldn't find out about you and Nate!" He threw a ceramic lamp across the room.

"I see how he fucking looks at you, Iris!" He yanked me off the bed.

I was losing hope. I *truly* believed I was going to die that night.

"I'm not lying, Campbell. I'm not."

"Oh boo-fucking-hoo," Campbell mocked. "Don't cry, you fucking whore!"

"No, I'm not," I said through tears.

He laughed, "Oh you're not?! Huh?! You're not?!" he then grabbed me by the throat and slammed me into the wall. He began to squeeze.

"All you bitches are, are fucking whores!" he yelled as he looked at me in my eyes as I struggled to breathe. "You think you can fuck dudes behind my back?!" he squeezed tighter.

I tried to grab his hands and peel his fingers off my throat, but his grip was far too tight.

"You're mine, Iris. No one else's. You're not Nates, you're not no one else's. And you're not fucking going anywhere," he growled.

I felt every ounce of blood my body owns congregate in my face, seconds away from bursting at the seams and creating an explosion.

"What did I tell you?!"

Silence, as I couldn't breathe.

"Huh?!" he violently rattled me. "I told you nothing was changing between us."

I stared at him, losing consciousness.

"You dirty, fucking, bitch," he said inches from my face. "I should *fucking* kill you."

I went numb. Those words pierced me with fear and rattled it through my body that was like no other. It ricocheted off each organ, muscle, and bone. Landing in the pit of my stomach and sinking so far down, dragging me along with it. I truly believed it—he was going to fucking kill me.

But I guess the idea of keeping a toy, someone to use and abuse, let me live. Because right when I was almost at the bottom of that pit, he let go of me and forcefully threw me down to the floor.

I began coughing and choking, gasping for air, so desperate to fill my lungs with oxygen. I coughed and choked, coughed and choked. As I repeated this pattern, blood came up as well. I'm sure this was from when he punched me in my mouth.

Campbell got down to my level, grabbed me by my chin, and made me look at him. "If you *ever* do something like that again, I promise, I'll fucking kill you, Iris. I will fucking *kill* you."

I stared at him as I continued my cough-choke pattern. The hatred I felt for him, the fear I felt from him, and the sadness I felt because of him, made me wish he did just fucking kill me.

42

Chapter 42

In the morning, I got up and went into the bathroom to take a shower. I placed my hands on the vanity's sink as a suspension while I looked at myself in the mirror. I saw nothing but emptiness staring back at me. I pulled my shirt off, now standing in my bra and underwear as I gazed at my tiny, frail body in the mirror. I looked down at my neck. The darkest shades of purple and blue ran around it like some sort of scarf. I then looked down at my chest. Ugly hickeys from the night before last stared back at me. I looked at my upper arm and admired the matching purple and blue mark that illuminated it. I looked at my face. I gazed at the bruise on my cheek and the dried blood that was encrusted around my lip. Both acting as a medal for endeavoring a fight. I looked at everything he left. I looked at it all. I looked at it all and simply felt nothing, I didn't cry, I didn't scream. I just stared back at the reflection of the empty shell I had become.

After I finished my shower, I got dressed in sweatpants, a bagging shirt, and a hoodie. I returned to my room and began to dig in my suitcase for the scarf I let Bianca use to cover her bruised neck. As I searched, the door opened. I turned around and saw it was Campbell. This was the first time I was seeing him that day.

"Hey, baby," he smiled as he sat down on the bed and patted it, motioning for me to come sit next to him.

I was stunned by his "nice" demeanor. But I did as he said and got up and went to sit down next to him

"Hi," I swallowed.

He smiled and kissed me. He then began to stare at my throat. "That bruise is pretty bad."

I touched it and looked down, "It's no big deal." I said, trying to deflect the attention away from it.

"You can't make me behave this way. I don't want to hurt you," he said, victimizing himself.

I stared at him.

"You can't do these things that make me lose my temper."

"Campbell—" I tried to intervene.

"Iris," he said, now interrupting me. "I'm not talking about it anymore. I know what I saw and as I thought about it later, I've come to the conclusion that the only reason you'd do that is if I wasn't pleasing you. So, I'll just have to do that better."

"Campbell"—I swallowed hard—"Nothing happened between Nate and I. I promise. I went to the bathroom and when I opened the door, he tried to hit on me. I tried to go back downstairs to you, but he pushed me down, got on top of me, and kissed me."

"Well," Campbell said, "whatever the truth *really* is, Nate's where he belongs," he said coldly.

My heart dropped, "Where's that?"

He laughed, "The hospital. You should see his fucking face," he joked as he pulled out his phone.

My blood ran ice cold. How could he laugh at something like that?

"See," he said as he showed me a picture of Nate.

It was horrendous. Absolutely horrendous. Nate was lying in a hospital bed with both of his eyes black and swollen shut, his nose was broken, his face was covered in blood, and his lips were busted and swollen as well.

"Look, he even lost a tooth," Campbell said nonchalantly as he slid to the next photo.

This one was from the bathroom and was a close-up of Nate's face. His eyes were closed, presumably unconscious, and Campbell's finger was holding up Nate's upper lip to expose his teeth. And just as Campbell said, his front left tooth was missing.

I winced, putting my hand to my mouth, afraid if I didn't I'd throw up. "Oh my God. Campbell, that's horrible."

The smile on his face disappeared and turned to an ire expression, "No it's not," he said aggressively as he locked his phone and put it down. "He fucking deserves that, Iris. I caught you two fucking. You're lucky I love you or I would have just kept going."

I was petrified by his violence. It was absolutely fucking terrifying.

"But it's over now, and it's just you and me again," he smiled then kissed me.

I forced a smile once we pulled apart.

"Cover your neck up if you leave the room," he said as he looked down at my throat again. "I don't want people seeing you that way."

I looked down then nodded my head.

"I'll be back in a little," he kissed my head and got up to leave.

As I watched him walk to the bedroom door, thoughts flooded my mind. The way he could so easily talk about hurting someone and…killing them? Horrified me in ways that were unexplainable.

Two days later, everyone sat down at the kitchen table for dinner. Ginger placed a big pot of sauceless penne pasta onto the oven mitt that laid on the table.

"Eat up," she said as if we were pigs. She then tossed a spoon into the bowl.

I sat there staring at everyone taking turns serving themselves the pasta. I didn't want to eat though.

"Give me your plate, baby," Campbell said.

I gave it to him with no expression. John scoffed as he stuffed a forkful of pasta into his mouth. Campbell glared at him then dished pasta onto my plate. He served himself then we all began to eat.

As we ate, the front door opened and in Nate walked. He had a cast on his nose, dark rings around his eyes, and a wound closure bandage on his forehead. Campbell readjusted himself at the table with an ire face once he saw Nate come through the door. I looked down at my plate and twirled my pasta around. I couldn't bear to see what Campbell did to him.

"What the hell happened to you, boy?" John asked as he set down his fork.

"Shit," Ginger said.

"No one told you?" Nate asked with hostility. "I've been in the hospital. I got jumped Halloween night," he said as he shot Campbell a death stare. Campbell shot one back that was even meaner. "You didn't notice I haven't been here for two days?" Nate then asked John and Ginger with agitation.

John and Ginger looked at each other like *Oh shit.*

"Uh," John mumbled, "we did. Yeah, we knew you were in the hospital. Jeff here told us what happened," he smiled and clamped his hand on Jeff's shoulder, trying to seem convincing.

Jeff looked up at John with a twisted face, knowing he never told John anything.

"Yeah," Ginger added in the same unconfident, lying tone. "We knew. How you doing?"

Nate scoffed, not believing them one bit. I mean, you would've had to be an idiot to believe their act.

"I'm going upstairs," Nate said.

He walked towards the stairs then stopped and turned around.

"Nice to see you, Iris," he smirked, then looked at Campbell.

My jaw tightened and I immediately shot my eyes away from him and back down to my plate.

Out of the corner of my eye, I saw Campbell gripping his knife and fork so tightly that his knuckles were turning white. I looked up at his face and saw his nose and eye were twitching as he hatefully watched Nate walk up the stairs.

"What's the matter with you?" Ginger asked as she stared at Campbell in confusion.

"Nothing," he stabbed a group of penne pasta and put them aggressively into his mouth.

I looked down at my plate and pushed my food around some more.

Dinner continued in basically silence and I ate about three forkfuls of the poorly cooked pasta.

43

Chapter 43

Days passed by like they typically did, and it was now Tuesday, November fifth. Around eleven, I was in my room, digging through my suitcase trying to find a pair of thick socks as it was really cold that day. Campbell was outside smoking a cigarette with one of the housemates.

While scavenging, I found a picture I had of my mom, Colton, Leannah, and I. It was from three years ago when we went to Niagara Falls. That was such a great trip. It was about an eight-hour drive from Chicago and the whole way we laughed and jokingly sang songs together. I don't know how our little 1990 Honda Civic made it, but it did, and it was a great time.

The memories that were flooding back, disappeared as quickly as they came when my phone rang; Colton was FaceTiming me.

"Shit," I said.

I didn't want to answer because he would see the bruises on my face and neck, and the cut on my lip from Halloween. My face looked better, but it wasn't fully healed, and my neck was nowhere *close* to unnoticeable. But I couldn't decline because in my fucked-up head, I thought he would think something was up—even though something was.

I jumped up from the floor and rapidly began digging through my makeup bag. I was looking for my concealer as I quickly wrapped my scarf around my neck. I checked every pocket and slot there was in the makeup bag as my phone continued to play the default iPhone ringtone. The makeup was clearly nowhere to be found, so I gave up and answered his call before it ended.

"Hello?" I tried my best to keep the wounded side of my face out of the camera.

"Hey, Sis. I gotta tell you about this insane shit Leannah and I witnessed," Colton stated.

"Oh yeah? What happened?" I asked dully as I laid down on my bed, knowing this wasn't going to be a short call.

"Well, Mom was working late so we walked down to the diner to get something to eat when all of a sudden like five cop cars came blazing past us. We wanted to see what was going on, so we ran down the block to where they were. All the cops had their guns drawn on this man—"

I began to zone out, not hearing a word Colton was saying. I began staring at the picture of us four in front of the enormous waterfall. Everyone looked so happy and full of joy. Now, the only thing I was full of was desolation.

"Uh, hello? Iris? Did you hear what I said? The guy was one of Mom's ex-boyfriends, he had just robbed a bank and shot the teller."

"What?" snapping out of my trace. "Holy shit, which boyfriend? Is the teller okay?"

"Lance. And yeah, he's okay. He got shot in the arm."

"Wow," I said blandly.

"Yeah," Colton said with no confidence. I could tell he knew something was up with me.

"Everything okay, Iris?" he then asked.

"Yeah, yeah everything's fine," I lied. "I just didn't have a good night's sleep, that's all."

He gave me a look like he pretended to believe what I said.

"Well, I'm gonna go take a nap, recharge a little you know," I said, trying to avoid this situation further.

"Alright, well enjoy. I hope it helps," he said.

"Thanks, Colton, I love you."

"I love you too, Sis."

I hung up the phone and laid down on my back, sighing at the ceiling.

A few minutes later, Campbell opened the door and peeked his head in. "I'll be back later. I'm going to this bar with Ricky."

"Okay," I sat up. I was confused though as he never seemed to be too friendly with Ricky.

He opened the door further and walked towards me, "Can I trust you to be here alone for a couple hours?" he asked sternly.

I looked at him with desperate eyes. I felt disgusted. I wasn't a child. I wasn't his property. And I didn't do *anything* wrong.

"Yeah," I answered blandly as I had my head down.

"Iris?" he repeated in the same stern tone.

I looked up at him.

"Can I?" he repeated.

"Yeah, you can," I said, still blandly but more convincing.

"Good. That's my girl," he kissed my head and then exited our room.

I laid back down on the bed once he closed the door. Tears welled into my eyes as the feeling of shame, embarrassment, and humiliation washed over me. I felt dirty, I felt bad about myself, and I felt exactly like what he called me: a whore. And I didn't even do what he thinks I did to deserve those types of feelings.

I must have somehow fallen asleep because I woke up to my phone buzzing. I adjusted my eyes and picked up my phone. It was a text message from Colton.

Can we talk, alone? It's important, it read. I knew it was about how I acted earlier.

Yeah sure, I wrote back.

Seconds later my phone rang.

Hello?" I said, answering his phone call.

"Hey. Alright, what's up, Iris? Why were you acting so weird on the phone today?"

"What do you mean?" I tried to act confused. "I don't think I was acting weird."

"Oh, come on," Colton scoffed. "Any other time you would be all ears in something I had to tell you, and you *never* give dry responses. Especially over something like, oh, I don't know, Mom's ex-boyfriend shooting a bank teller, robbing a bank, and running from the police," Colton said fretfully.

"I told you I didn't get a good nigh''s sleep last night and I was tired."

"Iris, you haven't sounded like yourself in weeks."

"Colton, everything's fine. I must seem off because I'm bored," I lied poorly. "There's just nothing to do here. The whole environment is *so* different from back home."

There was a pause. "You sure that's why?" Colton asked coldly.

"I don't know what else it could be." I said.

"Well, maybe it's to hide something," Colton said pensively. "Or to cover something up."

There was another pause.

"What are you talking about?" I tried to play stupid, but I knew he was on to me.

"You think I wouldn't notice the bruise on your face, Iris?" Colton asked discontentedly. "And the scarf? You haven't worn a scarf since you were like twelve. What happened? Who gave you the bruise?"

"It's nothing, Colton," I said dismissively.

"*Who* did that to you, Iris?" he asked again sternly, not giving up.

After a seconds-long pause, I sighed and answered quietly and reluctantly. "Campbell did it."

"What?" I could feel his heart drop.

I paused. "Campbell did it," I faltered, head down.

"What do you mean, 'Campbell did it'?"

I didn't say anything.

"Iris," Colton said with complete seriousness, "what did Campbell do to you?"

I swallowed hard as my eyes shifted from the left of the room to the right. I took a moment then I spoke. "Campbell, Campbell and I, were uh, dating for about three weeks, before uh"—I paused—"before things kinda got bad."

"What do you mean 'bad'?" I could feel the tension of his anxiety and worry so strongly through the phone.

"I didn't want to have sex with him one night," I said trailing off.

I could feel the suspense break as I knew Colton knew exactly what I was going to tell him.

"But he made me, and ever since he's been a completely different person. Before, he would compliment me, protect me, buy me gifts, and was just the best boyfriend I could ask for. Now, all he does is yell at me, calls me names…he's hit me. He makes me have sex with him still," I went silent for a minute, clenching my jaw.

"He threatens me, he likes having control. I think he likes to see me scared, but"—I tried hard to hold back my tears as I became choked up—"But, Colton, I am scared," I began to cry. "I'm really scared. I'm terrified. If I was in Chicago, if I was home, it'd be different. I could just go away. I could leave him. I could get on a bus, or a train and

I could go. I could just go away, but, Colton, here, there's no way, there's nowhere, Colton," I capsized, spilling over with emotion like I never had before.

"There's fucking nothing around here!" I exclaimed. "And all the other housemates are guys, and the hosts are mean and there's just nowhere, Colton. There's nowhere," I cried as Colton was silent for a moment from shock.

"I'm going to *fucking* kill him," Campbell said with anger in his voice. "How long has this been going on for?!"

"About a month," I said with my head down.

"A month?! Why didn't you tell me sooner?!" he sounded heartbroken.

"Because"—my eyes welled back up with tears—"you'd worry about me. You have already dealt with so much between the three of us," I said, talking about my mom, Leannah, and I.

"Well of course I'd worry about you!" he cried. "You're my sister. How could I sit back and let some man almost double your age take advantage of you and hurt you?"

I shook my head as I began to weep.

"What has he done?" Colton asked in a low voice, not really wanting to know the answer.

I clenched my jaw to keep from crying and sniffled before I spoke. "He first slapped me. He hadn't hit me since but on Halloween"—I paused to swallow my emotions—"on Halloween, this guy pushed me down and kissed me and Campbell saw. He swears we had sex, and he bludgeoned the guy so bad he was in the hospital for two days," I began to cry. "He beat me up that night, Colton," I said through tears. "He punched me. That's why I have a bruise on my face and a cut on my lip. He choked me, Colton," I paused to take a deep breath. "He choked me really, really badly. There's a disgusting bruise around my neck from it. That's why I had the scarf on."

"Iris—" Colton said in dismal.

"He told me he'd fucking kill me if I did something like that again." I interjected before he could finish. "But I didn't do anything, Colton!" I yelled as I cried. "I've *never* had sex with anyone else at this house and he's been treating me like a slut. He even called me one! The things he says to me are awful, Colton," more tears streamed down my face.

"Iris," Colton said again. "You need to go. You need to leave. I'll come get you."

"No, Colton, I can't, I can't go."

"Yes, you can! What are you talking about? There's not a chance in hell I'm letting you stay there one more day with him," Colton cried. "I'm coming to get you."

"No, Colton, no!" I yelled. "I'm not going anywhere!"

"Why?!" he exclaimed with emotion.

"Because I can't, Colton! I came here for you guys, for us, for mom, I can't just leave! This whole thing would be pointless!"

"You're not staying there with Campbell! I don't care if we would get a trillion dollars from you being there, I'd *never* have you stay someplace you aren't safe."

"And what is safe anyway, Colton?!" I barked while crying. "No where's safe! School wasn't safe, Camp wasn't safe, our own fucking house wasn't safe! I'll just come home, and the same shit will happen!" I took a pause, breathing heavy. "There's no place, Colton…there's nowhere."

Silence fell over the phone for a minute.

"Iris," he said in a tone that sounded like he was holding back tears. "You can't stay there."

My eyes flooded with tears at the sound of his heartbroken voice.

"How do you think I'll be able to sleep at night, to eat, to breathe, knowing you're there with that monster?!" he exclaimed passionately.

"I can't let him use you like that."

I hung my head, not knowing what to say.

"Iris," I could hear Colton crying. I only ever saw Colton cry *once*. When my mom almost died from an OD. There was no other time I *ever* saw him cry. "I can't let that happen to you. That breaks my fucking heart."

I squeezed my face together, trying to hold back my tears. Hearing him be this upset, broke me in ways I couldn't explain.

"I have to do something. I can't just stand here, knowing this shit is happening to you and do nothing,."

Tears ran down my face.

"I should be leaving soon," I said after a moment.

"How do you know that?!"

"I don't know," I sighed, shaking my head in distress.

There was a moment of silence. We both didn't know what to say, I knew this caused Colton affliction.

"So, what's your plan then?" Colton asked angrily at the thought of me being there with Campbell. "Stay there and let this man violate you?"

"I don't know, Colton. There's no other choice."

"Don't say *that*," he cried. "What if you don't leave for months? Huh?! I can't let this keep happening to you, Iris. Not for a month, not for a week, not for a day."

More tears struck my shirt, "I don't know what to say, Colton. I don't."

There was another pause. "Campbell's not gonna continue doing this shit to you, Iris. He's just not. I'm sorry, I'm coming to get you—"

"No!" I screamed, now angry. "I swear to fucking God if you come here, I'll *never* fucking speak to you again."

There was a pause. I knew what I said was bold. It was *very* bold. I guess I didn't *truly* mean it. But I did *not* want Colton coming to get me. It had already been a month. I wasn't going to endure all this to go home with nothing.

"Iris," he said, taken aback. "What the fuck is wrong with you?"

"I don't want you coming here, Colton. I don't. Just please, just let me handle this on my own. I know it's hard to stomach, I know that. It's fucking hard for me too. I'm terrified every fucking day, but I didn't come here, and endure all this just to leave empty handed. I'll be fine and I know you hate when I say that, but I will. Just please, just let me vent and cry to you, you don't have to lecture me…I need you right now."

There was a long silence. I think those were the words he needed to hear. I think he needed to be reminded that sometimes, all I needed was his support, not his words.

"Iris," he said after a minute. "I don't know how you'll *ever* expect me to just go about my life knowing what's going on with you. Because right now, the only thing on my mind is putting that fucker six feet under," he paused for another minute. "But, at the end of the day, I want to do what *you* want me to do, and what you *need* me to do. So, as much as it kills me, and I'm really not sure how I'm going to be able to"—Colton really didn't want to say his next sentence—"I won't come get you," he said through clenched teeth.

I looked down, "Thank you."

He didn't say anything.

"You call me any fucking time you need me. I don't care if it's two in the morning or four in the afternoon. You call me. And if at any second you want to leave, I'll be there in a heartbeat. You hear me?"

I nodded my head, "Yeah, thanks, Colton."

There was another pause.

"I can't believe I'm fucking doing this," he said aloud in exasperation.

"Colton," I said, trying to put his feelings to rest. "It's okay—"

"It's not okay, Iris. None of this is okay," he sniped.

There was a pause. "I'm sorry," he said. "It's just hard to hear all this and not be able to do anything."

"You are," I said. "By letting me talk to you and just being there for me."

There was another pause, like Colton was thinking about what I said.

"I love you, Sis."

"I love you too."

Colton sighed.

I knew he wasn't okay with this, and maybe deep down inside, I wasn't either. But it had to be okay, it had to. There was no other way, there was nowhere.

44

Chapter 44

November twelfth is Colton's birthday. The first thing I did when I woke up was throw on some clothes and went outside to call him. It was around nine, so Campbell was still asleep.

"Happy Birthday to you, happy birthday to you, happy birthday dear, Colton, happy birthday to you," I sang over the phone once he answered.

"Aw, thank you, Sis. I love you!"

I smiled, hearing his voice made me happy.

"You're welcome. I love you more. What are you guys doing today?"

"Well, Mom's cooking my favorite dinner and Leannah's making me a cake. They just left for the grocery store actually."

"That sounds awesome," I smiled.

"Yeah," Colton trailed off. I could tell he wanted to ask something else.

"So, uh, how are you, Sis? It's uh, it's really been killing me, what you told me and all," Colton sounded like he was holding down being choked up.

"I'm okay. Look, I don't want to talk about this on your birthday, I just want you to have a great day with Mom and Leannah."

Colton sighed, "I'll try, Iris."

"Please? For me? Everything's gonna be okay, I promise."

I think I was trying to convince myself of this as much as I was Colton. Because the truth is, I didn't know what was going to happen, or how long I'd be there. I didn't know anything, but I couldn't make Colton worry.

"Go enjoy your day. Especially that lasagna dinner and cake Leannah is gonna make for you. And tell her that when I get back, she better make one for my birthday that she missed," I joked, trying to enlighten both of our moods.

Colton chuckled, "Alright, I'll tell her, I love you. Call me if you need anything…anything."

"I will, I love you too. Happy birthday, Colton," I smiled.

"Thanks, Sis, see you."

"Bye," I hung up the phone, and once I did, I felt that little bit of happiness escape from my body. That little happiness I got from talking to Colton on the phone was now replaced with the reality of living with Campbell and the fear it brought.

I sighed knowing I couldn't stay out there forever. So, after some time alone, I headed back inside.

Sometime later, I was laying down on my bed when Campbell came in and started complaining about how bored he was.

"There's nothing to fucking do," he said as he sat down on the bed and lit a cigarette.

I didn't say anything.

"Come on, let's go drive around," he grabbed my hand and tried to pull me off the bed as he put the cigarette in his mouth.

"No, Campbell, stop. I don't want to go drive around," I pulled my hand back. "I want to lay down. I'm tired," I turned away from him.

He sat back down and started stroking my inner thigh, smirking as he took the cigarette out of his mouth and exhaled.

"You want to stay here instead?" taunting me with his control, "Because I have no problem staying here in this bed with you."

I gave him a cold, blank look. I *hated* him.

"That's what I thought, now let's go," he put the cigarette back in his mouth.

We got into his car and drove around for some time until we stopped at a gas station. Campbell got out and started pumping the gas.

"I gotta go piss," he said to me through the car window as he walked towards the convenience store.

I sat there, playing with the charm that hung off my bracelet. I shifted my focus from the bracelet to the gas pump. I fixated my eyes on the numbers climbing and climbing so rapidly. I then started looking at the convenience store that Campbell had gone into. A thought came into my mind. I stared back at the pump; it was still filling up the car. I looked back at the store; Campbell still hadn't come out. My heart started to pound as I alternated my attention between the gas pump and the store. *Get out and run,* my mind said to me. I looked at the pump, then I rapidly looked at the store, my eyes did this a couple more times. *Do it. Do it* now. So, I did. I opened the car door, got out, and ran. I ran, and I ran, and I ran. I ran down the highway, jumped over the guardrail, ran into the woods, through the trees, and down to the creek.

I looked around realizing what I had just done. I had no idea why I did that. I just wanted to escape, I wanted to be free, but there was no freedom. Everyone knows freedom isn't free.

Completely distressed, I slid my hands into my hair pulling on it, knowing I only just made everything worse.

"Stupid, stupid, *stupid*!" I pounded my fist on my head. "Why are you so fucking stupid?!" I collapsed down onto a rock and cried. "I hate you, Iris," I cried. "I fucking *hate* you."

After spending time in the woods not knowing what to do, I decided I had to walk home. It took me hours from wherever I was to get there. It was dark and cold and even started to drizzle at one point. But to tell you the truth, I think I would much rather stay outside all night than have had to go back into Campbell's arms.

It was very late when I finally arrived back at John and Ginger's home. I unwillingly walked up the porch stairs and opened the door into the house.

"Motherfucker, there she is!" John yelled.

"Where have you fucking been, Iris?!" Ginger shouted at me, "Did you run away?!"

I looked at Campbell who stood up from his seat, looking unpleasant.

"No, no," I cried out in desperation.

"Iris, where did you go? Why did you leave my car?" Campbell questioned.

"I-I-I don't know. I, I saw a dog run down the street and I chased after him so he wouldn't get hit by a car, but I got lost and you were gone when I got back to the gas station," I lied, hoping it would make things better.

He came over and hugged me, "I'm so glad you're okay, I was worried sick."

He pretended to be sympathetic towards me in front of John and Ginger. I knew it was only an act, I was terrified.

"Don't be doing that shit!" John snapped. "Ginger and I can get in some real fucking trouble if we lose one of you bastards!"

"Just go up to your room and don't be playing these games no more, you hear me, girl?!" Ginger roared.

My eyes welled up with tears as I looked at them all, absolutely defeated. How could John and Ginger not see the abuse? Maybe they did and maybe they just didn't care. I had never met more selfish, blind, or pathetic people in my whole entire life.

When we got into our room Campbell closed the door.

"What the fuck was that?!" he growled.

My heart sank. I was scared to death. "Campbell—" I put my hands up defensively.

"Why did you run away from me, Iris?" Campbell scorned.

"I didn't run away. I told you, I chased after a dog," still clinging to the hope that he may believe my lie.

"I'm not fucking stupid. Don't lie to me," he shoved me into the wall.

"Campbell," I began to capsize, "Please don't be mad, I'm sorry—"

Just then gripped up my shirt and pinned me to the wall. "I'll ask you again. Did you fucking run away from me?"

My eyes filled up with tears.

"Did you?!" he now screamed inches from my face, rattling me against the wall.

"Campbell—" I cried.

Just then he grinned and slid his hand around the front of my throat, clearly pleased from scaring me, "You're so pretty, you know that, my Iris."

I swallowed hard, feeling his grip tighten.

"Did you run away from me, Iris?" he asked a moment later.

I stared into his once beautiful green but now dark eyes; all hope lost.

"Did you fucking run away?" he shouted as he slammed me into the wall, hand still tight around my throat.

"Okay, fine, fine," I finally broke. "Yes—"

Campbell snickered. I was expecting a punch, a slap, something, but he didn't. All he did was snicker, with his hand fixed around my throat.

"You think you're so slick don't you, baby?"

I swallowed hard, keeping my eyes on his.

"You're not. I hate to break it to you."

He then loosened his grip on my throat and began to caress the side of my face. He looked deep into my eyes as he thought about something. I never broke my gaze as I was frozen still, scared to death.

He led his hand down the side of my neck, brushing my hair behind my shoulder.

"You're lucky I love you."

45

Chapter 45

The next morning, in the bathroom, I turned the bathtub's faucet on and began to run water for a bath. I ran my hand under the water and tried to make it as warm as possible. John and Ginger still never did anything about the water situation so lukewarm was as good as it got.

I pulled the lever up on the faucet to change the water to come out of the shower head instead. I then slipped my clothes off and stepped into the tub. I began to break down and sob.

"I'm sorry," I cried, looking up to the ceiling as the water came crashing down like meteors.

"I'm sorry, God…I'm so sorry," I panted as I cried. "I can't do it anymore. I can't. Will you please just take me? You don't have to keep me here anymore. I don't want to be here," I begged in despair.

"Please God, just take me. Will you? Please? Just make sure Mom, Leannah, and Colton are okay and then you can take me. That's it. That's all I want. Whichever way you want to do it is fine. I promise. Please?"

After a moment, I turned over on my side and closed my eyes, "Just let me go, God. Just please let me go."

46

Chapter 46

Ten days later, on Saturday, November twenty-third, I guess God did hear me because he answered my prayers. But not in the way I wanted him to. Which in hindsight, I was grateful for.

It was around eight in the evening when Campbell and I were laying on our bed. He was smoking a cigarette and I was laying on my side, staring out of the window.

John called everyone downstairs. As we got into the living room, I saw he was holding a stack of paper in his hands and Ginger was in the door frame, smoking a cigarette. We joined the rest of the housemates, sitting down in the loveseat.

"Y'all are leaving in two days," John said, passing out our packets.

A spark of life ignited inside of me, and I smiled. Unfortunately, it was a very small spark and burned out quickly. It simply wasn't bright enough, nor strong enough to reverse the damage Campbell created.

"On to a new batch," Ginger said as she rolled her eyes and exhaled smoke into the cold New Haven climate.

I looked over at her with a contorted face. I never knew why she was so miserable. She was the most tragic woman I had *ever* met.

248

John made his way over to Campbell and I and he handed us our packets.

Boston, Massachusetts, mine read on the top. I smiled again, knowing this was all finally almost over. I just hoped I wouldn't meet someone like him in Boston.

"Where are you going?' Campbell asked in an uncontrolled tone.

"Boston," I answered. "You?"

"Salt Lake City, Utah," Campbell said in somewhat of an aggravated tone. I know he wasn't used to not being in control. I guess he was upset his "toy" was finally escaping him.

"Oh okay," I said. I began to flip through my packet and read all the various information it had.

Campbell pulled out his phone. "It's about a nine-hour drive from here."

"That's not too bad.".

"Yeah. Whatever, I guess," he said agitatedly.

There was a slight pause. "I'm really going to miss you," he said as he wrapped his hand around my thigh.

I looked down at his hand, swallowing hard, "I'm going to miss you too, Campbell."

He grinned then kissed me.

"Oh, cut it out, lovebirds," Ginger said in disgust as she flicked her cigarette in the yard and came walking into the living room. "You'll see each other someday."

I looked at her then fixed my gaze to the floor.

"Come on, Iris," Campbell said sternly as he looked at Ginger and gave her an ire face. "Let's go upstairs."

I stood up and took his hand that was extended to me and we went up the stairs to our room.

"What time's your flight?" Campbell asked as I sat down on our bed and he opened the window to smoke, letting all the cold air in.

"Twelve," I said monotonously.

"What airport are you flying out of?" he asked.

"Region Airport, it's an hour and a half away."

"So what time is the taxi getting you then?" he asked, lighting his cigarette, and taking the initial puff.

"Eight," I responded.

"Oh okay," he exhaled the smoke.

I paused, then spoke, trying to make conversation to evade problems. "Well, what time are you leaving?"

"I guess the same time as you, eight."

"Oh, okay," I said, looking down at my feet.

He walked over to me, still holding the cigarette as he picked my head up by my chin and stared into my eyes, "I love you, my Iris."

I stared back, rapidly alternating between both of his eyes then I swallowed hard. "I love you too, Campbell."

He smiled as he brushed the hair behind my ears. I watched his cheeks suck in from pulling on the cigarette. He then pulled me in for a hug and rubbed my back. As he did, my face twisted into repugnance as my head rested on his chest. The smell of cigarette smoke filled my nose as I closed my eyes. I could not *wait* to leave.

47

Chapter 47

The best sound I've ever heard was my alarm blaring at seven a.m. two days later. This was it. It was all over.

When I told Colton the day before that I was leaving, to say he was ecstatic and relieved would be an understatement. He was *overjoyed*. When we talked though I started to feel guilty. I should have listened to him when he warned me about him. Maybe then none of this would ever have happened. But Colton quickly put a stop to those thoughts before they could take off. He told me I was stronger than I knew and I still think about that to this day.

I sat on the couch and watched as cabs began to drive up and down the dirt driveway. I looked down at my bracelet and played with its charm. I smiled. It was a small smile, but it was sincere. I was so happy to be leaving.

"Iris, your cab's here," Campbell said as he walked back into the house.

"Okay," I got up and walked over to my things.

"I got it," he said.

I backed off and strapped my duffle bag onto my suitcase, extended the handle, and headed outside.

"Thanks for everything," I said blandly to John and Ginger as I passed them. Although they didn't do shit for me.

"So long, sweetheart," John smiled. He was just happy to get rid of me.

Ginger didn't say anything, she just smirked. I looked past her and followed Campbell outside.

"Iris Cooke? Ma'am, are you Miss Cooke?" an older Black man asked me as I walked down the porch stairs.

"Yeah, I am."

Campbell carried my bags down the steps and we both went to the back of the trunk.

"Let me get that for you, sir," the driver said to Campbell as he opened the trunk.

"Thanks," Campbell said, flashing his award-winning smile.

Campbell loaded the bags and then closed the lid.

"I'll give you two a moment," the driver smiled as he walked around the cab and got into it.

"I'll miss you, Iris," he said, pulling me close to him by my waist.

I swallowed hard and met his eyes, "I'm going to miss you too, Campbell."

He sighed, "What am I gonna do without you each day?" he asked as he brushed my hair out of my eyes.

I lightly shrugged, "I don't know."

"You'll always be my girl, you know that? Always."

I swallowed the lump in my throat. I couldn't cry. So instead I forced a smile and nodded my head. Campbell began to rub my back then cupped my face and kissed me. It was the longest, loathsome kiss I had ever experienced.

"I'll see you again, someday," he grinned as he pulled away from me.

Those words sent a shiver down my spine.

"I hope," I choked out.

"You will. You're mine, remember?" he asked.

I clenched my jaw and swallowed hard, "Hmm hm."

He then pulled me in and gave me one final hug.

Just then the driver got out of his car gently, "I hate to interrupt," he said genuinely, "but Miss Cooke, we got to get rolling. You two lovebirds finish up, okay?"

"Yeah, okay," I said. "I'm sorry."

"No, no. Don't be sorry, baby," he smiled and then got back into the cab.

Campbell scoffed, "Baby?" he said in response to the man's term of endearment. "Try not to fuck him on the way to the airport," he joked. Although nothing was funny about that.

Repugnance flooded into me as I looked at him with hate.

"I'm just kidding," he laughed. "Come on, don't be a bitch the last few minutes we have together."

I stared at him blankly then flashed a smile, "You're right. I'm sorry."

He pulled me close to him, "Goodbye, Iris," he whispered into my ear. "Remember, nobody will *ever* love you like I will."

I swallowed as chills shot down my back, "I know. Goodbye, Campbell."

He pulled away and I walked to the side of the taxi and got in. The cab driver put the vehicle into drive, and we headed down the long dirt driveway.

"That your boyfriend?" the man asked.

"No, not at all," I said coldly as I stared out of the window.

"Oh," the man seemed confused, "well, you'll get to see him one day," he then added with optimism, not knowing what else to say.

There was a pause. "I hope I never do," I said monotonously as I still stared out of the window. "I hope I never, fucking, do."

48

Chapter 48

The taxi pulled up the cobblestone driveway after an exhaustive six-and-a-half hour flight. I was in complete awe. The house was *gigantic*. It was gorgeous. It was a dark brown and charcoal-colored stone mansion in a somewhat secluded area of Boston. I was intimidated by the size of this home. I mean, I had never seen a house *that* big before in real life.

I walked to the back of the cab, gathering all my things, then proceeded up to the stone stairs that led up to the front door, I rang the doorbell, and I could hear a beautiful tone play inside the house.

"Hey," a late-thirties, early-forties woman said with a smile as she opened the door.

She had bright, dyed red hair, and was wearing sweatpants and a hoodie.

"Hi, I'm Iris Cooke. I'm with The Stay program," I said.

"Oh, cool!" she exclaimed. "I'm Kalista. It's nice to meet you."

I smiled at her, "It's nice to meet you too," she seemed very laid back and chill.

"Well, come on inside, it's cold out here!"

"Thank you," I said, following her lead into her home.

The house was even more amazing on the inside than on the out. There were antiques everywhere, all the countertops were granite, the floors were made of marble, there were gorgeous throw rugs on the floor, the furniture and curtains were like nothing I had seen before, there were high-rise ceilings, it was all just *so* incredible. I felt like I was in a movie or something.

"Wow," I said as I stared up and looked around in awe. "Your home is beautiful."

"Aw, thanks," Kalista said. Then after a beat, "Well, let me show you around!"

She showed me every room in her home while we waited for others to arrive. They all were as exquisite as the next.

"And this will be your room," Kalista said as she opened the door to one of the bedrooms.

My eyes tripled in size. I was pretty sure that the room was as big as my entire house. It was huge, to say the least. It had a bathroom attached to it, a walk-in closet, which was something I could only dream about, and two queen size beds. You could have easily fit two or three more beds of the same size and *still* have plenty of room for everyone.

"This is incredible," I said, not knowing what else to say. I was speechless.

She chuckled, "Everyone has that reaction."

"I don't blame them."

Just then the doorbell rang.

"More people must be here," she said. "I'm gonna go downstairs. You can start unpacking if you want, or if you wanna keep looking around, that's cool too. Help yourself to anything."

I smiled, "Thanks."

I watched as she exited the room.

She seemed pretty cool, which made me feel at ease that at least I wouldn't have hosts like I did in New Haven.

I walked towards the window and looked out of it. I saw a girl, about my age, getting out of a taxicab. I watched as the driver helped her unload two medium sized suitcases from the trunk. As I watched, I prayed I'd have a normal roommate and an easy time here.

After a couple minutes, I went downstairs and approached the front door where the girl that I saw get out of the taxicab, now was. Kalista was talking to her and helping her bring her bags in.

"Hey, Iris," Kalista turned around and said to me. "This is Jolene. Jolene, this is Iris."

"Hey, nice to meet you," Jolene said.

"Nice to meet you too."

Kalista smiled, "Now, Iris already knows the room she's in, but let me find out where you are, Jolene. Then you guys can go unpack or whatever else you wanna do while I wait for the other guests."

"Okay, cool," Jolene said. "Thanks."

Kalista walked over to the small table that was by the front door. She picked up the piece of paper that was sitting on it and began to read it.

"Huh, it looks like you guys are actually roommates," she said as she read the paper. "Yup, Iris Cooke, room twelve, and Jolene Mulvoy, room twelve as well."

I looked at Jolene and smiled politely.

"Alright, awesome. Thank you, Kalista," Jolene said.

"Of course, let me know if you two need anything," Kalista said.

"Will do, thanks," Jolene smiled.

"Yeah, thank you," I added.

"No problem," Kalista said as she took a seat in a nearby chair.

Jolene began to grab both of her bags.

"I can get one," I said.

"Oh, thanks," she said with a smile.

I took one of her suitcases and the two of us then headed upstairs to our room.

"This house is incredible," Jolene said as we walked up the marble stairs. "I've never seen, let alone *been*, in a house this big or this nice before."

"I know right, it is a gorgeous home," I said as we rounded the corner to our room.

"Holy shit!" Jolene exclaimed as we entered. She paused in her tracks and looked around, "*This* is our room?"

"I can't believe it either."

She wheeled her suitcase further into the room.

"There's a walk-in closet?" she asked rhetorically. "*And* a bathroom? Wow, I've *never* seen *anything* like this."

I smiled."

"So, where are you from?" she asked as she put both of her suitcases on the bed I hadn't claimed.

"Chicago. You?" I replied as I walked over to my suitcase.

"No way! I'm from Springfield," she said joyfully.

"Oh wow, that's really cool," my emotionless mood gained some life to it as I unstrapped the duffle bag from my suitcase.

"Yeah, they're only like three hours away from each other."

"Right," I put my duffle bag on my bed followed by my suitcase.

"Have you lived there your whole life?" she questioned as she unzipped her suitcases.

"Yeah, I was born and raised there," I answered. "How about you?"

"Uh, yes and no," she said. "I was born there, but a couple of years later we moved to New York City. We moved back to Springfield not too long after and I've been there ever since."

"Oh, cool. I've never been to New York," I said, unzipping my bags.

"It's nice," she smiled slightly. "I was super little though when I was there. I was three when we moved there and seven when we left."

"How old are you now then?" I asked.

"I'm eighteen, you?"

"I just turned seventeen," I answered. "My birthday was in September."

"Oh, awesome, happy belated birthday," Jolene chuckled.

I smiled slightly, "Thanks."

The conversation continued with the typical small talk: my siblings and her lack thereof, how she was close with her dad, etc. Soon, she gathered her things to take a shower and went into the bathroom.

She opened the door back up as soon as she latched it, "Oh, you can just call me Jo by the way."

I smiled, "Sounds good."

She smiled then closed the bathroom door again.

I let my smile go and plopped down on my bed. I sighed wishing I was happy, too.

49

Chapter 49

Jo and I were just unpacking and getting to know one another more when we were interrupted by a knock at the door. It was Kalista telling us that dinner was ready.

We entered the dining room, and it was just as beautiful as the rest of the house. There was a very long, rectangular wooden table that ran down the room, beautiful oak chairs with elegant wood carvings, and glass cabinets that housed all different types of chinaware. Plates and silverware sat at each spot, on top of placemats. I had never seen such a formal dining room before.

"This is incredible," Jo said to me.

I nodded my head and smiled.

We looked around for two empty seats as there were already at least twenty people sitting down and serving themselves food.

"There's two seats back there," Jo said as she pointed to the far end of the table.

We walked towards them. "I didn't realize there'd be this many people here," I said.

"I know right," she said. "Guess it makes sense though, this place is huge."

"True."

We took our seats and looked in front of us at the food. There were two kinds of baked ziti. One with meat, one without. Everyone began serving themselves and eating. I looked around and noticed everyone was talking and laughing, having a good time.

"Okay—okay, everybody," Kalista stood up and interrupted all the talking. "Every time new guests come, I make a special dinner to celebrate and welcome them into their new home. So, I hope you all enjoy and help yourself to anything you find here."

There was cheering and toasts being made.

"Also—hey, hey," Kalista interrupted again, "I like for everyone to at least know one another's name. So, let's all go around the table, say our names and where we're from. You start," Kalista said to the girl that sat to her left. Kalista then sat down.

I sighed as I looked around. One by one, people said their name and where they were from. It finally came around to Jo and me.

"Hi, my name is Jolene. I go by Jo, and I'm from Springfield, Illinois."

"Uh, hi," I said. "I'm Iris Cooke and I'm from Chicago, Illinois," I said monotonously.

There were two people left then Kalista spoke.

"Alright cool," she smiled. "Now everyone knows one another."

When dinner was over, mostly everyone carried their plates into the kitchen which was a room over and put them into the dishwasher.

The kitchen was also extremely nice. It was very large, had a six-person table, along with a bar attached to the island, black and white tile flooring, big windows, and multiple modern and luxury appliances.

"Kalista seems nice," Jo said, trying to make conversation as we entered back into our bedrooms.

"Yeah, she does," I said blandly.

I saw Jo nod her head with pursed lips like she was defeated at making a conversation with me.

"I'm—I'm sorry," I said. "I don't mean to be short or sound uninterested, I'm just really tired," although I wasn't tired. Maybe of life. But I wasn't going to tell this girl, who I just met, what was *truly* wrong.

"No, no it's fine," she smiled. "I understand."

"Thanks…I'm gonna go take a shower now."

"Okay."

I grabbed a few things from my suitcase, grabbed a towel, and headed for the bathroom.

As I was getting undressed, I stared at myself in the mirror. I stared at myself, still feeling nothing. I felt blank, emotionless, and numb. I didn't feel like my old self. I looked at the hickeys that were still on my chest, the bruises down my arms, the leftover, and finally fading bruise on my neck, and everything else Campbell left me.

It made me think about him—about Campbell. How many other girls has he done this to before me? And how many girls would he *continue* to do this too? I started to feel guilty, like I should have told somebody, but I had nobody *to* tell. I shook that feeling off as I continued to stare at myself, disgusted with what stared back at me.

After my long, finally hot, shower, I got out, dried off, and reached for the oversized, long-sleeved, T-shirt. With it in hand, I realized it was short-sleeved and that I grabbed it from my suitcase by mistake. I angrily threw it in the trash, let out a huff, and rolled my eyes.

I tied the robe that Kalista laid out for us in the bathroom, around myself and walked out of the bathroom, irritated. I began rifling through my drawers to find my long-sleeved T-shirt. Jo was laying on her bed, reading a magazine.

I could see her out of the corner of my eye begin to watch me as I was messing up everything in my drawer that I had just organized.

"Iris, are you okay?"

I put one hand on the drawer, looking down, and used my other hand to keep my robe tightly closed. As I didn't want it to expose anything it hid away.

"Yeah, I'm fine," I said agitatedly. "I just can't find the stupid long-sleeved T-shirt I wear to bed."

She stood up with a confused face.

"Here, you can have this one," she said as she picked up a blue NASCAR printed long sleeve T-shirt from her suitcase. "It's an extra one of my dad's, I like to sleep in big shirts too," she smiled, handing me the shirt.

I met her eyes, "Thank you."

"Yeah, of course. No worries."

I went back into the bathroom to get dressed. I then sat down at the desk to braid my hair. Jo was back to looking at her magazine. As I was doing my hair, I happened to see Kalista through the window getting into a taxicab.

I frowned, "Did Kalista say she was going someplace while I was in the shower?"

"No," she seemed confused. "Why?"

"Well, look"—I pointed out the window—"she's leaving right now."

Jo got off her bed and came over to the window to look through it.

"Oh, yeah. Hm, that's weird she didn't tell anyone."

I shrugged, "Well, maybe she told somebody else?"

"Maybe," Jo said. "I just know hosts aren't supposed to leave their homes after a certain time, and most of them don't like to leave their guests unintended at all."

"True, well, I don't know then," I uttered.

We both stared out the window in confusion as the taxi with Kalista in it, pulled off the property, and disappeared into the darkness.

50

Chapter 50

I woke up around nine the next morning. Jo was still sleeping and as I laid in bed, I realized I hadn't called my family the night before like I told them I would once I got to Boston. I sighed remembering this, not because I *didn't* want to talk to them, but because I really wasn't in the mood *to* talk. Regardless, I forced myself out of my bed, threw on some pajama pants, and did my makeup. Once I was ready, I went downstairs, made a coffee, and headed down the hall to the lounge room.

I sat down on the white leather couch and dialed my home number.

"Hello?" Colton answered.

"Hey, Colton," I said.

"Hey, Sis. Are you in Boston?"

"Yeah, I am. Sorry I didn't call last night. I got distracted unpacking and then forgot before I fell asleep," I explained.

"It's all good," he said. "Don't even worry about it."

"Is Mom and Leannah home?"

"No, actually. Mom just left to take Leannah to school."

I took my phone away from my ear and looked at the time, "Isn't it kinda late? It's almost eleven there, right?"

"Yeah," Colton answered. "She skipped her two free periods this morning."

"Oh, okay," I said. "And what about you?"

"I'm off."

"Why?"

"It's senior skip day."

I made a confused face, "November twenty-six seems pretty random for that, don't you think?"

He chuckled, "That's what I thought, too but I won't argue with a day off."

I smiled softly, "Right."

There was a slight pause.

"Well, would you let them know I'm here, please?"

"Of course," Colton replied.

There was another pause of anticipation.

"So, uh, how is this house? Have you, uh, met your roommate?" he asked, afraid of my answer.

"Colton, the house is gorgeous. It's literally a mansion."

"Oh shit, really?" he said. "That's pretty cool."

"It's amazing. I'll have to send you some pictures."

"For sure, I want to see."

I smiled. "And yeah, I met my roommate. Her name is Jolene, well she goes by Jo. She seems nice. She's asleep right now, that's why I came downstairs to talk to you."

"Oh good," I could hear the relief in Colton's voice. "I hope you guys make good friends."

"Yeah," I said monotonously. "Well, I just wanted to call and let you know I'm here. I'll let you get back to your day off, don't want to interrupt that," I tried to joke but it felt so forced.

Colton chuckled, "You never would."

I chuckled, "Thanks. I'll talk to you soon, Colton, I love you. Let

Mom and Leannah know I love them too."

"Will do, Sis, I love you too. See you."

"Bye," I said, hanging up the phone.

I sat there for a moment just thinking, really about everything as I played with the corner of one of the pillows. Eventually though, around ten, I went back up the stairs to start my day. At this time, Jo was awake and doing her makeup.

"Good morning," she said to me as I entered the room.

"Morning, Jo," I said as I began making my bed.

"How did you sleep?" she asked.

"Good, thanks," I replied. "How about you?"

"Good, I needed that sleep. I was so tired."

"I can believe it, twenty hours on a train is a lot," I said.

Jo had just come from Spencer, West Virginia.

"It is. So, anything you want to do today?" she asked.

Lay in bed all day, I thought.

I looked out the window as it began to rain. "Well, it looks like it's starting to rain. Maybe we could check out the billiard room first and then go out later if it stops?"

"Yeah, that sounds good."

I smiled as I finished making my bed and pulled out clothes to wear for the day. I grabbed my favorite, most comfortable long sleeve shirt and a pair of jeans. I then went into the bathroom to change. After I was done, I entered back into our room holding the blue NASCAR shirt. I tried to give it back to Jo but she told me I could keep it.

On the way to the billiard room, we got stopped by some of our housemates.

"Hey, guys. Have either of you seen Kalista, we can't find her?" Audrey asked. She had three other people with her.

"No, we haven't seen her since dinner. But around ten-thirty last night, Iris and I saw her get into a taxicab and leave," Jo stated.

"Really?" Audrey asked in surprise. "Do you know where she went?"

"No idea," Jo replied.

"That's so weird…Alright, well thanks, guys. I'll let you know if we find her or hear from her."

"Alright cool, thank you," Jo said.

Audrey and the three others went off down the hall in the opposite direction of us.

"I guess Kalista still isn't home yet," Jo said.

"Yeah, I guess not. I wonder where she is," I questioned.

"Maybe she's at her boyfriend's house?"

"I don't know if she has one. But maybe, if she does. But you would think she wouldn't want to leave a house this beautiful to some random strangers to be in charge of," I said.

"Yeah, well whatever the case is, I guess it's not our business," Jo said.

"Guess not," I said as we entered the room.

We got our cues and racked the balls. Minutes later, we were ready to play. Jo crouched down to the cue ball to break. The white ball smacked against all the solid and striped pool balls, sending them in various directions. Jo made the orange solid ball into one of the pockets, so she continued her turn. When it was my turn, I got two balls in two pockets with just one hit of the cue ball.

"Damn, how did you know how to do that?" Jo asked, impressed.

I chuckled slightly, "When I was home in Chicago, my brother, sister, and I spent many nights at this bowling alley, pool room place. So, I guess since I played a lot, I gained some skills."

"I'd say so, that was awesome," Jo said.

I smiled softly at her, "Thanks."

"Having siblings sounds fun, I never had the chance to do any of that stuff," Jo stated.

"Yeah, it's nice, but I guess only if you're close with them. I don't think it'd be that great if you had siblings that you weren't close with. Well, at least I couldn't imagine not being close with mine," I said.

Jo struck the cue ball hitting the solid purple ball, almost sinking it into a pocket, "Yeah, that's true. I guess not."

"Hey, nice shot," I said.

"Thanks," she smiled.

"So, what about your dad though?" I asked as I switched places with her, getting ready to strike the cue ball. "You said you're super close with him, didn't you ever do fun stuff with him?"

"Yeah, of course, but he works a lot. Especially when I was younger," Jo explained. "He always tried to make sure we made ends meet. So yeah, we did fun stuff, just not all the time. I guess it's still like that today."

"Oh, okay. I understand," the cue ball struck the green striped ball and fell into the pocket. "My mom works a lot too. Same kind of thing: making sure we have enough money to pay the bills, feed us, that kind of thing," I sunk another ball in. "She never really used to though, but now that she's clean, she's doing a lot better."

"I'm really happy to hear that," Jo said smiling.

The night before, when we were talking, I told her about my mom's addiction and how she's now in recovery. She seemed very sympathetic about everything I had to say.

"Thanks," I said with a little smile. "What about your mom? Does she work?"

"Uh, no, no," Jo said vulnerably. "My mom, uh, she died when I was six."

The mood instantly turned serious and melancholic.

"I, uh, I'm so sorry, I shouldn't have asked—"

"No, no, it's fine...really," Jo said, faking a smile, I knew this was a tender topic.

She put her pool cue down on the pool table and leaned her back up against the table, placing her hands on it.

"We moved to New York City for my mom's job. She got a corporate job that was going to pay pretty well. This was great news because, from what I was told, my parents were really poor. After my mom had me, she worked her ass off to get the job in New York so that I wouldn't have to grow up in a struggling household. So, we moved, and everything was going great at her new job. We were all settling in, she was earning more money, life couldn't seem to get better." She took a deep breath and a long pause, "Well…that job was in the Twin Towers."

My heart tightened at her words. It became so heavy that it sank right through my chest and into the floorboards.

She looked down at her hands as she picked at her nails, holding back tears.

"My mom was on the eighty-first floor of the South Tower."

She took another long pause, struggling to hold back tears. I was in shock, staring at her, absolutely heartbroken.

"The plane hit between the seventy-seventh and the eighty-fifth floor, so, she never, she never had a chance," she took another pause. "I like to think she wasn't in pain though…that she wasn't afraid and scared"—she stopped talking, taking a moment to breathe.

"I remember my dad picking me up from school, I was in first grade. I knew something was wrong because he didn't say a word the whole ride home. And they let us out of school early which was weird, they didn't tell us why," she paused again, letting out a sigh.

"When we got home, my dad sat me down on his lap and he said to me, 'You know Jo-Jo, the reason why you got out of school early is because'"—she paused as she choked up again.

I went over to her and put my arm around her, leaning my head on her shoulder.

"'The reason your school was let out was because bad people from another country, that don't like us, took over planes and flew them into different buildings.' And at first, I didn't realize my dad meant buildings that were near us and my mom's work, so I said, 'Well, why did they close school if this didn't happen around here?' My dad said, 'No, baby, it did happen around here.' And I guess, I guess I just knew by the look on his face"—she began to get more choked up.

"I asked my dad where Mommy was as my little eyes just filled up with tears, somehow knowing she was gone. He said, 'Jo-Jo, Mommy went to heaven,' as he choked up himself, brushing my hair behind my ear. 'One of the planes that crashed, crashed into Mommy's building.'"

Jo's head hung low as tears overflowed from her eyes and onto her cheeks, streaming down her face.

I turned to her, hugging her, holding her so tight. Tears streamed silently down my face.

"I am so, so, so sorry, Jolene," I said quietly to her, trying not to let her hear me cry.

There was a slight moment of silence.

"My dad loved her so much," she uttered quietly through her tears, hugging me tighter. "She was my best friend."

More tears streamed down my face as I bit my lip. I wanted to burst into tears, my heart felt like it had shattered into a million pieces. My biggest fear was something bad ever happening to my family, I couldn't *ever* imagine Jo's pain.

We hugged for a couple more seconds until Jo let go. I think she needed that. I waited for her to let go. I never let go first, ever.

She pulled away, wiping her eyes with the back of her palm, "I'm sorry, I shouldn't have—"

"No, no stop," I interrupted. "Don't be sorry, there's *nothing* to be sorry about."

She smiled, "Thank you."

There then there was a pause and Jo's smile faded away.

"I've just always felt like an outcast, like I was never like anybody else. We moved back to Springfield almost a year after Nine-Eleven and I never fit in with the other kids I went to school with. They all had moms and dads and lived in the suburbs, and I just had a dad and lived in the city. My dad struggled a lot trying to provide for me since my mom was the one who brought in most of the money. Because of this, I grew up poor which only added to my feelings of exclusion. But after finding this program and coming here, I realized there's a lot of people like me and it for once makes me feel...not alone. I don't know, it's a nice feeling, it's just something I've never really felt before."

I smiled ruefully at Jo. "I know how you feel. And trust me, you're not alone."

She smiled in the same way, "Thank you."

A silence fell between us then moments later I spoke.

"My dad cheated on my mom when I was seven and then left us for her." I stopped for a second, "So, I uh, I know what you mean when you say you feel like an outcast."

Jo stopped and looked at me.

"Oh, wow. I'm sorry to hear that," she said.

"No, no, don't be. He never really cared about any of us, he was an asshole anyway," I said. "I've just always felt just like you. Like nobody else was like me, like nobody else was like my family...I don't know, I just wanted you to know I can relate."

She smiled slightly, "Thank you, Iris."

I nodded my head and smiled back.

Jo picked up the pool cues and handed me one.

"Want to continue playing?" she asked with a smile, trying to change the dreary mood.

I smiled back, "Yeah sure, you're on."

271

51

Chapter 51

Around six-thirty, we were hungry for dinner. There was still no sign of Kalista so we went to the kitchen to see what we could find to eat. I guess everyone else had the same idea because out of the twenty-three other people who stayed at that house, more than half were in the kitchen looking for food.

"Holy shit," Jo said in shock.

My eyes widened as I watched all the guests go through the fridge and each drawer, cabinet, pantry, and closet there was, to find something to eat. Some people even started getting into Kalista's alcohol, which I knew was only going to lead to trouble.

"What a nightmare," I said monotonously while shaking my head.

"Good luck trying to find anything," some girl said to us as she passed by, clearly annoyed that there was nothing to eat.

"How is there nothing to eat? We had a feast last night!" Jo exclaimed.

"Everyone probably already ate it all. There's twenty-three other people here," I said.

"Yeah, I guess that makes sense," Jo paused. "Where is she anyway? Why wouldn't she be back by now?"

I shrugged, "Who knows, Jo. I've heard that a lot of these hosts are real weirdos."

I knew how true that was due to my own experience with John and Ginger.

"Oh, I know it," she added with confidence. "Whatever, I'm hungry, let's take a bus down to a diner and get something to eat there."

"Alright," I said.

We made it to the diner, had our food and were soon enough back at Kalista's, where she still was nowhere to be found. What we did find, however, made our jaws drop. All our housemates were throwing a party. Now, this wouldn't have been a big deal if they were respectful and it was just something small, but this party was *far* from that. Lamps were broken, curtains were ripped, carpets were wet and stained with various cocktail drinks, the couch had throw-up on it, party cups and snacks were everywhere, it was a complete and total nightmare, and that was just to name a few things that went wrong.

"Oh my God," we both said, bewilderment scribbled across our faces.

"What the hell are you guys doing?!" Jo turned off the music and flipped the lightswitch.

Everyone was *extremely* drunk and fucked up on so many different types of drugs, that they most definitely didn't know what was going on.

"W-w-what are you two losers doing? The party's just starting," some guy slurred as he hung his arm around my shoulder.

I froze but quickly recovered, frowning and throwing his arm off me.

"Do you guys have any idea how much trouble you all put us in?! Look at all the shit you broke! Look at the carpets and the curtains!"

Jo yelled.

Some people who were just intoxicated from alcohol, began to sober up a little. Overall, though, Jo was better off talking to a brick wall.

"Iris, what are we gonna do?" Jo asked. "This place looks like hell!"

"Alright, well how about you just get everyone back to their rooms and I'll start to clean the big issues. I doubt Kalista will be back tonight, so in the morning when everyone is sober, they can do the rest," I said.

"Alright, sounds good," Jo said.

"Yell if you need me."

"You too."

Jo started getting everyone back to their rooms while I grabbed all the cleaning products that I could find under the kitchen sink. I began working on the stained rugs, curtains, and the couch that had throw-up on it. Luckily, I had a lot of cleaning tricks under my belt from doing it all of my life. There weren't too many stains or messes I couldn't eradicate.

I let the cleaning products sit as I swept up all the broken glass bottles, lamp bases, chips, bottle caps, cigarette butts, and more.

After about fifteen minutes, Jo came back downstairs and opened a big black trash bag, filling it with everyone's garbage. We stayed up until two in the morning just cleaning everything. We tried our best, but curtains were destroyed, lamps were broken, and certain stains just don't like to come out of white carpet too much. We made it look ten times better for sure, but Kalista was going to see everything else that couldn't be fixed. I felt really bad. Jo and I both did.

We both walked four large trash bags down to the end of the long cobblestone driveway and put them on the curb for the trashman to take in the morning.

Jo let out a big sigh and leaned up against the stone pillars that the gate doors were connected to. I sat down on the curb, rubbed my face, and then ran my hands through my hair.

"What a fucking disaster," Jo said as she pulled a cigarette and lighter out from her pocket and lit it. She exhaled and with the streetlamp being the only light source around, I watched the smoke disappear into the night sky.

"Want a drag?"

"Sure."

She handed me the cigarette and I took one big pull off it, then gave it back to Jo. I sighed as I exhaled, "I wonder how Kalista will react to all her stuff getting messed up."

Jo rolled her eyes and shook her head in disapproval, "I know, it's so fucked up." She took a pull on her cigarette.

After a couple of seconds, she handed me the cigarette again and I took another pull off it. When I was done, I handed the cigarette back to Jo and I stood up.

"Come on, let's go. It's cold," I grabbed her by her forearm.

She took one last pull off her cigarette then threw it down to the ground. She then interlocked arms with me, and we walked back up the driveway, soon taking turns showering and finally, crashing into bed.

Chapter 52

"So now what?" Jo asked as she plopped down onto her bed. It was eleven-thirty the next morning. Two of our housemates, Christina and Asher, thanked us for cleaning up last night. They told us they planned to go to the mall that day to try to buy replacement curtains and lamps. I figured the gesture was nice enough but I still didn't know how it'd blow over with Kalista—if she ever returned home that is.

I shrugged my shoulders as I walked over to the pile of unfolded clothes that sat on my dresser and began to fold them.

"Do you want to go somewhere?" Jo asked as she sat up against the headboard.

"Sure, where do you want to go?" I replied as I continued to fold my clothes.

"That's the thing, I have no clue what's around here," she said.

"Yeah, neither do I," I said, with full attention on my clothes.

There was a slight pause.

"Hey, Iris, what's that?" Jo asked.

"What's what?"

"That mark on your chest?" she asked.

I looked down and saw my hoodie zipper had slipped down. I quickly zipped my hoodie back up.

"Oh, nothing, nothing—it's just a birthmark," I lied, not wanting her to know what it actually was.

I could tell she didn't believe me by the look on her face.

"Well, most people don't hide birthmarks," she said, with a frown, knowing it was something else.

"Well, I'm just embarrassed by mine," I said as I turned away from her and continued to fold my clothes.

"It looks like a hickey," she said coldly.

"It's not," I quickly said, lying again.

There was another pause.

"Did you *want* the hickey?" Jo asked in a low pensive voice.

"It's not a hickey, Jo," I said as I tried to walk out of the room.

Jo jumped up from her bed and stood in front of me, stopping me before I could exit.

"Iris, is everything okay?" she asked, very concerned.

"Everything's fine, Jo," I tried to walk past her, but she stopped me again.

"I know we just met but you can talk to me about anything," she said looking directly into my eyes. "I'm here for you."

I stared blankly at her for a moment, "Thanks."

I pushed past her and left the room. I went into the hallway bathroom, sat down on the floor, and just cried. Maybe a part of me wanted to just explode and tell her everything, but I just couldn't. I hated how I felt.

I only stayed in the bathroom for five minutes tops. I wiped my tears, fixed my makeup, straightened my shoulders, then walked back into our room.

"I'm sorry, Iris, I didn't mean to—"

"No, it's fine, it's okay," I said, interrupting Jo while my back was towards her.

I quickly finished putting my clothes away then turned around to face Jo.

"So, what do you want to do?" I said, trying to act like nothing just happened.

"Uh, do you wanna go down to the game room and hang out there?" Jo suggested trying to act like nothing just happened as well.

"Sure."

We played Air Hockey, the WII, racing games, and all other sorts of fun stuff. It really changed the mood and made us, well me at least, forget about earlier.

We both got hungry around two-thirty. We knew there was no food in the house to eat, so we had to go out. Instead of going to a restaurant, we decided to go to a grocery store. We figured it would be cheaper and besides, neither of us knew when Kalista would be back. We figured we should stock up.

We went back upstairs to our rooms to get our coats and purses. I put on my brown faux fur coat that I always wore and counted all the cash I had in my purse. I had eighty-five dollars and Jo had ninety-five. We went down the stairs, heading for the door when we passed Asher and Christina. We didn't say anything to them, but we saw them hanging brand new curtains. I noticed new lamps as well.

We walked ten minutes to the bus stop, and we were in luck. Right when we approached the stop, the bus pulled up. We got on and found ourselves two empty seats in the back. The bus was packed that afternoon. I guess it was due to work travel and last-minute stops before Thanksgiving tomorrow. When we got off the bus—about twenty-five minutes later—at the Shoppin' Mart on Bethel Avenue, Jo grabbed a cart, and we began down the aisles.

"How about cereal? For breakfast or a snack," Jo asked as she held out a box of Reese's Puffs.

"Good thinking, two birds, one stone," I chuckled. I took the cereal out of her hand and placed it in the cart. "But if you're going to get cereal, at least do me a favor and get a *good* one, like Golden Graham."

"No way. Please don't tell me you *don't* like Reese's Puffs."

"I do, I do. Golden Grahams are just better."

"I don't know about that," she said.

"It's a fact," I teased, feeling a happy mood for once.

Jo rolled her eyes playfully as we strolled down the aisle.

"Let's get some milk before we forget," Jo said.

We got to the milk aisle and put a gallon of whole milk into our cart. We then decided to get TV dinners for that night.

"Aisle seven should have them," I said as I pushed the shopping cart in that direction. "A lot of times they're on sale too, like two for five or something like that."

"Yeah, you're right. I saw that all the time in the grocery stores back home," Jo said.

"Yeah, when my mom wasn't doing the best, my siblings and I lived off TV dinners. Hell, even when my mom was doing well, we lived off them. Being poor, I grew up on these."

"Me too!" Jo exclaimed "Many nights my dad worked late, and I was left to heat one up for myself in the microwave. They're actually pretty good."

"They really are," I said as I stopped the cart beside the glass door that stored the dinners behind it. They were on sale for two for four. We grabbed the kind that had turkey with mashed potatoes and stuffing; figuring it was as close to a Thanksgiving meal as we'd get.

"Thanksgiving, well holidays in general, never were really special when I was younger because of my mom being drunk and then strung out on drugs," I said. "She'd either not know what day it was and completely forget, be passed out that day, or she'd be having a blowout fight with my dad or one of her award-winning boyfriend's," I said sarcastically. "Colton, my brother, would cook my sister and me a special meal on those days. He always tried his best for us; for things to be normal."

Jo smiled, "He sounds like a great brother."

"Yeah, he most definitely is," I smiled as I thought about him. "But as I got older and into my teenage years, my mom finally got clean and stopped dating, so holidays got better."

"That's really great," Jo smiled as we continued down the aisle.

"What were holidays back home like for you?"

"Well, when my mom was alive, they were awesome. She was the best cook, and we weren't struggling financially, so they were like any other holiday for any other "normal" kid. But when my mom died, the first few holidays without her were really, really hard. My dad tried to make them normal for me, but I knew how difficult it was for him. I missed her so much more during those times too, I still do. It was hard for him financially too, it still is, so he's always tried to do the best he could, but they were always small. Truthfully though, all I could ask for was him, so I've been content," Jo said as we turned the corner and began to head down the aisle with premade sandwiches.

"I know what you mean when you say your holidays were small. I've always been poor, so the gifts were always minimal, if at all. But like you said, having my family was most important. When my mom was absent, I relied heavily on my brother. My sister and I both did. Really, we *all* relied on one another. That's one of the reasons we've always been so close," I said, stopping the cart in front of some deli sandwiches.

"That's amazing. So many people hate their siblings, so it's great to hear how close you all are. Although it must be hard to be away from them," Jo said.

"Yeah," I sighed. "It is hard. I don't know what I'd do without them, you know? But my drive each day is that I'm making things easier for them and my mom," I said, trying not to get down.

Jo smiled at me, "That's really admirable of you."

I smiled, "You're doing the same for your dad."

"Yeah, I guess that's true."

We returned to the previous lighthearted mood as we put two ham and honey mustard sandwiches on a pretzel bun in our cart. That concluded our shopping spree and we made our way to the long check out line. Last minute Thanksgiving shopping, I supposed. It wasn't long until we were claiming our bags and heading back to the bus stop.

53

Chapter 53

On Jo and I's ten-minute walk back to Kalista's house from the bus stop, she told me there's a mini-fridge and freezer in our bathroom. This was news to me. Typically, I was a very observant person, but after Jo showed me where it was, it made sense why I didn't spot it sooner. Not only had I been in a fog recently, but the damn thing was hidden behind a half wall on the opposite side of where the shower, toilet, and sinks were. For a house as incredible as Kalista's, that design was definitely flawed. Nevertheless, having the mini-fridge and freezer was a life saver. This meant we could keep our food from being eaten by the other hungry housemates.

"Alright, where are those sandwiches?" Jo asked as soon as we finished putting the perishables away.

I chuckled as I led the way out of the bathroom, "Here you go," I handed her the sandwich.

"Yesss, I'm *starving*," she joked dramatically.

I just laughed and shook my head as I unwrapped my sandwich.

We ate our lunch and once we were finished, we decided to throw out our trash in the kitchen as opposed to our room. We figured it would prevent attracting bugs or rodents that way.

We wandered down into the kitchen where three guys were hanging out and drinking. I didn't say anything to any of them. Jo threw out our trash then began texting on her phone as I walked over to the sink to wash my hands.

"Hey," one of the guys said. "What y'all girls up to? You wanna hang out?"

He had on jeans and a hoodie. His hair was blonde and somewhat unkempt. He had blue eyes that pierced your soul, but not in a good way. They reminded me about what Susan said about crazy eyes.

The three guys were sitting at the island behind me, and Jo was standing in front of me, facing me while she was on her phone. Jo looked up at me and didn't say anything. I stared back at her for a couple of seconds, then looked down, beginning to dry my hands, slowly.

"Hey, I'm talking to you guys," the same blonde-haired and blue-eyed guy said in a fake friendly voice as he stood up and approached us.

"We wanna hang out with you guys, you're both really pretty," he said as he was now standing next to me, trying to get me to face him. The other two stood up and walked over as well. They all reeked of alcohol.

"We're not interested," Jo said as she came over to the other side of me and grabbed my wrist pulling me from the situation.

I turned to go with her but a different guy with brown hair, sweatpants, and a flannel put his hand on my other wrist and pulled me back to face him.

"Hey, we just want to hang out," he said.

I froze, *Deer in the headlights* at him for a minute. I felt my soul leave my body, leave Kalista's house, and travel all the way back to New Haven, back to Campbell.

It's not him.

"We're not interested," I said, in a tone so soft you could barely hear me.

He and his friends laughed, "Oh, come on, don't you guys wanna have fun?"

"Come on, Iris," Jo said to me quietly as she lightly tugged on my arm.

I stared fearfully at the guys for another moment but soon regained mobility, now able to move.

"Oh, whatever!" I heard the brown-haired guy yell in a pissed-off tone.

Back in our room, I locked the door and exhaled all my pent up air.

"You okay?" Jo asked as she turned around.

"Oh, yeah, yeah, I'm fine," I then looked at the door's lock, where Jo was looking too. "Just in case."

There was a short moment of silence.

"Alright, I'm gonna go take a shower. I feel dirty and I'm kinda cold."

"Alright," I said as I laid down on my bed. "Enjoy."

"Thanks," Jo smiled ruefully, knowing something was wrong with me.

I turned over onto my side, facing away from her, to avoid any kind of conversation like earlier.

I didn't hear her move for a second, almost like she was defeated or something. But within seconds, I heard her gather her things then close the bathroom door behind her.

I stared at the wall. Any happiness I felt in the grocery store was sucked out, replaced with the numb and blank mood I was constantly subjected too. I closed my eyes, trying to snuff out the thoughts and emotions I knew were brewing; hoping it would ease the emotional and mental torment. Thankfully, it worked, I soon drifted off to sleep.

54

Chapter 54

The next morning was November twenty-eighth. It was Thanksgiving. I woke up around eight o'clock and quietly got out of bed as Jo was still sleeping. I then gathered my things to take a shower.

Once in the bathroom, I pulled my shirt off and looked at myself in the mirror as I typically did. I hated what I saw. I hated what I saw so much that it started to make me hate myself. It wasn't what I saw staring back at me and the empty hole of nothingness I felt that was what made me hate myself. No. It came from the inside. It was the confidence I now lacked, the sadness I now felt, the anger I now suppressed, the things I let happen, the regrets I had, and the wishes and prayers I wanted more than anything, that collectively made me hate myself. All the things I never felt before and it was all thanks to Campbell. It was the lack of *Iris* that made me hate myself.

As I stared into my eyes in my reflection, I sighed and swallowed hard. After a moment, I finally turned away and twisted the shower knob, turning on the water. As the water struck down, the feeling of morose submerged itself into me with each droplet of water that fell. But there was nothing I could do, I just had to continue with life like I always did.

I finished showering, got dressed, and did my makeup. Once I was done, I left the bathroom. I saw Jo was still sleeping, so I decided to grab my jacket and go outside to call my family.

As I put on my faux fur jacket and sat down to tie up my high-top Vans, I looked next to me into my purse. At the very bottom, I saw Melanie's cigarette that I took from her that day at the Space Needle. I guess I never gave it back. It was somewhat squished but still intact. I picked up the skinny, white, object and stared at it for a moment, twisting it around my fingers. After another moment, I closed my palm, stood up, and grabbed Jo's lighter that was sitting on her dresser. I then went down the hall to the stairs and into the frigid Boston air.

"Happy Thanksgiving, Iris!"

"Thanks, Mom. Happy Thanksgiving to you too," I said, finally successfully lighting the cigarette and taking the initial pull.

"One sec, let me get your brother and sister," she said.

"Alright," I said as I exhaled.

"Happy Thanksgiving, Sis!" Colton and Leannah both said.

I smiled, "Happy Thanksgiving, guys. What are you all doing today?" Taking another pull on my cigarette.

"Well, I'm getting the turkey ready now, then in a little bit Colton, Leannah, and I are gonna do the rest of the cooking," my mom said.

I bitterly took another puff of the cigarette. I was jealous. I wanted to be home and help them cook. I wanted to laugh and smile with them. I didn't want to be here, feeling this way, but being upset wasn't going to change anything.

"Oh yeah?" I asked exhaling, "What are you guys making?"

"Mac and cheese, mashed potatoes, asparagus, stuffing, all the typical stuff," my mom answered.

"Sounds good," I said, trying not to sound envious.

"What are you doing today, Iris?" Leannah asked.

"I don't know yet," I answered.

"You haven't heard from your host yet?" Colton asked. I had filled them in on Kalista going MIA days ago.

I pulled on my cigarette, slightly delaying my response to him, "Nope, no one's seen or heard from her."

"Really? Are you gonna call the cops?" Colton asked.

"Yeah, I will tonight or tomorrow morning if she doesn't come back by then," I assured.

"Oh alright," Colton said.

"Well, what are you gonna do for Thanksgiving dinner?" Leannah asked.

"Probably nothing. Jo and I bought Hungry Man turkey dinners yesterday for tonight, so," I said as I pulled again on my cigarette.

"Oh, honey," my mom said sympathetically.

"It's fine, guys," I exhaled smoke. "I didn't expect holidays to be anything special in this program. It's just another day."

"I'm sorry, Sis. We can't wait for you to get home," Colton said, trying to cheer me up.

"Thanks, Colton."

"Alright, well I'll let you guys go. I hope you all have a great time today. I love you," I said, not in the mood to talk anymore.

"Thanks, Sis, I love you," Leannah said.

"I love you, baby. Have a great day, I hope it goes better than planned," my mom said.

I smiled slightly, "Thanks, Mom."

"You're welcome, baby."

"Hey, Iris, I wanna talk to you for a sec," Colton said.

"Alright," I pulled on my cigarette, knowing what this was about.

I then heard the storm door close behind him.

"How have you been doing, Iris? You know…since everything with Campbell?"

I exhaled the cigarette smoke, "I've been fine," I lied emotionlessly.

"You don't sound fine, and you haven't sounded fine all the times we've talked on the phone since."

There was a pause. My eyes welled up with tears as everything held inside was trying to reach the surface. I pulled deeply on my cigarette, trying to fight down my emotions.

"It's hard, Colton," I mumbled, exhaling my cigarette smoke, trying not to cry.

"I know, Iris. I know," Colton sighed. I knew he felt defeated and helpless.

"I know our life's been rough but this…this is just different," I confessed.

"It's alright, Iris. I get it. You know you can come home whenever, if you need to. None of us will be mad at you."

I shook my head, "No, no, I'm not doing that."

"Alright, I'm just saying," Colton said.

"I'm fine, Colton," I said as I exhaled. "I'm going to be fine, just like I always have been."

"I know, Sis, but just know it's okay to *not* be okay. You never gotta pretend to me that you're okay."

"I know…Hey, Colton?"

"Yeah, Sis?"

"I love you a lot you know?" tears welled up again and fell onto my cheeks. I tried to push them away with my wrist while the cigarette sat in between my two fingers. "And thank you…for everything."

"Of course, Sis. I told you I'd do anything for you guys, and I mean it. I meant it ten years ago and I still mean it today…and I always will."

My lip quivered as more tears fell out of my eyes and rolled down my cheeks. I swallowed hard, pushing down my feelings so that I could speak. "Thank you."

"I love you, Sis. Go chill out and have a good Thanksgiving. I'll talk to you soon."

"Alright...I love you too, bye."

I then hung up the phone.

I didn't know it then, but Thanksgiving that year would be anything from good. It actually turned into the *worst* Thanksgiving I ever had, and that said a lot for me.

55

Chapter 55

I entered back into the house and walked to the staircase to go up to my room. Once inside, I saw Jo was now awake, but still lying in bed.

I pursed my lips, "Here. Sorry, I borrowed this," I showed her the lighter then placed it on her dresser.

Jo sat up, "Oh, no worries. It's fine."

I took a few steps then said, "The cigarette wasn't one of yours. I was tying my shoes and saw one of my old roommate's in my bag."

"Oh, okay. Well, you could have had one of mine, I wouldn't care."

"Thanks," I said as I began to take off my coat.

"Is everything okay though?" Jo asked. "You told me you don't typically smoke."

"No, I'm fine. I don't know. I just wanted one once I saw it," I said, somewhat lying.

"I guess it's like that sometimes," Jo said as she got out of bed and came over to me. "Happy Thanksgiving, Iris. I'm thankful for a friend like you," she said as she pulled me into a hug.

I was caught off guard, but then embraced her hug. Feelings of bliss that I so desperately needed flooded into me.

"Thank you, Jo. I'm grateful to have a friend like you, too."

The day passed by and we decided to play some pool. To our surprise, when we entered, there were already three other people in there.

"Hello," Jo said as she gave a little smile, "I'm Jo and this is Iris."

I didn't say anything, I just smiled.

"I'm Rachel and this is Sebastian and that's Carter," the girl with dirty blonde hair said.

"Nice to meet you, guys," Jo said. "So could we join?"

"Yeah sure," Carter said. "Let me re-rack the balls."

Carter began racking all the balls for a new game while Rachel and Sebastian put chalk on their cue sticks. I walked over to the corner of the room where the rest of the cues were and got two. Walking back over to Jo, I handed her a stick and we both began chalking ours.

"Alright, who wants to break?" Carter asked as he removed the rack from the balls.

"I'll go," Rachel said.

We all watched as she walked around the table and bent down to take her shot. Seconds later, all fifteen of the pool balls split apart and were sent into different directions. None of them made it into any pockets though.

"Nice break," Sebastian said, giving her a fist bump as she walked back over to him.

She smiled at him but seemed disappointed she didn't make any balls in.

"Iris, why don't you go?" Carter asked. "Then you, Jo."

I silently walked over to where the cue ball was and bent down. I pulled back a couple of times, preparing to strike the four ball, as I looked at the reflection of the lights on the balls.

Bang! The cue ball slammed into the solid purple ball, and it fell into a pocket. The solid green number six was also struck and as well fell into a pocket.

"Damn, girl, nice shot," Sebastian said.

I smiled then walked around the table to the cue ball and bent down to take a second shot. This time, I didn't have a clear shot, so I had to work off the diamonds.

Bang! The cue ball smacked into the wood siding then struck the solid orange number five ball, sending it into a pocket.

More praise rang out. "You go," I said to Jo. We were all just taking turns hitting the balls, not actually playing a real game. I'm not even sure if you can play a real game of pool with more than two people.

Soon enough, all the balls were in the pockets and Carter began to re-rack them again. We began to play two on two for a while and I beat everyone, pool was one of the few things I was actually good at.

A few hours had passed, and it was now almost one. Carter invited Jo and I to eat at Bethany's Diner with him and the others as they were all starting to get hungry. Since Jo and I were too, we agreed. Rachel told us Carter had his car here so after Jo and I went to our room to get our purses and my coat—and the cigarette pack that was sitting on my dresser, we met the three at the door and we all walked outside and got into Carter's burgundy 2000 Nissan Altima.

"So, where are you guys from?" Sebastian asked.

"I'm from Springfield, Illinois."

"Yeah, and I'm from Chicago."

"Oh, cool, so you're both from Illinois," Sebastian said.

"Yeah, where are you guys from?" Jo asked.

"I'm from Minnesota," Rachel said.

"Nevada," Carter said.

"I'm from Florida," Sebastian finalized.

"Oh, wow, all very different places," Jo said.

"Yeah, that's the truth," Carter chuckled.

"I've never been to any of those states," Jo claimed. "At least yet."

"Yeah same," I added quietly.

"Iris, you don't talk much, do you?" Sebastian smiled.

I looked up at him blankly in the passenger's seat, "I do."

He laughed, "You've said like five words since I've introduced myself."

"Bro, chill," Carter said to Sebastian quietly.

"You don't even know me," I said monotonously, slightly offended.

"I was just saying it seems like you don't really talk a lot," Sebastian said.

"Alright, well it doesn't matter if she does or doesn't, just leave it alone," Jo chimed in.

I looked over at her and smiled.

Sebastian didn't say anything, he seemed embarrassed.

It was quiet for a couple of minutes, but small talk quickly resumed. And soon enough, we arrived at the diner.

We all got out of Carter's car and headed inside. The restaurant wasn't busy, and we immediately got seated at a booth. Rachel, Sebastian, and Carter sat on one side while Jo and I sat on the other.

"Do I want a grilled cheese or a bacon cheeseburger?" Carter asked aloud.

"Grilled cheese," I said as I continued looking at my menu.

Jo laughed, "That was an easy decision for you, since you don't eat meat."

I chuckled, "You're right."

"You don't eat meat?" Carter questioned.

"No, I don't—well red meat anyway," I clarified.

"Any reason?" Carter asked.

I shrugged, "I just never liked it, that's the only reason."

"Oh okay, well that's cool," he smiled at me, meeting my eyes.

Feeling self-conscious, I looked down at my menu.

The waiter came back around, taking our orders, then scooping up our menus and walked away.

"So, what do you guys like to do for fun?" Sebastian asked Jo and I as he took a sip of his water.

"Uh, well, I don't know," Jo looked at me. "We like to go out and find new things, play pool, simple stuff like that."

"Alright, alright, what kind of things do you like to "find"?" Sebastian asked, using finger quotes.

"You know, go around town and see what's going on and then just get into things," I explained.

"Sounds fun," Rachel said as she grabbed her glass of water to take a sip.

"Yeah, it does," Carter added, looking at me. "I like to do that kind of thing too."

"Do you guys' party?" Sebastian asked.

"No—well, I don't at least," Jo said, looking down.

"I don't really either," I added.

Sebastian sucked his teeth, "You guys *seriously* don't party?"

I just looked at him blankly, not saying anything.

"So, I'm guessing you guys didn't come to that rager I threw a couple of nights ago?"

"That was you?" Jo asked with annoyance in her voice.

"Yeah, why?" Sebastian asked.

"Because we were the ones who cleaned the whole thing up at one in the morning," I now said, bitterly then took a sip of my water.

"Oh shit, that was you guys?" Sebastian questioned. "I heard two girls cleaned it up, but I didn't know who. Yeah, that shit got wild."

Carter scoffed and rolled his eyes as did Rachel.

"I'm really sorry about that, guys," Rachel said. "We tried to stop him but he never listens," she glared at Sebastian.

"Yeah, that was really nice of you two to do that," Carter added. Sebastian scoffed.

I rolled my eyes, growing annoyed at Sebastian's behavior. I was liking him less and less.

"So, Iris, how are you so good at pool?" Carter asked, changing the topic.

"Back home my brother, sister, and I would walk to this bowling alley that had a bunch of pool tables in it. We always played. My brother taught me a lot," I said.

"Oh, wow, that's pretty cool. How old are your siblings?" he asked.

"My sister is fourteen and my brother just turned nineteen."

"Oh, nice, my little brother is fourteen."

I smiled shyly, nodding my head.

"How old are you then?" he asked.

"Uh," I looked down, "I'm seventeen."

"Oh, wow, you look older than seventeen," Carter said, surprised.

I thought you were at least twenty. You look old for your age.

Campbell's words echoed in my mind. I swallowed the rising lump in my throat. My hand shook on my water glass.

Jo must have noticed because she jumped to ask Carter how old he was, removing any attention from me. Carter was twenty, Rachel was also twenty and Sebastian was twenty-one, making me once again, the youngest in the group.

Our food soon arrived and everyone began to dig in, except for me. I pushed around the food on my plate, my appetite long gone.

$$56$$

Chapter 56

"Yo, Carter, you trying to drop me off at The Poppy?" Sebastian asked as we all climbed back into Carter's car. It was now around three o'clock.

"If I do, you gotta get a cab home unless you seriously need me," Carter replied.

"Nah, I'll get a cab. Thanks, man."

"What's The Poppy?" I asked.

"It's a bar about ten minutes from here," Rachel answered.

"Yeah, figured I'd start early," Sebastian snickered.

I just frowned. He thought he was so cool.

Carter put the directions into his phone then backed out of the parking spot, exiting onto the main road.

"So you guys said you don't party, does that mean you don't drink?" Sebastian asked, still on this.

"Uh, not really…anymore at least," Jo answered unnervingly.

I watched as Jo became uncomfortable.

Sebastian dramatically sighed, "You don't party *or* drink? Your lives must be pretty fucking boring. Iris, do *you* at least drink?"

Something in me snapped.

"You know, partying and drinking and doing drugs isn't the only fun thing in life and if you think it is, then you're the one who's pretty fucking boring and pathetic. Stop asking people what they do and don't do every second you get because you want someone to be as two-dimensional as you are."

The car went silent for a second. I think everyone was shocked that all of that came from the girl who has "barely said five words." Please.

Sebastian just laughed and shook his head as he lit a cigarette, not saying a word to me.

No one said anything for the rest of the car ride there. Although Jo did look at me and smirk, satisfied that Sebastian was put in his place.

After we dropped him off, Rachel got out and moved into the front seat.

"Sorry about him," Carter said. "I think it's cool you both don't really drink."

I scoffed and rolled my eyes. Why did that have to be "cool?" "Can we just go, please?"

"Uh, yeah," Carter said in a confused tone. "I gotta get gas on the way back though."

"No problem," I said as I stared out the window.

After about ten minutes, we pulled up to a Mobil. Carter said he was going in for a coffee, which sounded good so I went as well. We got to the coffee makers and began making ourselves our cups.

"I'm sorry about Sebastian though," Carter said as he stood close to me. "He can be a bit much and careless sometimes."

I backed away timidly, "It's okay."

"He just doesn't know how to act around girls or talk to them."

I looked at him blankly for a second as I unscrewed the milk.

"I mean, he probably thinks Jo, or you, are really pretty," he smiled as he got closer to me again.

I swallowed hard.

"I mean, *I* think you're really pretty, Iris."

You're so pretty, you know that, my Iris.

I moved away from him as I put the milk away and grabbed two packets of sugar.

"Do you think maybe we could hang out alone tonight or go someplace?" Carter turned to me.

"Uh," I swallowed.

You're mine, Iris. No one else's.

"I'm sorry, I'm not interested," I grabbed my coffee and tried to swiftly walk away, discomfort growing inside of me.

"Hey!" He stopped me by grabbing my waist, abruptly turning me around.

"Iris, I *really* think you're pretty and cool. Maybe you could just give me a chance?" he asked once more, trying to be kind. Although his kindness was not genuine.

I swallowed hard.

Nobody will ever *love you like I will.*

I took a breath, "No. I said no."

He contorted his face and scoffed, "Your loss. I'm fun to be with. Sebastian was right. You and your little friend are fucking boring."

Timidness dispersing, I narrowed my eyes, "Fuck you," I stormed out of the store without my coffee.

I rounded the side of the building and began scurrying down the sidewalk. Jo must have noticed as I heard a car door close and footsteps pattering on the ground behind me.

"Iris! Iris!"

I kept chugging forward.

"Iris!" Jo caught up to me, clasping my shoulder and spinning me to face her. "Iris, what's wrong?"

I looked into her deep blue eyes. Seeing the concerned inside of them broke something inside of me. "Carter tried flirting with me then when I told him no, he said Sebastian was right, you and I are fucking boring."

"What? Are you kidding me? That's fucked up," Jo said passionately.

"When I tried to walk away, he grabbed me," I said softly.

"Iris," Jo's face softened with sympathy. "Are you okay?"

"I'm fine," I said.

Jo smiled ruefully and hugged from the side.

I swung my arm around her and squeezed back, a smile growing onto my face. I know I hadn't known her for long, but that was when I knew she'd be my best friend.

"So, how far to the bus stop?" I exhaled smoke into the cold air from the cigarette Jo gave me. Neither of us had money for a cab.

"Uh," Jo began pressing the screen of her phone, "thirty-minutes."

I inhaled, then exhaled the smoke, "Why is the bus stop so far from here? Boston should be crawling with them."

"I don't know. We're on the outside of the city right now so maybe that's why," Jo explained.

I inhaled one final time then threw my half-used cigarette to the ground, "Alright, well we might as hurry. It's almost four, it'll be dark soon," I stuffed my hands into my pockets, trying to keep them warm.

Jo trailed behind.

"I'm sorry, Jo," I said a beat later. "If I didn't get so emotional we wouldn't be here right now."

"Iris, stop. Are you kidding me? I wouldn't have wanted to go with them after Carter was an asshole to you. And anyway, I wouldn't just leave you to walk all this way by yourself, that's not what friends do."

I smiled slightly, met her eyes, then looked straight ahead.

"I've had so many friends that have either left me and I've had to walk home alone at night, or they chose someone who has wronged me, over me. Betrayal hurts, trust me. Don't ever apologize. Whether it's thirty minutes or thirty miles, we're doing it together."

I looked at her, "Thanks, Jo. Not many people would do that."

She smiled, "I know, trust me. Just forget about it though, seriously. There's nothing to be sorry about."

I smiled and we continued down the sidewalk.

We walked several more minutes down the idle road when a red Dodge Charger pulled up real slow behind us.

"Hey!" a male's voice shouted out to us. "Y'all girls need a ride or something?"

Unbeknownst to me at the time, he appeared to be about forty-five years old. He had dirty, semi-long brown hair that was coming out from underneath a baseball hat.

"Don't say anything," I said to Jo as she turned around.

She turned back, facing forward, and we both kept walking, ignoring the man who was still slowly creeping behind us.

"Hey!" he yelled again. "I'm talking to you guys."

"No, we're fine," I shouted, still not facing the man.

He sped up and stopped his car about ten feet in front of us, parked the car, and then stepped out.

Jo and I froze. Fear began pinballing around my insides with a *ping*.

"I was just asking if you guys need a ride," he said.

"She said we're fine," Jo said coldly, trying to bolster her confidence.

The man began walking towards us, "Well, can I take you guys out someplace? You're both very pretty."

Jo and I stepped back. *Ping, ping, ping.*

I mustered up all my courage, forcing the ball of fear to still, "No.

Just leave us alone."

"Come on now, don't be difficult," he said as inched forward toward us.

We do it all the time. Don't make this harder than it needs to be.

"Just leave us alone!" Jo yelled.

The man then lunged for Jo and grabbed her arm. He yanked her towards him, wrapping his large arms around her, and quickly dragging her to his car.

"Jo!" I screamed *Ping, ping, ping, ping, ping.* I ran towards them both. I grabbed at her, trying to pull her back with all my strength.

The man then grabbed me as well. He wrapped his big, muscular arm around my waist as Jo was sandwiched in between us. He opened his car's back door and tried shoving both of us in, but we fought to get free. I somehow broke out of his clutch and fell to the ground, scraping my arm and palms. With me being free, he now got a better grip on Jo. He shoved her into the car and began closing the door. Once I saw this, I quickly staggered to my feet and jumped on top of him before he could close it all the way. He stumbled and lost his balance which forced him out of the doorframe. Jo was then able to jump up and escape from the car. The man and I began to tussle and when he saw Jo get out of his car, he shoved her to the ground. He then tried shoving me in the car, but I let out an ear-piercing scream. He covered my mouth as he pushed me down onto the seat, but I bit his hand as hard as I could, drawing blood. Jo scrambled off the pavement with blood running from her forehead and shoved him with all her strength. The man tripped on the curb and stumbled onto the ground. I heard Jo scream as he had grabbed her ankle, swiping her down to the ground with him. I saw a baseball bat laying across the backseat which I instinctively grabbed and jumped out of the car.

Ping, ping, ping, ping, ping.

"Jo, watch out!" I yelled as I swung with all my strength at the man, who was on his knees, stumbling to stand up.

Jo saw the bat in my hands and rolled to the side, getting out of my way.

I hit him in his side, right where his ribs were. The sound of those bones cracking, and a grown man's gut-wrenching scream filled our ears as he naturally fell back to the ground. Jo stumbled to her knees as I swung the bat once again and hit him in the same spot. He screamed out in pain as he turned over into a fetal position, holding his side. I threw the bat down and helped Jo to her feet.

"Come on, Jo. Run!" I yelled at her as I held her forearms.

I pulled us down the sidewalk and we took off running. *Ping, ping, ping* with each footstep I took.

After a couple of seconds, I looked back, and the man was trying to get up as he held his side in pain. I looked forward and grabbed Jo's hand, making sure she wouldn't falter behind.

We ran some more but eventually we came to a building. We quickly turned the corner to catch our breath and be out of sight of the man.

"Are—are—are you okay?" Jo asked me as she desperately tried to fill her lungs with air.

I placed my scraped hand on the wall for support.

"I'm okay—I'm okay," I said in between gasps. "Are you?" I asked as I pulled her bloody blonde hair off her forehead wound.

She pushed her hair behind her ear and touched the wound. Her fingers were covered in crimson.

She wiped the blood on her black jeans and nodded her head repeatedly, "Yeah—yeah, I'm good."

We stood there catching our breath for a couple more seconds when suddenly, we heard a car's engine roar from the direction we had just run from.

We both froze. *Ping, ping, ping, ping.*

"That's gotta be him," Jo's words dripped with fear.

"Come one, let's go. He can't find us, we gotta make it to the bus stop!" I said desperately.

"Alright, come on!" Jo grabbed my arm, and we took off parallel to the building.

We ran a couple of blocks, changing our direction frequently so it would be harder for that freak to catch us.

"Iris!" Jo shouted. "The bus is leaving!"

We ran towards the bus as it was beginning to slowly pull away. We both ran up to the bus and started banging on the doors. It came to a halt. The driver opened the doors, and we practically threw ourselves into it.

"Thank you—thank you. We're so sorry," Jo frantically stuffed four crumbled-up dollars into the fare box.

"Come on, take your seats. I got a schedule to stay on," the unfriendly female driver said.

Jo and I threw ourselves into two seats and exhaled deeply.

"You okay?" I asked Jo.

"I'm okay. Are you?" Jo tried to be strong, but I could hear the tremble in her voice.

"I'm okay," I lied, side hugged Jo. "It's all good, we're safe now."

The *Pings* finally came to a halt.

She leaned her head on my shoulder. I then closed my saturated eyes, tears escaping down my cheeks. That Thanksgiving, I was simply thankful to be alive.

57

Chapter 57

"Alright, let me clean your cut," I said to Jo after I took my coat off. It was around six forty-five when we finally made it back to our room.

"Oh—you sure? Thanks."

In the bathroom, Jo sat up on the sink, taking her coat off and tossing it to the floor. She kicked off her shoes as I washed my hands. I then pulled out a bin of first aid supplies from under the sink.

I poured alcohol onto a cotton ball and pushed her hair behind her ear, "This may sting a little."

I proceeded to dab it on her head as she wrinkled her face, it was tender. It was quiet while I continued to clean it.

"You know when I was younger, like sixteen, I used to drink a lot," Jo said, looking up to the ceiling as I wiped the encrusted blood from the surrounding area.

"I was at a party this one night and I got pretty messed up. I was stumbling all around and banging into things and at one point, I bumped into a side table and knocked over some vase. It hit the ground and shattered. The girl who was throwing the party got super pissed. Apparently, it was her mom's and was super expensive. I didn't even know her, she was a friend of an acquaintance, so that also kinda made things worse. So anyway, she started yelling at me and told me to get out. I didn't have anywhere to go except home, but I didn't have anyone or the money to take me there. I was standing outside her house, drunk, on the curb in the cold. I figured I would still call a cab. I knew I didn't have any money for it but in my delusional state, I figured somehow it would work. So about fifteen minutes later, my cab arrives. I got in and I remember it was this, like, thirty-something-year-old man. He had dark hair, his skin was that dark-olive color, and dark brown eyes. I gave him my home address and we got about five minutes down the road when I started slurring out that I had no money to pay him. He turned around looking really angry and yelled out, 'You don't have any money? Why did you call me and waste my time?' I was taken aback by his anger as he pulled the car over to the side of the road. He kept screaming at me, all different things that I can't exactly remember, but he was beyond pissed. I was terrified and didn't know what to say. He then twisted towards me, got halfway into the backseat, opened my door, and began pushing me out of the car. I drunkenly tried to resist but he violently shoved me out onto the ground, where I fell and scraped my head."

Jo then chuckled, "Kinda funny, in the same spot as this cut," she then got serious again. "He took off, speeding down the dark road. I started bawling my eyes out. Not only did he scare the hell out of me, but I started to realize that I did it to myself. I did a lot of shit to myself and didn't even realize it," Jo sighed once more as I slowly dapped some Neosporin on her cut with a Q-tip.

"I got up and started to walk home. That whole hour walking home, I beat myself up. Man, did I beat myself up. I told myself things like, 'Maybe if you weren't such an alcoholic and a loser, Jolene, you wouldn't have broken the vase. And maybe you wouldn't have called a cab knowing you had no money. And maybe you wouldn't have met that man, and he wouldn't have kicked you out onto the ground and you wouldn't have a bashed-up face,'" Jo shook her head, disappointed with herself.

"'If you weren't such a *loser* and had to drink all of your issues away, maybe bad shit wouldn't happen to you.' That whole walk home I just beat myself up over and over and over again. I had hit rock bottom and I finally thought, 'You know, Jolene, maybe if you didn't get so fucked up all the time then maybe this shit just wouldn't happen.' So that's exactly what I did. I stopped drinking completely, in hopes that the bad shit would stop too and I've been sober ever since but it's funny"—Jo chuckled again—"'cause bad shit still happens. I'm sitting here with another cut in the same spot as that night. I've realized it's inevitable and you can't escape the inevitable."

Extreme disappointment hit me like a ton of bricks. I sighed while holding a Band-Aid, "Jo I'm—"

"And I'm not telling you this at all to make you feel guilty," she jumped to say. "What I said back at the gas station was true and it'll always be true. I would walk a *hundred* miles with you if it meant you wouldn't walk alone, and it meant I wasn't supporting someone who's against you. Tonight just made me realize even more, that there's no escaping bad things. No matter what you do, you just can't," Jo paused for a second. "And anyway, if I didn't come with you, it would've still happened to you, and if you didn't go at all, it'd be someone else."

Jo looked down at me and made eye contact for the first time. I smiled ruefully then looked down at the Band-Aid, unpeeling the wrapper.

"I know what you mean. I really do," I said. "I've felt that a lot in my life. My brother would always worry about me going here or there, but bad things have happened in so many different places, that there's really no use in worrying because nowhere is safe," I exhaled deeply and paused as I took the final wrapping off the Band-Aid. "I'm sorry you went through all that, Jo. For what it's worth, I'm really proud of you."

I stuck the Band-Aid over Jo's wound and smoothed out the edges with my fingers. Jo then hopped down off the sink.

"It's alright, thanks, Iris. Everything is always okay in the end," she smiled and I wanted to believe her.

58

Chapter 58

I turned on the shower faucet and ran my fingers under the water as it soon became warm. I stared at the water for a couple of minutes as emotions overwhelmed me. Sadness, anger, bitterness, resentment, and sorrow seeped out of me as I began to cry uncontrollably. I cried so hard I shook. I cried so hard I feared I'd vomit. I covered my mouth to prevent Jo from hearing me as I hiccuped. I cried and cried until there was nothing left in me.

Eventually, I calmed down and got out of the shower. I got dressed then walked back into our room. I walked towards my vanity, towel in hand, that sat against the window. That's when I saw it.

I placed the towel on the back of the vanity chair and leaned on it as I peered out the window at the black sedan car that pulled up.

"Oh my God. It's Kalista," I said in shock as I had lost hope she was coming back anytime soon.

"What?" Jo jumped up from her bed and came over to the window. She pulled the other side of the curtain open to get a better view.

"Holy shit, it is her," she said as we saw Kalista get out of the car and walk to the door.

We let go of the curtains and they naturally fell back together.

"Should we go see where she's been?" Jo asked.

Just then we heard our housemates whose rooms were in the same hallway as ours, open their doors and go downstairs.

"I guess they had the same idea as you," I said.

We began walking down the stairs and Kalista was now entering her home. Immediately I knew she was drunk. Although it wasn't very hard, I could tell someone was intoxicated in a minute tops when I was around them. Being born into a family where both my parents were alcoholics (and my mom an opioid addict later) would do that to you. One of my earliest memories is my mom asking me to pour her another shot of whiskey. I was four.

We got to the base of the stairs as more people were coming from different directions. Carter took a seat on one of the couches. We made eye contact and he smirked at me, making my skin crawl. I quickly looked away back to the floor.

No matter what you do, no one will ever believe you.

"Hey, everybody. Sorry, I know I've been—I've been gone a couple of days," she slurred her words and stumbled.

She stunk like alcohol, her eyes were bloodshot, and her pupils were the size of meteors. She looked like a mess. A completely and utterly different person than who welcomed us in.

I couldn't deal with it.

It brought me right back to when I was a kid. Watching my mom drink, pass out, throw up, repeat. Watching my mom and dad fight, spewing drunken words at one another while me and my siblings stood in the shrapnel. Watching random men after random men come into our house. Watching Colton grow up too fast to take care of Leannah and me. Watching us move from one shitty place to another shitty place. Watching it not be enough anymore and leading to pills. Watching my mom fall apart then promise us she'd change only to fall apart again. Watching everything go up in flames around you. Watching the destruction, the heartbreak, and the desperation, time after time again.

I couldn't deal with it. I barely had time to process what happened earlier. I barely could keep my head above water from everything with Campbell. I could carry this too. I couldn't deal with it, so I simply walked away.

"Where you going, Iris?" Kalista slurred through a laugh.

"Don't," I said, all stone.

"Aw, come on! Let's have some fun!" she grabbed my hands but I yanked them away.

"*Don't*," I said, voice almost trembling. "Just please, *don't.*"

Everything went quiet. Jo, face full of concern, looked at me. I scurried up the stairs and into my room, collapsing on my bed, only now allowing the tears to run free.

What was I even crying about? Was it Campbell? Almost being kidnapped? My mom? I wasn't sure. The old Iris rarely cried. The old Iris would have told Kalista off. Would have told her how irresponsible she was and that we had no food and no way to contact her. Would have called her out on her drinking. Her voice would have been steel, confidence aplenty, and she wouldn't cower to a boy like Carter or anyone for that matter. The old Iris was fierce, fearless, and courageous. But that Iris died on October seventh, leaving only a shell of her behind.

"Iris!" Jo hurried into our room. "What's wrong? Are you okay?"

She came over to where I laid, kneeling down to my level. My tear-filled eyes met hers. I couldn't tell her the truth, but I also couldn't lie to her. So, I met somewhere in the middle.

"I don't know. I guess I'm shaken up from earlier and seeing Kalista that way is hard because my mom used to be like that all the time."

Jo looked at me. Half pensive, half sympathy, like she was deciding if she believed me. I don't think she did. I think she knew there was something much bigger underneath the surface but didn't want to push.

"I'm sorry, Iris. Everything is okay though. We're here safe, your mom is healthy, everything is good," she pulled me into a hug. "I love you, Iris."

I squeezed her tight. "I love you too, Jo."

59

Chapter 59

I woke up around three a.m. having to go to the bathroom. I quietly walked into our bathroom, went pee, and then began to wash my hands. I wrinkled my face as the water struck my scraped hand, inflicting a stinging sensation. I then gazed up into the mirror where I fixated on the image of myself reflecting back at me. I felt sad staring at myself in that mirror at three a.m. I missed my mom, my brother and my sister. I turned around and leaned up against the sink as I let out a sigh while playing with my bracelet. The glowing white moon then caught my eye in the black night sky through the small bathroom window. As I gazed up at it, I decided I would go outside and just be alone with the moon—finally *completely* alone.

I walked down the driveway to the sidewalk and sat down, pulling the sides of my faux fur jacket together to warm myself. I gazed up into the sky and fixated my eyes on the moon. It was so huge and beautiful. That always seemed to make everything better. When you look up into the sky and see the moon or mountains or cliffs, even buildings. Things so much bigger than you make you feel so small and your problems insignificant. And in that time, you feel peaceful and like none of it is even there. That's how I felt that night looking up into the moon. Everything I had been feeling, disappeared and although it was only for a short amount of time, it was enough. It was enough for me to gain hope, it was enough to let go of some of the sadness, it was enough to remember why I was even here in the first place.

Around ten, I was making my bed when Jo walked in.

"Oh, hey, you're up," she said as she had two coffees in her hand.

"Hey, good morning."

"Here, this is for you. I figured you'd be up soon," she smiled as she handed me the coffee.

"Thanks," I took a sip then set it on my nightstand to continue making my bed.

"How are you feeling?" Jo asked, sipping her own coffee.

"I'm okay." After a beat, "Thank you…for everything."

Jo smiled but it was laced with sadness, "You know I'm always here for you, Iris."

I smiled then looked down. "So," I said, changing the subject. "What do we want to do today?"

"Well, we could go into the city and see what's going to be on sale in all of those little stores they have downtown."

"Oh yeah, that's right, today's Black Friday," I said, having forgotten.

"Yeah, we may find some unique things, and it'll give us something to do," Jo said.

"Yeah totally. Let me get dressed and we'll head out," I set my coffee down and walked towards my closet.

We made it to downtown Boston shortly after. As we got off the bus, we looked around and saw all the vendors and shops that were set up along the road.

"Oooo this looks so cool!" Jo exclaimed.

I smiled, "Yeah it does. Come on, let's go," I grabbed her arm and we hurried to the other side of the street. We began to window shop and admire all the unique and interesting things that were for sale. Soon enough, we came to a custom bracelet stand.

"Oh, this is cool. Look at this, Jo," I said as I stood in front of a sign that read, "Engraved Bracelets: Two for Ten," and a basket full of those braided faux leather bracelets that have a flat side for engraving.

"Oh yeah, I've seen these before at carnivals!" Jo exclaimed.

"Hello, ladies. How you?" the Asian man who owned the store said in his thick accent.

"We're good, thank you," Jo said with a smile.

"You like bracelet?" he asked.

"Yeah, they're pretty cool," Jo answered.

"Okay, I do for you. If you get bracelets, I give to you, two for five!" the man exclaimed, trying to strike a deal.

Jo and I looked at each other like *What the hell, why not?*

"Okay, sure," I said.

"Okay, okay," the man smiled. "Pick out your color, honey, then write down what you want on this paper here, okay?"

"Okay," Jo smiled. "Thanks."

The man then sat back down on his stool several feet from us while he waited.

"What should we get engraved?" I asked.

"Well, how about matching bracelets? Like maybe our initials on the inside?" Jo suggested.

I smiled, "Yeah, I'd like that. I have my mom's, brother's, and sister's on this one." I said, lifting my arm so she could see.

"That's beautiful! I never noticed that," she said, examining the charm.

I put my arm back down, pulling my sleeves to my fingers. "It was a gift from them for my seventeenth birthday."

"That's so sweet."

I smiled, looking down at the colorful faux leather bands. I picked out a rustic pink one and Jo picked out a brown one.

"What's your middle name?" Jo asked me as she picked up the pen and had already written an *I* on the paper.

"It's Dallas," I said.

"Really? That's such a cool name."

"Thanks. My mom found out she was pregnant with me there. So, she figured, why not make that her middle name," I then picked up my pen.

"That's awesome."

"What's yours?" I asked.

"Savannah, that was my mom's name so it's pretty special to me. Actually, my whole name is. My mom *loved* Dolly Parton. I mean, like, *loved* her. Her favorite song, well album too, was *Jolene,* so that's where she got my name from. And then my dad always loved her name and wanted my middle name to be her first name."

"That is really special."

"Yeah, I really like it," Jo smiled as she wrote *IDC* on her paper.

I wrote *JSM* on my paper and handed it to the man.

We talked for a couple more minutes while the man worked on our bracelets. Soon enough, he approached us at the counter with the two bracelets.

"Okay, here you go. They all done for you."

Jo and I grabbed our bracelets, excited to see the finished product. We flipped them over to see the initials and they were perfect, just what we wanted.

"Oh wow, these look great!" Jo exclaimed. "Thank you so much!"

"Yeah, these look awesome. Thank you," I added.

"Good, good," the man said, smiling.

We paid the man then jumped back into the moving crowd and continued to the next stand that would catch our eyes. We did this for about two more hours, just checking out different stores and window shopping since we didn't have any extra money to spare. Eventually though, we got hungry.

"You wanna get something to eat? I'm pretty hungry," Jo said.

"Alright. What do you wanna eat?" I asked.

"I don't care. We could go inside this hall and see what's all in there," Jo suggested as she pointed to a sign that read *The Market at Liberty Place. Food Court/Market.*

"Alright, yeah. Let's try that."

We opened the door to the building and we went in.

There were a bunch of different vendors serving all different kinds of food. Pizza, burgers, Mexican, bakery items, BBQ, there even was a bar. It was pretty cool.

"Some pizza sounds good," Jo said as she stared up at the vendor's sign.

"It does, I'm thinking Mexican though. A burrito with some rice and beans sounds good," I said as I looked at another vendor's sign.

"Alright, why don't you get your food and I'll get mine? I'll probably be done before you, so I'll grab us a table," Jo suggested.

"Okay, cool."

We went our separate ways. I got into line, which was a decent length. I looked around and took in the place as I patiently waited to be next.

The hall was somewhat big but since there was so much inside of it, it felt small. It felt like a cafeteria to me, or like a community dining center. Which, technically it was, but it really emphasized my feelings of being disconnected from home and astray.

The line moved forward, and a couple of more people joined, distracting me from my thoughts for just a moment. I watched everyone around me as the environment put me into a morose mood. Men and women, children and elders, all getting food and sitting with their loved ones. Laughing and having a good time. They probably come to this Black Friday Fair each year then go back to their cozy, decorated homes, in their heated cars. Happy and content with life, no issues. Then there was me. All alone. With no family, no friends—except Jo—and no car; living in a place that wasn't home and doing it because we weren't happy and content with life. Because *we* were the ones with all the issues.

I got my food then found my way to Jo. The two of us ate and talked and once we finished, we decided we would head home.

We walked outside and down a block to get out of the way of everyone so that we could google the nearest bus stop. We stood at a corner of a building while Jo lit a cigarette and went on her phone.

"Okay, let's see—current location—bus stop—" she said to herself as she touched the screen of her phone.

I went in my purse and got a cigarette out of the pack I bought at one of the stands. It took me a couple of tries to get it to light due to the aggressive wind that ripped through the gray, gloomy sky.

Once it was finally lit, I inhaled and exhaled the gray smoke into the air, feeling the calming sensation that I needed, take over my body.

"Alright, it says the closest bus stop from here is a twenty-minute walk," Jo pulled on her cigarette.

Ping, ping, ping. The pinball of fear began to fire.

I swallowed. *Breathe, Iris.* I pulled on my cigarette then exhaled deeply. "Okay…well, we better go now then. The sky's getting darker."

"Okay, it says we go down this street for ten blocks then take a left onto Orange Street, walk another ten blocks, and we'll run right into it."

Ping, ping.

Breathe, *Iris. Please.*

"Alright," taking another deep drag from my cigarette.

We walked and the roar of thunder filled our ears as the sky began to blacken and the wind began to intensify.

"Oh shit, it's about to pour," Jo said as she stopped to look up at the sky.

I gazed up at the sky and the dark clouds, "Come on, we gotta hurry."

I pulled on Jo's arm, and we began to run down the sidewalk as we felt raindrops strike us.

"Shit," I heard Jo say as we ran.

We continued running and the rain only grew stronger. Within minutes, it was full out pouring.

"Iris, that sign says Orange Street, make a left there!" Jo yelled to me over the loud claps of thunder.

"Okay!"

We turned left onto Orange Street and continued running. We ran for ten more blocks through the rain and thunder, splashing mud all over us. We saw lightning bolts in the distance strike down at the earth. The sky was as black as it should be at midnight, not three o'clock in the afternoon.

"Hey! There's the bus stop!" I called out to Jo.

"Oh, yeah!" she yelled back.

We ran one more block then practically dove into the small bus shelter. sitting down to catch our breath.

"Holy fucking shit," Jo said, struggling to breathe.

I wiped the running mascara off my cheeks as I gasped for air.

"It's fucking cold," I shivered as I tried to pull my soaking wet faux fur coat to my body for warmth.

Jo slid over to me as she continued trying to catch her breath. She shivered as she put her arm around me, leaning her head on my shoulder.

We waited twenty minutes in the blistering cold, soaking wet, and covered in mud for the bus to come. By the time it did, the rain had slowed to a drizzle.

60

Chapter 60

The first thing Jo and I did when we got home was take showers. After that, we went into the lounge with a bowl of popcorn and watched a *Full House* marathon. Watching the sitcom and the antics of the Tanner family members, I felt content. It was a nice distraction from the prison that was my mind.

After dinner, the two of us went back to our rooms, and changed into what we'd be sleeping in. I got changed in the bathroom like I normally did and once I was done, I walked back into our room where Jo was finishing getting dressed. I carried my dirty clothes to our overflowing hamper, not even attempting to try to make them fit.

"I think I'm gonna go do some laundry," I said as I pulled the bag out.

"Here, separate them first. You don't have to do my clothes, Iris," Jo said as she walked over to me.

"No, no, it's fine. I don't mind at all, seriously."

Jo frowned, "Are you sure? You really don't have to."

"Yes, I'm sure. I'm doing wash regardless, so it only makes sense."

Jo smiled, "Thanks, I'll do them next time." She walked back over to her vanity.

I chuckled, "Don't worry about it, Jo, seriously. I'll be back."

After I put our clothes in the washing machine, Jo and I just hung out until my timer went off to put the clothes in the driver. This naturally only took a couple of minutes. So, I was done and headed back to our room relatively quickly.

I sighed as I entered our room and plopped down onto Jo's bed next to her. "I'm so tired."

"Me too," Jo said while she laid on her back with her eyes closed.

I closed mine just to rest but we all know how that goes.

Suddenly, it was now eight-thirty the next morning. I rubbed my eyes as I turned the lamp off that was accidentally left on overnight. I yawned as I looked over at Jo who also fell asleep. She was still sleeping, so I decided I would go make us coffee and grab our clothes out of the drying machine.

I got up, quietly changed into sweatpants and a normal-fitting long sleeve T-shirt and put my socks and shoes on. I then went to the laundry room, got our clothes, dropped them off at our room, then made my way to the kitchen. After getting our coffees, I walked back to our room, where Jo was now waking up.

"Good morning," Not a hand available, I used my foot to push the door closed, "Here, this is for you."

"Oh, awesome, thanks," she said as she sat up and took the coffee out of my hand. "This is just what I needed." She took her first sip.

I sat down on my bed, "You know we fell asleep last night."

"Yeah, I realized that when I woke up and saw the basket of clothes," she chuckled.

"Yeah," I chuckled lightly and sipped my coffee. I then pulled the basket of laundry to my bed and sat crisscrossed to fold the clothes. Jo reached over, set her coffee down on the nightstand, and then grabbed some clothes to fold as well.

"Want me to separate ours first or just fold them?" she asked.

"Uhm, I guess separate them. I think it may be easier that way," I replied.

"I was thinking the same thing," she said.

We started separating and folding clothes as we talked for a couple of minutes until Jo suddenly stopped.

"Iris? What's that?" she asked, fear dripping from her words.

"What?" I asked her.

"That mark on your arm?" her voice was serious and concerned.

I looked down at my wrist that was exposed. A habit I never broke; pushing my sleeves up when I did laundry, dishes, etc. I quickly pulled it back down.

"Nothing, nothing," I deflected.

"Iris, yes, it is," she said, seriousness laced with concern. She grabbed my arm and pushed up my sleeve. She looked up at me as her face crumbled, "Iris, is that a cigarette burn?"

I pushed her hand off and looked down. I swallowed hard then said, "No, it's a scar from when I was younger."

But that was a lie. It was a cigarette burn. A cigarette burn from Campbell. One night, when he was already in a bad mood, he saw me in the living room with one of the housemates. I was watching TV when the housemate—Shawn—came in and innocently joined me. Of course Campbell didn't see it that way. He asked if he could talk to me alone in our room. Knowing it was not going to end well, I began to shake as I followed. He lit a cigarette then started yelling at me, followed by him through things, followed by him shoving me. He called me cruel names and accused me of being disloyal. He pushed the hot end into my skin, burning me. It was dreadful.

I bet you'll think of this the next time you want to be a whore.

I closed my eyes, swallowing.

No matter what you do, no one will ever believe you.

"What else scars like that, Iris?" Jo asked with agitation in her voice, ripping me from my thoughts. She knew I was lying.

"I burned myself on the stove," it was a terrible lie, but I tried.

Jo scoffed as she stood up from her bed.

"Oh, come on. How would you get a *perfectly* circular burn from the stove in that spot on your wrist?" she questioned. "And anyway, it doesn't look years old, it still looks new."

I got up from my bed trying to evade this confrontation. "I don't know what to tell you, Jo. It's a scar from when I was younger, from my stove."

I approached the door while there was silence.

"You think I didn't notice the fading yellow on your eye when we met?"

I stooped, frozen in my tracks. *Ping.*

"You think I didn't notice the fading bruise on your neck?" she asked.

I turned around and stared at her intently, not saying a word.

"You think I haven't noticed how emotionless you always are, Iris? How *dismal* you are? You think I haven't noticed the things that make you jump or make you freeze? You think I don't know why you won't get changed in front of me? You think I *really* believed that the mark on your chest was a hickey the other day?" Jo asked with passion. "I've noticed it all. I've noticed everything."

She spoke with a plea in her voice, she wanted to help me. She wanted me to let her in. But I just stood there, staring at her, starting to pant.

No matter what you do, no one will ever believe you.

All the dark, ugly secrets that I fought so hard to keep inside were breaking their way out. It was too much. I couldn't handle it.

Breathe, Iris. Please.

Before Jo could say anything else, I snatched up my purse and jacket and rushed out of our room.

"Iris!" Jo yelled as I fled down the hall to the staircase.

I ignored her as I began to run. I ran out of the house, down the driveway, down the sidewalk, all the way to the bus stop, where I finally ceased, collapsing to my knees.

Then, I screamed. I screamed loud enough to scare the birds. Loud enough to scurry off the squirrels. Loud enough to drown out the dog barking nearby. Loud enough to cease car engines. Loud enough to silence the chainsaw being used to cut up a fallen tree. Loud enough to ricochet off the houses, shoot into the sky, pierce the ozone layer, and crash into outer space.

And then, only when my throat was ripped raw and my vocal cords snapped did I cry.

61

Chapter 61

Pulling my knees to my chest, I finally exhausted myself. I sniffled, hiccuped, and caught my breath, beginning to calm down. I looked around and saw no one, hardly anything. No cars, no people, no noise, it was just me. I pulled my coat from the ground next to me, onto my body. I then dragged my purse to me and pulled out my cigarettes. I leaned against the bench while I lit the cigarette. As I inhaled, tranquility washed over me and I exhaled, finally being able to breathe. Inhale, exhale, repeat. Inhale, exhale, repeat. I watched the smoke dance into the sky.

After I finished my cigarette, I pulled out my phone from my purse and was met with about a dozen phone calls and two dozen texts from Jo. I locked my phone without bothering to respond or really even read them. I *just* needed to be alone.

About ten minutes later, the bus pulled up. I stood up and approached the door. I walked up the three steps the bus had and stuffed my two dollars into the farebox. The lady stared at me, hard. I don't blame her, I looked disgusting. My hair was a mess, my makeup was half worn off, half smudged across my face, my breath probably stunk, I hadn't showered…I was gross.

"You okay, baby?" the middle-aged White woman asked me.

I stared at her for a moment, expressionless. "Yeah, I'm fine."

She nodded her head reluctantly as I walked by and sat down towards the back.

Surprisingly there were about five or six other passengers on the bus. They didn't pay me any mind and I didn't pay them any mind either. I just slumped down in my seat and gazed out the window. We began to move down the road, and I watched everything pass by. I watched little snowflakes begin to fall from the sky and kiss the ground. The more I watched, the more therapeutic it became. It was almost the same feeling I had that night outside with the moon. I smiled slightly as I closed my eyes.

I stayed on that bus for almost two hours, not caring where it took me. Eventually though, I had to get off at the last stop which was at the very bottom of Boston. It was called Lansdale. I got off at Claymont Park Avenue at Benton Square. It was a suburban area, a little run down, but nothing like back home in Chicago. I took out my phone to check the time, it was eleven-thirty. I scrolled through all the messages Jo had sent me and sighed. They mostly were asking if I was okay and where I was. I sighed again as I decided I had to text her back, it was only right.

Got on the bus, wanted to be alone, I hit send. *Love you...*I sent a second message.

A couple of seconds later she wrote back: *Alright, call if you need me. Please be safe...love you too.*

I read the message then locked my phone. I looked up and exhaled, I was hungry. As I looked around, I saw there was a Dunkin' Donuts right across the street. I put my phone in my purse then crossed the road.

I entered the store and ordered a large black coffee and a bacon, egg, and cheese on a croissant. I took my food outside and ate it while I passed several homes. It was cold but it wasn't snowing like northern Boston was, so that was good.

I walked a couple more minutes until I reached a Mobil. I had to use the bathroom so I decided I would go in.

I entered the Mobil and went into the bathroom. It was a typical gas station bathroom, dirty and run-down. That stuff never bothered me too much though. I flushed the toilet and began washing my hands. As I did, I pushed up my sleeve and ran my fingers over the cigarette burn that caused all this. I stared at it for a moment then sighed, turning off the water. Finished with drying my hands, I balled up the paper towels, tossed them, and walked out of the bathroom.

When I did, I saw a girl, about fourteen, and her, I assume, little sister, about six, at the register. The older girl was helping the younger girl make sure she had the right amount of money to pay for the things they were buying. It made me smile as I headed for the door. They reminded me so much of Leannah and me. We used to go down to the corner store all the time and I would do the same thing for her; make sure she had enough money, was counting it right, things like that. I taught her how to save. I remember her stashing every dollar she got in a cute little purse that Colton gave her. I cherish those kinds of memories.

I put my hand on the door to push it open but before I did, I looked back at the little girl who was looking at me and smiling. Big, toothless, innocent. I smiled back then exited the store.

The more I walked, the more my head became clearer. I started to think about—well, everything. The good in my life, the bad, I thought about my family and Jo and how she was the greatest friend I ever had. I just thought about it all. I walked several more miles. Actually I walked for two hours since I left the bus stop. I had made my way all the way back up to Alton Street. It was now almost one-thirty.

Deciding I should go back, I got on the bus and made my way to the bus stop near Kalista's. As I began to walk the short distance to her house, I realized I would soon have to face the music. Not a fiber in me wanted to. I don't even think I had the emotional bandwidth to do so, however, my other option was to keep aimlessly wandering around Boston. Not a terrible idea but it had grown colder and the snow was intensifying.

About ten minutes later I was at Kalista's house. I walked up the cobblestone driveway and made my way inside. I didn't want to be there but I walked through the hall, up the stairs, and to our room. I opened the door and to my surprise, it was empty. I threw down my bag, took my coat off, and laid on my bed.

As I did, I picked up the white Bic lighter that sat on my nightstand and started to flick it. In some weird way, the little, tiny fire that danced before my eyes was always so comforting and calming to me. My eyes soon began to feel like paperweights, and I drifted off to sleep.

62

Chapter 62

I squinted my eyes as the light from the lamp felt like the sun. Once my eyes adjusted, I reached for my phone on the nightstand and checked the time. I couldn't believe it was almost nine p.m. I was asleep for five hours. Putting my phone back down, I rolled onto my back. I scrubbed my face, running a hand through my hair as I heard the doorknob twist and Jo walked in.

"Oh, hey, you're up," she said. "I came in earlier and saw you were here, but I didn't want to wake you. I thought you'd be up by now though."

"Yeah, thanks, I just did." I sat up, pushed the covers off me, and put my feet on the floor.

Jo sighed and approached me, "Look, Iris, we gotta talk about earlier."

"No, no, we don't." I stood up and walked past her. I grabbed my towel from the back of my chair and proceeded to the bathroom to take a shower.

"Iris, you're not okay and I can tell. Just let me in, I'm here for you," Jo pleaded.

"Jo, I'm fine," I lied as I approached the bathroom door, my back facing towards Jo.

There was a beat of silence as I reached the door and grabbed the handle.

"When I was twelve, my dad had a friend named Ian," Jo spoke earnestly.

I paused in my tracks, still holding the doorknob. *Ping.*

"He was a really nice guy in the beginning. My dad met him at a car show. They got close quickly. They went to car shows together, auctions, the bar, he even took on an uncle roll for me since I never had one. He always bought me gifts and picked me up from school, friends' houses, and any appointment if my dad couldn't. No one ever suspected him to be a bad guy, ever."

I stared hard at the door listening to her words knowing exactly where they were going to lead. *Ping, ping.*

"But when I was fourteen, things changed. I'd catch Ian in my room "putting away my clothes" and he started to make me feel uncomfortable by the way he'd look at me or how close he would stay to me. He started offering to pick me up from school more often so that my dad wouldn't have to or so that I wouldn't have to take the bus. I never said anything to my dad because I thought it was all in my head. I thought I was making a good person out to be someone they weren't. But God I wish I never thought that. I wish I told my dad because he would have stopped it all."

My eyes were now burning a hole into the wooden door from how hard I stared. My eyes welled up with tears as she spoke, I turned my head slightly towards her.

"He started with little things. Like he'd pat me on the back or give me one too many hugs. On the rides home from school, he'd ask how my day was and when I told him it was good, he'd pat my thigh and say things like, 'That's awesome, kiddo' or 'Good, I'm glad, sweetheart,' but he never would take his hand off my thigh. He'd just leave it there and I began to dread the end of school every single day. I started to hate when he'd come over, and…I don't know…I still just never said anything to my dad or anyone for that matter."

Jo took a deep breath.

"One night when I was fourteen, my dad was running late at work. I was in my bed, sleeping when I woke up to a noise. It was the front door opening and closing. I didn't think anything of it because I figured it was just my dad coming home. So, I closed my eyes and began to try to go back to sleep. But…it didn't take me long to realize the footsteps moving around downstairs weren't my dad's. Even though I knew they weren't his, they didn't sound completely foreign. I listened more and that's when I recognized them to be Ian's. I was really confused because although Ian and my dad were close, he didn't have a key to our house. And he *never* was there that late, especially when my dad wasn't home. I continued to try to come up with an explanation when I heard footsteps climb the stairs. It wasn't long until Ian cracked open my bedroom door. I snapped my eyes shut, pretending I was sleeping. I figured this would make him go away, but it didn't. He crept over to my bed and sat down, beginning to stroke my hair. I clenched my jaw and tried not to move a muscle, still hoping he would just leave. Well"—Jo took a deep breath—"a moment later, he leaned down and kissed me."

Ping, ping, ping. My eyebrows were squeezed together so tight as disgust and sadness rushed into my cells.

"I shoved him, which caught him off guard, and I jumped out of my bed. I backed towards the wall as I mustered up all my courage to scream at him to leave. He tried to be all sweet and say he was 'just playing' but I held my ground, although on the inside, I was trembling with fear. I screamed at him once again to leave but this time, he yelled at me to be quiet. I stood frozen for a moment until my flight senses kicked in and I tried to take off for the door. But I wasn't quick enough, and he grabbed me, putting his hand over my mouth. I tried to fight him, I tried to kick and scream and bite his hand, but no one was there to help me."

Tears began to roll down my face. I looked back at her and then turned to face her.

"He pinned me down on the floor and began to kiss me. I kicked at him and tried to wiggle myself free, but he held me still. It uh"—telling the story became more difficult for Jo—"it didn't take much for him to uh…win…if you know what I…uh, mean."

I stared at her pensively as the tears continued to flow freely from my eyes.

"As it was happening, I heard my front door open again and this time, I knew it was my dad. I somehow managed to pull up my leg and kicked Ian in the stomach as hard as I could. This caused him to, uh…take himself…uh, pull himself out—pull away from me, and reach for his stomach.

"At that time, I screamed for my dad as I pulled my pajama pants back up and scurried away from Ian. I heard my dad yell my name followed by the sound of his footsteps barreling up the stairs. My dad swung open my door and when he did, he saw Ian with his pants down. He knew what happened. It didn't take a genius to figure it out. A look crossed my dad's face I had *never* seen before. It was the worst form of sadness, hate, betrayal, wrath, and resentment all at once. He charged at Ian and slammed him into the side of my bed. My dad screamed at me to go downstairs and call the police. I did as I was told, and I remember hearing my dad repeatedly punch and kick Ian followed by Ian's moans and cries of pain. I remember crying to the nine-one-one operator and how kind and gentle her voice was. Chaos never ended upstairs until the police got there about five minutes later. They had to drag my dad off Ian, who was barely alive at that point. They never charged my dad with anything though, thankfully. We went through the whole court process, which was terrible and traumatizing in and of itself but Ian was sentenced to seventy-five years in prison so he'll rot and die in there like he should."

Jo took a deep breath. I stared at her absolutely speechless. Tears cascaded down my face, a dam that had burst free.

"Life got pretty hard after that. I dealt with a lot of issues from that assault and when I was sixteen, I uh…I"—Jo's words began to slow down as she struggled to get out what she wanted to say—"I tried to take my life. I just wanted to be with my mom. Whenever I was hurt or sad or angry or anything, my mom had this special way of making anything and everything better. It's like, no matter what was wrong in my life, if my mom knew, it would all disappear, and the pain would go away. So, I figured if life was so terrible and she wasn't here to make it better, then maybe if I went to her, it *would* be better. Maybe if I went to her, she *could* make it better.

"So…one day after school, when my dad was at work, I took an entire bottle of Tylenol and washed them all down with some vodka. I know I told you the story about me hitting rock bottom and quitting drinking, well, that wasn't the last time. It was for a couple weeks but this was *actually* the last time. And that's the *real* reason I don't drink anymore. Because I tried to kill myself with it, nothing else. I just laid on the bathroom floor crying. I started to feel terrible and then I blacked out. The next thing I remember was waking up in the hospital with my dad crying and holding my hand. They had pumped my stomach. They said I was lucky to be alive. It was right there in that moment, seeing the pure sadness on my dad's face, that I knew I had done the worst thing I possibly could ever do to him. I mean how could I have been so selfish? The love of his life died in a terrorist attack, and he just almost lost his sixteen-year-old daughter to suicide after walking in on his best friend raping her. How could

I have almost left my dad here all alone?"

This was the first time that Jo's voice wavered and her eyes saturated.

My tears never halted. "Jo, I—"

"Iris, I'm not telling you this to make you feel sorry for me or make you tell me what you're dealing with," she said. "I'm telling you this because I see my fourteen, fifteen, sixteen, year-old self in you right now. I was distant from others. I held everything in. I was depressed. I had whittled away to nothing and that's when I thought there was nothing else for me. That's when I truly believed that being dead was going to fix my issues, not realizing it would only create them for the people I loved most. I can't tell you how glad I am that my dad found me because I wouldn't be here right now if he didn't."

There was a slight pause.

"I can see what you're going through, Iris. And know that I can relate. And that I'm *always, always* here," Jo blinked and the tears finally ran down her face. "Iris, I just don't want you to whittle away…please, please don't whittle away."

Her voice cracked as she said that final sentence. That was the sentence that broke me. *Please don't whittle away.* And that's exactly what I was doing.

I grabbed a hold of Jo, hanging onto her like the lifebuoy I needed. I held onto her as the tears ran marathons down my cheeks. I sobbed, ugly crying in a way I didn't think was possible. And Jo held me tight, never faltering, absorbing all my pain so that for just a moment, it was lighter for me to carry.

63

Chapter 63

I told Jo about Campbell. I told her everything. Everything from the day he first walked into room ninety-three to the day I looked at him for the last time through the taxicab window. I told her about the home fries, the kiss in the rain, and Devil's Tower. I told her about October seventh, Halloween, and the scar. I told her everything, leaving not a detail to spare. Once I started, there was no stopping it and I word-vomited until I heaved, completely empty.

She listened to me. Every word I spoke she heard at one hundred percent volume, soaking them up like a sponge. Never smiling at the good parts or wincing at the bad ones. She kept her eyes locked with mine, never looking away. She was there. She was present. Just like she said she would be. I felt lighter, clearer, free*er*. Jo, she believed me.

It was the next day; Sunday, December first. Kalista, while she still drank, hadn't disappeared again. I kept her at arms reach; not cutting her out completely but not letting my guard down either.

Jo and I were in the kitchen cleaning up from breakfast when Kalista came in and asked if we wanted to go to the grocery store for her. We agreed as we had nothing else better to do.

"Great, thank you! So here's the list," she handed Jo a piece of paper. "And here's my credit card to pay for the groceries and the fare for the cab." She handed me her card and some cash. "Just go to the Whole Foods on Brecknock Street, it's about ten minutes from here, so forty dollars should be enough to get you there and back."

"Sounds good," Jo said.

While we waited outside for the cab, Jo lit up a cigarette. She gazed at the list as her cheeks sucked in, taking a puff.

"Damn, this list is long," she said, exhaling smoke.

"Let me see," I took the list from her. "Shit."

Jo snickered as she took another hit. "Want some?" she asked, holding up her hand that held her cigarette.

"Oh, nah." I said, a small smile creeping onto my face. "I'm okay."

Jo smiled and we began talking about the irony and well— idioticness of Kalista giving us her credit card. Not that Jo or I were going to use it for any other reason than the one she gave it to us for, but you'd think you wouldn't hand something like that over to two practically strangers that are in a program for the poor. We laughed and for the first time in a while, it didn't feel forced.

Soon enough, the cab arrived and took us to the Whole Foods where we entered inside.

"Okay, well first thing's first. I know we'll need a cart," Jo said as she pulled one out of the cluster.

"This grocery store screams rich," I said, looking up and around.

Jo chuckled. "Right? I'm used to Save A Lot or Walmart."

I snickered, "Same."

We began to walk.

"I've never seen a Whole Foods. I've heard of them but never been to one till now. They don't have that in Springfield. I think the closest one is like almost two hours away," Jo said.

"Oh, wow."

Jo then stopped walking as she exhaled, consulting the list as to where to start first. "Well, she needs…well, everything."

I took the list from her, looked it over, then gave it back. "Let's start with the non-cold items," I suggested. "She needs ketchup and stuff like that so let's go to that aisle."

"Sounds good," Jo said, pushing the cart forward.

It wasn't particularly crowded or busy. I assumed this was because it was somewhat early; ten forty-five. I also assumed that since Thanksgiving was a couple days ago, people didn't really need anything at the grocery store.

We made it to the condiment's aisle, and got the required ketchup, mustard, mayo, hot sauce, and teriyaki sauce. After those were in the cart, we headed to aisle fourteen where the boxed pastas would be. We got those then carried on shopping, collecting all the items that Kalista needed.

By the time we had everything that was on the list, the cart was basically filled to the brim.

"Alright, I think we got everything," Jo said as she looked over the list.

"Yeah, I think so," I said. "Let's go to register seven, there's only one person in line."

"Okay, cool."

Jo pushed the cart with me following behind. We stood in line and waited until we could put our items on the belt.

"Damn it's already almost twelve-thirty," Jo said as she looked down at her phone.

"Is it really?" I questioned not knowing we had been in the grocery store for almost two hours.

"Yeah," Jo said with a chuckle, still looking down at her phone. She couldn't believe how long it had been either. "Look at this picture my dad just sent me," Jo smiled as she turned the phone towards me.

It was a picture of her when she was younger in a long dirty blonde wig, wearing a colorful and glittery outfit, holding a microphone. A man was standing next to her and had on a mullet wig, a fake mustache, and a bandana. They both were standing back-to-back making funny faces.

"That's my dad and I on Halloween six years ago," she laughed. "I loved *Hannah Montana* when I was younger, so I dressed up like her, and my dad dressed up like her dad."

"Oh my God," I laughed as I took the phone from her and inspected the picture closer. "Look at you guys! That's hysterical," I smiled as I handed her back the phone.

Jo looked at the photo, smiling ruefully, "Yeah, I was twelve. I never really had a lot of friends, so I didn't usually have someone to dress up with. But my dad always dressed up with me if I wanted him to. He didn't care if he was a badass biker one year and a Disney Princess the next. As long as I was happy, that's all that he cared about," she locked her phone and put it in her coat pocket.

I smiled, "He sounds like an amazing guy, Jo."

"Yeah, he totally is. He'll do anything for me."

I smiled and we moved up in line and were now able to start putting our items on the belt.

"Friends are overrated anyway," I put cans of soup onto the belt. "Family's forever."

Jo smiled, genuinely this time, putting frozen meats on the belt, "Yeah, you're right. Except you, at least."

I smiled, finally genuine as well.

Chapter 64

We got back to Kalista's, and she had some of the housemates bring in the bags as she began to put everything away in her cabinets. She offered to make us lunch, but Jo and I declined as neither of us were hungry.

"Hey, my mom texted me wanting me to call her today. I'm gonna go do that. I'll be up once I'm done," I said to Jo as we walked to the stairwell.

"Okay, yeah, no worries."

I smiled and proceeded back outside as Jo headed upstairs to our room and I dialed my mom's number.

"Hey, baby," my mom said through the phone. "How're you doing?"

"Good, how are you?"

"I'm good too. Whatcha been up to?"

"Oh, nothing much. Jo and I just got back from the grocery store. We picked up some things for our host. Well, more like a *lot* of things."

My mom chuckled, "Oh, yeah? It was a lot of stuff?"

"Mom, the total was almost six hundred dollars." When the cashier told me that I almost melted into a puddle on the floor. I think the only reason I didn't was because I remembered it was Kalista's money, not mine.

"Six hundred dollars?!" my mom exclaimed. "Where the hell did you two go?"

"She sent us to Whole Foods. You know, that really expensive place?"

"Oh my God," my mom laughed. "That's why."

"Yeah, it was crazy."

"Oh, look who it is," my mom teased, obviously talking to someone else. "Y'all are just in time, your sister's on the phone."

There was a pause and indistinct chatter in the background.

"Leannah and Colton just walked in," my mom said to me. "You're on speaker now, baby."

"Hey, Iris!" they both yelled.

"Hey, Le. Hey, Colton. How are you guys?" I asked.

"We're good," Leannah said. "We went down to the Dollar General and got stuff to make s'mores and hot chocolate."

"S'mores?" I questioned with confusion, knowing we didn't have a fire pit or fireplace to roast them. "Where are you gonna make s'mores?"

They both laughed.

"On the stove," Leannah said.

I laughed, "That's pretty fucking smart. Damn, now you guys got me wanting s'mores!"

"We can make them again when you're back home," Colton said with a chuckle.

I laughed, "I'll have to take you up on that."

"Iris, they're getting more and more creative each day you're gone," my mom laughed.

"Ma, don't you complain you got s'mores coming up!"

"Oh, I know, and I'm excited for them!"

I laughed, shaking my head, "Well, I'll let you guys go have your s'mores fun. I'm gonna go see what Jo wants to do now."

"Alright, baby. I love you and we'll talk to you soon," my mom said.

"Love you, Iris," Leannah chimed in.

"I love you guys too, talk to you all soon," I said.

"Mom, can I see the phone?" I heard Colton ask. "I wanna ask Iris something."

"What's up, Colton?" I asked as I heard him go outside.

"You seem pretty happy today compared to recently. What's up?" he asked.

"What? I can't be happy?" I teased. "Just kidding. You know, Colton, I was gonna tell you, just have been busy this morning but I told Jo about Campbell."

"Oh really?" he asked. "How'd that happen?"

"It's actually a long story…"

I then proceeded to tell him everything that occurred yesterday. I told him how Jo saw the mark on my wrist, and how I lied about how it happened. I told him about the confrontation and how she's noticed other things. I told him how I ran away and spent the day in southern Boston. I told him about getting home, falling asleep, then Jo wanting to talk more once I was awake. I told him how Jo shared a really personal story with me and how she tried to take her life because of it. And I told him how, with her doing all that, something broke loose inside of me and I was finally able to vocalize the words I couldn't before. I could tell her. And by doing so, the weight I carried for weeks had dissipated.

"Oh, wow," Colton was taken aback. There was so much for him to take in. "I'm so happy to hear that, Sis. I'm proud of you."

I smiled, "Thanks, Colton."

"I know talking with her is probably a hundred times easier than talking to me," he chuckled softly. "I know I can be overbearing sometimes, and I will never understand like Jo does, being a female and having a similar situation, but I try my best and I always will. You always have me, Iris. "

"Thanks, Colton. I appreciate that and I know I always have you, and you always have me. And you're not as overbearing as you think, so don't be so hard on yourself."

"Thanks, Sis." After a beat, "So uh, what mark was she talking about?"

I quietly exhaled as I looked down, "It's a uh, a…uh, a cigarette…uh, burn."

There was a pause. I swear I could feel Colton's rage penetrate through the phone. I could feel his chest rising, heart pumping, eyes flickering. He tamed it though, somehow. If he wasn't using my mom's phone, he'd probably break it in half.

"How uh, how did that happen?" he asked through a swallow.

Breathe, Iris.

"He smokes, as you know and uh, one night, he saw me downstairs watching TV with another housemate. He thought something was up, nothing was. But that didn't stop him from yelling at me and then uh…yeah." Those words I still couldn't manage a way out.

There was another pause. I'm sure a silent scream from Colton.

"I'm so glad you're out of that fucking house," Colton said, venom in his voice.

My eyes swelled and I bit my lip hard to keep from crying. *Breathe, Iris, breathe.* "Me too."

I heard him exhale, letting the fury escape. "I love you, Sis. You know there's nothing I wouldn't do for you. You call me anytime you need to talk or need anything."

"Thank you, I will. I love you, Colton." My voice began to waver, "I miss you."

"I miss you too, kid," Colton said playfully, trying to enlighten the mood. "I love you more and I'll talk to you soon, 'kay?"

"For sure, bye." I squeaked, ending the call.

I hung up the phone and squeezed it hard, beginning to shake. Holding in a scream, I felt emotions push their way to the surface.

Breathe, Iris, breathe.

No matter what you do, no one will ever believe you.

Breathe, Iris. Please, breathe.

Remember, nobody will ever love you like I will.

No.

Stop.

Breathe, Iris, breathe.

Please.

I love you, Sis. You know there's nothing I wouldn't do for you.

My grip loosened.

I love you, Sis.

The shaking stopped.

I love you, Sis.

The scream dissipated.

I love you, Sis.

The emotions finally laid to rest.

I love you, Sis.

65

Chapter 65

Life was pretty normal for the few days that followed. Jo and I found our own fun by walking around the city of Boston (which was beautifully decorated for Christmas that was quickly approaching), walking around various malls, doing little errands for Kalista to keep us busy, and playing board and card games. But they always say good things must end, and Friday, December sixth was the start of that.

It was early and Jo and I were hungry. So, we slipped on pajama pants, slippers, and made our way to the kitchen. When we got there, we saw a couple of our housemates looking in the fridge and cabinets.

"That's not a good sign," I said.

"What?" Jo asked.

"Look," I pointed to all the people scrounging for food.

"Oh shit," Jo said in realization. After a beat, her voice fell, "Kalista isn't here, is she?"

I looked at everyone lost in their search, then looked down, "Guess not."

There was a slight pause.

"Well, we don't know that yet," Jo rationalized, trying to be optimistic. "Maybe she's still asleep or went to the store to get stuff to make for breakfast."

"Yeah maybe."

"Let's just see if there's anything to eat," Jo said.

"Alright."

The two of us walked over to the pantry and began looking. A few minutes of searching passed, and we came up with not one single thing. We made our way through some people and got to the fridge.

"There's nothing in there," Asher said with annoyance.

We both looked at him.

"Unless you want leftover pizza for breakfast," he then added.

"There's *nothing* in there?" Jo asked, as she opened the fridge door, not fully believing him.

"Well, there is—" Asher said, "but it's just random shit. Condiments, drinks, the pizza, some vegetables—"

Jo sighed and closed the fridge door after she witnessed exactly what Asher was talking about.

"Is Kalista home?" I asked.

"Uh, I'm not really sure. She might be. I just got up," he responded.

"Let's go see," Jo said as she grabbed my arm.

We went up the stairs and proceeded to Kalista's room. The big wooden doors were shut. As we knocked, the door crept open. Jo and I looked at one another. The lights inside were off.

"Kalista?" Jo asked as she slowly pushed the door open.

There was no response.

"Should we go in?" I asked.

Jo shrugged, "I guess," she replied unsurely.

Jo pushed the door open further, "Kalista?"

We stepped inside her room, and I turned on the light. We began to look around and could now tell Kalista was *definitely* not home.

Her bed was made, her purse and phone were nowhere to be found, and the biggest give away, a bright orange suitcase I noticed before, was gone.

"Kalista left again," I said, matter of factly.

"Well, maybe she'll be back tonight. Maybe she's not "gone, gone,"" Jo said.

"The orange suitcase is gone. She's "gone, gone," Jo," I said with finger quotes.

"What orange suitcase?" she asked.

"I came in here the other day to give Kalista her credit card back. There was this ugly, bright orange suitcase against that wall," I pointed to the opposing wall. "Now, it's not."

Jo sighed knowingly in defeat.

"She's on a bender again," I said.

Jo shook her head. "Don't worry, we'll figure it out."

"I don't know, Jo," I shook my head. "I don't have any money to eat. She's supposed to be here."

"I know," Jo looked down. "Let's just go to Dunkin' and go from there, okay?"

"Yeah, alright," I said.

We arrived at the Dunkin' and ordered our food. As we ate, we decided we'd count our money when we were done to see how much we were working with. Kalista wasn't gone for long the last time but if I knew anything about a bender, it's that they can last for longer than three days. *Way* longer.

We finished our breakfast and then pulled out our wallets.

Jo began to count her money, "Twenty, twenty-five, thirty, thirty-five, forty, forty-one, two, three"—she began to count out her change—"and eighty-seven cents."

"Five, ten, fifteen, sixteen, seventeen, eighteen, and twenty-five, fifty, one, two, three," I said as I counted my change. "I have eighteen dollars and fifty-three cents."

"Well, we have sixty-two, forty combined," Jo said. "We can stretch that."

I sighed, "I really hope Kalista comes back because I don't know what we'll do when that money runs out, Jo."

Jo looked at me with distress.

"I mean, I can't ask my family. The whole reason I came here is for them to save up money," I added.

"Yeah, same," Jo said looking down.

"We'll figure it out," I said seconds later, trying to keep both of our spirits alive.

"Yeah," Jo said, trying to be optimistic.

At this point, I had no idea how involved and serious this would turn out to be. Never in a *million* years would I have guessed how detrimental it would turn. But it did, and Jo and I did everything we could to stay afloat. I guess when life turns into a game of survival, you'll do anything to win.

66

Chapter 66

Three days had passed, and it was now Monday, December ninth. In those three days, there was still no Kalista. Jo and I tried to save as much money as we could—not knowing when she'd return—but it was hard given the circumstances. We ate leftover pizza, canned soup we found in the back of the pantry, and a lot of Top Ramen from the Dollar Tree.

It was around three-thirty when Jo and I were sitting on our beds feeling hopeless.

"Alright," I said, jumping up. "We have to do something to try to get Kalista to come back."

Jo stood up, "What are you thinking?"

"I don't know. But I know someone here *has* got to have her phone number. I mean, there's twenty-three people in this house."

"Alright, well, let's go ask around," Jo said.

We left our room and went to the room directly next to ours. We knocked and waited for a response.

"Yeah?" Jasmine—a light-skinned Black girl—said as she opened the door.

"Do you have Kalista's phone number?" Jo asked.

"No," Jasmine said in despair. "I'm trying to find her too."

"Do you know anyone that may have it?" I asked.

"I don't, no," she said. "But if you hear anything about her, let me know?"

"Will do," Jo said.

Jasmine smiled then closed the door.

Jo and I then proceeded to the next room. We knocked again and waited once more.

"Hey, what's up?" Asher asked as he opened the door.

"Hey, do you have Kalista's number by chance?" I asked. "Jo and I are trying to get a hold of her."

"Hey, Iris. Hey, Jo," Ben, his roommate asked as he now approached the door.

"Nah, I don't," Asher said.

"Do you?" Jo asked Ben.

He shook his head, "Nope."

I sighed, "Alright, thanks."

"What, are you guys trying to call her or something?" Ben asked.

"Yeah," Jo said. "She's been gone for three days now, and she needs to get her ass back here before there's literally only ketchup and stale chips left."

Ben laughed, "Yeah, we've been eating Chinese food and Top Ramen like it's nobody's business."

I cracked a smile, but I was still in despair.

"Well, let us know if you hear anything or somehow get her number," I said as I turned away to go to the next room.

"Will do," Asher said.

I walked away and Jo followed behind. We then stopped at the next room, and I knocked. There was no answer. Jo then tried knocking, there was still no answer.

"They're probably not in there. Let's just go to the next room," I said.

We went around to all the rooms on our floor and had the same luck as the rooms we tried before. We headed upstairs to see if our luck would be any better there. It wasn't. We got the same answer as before: no one had Kalista's number. We came to the end of the hall and knocked on the door. It opened and to our surprise, Carter answered. We didn't know where their room was before this moment.

I took a step back. *Ping.*

Breathe, Iris, breathe.

Noticing my unease, Carter smirked, "What do you guys want?"

Jo scoffed, "Not jack shit from you," she then turned away.

I followed behind; classic new Iris—tail between her legs.

"I heard you guys are looking for Kalista's phone number," Carter said, crossing his arms and leaning against the doorframe.

Jo turned around, "And why do you think that?"

"Trevor texted me saying you two were walking around asking everybody if they had her number," he then laughed, "Pretty fucking pathetic."

Jo narrowed her eyes, "Do you have a better idea?"

"Yeah—not worrying about it."

Jo scoffed, "That'll get you real far."

He shrugged, "You guys are making this a big deal."

It's not that fucking serious. You're making this such a big deal.

I swallowed, heart picking up its pace.

Breathe, Iris, please.

Jo looked at me. A knowing look crossed her face. She turned to Carter, "Whatever." She then looped her arm through mine and ushered us down the hallway.

"Thank you," I said after a moment.

Jo smiled then pulled away to meet my eyes. "Let's go see if anyone else has Kalista's number. Can't let that jackass stop us."

A small smirk formed, "Alright."

The day passed on and we asked every person in the house if they had Kalista's number. To which they all answered with no. We even tried looking through all the papers the program had given us *and* Google to see if there was some kind of number to report a host. Again, there was nothing.

"So now what?' Jo asked as we stood outside and she lit up a cigarette, exhaling the smoke.

"I'm not sure," I said. "I guess we should wait a couple more days and if she doesn't come back by then, we could try to get a job?"

Jo exhaled more smoke, "That's not a bad idea." Jo held out the cigarette, nudging me with her eyes to see I wanted a drag.

"Sure, thanks," I said as I took the cigarette from her and pulled on it.

"Do you think someone will hire us?" I asked. "You know, with probably not being here long."

"Christmas is coming up, I'm sure *plenty* of places need extra seasonal help," Jo said.

"Yeah, you're right. That's a good point," I took another pull on the cigarette.

"Let's just see if she comes back in a couple of days. It's Monday, maybe she just left for the weekend and will be back tomorrow or Wednesday," Jo said.

I blew out smoke and handed her back the cigarette, "Alright."

67

Chapter 67

Four days passed, it was now Friday, December thirteenth. The more days that passed by, the more hopeless Jo and I grew. It had been a week at this point since Kalista first left. No one had heard from here, seen here, or knew where she went. Although, we all assumed it was the same place she disappeared off to last time.

With our initial food supply from the Dollar Tree dwindling, we had no choice but to get more. Although we really didn't want to as we only had forty-one dollars between the two of us left.

"Okay," Jo sighed as we entered the Dollar Tree. "What do we wanna get?"

I shrugged. "I guess just the most food we can for the littlest amount"

"Alright."

I grabbed a basket sitting next to us and we proceeded down the aisles and towards the back of the store where the food items were. Jo went to the cold stuff while I hit the dry items.

I put three packs of the Top Ramen six packs into our baskets then moved to the aisle with the soups. I began grabbing a variety and putting them into our basket. I froze once my eyes landed on the

353

red and white can in my hand.

Campbell's Chicken Noodle Soup.

Ping. I dropped the can like it was acid burning my skin.

Breathe, Iris, breathe.

I swallowed.

It's a stupid can of soup, Iris, stop it.

I bent down and picked up the can. My eyes lingered on *Campbell's.*

I'll see you again, someday.

Stop it.

You're mine, remember?

Please.

Nothing's changing between you and I, Iris. Got it?

I'm begging you.

Remember, nobody will ever love you like I will.

STOP IT.

Breathe, Iris, breathe.

I promise, I'll fucking kill you, Iris. I will fucking kill you.

"STOP IT!"

I threw the can with force down the aisle.

"Iris?" Jo asked, rounding the corner. "Iris!" She ran to me. "Iris, are you okay?"

Tears clouded my vision as I breathed heavily.

"Iris?"

Breathe, Iris, breathe.

I love you, Sis.

You know there's nothing I wouldn't do for you.

"Iris? Are you okay?"

Just let me in, I'm here for you.

Please don't whittle away.

I snapped my head towards Jo, locking my eyes with hers.

"Iris?" her blue eyes shook with concern.

I blinked. Unaware of how saturated my eyes were, tears fell from both my eyes.

"I'm...I'm okay."

Breathe, Iris, breathe.

I took a deep breath, "I'm okay."

Jo latched onto me, pulling me into a tight hug, not letting go. I clutched her back just as hard.

I was okay.

Chapter 68

Jo and I stood in the kitchen making our Dollar Tree waffles. It was the next morning and even though the whole Soup Incident took place, we still bought a few things. We had twenty-eight dollars left and decided that today we'd go downtown and see who was hiring. I wasn't sure that someone would hire us due to being in this program but after some convincing from Jo (her saying we'd fill out the applications like normal and not tell them we were in The Stay program), I was in.

We ate our waffles and drank our coffee while we devised a plan to go to East Boston first as there were several stores we could try. With the one Walgreens being a seven minute walk, we decided to go there first.

The building was decorated with big red bows and silver snowflakes. As we walked inside, there was a Christmas tree set up with fake presents underneath it. There were also other little random Christmas decorations and several Christmas items in the front for sale.

"It looks nice in here," Jo said as she looked up and around.

"Can I help you ladies with something?" a forty-something-year-old White woman asked us. She had blonde shoulder length hair and was very petite.

"Oh, uh, yes," Jo said, turning towards the woman. "We're interested in getting a job here."

The woman smiled politely, "Oh that's very sweet, but we actually aren't hiring right now."

"You guys don't need any extra help?" I asked. "Not even with the holidays coming up?"

She shook her head disappointedly, "No, I'm sorry, we don't."

Jo and I looked at one another.

"Oh, okay. Well, thank you anyway," Jo said.

The woman smiled ruefully, "I'm sorry, guys. I hope you find something elsewhere."

"Thanks," I said.

We turned to exit the store and walked out of the automatic doors.

"Now what?" I asked.

Jo pulled out her phone and touched the screen several times, "CVS is on the street over, let's try there." She said then put her phone away and began walking.

I followed behind and within three minutes, we arrived at a shopping center that had about nine stores in it.

"Oh, great, it's a shopping center," I said. "If CVS doesn't want us, I'm sure one of these other places will."

"Exactly," Jo smiled, "Look, there's even a Marshall's. There's no way a clothing store wouldn't need extra help during Christmas time."

"For real. Should we try them first then?"

"Yeah, let's do that," Jo agreed.

We crossed the parking lot and headed inside of the Marshalls. It was *crowded.* The checkout line was miles long, the floor was flooded with people walking around, looking through clothing racks, and holding Christmas decorations.

"Holy shit, it's packed," Jo said as we looked around. "This is a good thing though. A busy place can always use more help."

"Right," I smiled. "Let's find a manager."

"Okay."

The two of us shuffled past several people. We slid through the crowd searching for an employee and within minutes, we found someone.

"Uhm, excuse me?" I asked the short Asian woman.

"Yes?"

"We're looking to work here. Is it possible that we could fill out an application?" I asked.

"Oh, sweetheart," she said in her native accent, "I just hired four new employees. I don't need any more."

"There's nothing you could use us for?" Jo asked desperately.

The woman shook her head.

"I mean, look how busy it is in here," I said, "I'm *sure* you could use our help. We're, we're reliable, and trustworthy—"

"Mhmm hmm," Jo agreed.

"And hard workers and—"

"Honey," the woman said, cutting me off. "I'm sorry, I just really don't need the help."

Disappointment washed over Jo and me.

"Alright, thank you anyway," I said dully.

The woman smiled then walked away.

I looked blankly at Jo.

"Come on, there's like eight other stores in this place that we can try," Jo said, being optimistic for the both of us.

"Alright," I said, trying to be optimistic as well.

We turned and walked back to the front of the store and then out of the same automatic doors that we came in from.

"Alright, should we try CVS now?" Jo asked.

"Well," I said as I looked at the several signs around us, "there's a Burger King, AutoZone, T-Mobile, CVS, and Shaw's. What do you think we have the best chance at?"

"Well, people are probably buying phones for Christmas from T-Mobile," Jo said. "Wanna try there before CVS?"

"Yeah, let's do that."

We walked two stores down and opened the black metal and glass doors and entered inside. The store was busy, but not jam packed.

"Hey, what brings you ladies in today?" a man with blonde hair and blue eyes wearing the black and pink T-Mobile shirt, asked us.

We told him we were looking for jobs but after telling him our ages, he told us we had to be at least twenty-one. Something about the company wanting employees that are closer to the age of the clientele. Whatever that means.

"Strike three," Jo said as we stood back outside. "I didn't think it'd be this hard."

"Yeah, me either," I added monotonously.

There was a slight moment of silence.

"Let's just try the CVS," Jo said.

"Alright."

We entered shortly after and went up to the cashier at the checkout counter. She was a small teenage girl with brunette hair. She paged someone by the name of Allison to the front and told us she'd be out momentarily. Within a minute, a Black woman with a head full of long braids, approached us.

"How can I help you?" she smiled.

"Hi, my name's Jolene and this is Iris. We were really hoping to get a job here. We're willing to do anything you may need us to."

I smiled and nodded my head in agreement.

"Oh, really?" Allison said, seeming pleased.

"Yes!" Jo said with more enthusiasm in her voice.

"Well, I can't promise that I'll need you guys once the holidays are over, but I could surely use the help now," Allison said.

Jo and I looked at each other and our faces lit up.

"That would be great, thank you!" I said.

Allison smiled, "No, thank *you*. Come on, let's go fill out some paperwork in the back."

She walked off and Jo and I followed her like two puppies after a bone.

We made it to the back of the store and Allison held the door open to her office for Jo and me to go into. We took our seats and Allison sat down at her spot.

"So, I'm Allison. I'm the store manager here," she said. "You said your name's Jolene, baby girl?" she asked as she looked at Jo.

"Yes, ma'am," Jo said.

"Okay, and you're Iris?" Allison asked as she now looked at me.

"Yup," I smiled.

"Really beautiful names. You guys' sisters?"

Jo and I looked at each other.

"No, just friends," I said.

"Oh, okay. I was gonna say you two don't look much alike to be sisters," Allison chuckled. "Okay, let's see here"—Allison leaned over in her seat and pulled open a filing cabinet drawer. She pulled out a Manilla folder and laid it in front of her.

"Here's the applications," she said as she opened the folders and handed one to Jo and one to myself. "Do you two ladies have your licenses on you?"

"Yeah, we do," I said as I picked my purse up from off the ground and took out my wallet.

Jo did the same and we both handed Allison our licenses.

She looked at them and made a confused face, "Illinois? Why do y'all's IDs say Illinois?"

I looked at Jo, unsure what to say.

"Uh, we're from there," Jo said. "But we just moved here. We just haven't gotten time to get Massachusetts licenses yet."

Allison's eyebrow shot up, "And where do you two live in Massachusetts?" I could tell she thought our story was BS.

"Boston," I said.

Allison narrowed her eyes at me, "I figured that. *Where* in Boston?"

"Uh, Miller Street?" I said.

"Uh, huh. Well, I'm going to need current Massachusetts licenses in order to hire you guys. I need proof of where you actually reside."

"We just told you, we live in Boston!" Jo said.

"And I said *proof*," Allsion sniped.

"It sounds like you just don't want to hire us," Jo said, crossing her arms.

"*Jo*," I said, shooting her a look.

If this was a year ago, I wouldn't be giving Jo daggers for her remark. I'd even be the one calling Allison out. That's who Iris used to be…

"I have every right to *not* hire you, thank you very much," Allsion said, rising to her feet, evident of this conversation being over.

"I think it's best you both take these and leave," she then added, handing us our licenses.

Jo stood up and took her license. I then did the same.

We left Allison's office without further words.

"Well, that blew over well. Where do you wanna try next?" Jo asked as we walked out from the CVS.

"Uhm," I looked around at the stores in the shopping center, "I guess the grocery store. I feel like it's a good chance they'd need help, with Chrtismas coming up and all."

"Alright, let's go."

Jo and I crossed the parking lot, soon entering through Shaw's automatic doors and proceeded to the customer service desk.

"Can I help you?" the Hispanic man asked from behind the desk.

"Uhm, yes. We're interested in working here. Could you get the manager or someone we could talk to about the hiring process?" Jo asked.

"Yep, give me one second," the man said as he got up from the stool he was sitting on and opened a door behind him. He then went into a separate room.

"What's our story this time when they ask for our ID?" Jo asked me quietly.

I shrugged, "Say the same thing? It's better to keep it consistent than to get all confused and jumbled up with several different stories."

"Okay, you're right, you're right," Jo said as she turned and looked out into the store.

It was busy, the lines were long and there were hundreds of people around.

"Hi, I'm Steven," a thirty-something-year-old man with dark hair and a beard said. He had a beer belly and was somewhat short.

I narrowed my eyes at his name. I thought about the Steven that Bianca met in Seattle.

"Hi," Jo said with a grin, "We're interested in working here. "Is there any way we could fill out an application?"

"Yeah, that'd be great! We could use the extra help!"

"Really?" I asked. "That would be wonderful."

"Yeah," he smiled. "Come on into the back and I can get you guys started on the application."

We exchanged names as we followed him to his office. We entered and took a seat on two plastic chairs. He handed us the applications and said he'd be back in a minute with another form for us to fill out—so far, so good. About three minutes later, Steven came back into the room and sat down.

"Okay, sorry about that. Here you guys go," he handed us the papers. "It's just a list of acceptable identification documents that you can provide to me."

Jo and I began to read the paper and I can't speak for her, but I know all the joy and feeling of like we were getting someplace, instantly vanished.

Under the title it read, *Employees may present one selection from List A or a combination of one selection from List B and one selection from List C.* I read all the forms of documentation in List A and realized I didn't have any of them. I began to look at List B, and while I had a driver's license, I didn't have anything from List C to combine with it.

Jo then looked at me with an expression that I knew meant she was in the same boat as I was.

"Uh," I said as I looked up at Steven.

"Yeah, what's wrong?" he asked.

"We only have driver's licenses," I looked at Jo. "We don't have anything else in List C to go with it."

"Oh, really?" he seemed disappointed.

"Yeah," I said dully.

"Are you able to bring your social security card or something else from List C, say, tomorrow?"

"Uh, we don't have them at all," Jo said.

He tilted his head at us, "I don't understand."

"I—" not having a reason to provide, I looked at Jo.

"We're from Illinois and recently moved to Massachusetts. I think they got lost or something because we haven't been able to find them since."

World's. Worst. Liars. Ever.

Steven frowned, "That's ironic you *both* can't find your social security cards."

I looked down, fiddling with my bracelet. That's exactly what I thought too, Steven.

"Well, I'm sorry girls, I don't know what to tell you. I legally can't hire you without something from List A or something from B and C," he said in an annoyed tone like we had wasted his time.

Jo looked at me.

"Alright, we understand. Thank you anyway," I said, standing up.

Jo stood up as well, "Yeah, thank you."

"Sure thing," he said blandly.

Back outside again, I asked, "How are we gonna get a job without our social security card or something from List C?"

"Well, I'm sure some places won't need it. Let's go to Burger King, they won't ask for it."

"Jo, I'm pretty sure if it's required by law, they're gonna ask."

"I don't know, some places are shady," Jo joked, trying to make light out of the shitty situation.

I chuckled softly, "Alright, let's go then."

We tried Burger King and AutoZone. We were turned down at Burger King—not hiring. At AutoZone—we got laughed at. I forgot, it's preposterous for a woman to work at an auto store. Silly me.

The two of us continued to walk around for the next several hours. We tried the B D Discount store, the Family Dollar, Dunkin' Donuts, various restaurants and cafes, and several grocery stores and gas stations. To which we all heard the same response—we're not hiring, you're not old enough, or they needed identifying documentation that we didn't have.

It was three forty-five when Jo and I sat on the wall, outside of a Dominos—where we were just rejected—smoking cigarettes. We decided we'd go downtown next. As we sat on the bus, Jo looked at her phone for the places we could try.

"Hey, look," she scooted closer to me and shared her phone. "It looks like there's some cafes and coffee places. Uh, a Shake Shack, another Marshall's and T.J. Maxx, Old Navy, DSW, Gap, Skechers—"

"Oh, so it seems like a lot of retail places," I said.

"Yeah," she responded.

"That's good," I said, feeling hopeful.

"Yeah, it is," Jo said as she continued to look around on the map. "There's a lot of shit, actually."

"Good," I said. "We'll definitely be able to find something then."

"For sure," Jo smiled, then locked her phone and put it back into her back pocket.

Getting off the bus, we looked around. It was now around four-twenty and still flurrying. It was pretty cold and the sun was beginning to set but none of these factors were going to stop Jo and me.

We decided to go a block over to where all the retail stores were. The two of us walked down the street and turned left onto Jefferson Avenue. From here, not only did we see a bunch of people, but we also saw several and various stores. The entire street was decorated for Christmas. Garland and bows wrapped around the lamp poles, Christmas music played, and string lights were hung from store to store. It was all so beautiful, and as I looked around, it filled me with peace.

"Well, I guess we should try Marshall's again, then T.J. Maxx," Jo said, interrupting me from my admiration. "They probably would need us more than McDonald's, GNC, or True Diamond."

The stores directly in front of us on the left were Dunkin' Donuts, Verizon, Marshall's, and T.J. Maxx. On the right there was Walgreens, McDonald's, True Diamond, and GNC.

"Yeah, you're right," I said. "Hopefully *this* Marshall's will be hiring."

"Seriously," Jo said. "Come on, let's go see."

We headed down the sidewalk through the crowds of people

and eventually came to the two sets of double doors that lead into Marshall's.

This Marshall's was even busier than the previous one—if that was even possible. Everyone scurried around, ripping through the clothing racks, checking customers out, hanging new inventory up, hustling to get to the checkout line, just so much occurring at once. Jo and I took this as a good thing though. We wanted to see busy places, because busy stores meant employers who could use as much help as they could receive.

Jo and I walked over to a young Indian woman putting the carts back and asked if we could speak to the manager. She paged her on her headset and within a few moments, a tall, slender, brunette woman wearing a headset came strutting towards us.

Jo and I stood up from the cardboard box of wrapping paper that we were leaning on when we noticed her. We assumed she was the manager.

"Hi, are you the two girls asking about employment?" the woman asked.

"Yes, ma'am," Jo said.

"Great," she smiled in relief. "I'm Debby," she extended her hand to ours.

Jo shook her hand, "I'm Jolene."

"And I'm Iris," I shook her hand as well.

"Nice to meet you two," she smiled.

"You too," Jo said. "So, are we able to fill out an application?"

"Oh my gosh, yes," Debby said desperately. "You two seem like lovely girls, I'm just going to hire you now. I'm sure you can see we're crazy busy. I could really use the extra help."

Jo and I looked at one another with smiles from ear to ear.

Finally, I thought to myself, *we found a job.* We got something and we're not going to have to worry about food or Kalista coming back to take care of us. By Jo's facial expression, I knew she thought the same thing.

"Let me take you guys to the back to do all the paperwork and then I'll see when I can get you guys' training."

"Thank you so much," Jo said with a huge smile.

The two of us followed Debby to the very back of the store and into her office.

"So what positions are you guys looking for?" Debby asked as she grabbed papers out of her desk drawer and two pens.

"Literally anything," I said. "We're willing to do anything you need us too."

"Oh, okay, great," she said in a surprised manner with a smile. "Well, I'll have you two fill these out"—she handed us papers that were clipped onto a clipboard—"and if I could just have your guys' licenses to scan them into the system that would be great."

Jo and I looked at each other nervously as the last time we handed our licenses over, everything went to shit. And we *really* didn't and couldn't have it go to shit this time.

"Uh, sure thing," I said.

The two of us dug out our wallets and took our licenses out from them. We then nervously handed them over.

"You guys are from Illinois, huh?" Debby asked as she inspected both of them.

Jo and I looked at one another.

"Uh, yeah," I said, "we, we just moved here."

"Oh, really?" she smiled as she looked up at us. "That's awesome. Well, welcome."

"Thank you," I smiled, then looked down, fiddling with my bracelet again.

"Well, I'll be right back with these. You ladies get started on that," Debby said as she headed past us to the door.

"It worked," Jo said enthusiastically but in a quiet manner in case Debby could still hear.

"I know," I smiled. "As long as she doesn't ask for another type of identification, we're golden."

"I know!" Jo smiled and looked behind me, out of the door, to make sure Debby wasn't coming back. "But she seems desperate, I doubt she'll care."

"I hope not," I said. "Let's just get these done so there's not a lot of room for questions when she gets back."

"Right."

The two of us filled out the application and other work-related papers. Several minutes later, I'm talking like ten, fifteen, went by and Debby still hadn't come back. It seemed like an awfully long time to scan our licenses into the system and have a copy of them. This thought made me somewhat nervous, but I ignored it as I was excited, we finally found something. I think I also didn't want to believe that something could be turning our table of luck.

A total of twenty minutes passed by when Debby finally came back into her office with our licenses in hand. Only this time, her cheery mood was gone and there wasn't a trace of a smile found on her face. Jo and I instantly noticed this and knew it wasn't going to be something good.

"Uh, we finished filling out the papers," Jo said, trying to somehow distract her from whatever she was thinking.

"Yeah, they're all done," I chimed in. "We're able to start whenever, even today if you'd like."

"Girls," Debby said with her hand up, "I scanned your guys' licenses. You're both in The Stay program?"

Jo and I looked at one another. I swallowed the rising lump in my throat.

"Uh, yeah...Is that a problem?" Jo asked politely.

"Well, you two just straight up lied to me," she said with a slight attitude.

"Uhhh," Jo said, drawn out.

"Jolene Mulvoy, Iris Cooke," she read off our licenses. "You guys didn't move here."

"Look, we can explain—" I said.

"I don't really care what the truth is anymore. I know all about The Stay program and I don't hire people from it," she said as she handed us back our licenses.

I frowned out of confusion, "Why?" I asked as I took the card from her.

"Because you guys are constantly bouncing from house to house. I can't hire someone that I don't know if they will be here for another month, four months, seven months—I just can't."

"We would tell you as soon as we found out though," Jo said. "And anyway, we aren't going to be leaving the house we're at for a while now."

Debby chuckled as she sat down in her chair, "I've heard that several times before."

"Listen, Debby, please," I begged. "We're willing to do anything. We *need* this job. Just give us a chance…please."

"I have, honey," Debby said. "And I refuse to do it again. Almost all the people in The Stay program are unreliable and I can't depend on them. I've had people stop showing up for work, call out daily, they're late, I mean the list goes on."

"Yeah, but we're not like that," Jo protested desperately. "We promise you, we'll never be late and we'll never miss a shift. I mean, we're willing to work any time you need us to, and we'll do anything you ask with no complaints. We can even pick up extra hours."

I nodded my head rapidly in agreement.

"Yeah, and we'd stay longer if you need us to, or, or come in early,"

I begged.

Debby shook her head, "I'm sorry, girls. I just can't do it."

"Debby, ma'am, please. I'm seriously begging you," I went on. "You don't get it, our host left and there's no food in the house to eat. We only have about twenty-five dollars between the two of us and no one in our house can get a hold of our host. There's—"

"Iris," Debby interrupted with her hand up, "I'm sorry, I don't get involved with all of that. I'm gonna have to ask you two to please leave."

"Ma'am," Jo pleaded, "please! We're willing to really, really work. We promise we won't let you down and we'll be the best employees you ever had. We need this job, as Iris said we don't have any food to eat—"

"Jolene," Debby said sternly, standing this time, "I'm sorry, but I need you guys to leave *now*."

Jo and I looked at each other absolutely defeated. Not knowing what else to say or what else to do, I caved.

"Alright," I said, standing up.

"No, wait," Jo said, standing up as well. "How did you know that we're in The Stay program?"

"The state of Massachusetts allows employers to scan potential employees' IDs to run quick and somewhat vague background checks on them," Debby said. "How many times you've been arrested, if at all, comes up, if you're on the sex offender list or not, comes up, things like that, and of course, if you're in The Stay program, that'll show up as well."

"Why?" Jo asked with agitation. "It's not like getting a job while in this program is illegal."

"No, it's not. But from what I understand, it's more for The Stay program itself. If the host needs to verify if you are really who you are, if they need to verify your address or age, anything like that, or any other issues."

"Wouldn't they need to scan it like you just did?" I asked.

"Oh, no, they can type your license number into their account."

Jo scoffed, "That's shady as fuck."

Debby looked confused, "No one ever told you girls that?"

"No," Jo said. "No one tells us shit. There's a lot of shit that doesn't make sense in this program."

Debby frowned, "I'm sorry about that. Well, if it makes you feel any better, it's not like they can look up loads of information on you guys. Basically, all they see is what's on your license, and like I said, if you've been in legal trouble."

"So, the same stuff that you see?" I asked.

"Yep," she said with a slight smile.

There was silence for a moment between the three of us.

"So, any time an employer scans our license, it pops up that we're in The Stay program?" Jo asked.

"Yeah," Debby answered.

Jo scoffed.

"How often do employers around here do that?" I asked.

"Mostly all of them," Debby said gently.

I sighed, shaking my head, "Come on, Jo. Let's just go."

We made it back into the flurries when I asked, "What are we supposed to do now, Jo?"

"We're going to find something, Iris," she said earnestly. "Look around. You see all the stores around here? She motioned with her hand. "And that's just on this *one* street in Boston. You can't *possibly* believe that every single one of the managers of these businesses are either gonna, A, scan our licenses, or B, care that we're in this program."

"You're right," I said, trying to believe her though my hope was running thin.

"There're a million places here, Iris. I'm telling you *someone* is going to hire us. Let's just keep trying. There'll be at least *one* place."

And after we each had a cigarette, that's exactly what we did until one a.m. when all the stores and restaurants closed. Jo and I tried a total of over forty stores that day and in some, fucked up way, that I will never understand, didn't have the slightest luck at any of them. And go figure, most of the stores denied us because we were in The Stay program. It sucked. Absolutely and positively, sucked. I didn't know what we'd do at this point. I was actually worried. We were running out of money and our only solid, golden (or at least we thought) plan, failed. I never thought we would have this much trouble finding a job and I *never* thought being in this program would be the reason behind it.

Chapter 69

Five painstaking days dragged by, and it was now Thursday, December nineteenth. Jo and I woke up that morning with nothing to eat. All the food that we got from the Dollar Tree the week before, was gone. We tried our best to make sure we still ate three meals, although the last two days we had eaten soup and Ramen for breakfast. I was so sick and tired of that salty, artery clogging shit, but I ate it anyway. Nevertheless, we now had no food, which meant we had to go get some more.

Since we didn't have enough money to pay for the bus fare that would take us to the previous Dollar Tree we had been to, we found that there was a closer one on Velmer Avenue. The catch, however, was that it was an hour walk away (since we couldn't take the route that included a ferry, and was a hell of a lot quicker). So, the two of us dressed warm and made sure we had everything we needed for our journey to the Dollar Tree.

It was cold that day in Boston. I checked my phone, and it said it was twenty-five degrees out. Thankfully, it wasn't snowing, so that was a plus. I still froze my ass off the entire way there though.

Jo and I had walked for several minutes when I thought about how

I used to walk everywhere with Colton and Leannah back home in Chicago, especially growing up before Colton and I could drive. We would walk to the grocery store, to the mini mart, to the gas station—where Colton worked, to fast-food places, we would walk just about anywhere. It didn't matter if it was cold and snowy or hot and humid, we walked wherever and whenever we wanted—well for the most part.

"What are you smiling about?" Jo asked lightheartedly. I hadn't realized I broke out into a grin.

"Oh, nothing," I said, still smiling. "Just about how Colton, Leannah, and I would walk just about everywhere back in Chicago. It wouldn't matter to us if it was freezing cold or hot as hell."

Jo smiled, "Sounds like it was pretty fun."

"Yeah," I looked down. "I was." After a beat, "So, what would you do all day in the summer? I know you said your dad worked a lot, so, what would you do?"

Jo exhaled, "Well, when we moved back to Springfield, I was still young and needed a babysitter. So, my Aunt Jenna—my dad's sister, would stay with me when my dad was at work. She was the best. We'd go biking, play all kinds of games, go net fishing at the park and then catch butterflies with those same nets"—Jo smiled—"Yeah, she was the best."

I smiled but then her words caught up to me. *Was.* She *was* the best.

I swallowed, "Was?"

"Yeah," Jo looked off at the traffic. "She died unexpectedly when I was twelve. Right before my dad met Ian."

Pity smothered me. How much can one person lose? "What happened? If you don't mind me asking."

Jo shook her head, "Of course not. Uh…a drunk driver hit her."

"Jo, that's awful," I said sympathetically. "I'm so sorry."

Jo smiled but it was rueful. "Yeah, I am too."

Silence fell over us for a moment.

"She was only thirty-five," Jo then said. "She was the closest thing I had to a mom after mine died. When I was younger, I'd be mad at like, like, the world or God or—I don't really know who. But I'd be mad because I felt like my Aunt Jenna was taken to be replaced by Ian; since my dad met him shortly after."

My face fell, "Jo—"

"I don't think that anymore though," she added genuinely. "But I don't know…I just don't think I was ever meant to have a mom."

I looked at Jo pensively for a moment, "I feel the same way about having a dad."

Jo met my gaze, "You do?"

"Yeah. I mean, the closest thing I've had to a dad is my nineteen-year-old brother," I said lightheartedly.

Jo chuckled.

"Anyone my mom dated after my dad left would have *never* been a good father figure, even if they tried. Sometimes, every here and there, my mom would meet a half-decent guy and I would get kinda hopeful like maybe I could finally have a dad but they always left once they discovered my mom's addiction and our shitty home life. So, one day, I just thought to myself, *Okay, Iris, a dad isn't coming for you. You aren't supposed to have one, so just accept what you have and love what you have.* And from there on, I stopped getting let down because I was no longer waiting for something that was never coming."

Jo looked away from me and down to the ground. "Well, I'm glad you can relate."

I smiled softly then looked away.

"You know, Iris," Jo stopped. I paused as well. "You're like my soulmate…My friend soulmate…my—friend-mate."

I smiled in a way that was more genuine than it had been in months. I swung my arm around her and rested my head on her shoulder, "Yes, we're friend-mates for life, Jo."

70

Chapter 70

We bought bread, peanut butter, jelly, breakfast sandwiches, frozen chicken sliders, Frosted Flakes, and a half-gallon of milk all totaling seven dollars. It wasn't the best but it wasn't terrible. We figured the bread would be versatile as well as the cereal—serving as options for any meal of the day.

Around six o'clock we sat on our beds listening to music and reading. Jo asked if I wanted to eat dinner—which I did—so the two of us got up and decided on what we wanted. Jo settled on the chicken sliders while I chose Frosted Flakes. Since Jo needed to use the microwave to make her food, we headed to the kitchen where there were several people, including Sebastian, Carter, Rachel, and the three drunk guys that tried to hit on Jo and me that one day in the kitchen. Their names were Jerry, Darren, and Mike. They all were playing beer pong and taking shots.

Ping, ping, ping.

"IRRRRIISSSSS, JOOLLEENNNEE," one girl, I think her name was Diana, slurred. She was clearly drunk. "Come take shots with us!" she said as she slung her arm over my shoulder.

"No thanks," I tossed her arm off me.

Jo set her things down on the counter next to the microwaves.

"Don't bother," Carter said, "they don't drink."

My jaw tightened as I swallowed, closing my eyes and not moving a muscle.

Breathe, Iris, breathe.

"Awww!" Diana exclaimed. "Why not?"

"Because we don't. 'Kay?" Jo whipped around and said sternly.

"You're no fun!" she pouted then walked over to Jerry and sat down on his lap.

I gingerly grabbed a bowl from the cabinet above and a spoon from the drawer beside me.

"They never have been," Sebastian snickered.

I inhaled deeply, tired of their bullshit, and exhaled slowly.

Jo was taking her food out of the microwave and placing it on a plate when Jennica—another girl that was drunk—knocked over the half full bottle of Crown Royal. It hit the marble floor and shattered, spilling its contents everywhere.

"Jennica!" Diana yelled. "You dumb fucking bitch, look what you did!"

Jo and I exchanged a look. Knowing this wasn't our problem, we gladly walked upstairs.

"What a piece of work," Jo said as she sat down on her bed with her plate on her lap.

"Tell me about it," I said.

I sat my bowl on my dresser and went into the bathroom to get the milk from our fridge. I poured cereal into my bowl first, then added milk. Sitting down carefully on my bed, I began to eat.

"Are those any good?" I motioned to Jo's chicken sliders with my spoon.

"Uhm," she looked at it. "Yeah. They are."

That made me break out into a grin. Jo was the worst liar ever.

"Bullshit," I smirked

Jo smirked as well, "Shut up."

It was around four in the morning when I woke up to a noise. At first, I couldn't make out what the noise exactly was. I looked around with groggy eyes to see if I could piece it together. As I looked around and my eyes got adjusted to the darkness, I saw Jo wasn't in her bed and her covers were all tumbled around and messed up. As I tried to figure out where she could have gone, I noticed a small gleam of light coming out from under the bathroom door. I realized Jo probably just got up to use the bathroom. But…that's when I heard it again: a gut wrenching, regurgitating and gagging sound. I paused and silently listened to hear the noise again, and sure enough, seconds later, I could hear someone—well Jo—throwing up.

I threw the covers off me and scurried over to the bathroom door, "Jo?" I knocked on the door. "You okay?"

She didn't respond but I heard her vomit again.

"Jo!" Now concerned, I turned the knob and flung open the door.

I saw Jo, sitting on the floor, hunched over the toilet, covered in sweat, and absolutely distraught looking.

"Jo!" I exclaimed. "What's wrong?!" I hurried over to her, sat down on the floor, and pulled her hair back.

"I think, I think the chicken made me sick," she struggled to get out as she breathed heavily.

"Really?" I asked. I plucked away the stray hairs that stuck to her face. I then touched her forehead, "Jo, you're burning up."

"I know," she said in a pant.

I stood up to get a wet rag.

"I woke up around one, feeling really nauseous," Jo began to explain as I ran a washcloth under the sink's cold water and then wrung it out.

"I thought maybe I was just dehydrated or something but then my stomach started to cramp really bad."

I sat back down on the floor with her and wiped the sweat away.

"I tossed and turned for a while, sweating when I felt like I was about to throw up. I rushed to the bathroom, and this is where I've been for the past hour and a half."

"Jo," my face fell as I dabbed her forehead with the rag.

Before she could speak, she threw up once more. I held her hair back as she continued to vomit. After a moment, she finally stopped as she hung over the toilet.

"Jo, why don't we go to the hospital?"

"No!" Her face was stricken with fear. "We don't have money for that."

"You're sick, Jo!" I exclaimed. "You can't just ignore food poisoning."

"Sure you can," she said as she forced herself to sit against the wall. "I've had it before and was fine after a day or two."

"But what if it's worse this time? My brother had it pretty bad once."

"I'll be fine," she said as she leaned her head back against the wall and sweat dripped down her face.

I looked over at her with despair and tenderness, "Well, what can I do?"

"Nothing, I'll be fine."

"No, Jo. If you won't let me take you to the hospital, at least let me get you some things from the store."

"No, we don't have money for that."

"Yes, we do," I stood up.

"Seriously, Iris! Don't!" Jo shouted as she sprung to her feet.

"Hey, hey, take it easy. Don't jump up like that," I said, putting my hands out.

"We don't have the money, Iris," Fear crossed her face once more.

I grabbed a hold of Jo's arms and made her meet my eyes, "I'm gonna go get you some Gatorade and some medicine. Don't worry about how much money we have or how I'm gonna get the stuff, okay? Just go lay down and call me if you need anything."

Jo looked at me like she wanted to reject what I was saying, but deep down she knew she didn't *really* want to.

"Alright," she said reluctantly. "Just be safe out there alone, okay?"

I swallowed, "I will."

Ping.

When Jo knew she wasn't going to throw up again, I helped her back to her bed.

"Do you need anything before I go?" I asked. "The fan on? Water? Anything?"

"No, I'm good," she said.

"Alright."

I put on my Vans and my faux fur coat and started to head out the door.

"Iris?" Jo said, stopping me.

"Yeah?"

"Thank you," she smiled.

I smiled, "Of course."

I opened Kalista's door and stepped outside, the frigid Boston air whipped around me. Snow kissed my head. It was dark out, very dark out.

Ping, ping, ping.

I looked around; no one was there. I listened; nothing.

Ping.

Breathe, Iris, breathe.

Swallowing down the fear, I took a deep breath.

You can do it, Iris.

I closed my eyes.

It's for Jo.

I opened my eyes and exhaled. Calmly, I stepped off the step and made my way to Walgreens.

I entered through the automatic doors and headed back towards the refrigerated drinks. As I passed through the store, I noticed it was pretty much empty. This didn't come as a surprise considering it was four-thirty in the morning. Nevertheless, I made my way to the drinks and began scanning what they had.

"Three-dollars for one Gatorade?!" I exclaimed to myself. I sighed, shaking my head. I stared at the blue, red, yellow, and purple bottles through the refrigerated glass doors. I contemplated if I should get them or not considering the price but Jo needed them. I stared at the drinks for a moment longer when I heard it.

Just take them.

I looked around me and saw no one.

Just do it. I opened the glass door and took out two blue and two purple. I stuffed them down into my purse, looked around once more, then headed to a different area of the store. I knew it was wrong, but there really was no other choice.

I made my way over to the medicine aisle. As I stood there, I was faced with all types of rectangular boxes, cylinder plastic bottles, and liquids; all filled with medicine. I knew Jo needed something, but I also knew there wasn't much for food poisoning. As I looked over my options, my eyes met with the numerous Tylenol bottles. I picked one up and looked at it pensively. I pictured Jo sitting on her bathroom floor, face wet with tears, as she poured the white oblong tablets into her hand and then washed them down with alcohol. Gulp after gulp after gulp until it was all gone. I swallowed the rising lump in my throat and blinked away the forming tears that the image created.

"Thank you for saving her," I whispered.

I grabbed a generic brand liquid fever reducer and stuffed the box into my purse. I then walked down the aisle towards the food. I figured that if I'm stealing, I might as well take some of that too—although I wasn't proud of that thought.

I entered the aisle and scanned what they had. Mostly cereals, snacks, chips, canned tuna, and other random food items filled the shelves. I knew I couldn't get away with a box of cereal or a family size bag of chips. But I *did* know that the tuna cans would be the perfect thing to slip into my purse. Not only that, but they would last a long time *and* were good for us. So, I grabbed a hold of about six cans and dropped them all into my purse.

At this time, I figured I better leave before I get caught and end up digging myself a deeper hole. I walked back towards the front of the store where the cashier was, with my head down. As I approached the doors, I felt her watching me. Not necessarily in a suspicious *I know you're stealing* kind of way, but more so, an odd or off feeling that I gave her. She never said anything to me though and I made it back onto the sidewalk, where I wasted no time getting home.

I made it back to Kalista's house right before five a.m. It was still dark out as the sun wouldn't rise for another two hours. I scurried up the steps and into our room where I found Jo, laying in her bed in a fetal position.

"Hey," I said gingerly as I approached her and sat down on the bed. "How you feeling?"

Jo turned her head to look at me then rolled onto her back, "Like death."

I smiled ruefully then touched her head, "You're still burning up."

Jo sighed and struggled to sit up, "I know."

"This should help," I said as I pulled the liquid fever reducer out of my purse.

"Fever reducer?" Jo exclaimed. "Why would you buy that? That shit must have cost like twelve bucks!"

I looked at Jo and went silent for a moment.

"What?" she asked.

"I didn't *buy* it…" I trailed off.

Jo looked at me with a confused frown, "Then how did you—did you steal it?" she asked in a shocked manner.

I nodded my head.

Jo moved her head slightly but still looked at me, "Iris, why did you—"

"And I got Gatorade and canned tuna," I said, interrupting her as I pulled out the items.

"Iris, why did you steal this stuff?"

"Because how else was I gonna get it, Jo?" I asked in a bitter tone. "The thirteen dollars we have sure wasn't gonna buy it."

Jo looked disappointed but didn't say anything because she knew I was right.

"I know…well, thank you…I appreciate it."

"Of course," I said genuinely.

I cracked the seal on one of the blue Gatorades then handed it to Jo. As she drank, I opened the fever reducer and poured the liquid into the measuring cup. When she was done drinking, I traded her the Gatorade for the medicine.

"So, is this our new plan?" Jo asked monotonously after she washed down the medicine. "To steal?"

I exhaled then swallowed, "I guess so. What other choice do we have?"

Jo shook her head then shrugged, "None."

I looked at Jo emotionlessly for a moment as I thought.

"We hold on to those thirteen dollars for as long as we can. We only use it for emergencies. Like when we have to ride the bus, or when we *have* to buy something that we can't steal. And we just ride out the stealing train for as long as we can," I said with full conviction.

"Yeah, and we'll be as sneaky and as careful as we can and try to avoid going to the same place multiple times," Jo added with conviction as well. "We can do this, Iris…we have to."

I nodded my head as, "Yeah, we can…I know, we have to."

71

Chapter 71

Four days passed and it was now December twenty-fourth: better known as Christmas Eve. Over the course of those few days, Jo got much better. By Christmas Eve, she was practically back to normal, and I thank God for A, the obvious reasons and B, we were in *no* position to go to the hospital or a doctor. Nevertheless, those four days were spent taking it easy, helping Jo when she needed it, and overall relaxing.

It was around one o'clock when Jo and I decided we'd go to the store to get some more food. Over the past couple days, we ran out of our breakfast sandwiches and cereal so instead of eating tuna or peanut butter and jelly sandwiches for breakfast, we decided to go get some more of the former. And anyway, we figured it'd be easier to steal on a crowded, busy day like Christmas Eve than any other day.

We settled on Seven-Eleven. It was a five minute walk from Kalista's and we knew they'd have breakfast foods. Being in the city meant a lack of chain corporation grocery stores. There was Shaw's, which was in walking-distance of Kalista's, but we figured it would be better to *not* steal from the place that we gave all our information to.

The Seven-Eleven was a very run down, squat, cream colored building with a supposedly homeless man sleeping out front. The building itself and the banner style "Seven-Eleven" sign was dirty and old looking.

"Well, I don't think we'll be the first ones to steal from here," Jo said sarcastically as we both stared at the building.

I snickered and rolled my eyes, "Come on."

I pulled open the single glass door and the two of us entered inside.

The clerk was a late-thirties, early-forties, year-old White guy. He was dirty and rugged looking. If you ask me, he looked like he was on drugs. I looked at Jo and the two of us headed towards the back of the store. There were hardly any people inside. I noticed two kids—probably about twelve—a woman nodding off as she stood in front of a selection of chips, and an average looking man taking two bottles of water out of the refrigerators and heading to the check out.

We continued walking down the aisle until we got to the refrigerated food section. Once we did, Jo nodded at me then trailed off several feet.

I opened a glass door, took out two of the individually wrapped Jimmy Dean breakfast sandwiches, then slyly put them in my purse.

I glanced over at Jo and saw she had put something in her bag as well.

I rounded the corner, walking away from Jo and the refrigerated section, and towards a snack aisle. There were granola bars, Pop-Tarts, protein bars, Goldfish, all sorts of small and singular items. I grabbed a handful of four granola bars, two packages of Pop-Tarts, two bags of Cheez-Its, and four Cliff bars. As I grabbed each item, I shoved them down into my purse quietly and swiftly.

I walked away from the area, heading to the front of the store. As

I did, Jo came out of an aisle and met me. The two of us walked past the cashier—who didn't pay us the slightest bit of mind—and went out of the front door, back down the sidewalk the way we came.

I let out all the breath I held inside while in the store, "I can't believe we just did that."

"I know," Jo said remorsefully, hiking her purse further up on her shoulder.

"Well," I said, trying to push aside the guilt as there was no changing what we did, "what did you take?"

"Breakfast burritos and like two of those plastic cups of cereal. You?"

"Breakfast sandwiches, some granola bars, Cliff bars, Pop-Tarts, and some Cheez-Its."

Jo nodded her head. I could tell she felt as bad as I did. "Well, we should be set on breakfast for a bit now."

"Yeah."

The two of us walked home in silence as we both felt pretty guilty about what we did. Although we had to just keep reminding ourselves, there was nothing else we really *could* do. We were innocently just trying to take care of ourselves—to whatever extent that meant.

Jo and I made it home a little after one-thirty. We put all our stolen food away and plopped down on our beds.

"How fucked up is it that we stole on Christmas Eve?" I asked, shaking my head. "Of all days, we choose *Christmas Eve* to be criminals."

Jo gave a disappointed face, "We gotta try to not feel guilty about it, Iris. We've tried other ways. We've tried using our own money and getting a job, we tried," Jo said passionately.

I looked down, sighed, and shook my head as sorrow washed over me.

"Iris," Jo repeated, "we're doing what we have to do."

I then looked up and caught Jo's eyes, "Why does feeling guilty about this make me feel guilty about Campbell?"

Jo gave me a perplexed look as she was not expecting me to say that.

"What do you mean?" she asked.

"Well, I feel guilty about stealing because I know we shouldn't do it, but I also keep trying to tell myself that we're just trying to survive. But the more I think about feeling guilty for stealing, the more I feel guilty about not saying anything about Campbell."

Jo got up from her bed with a concerned face and sat down next to me, "Iris, what are you talking about? Why do you feel that way?"

"Jo, I didn't tell *anybody* what he did. Nobody. I told my brother and you. That's it. And I've thought to myself a million times, because of this, because of me not telling anyone, he's still out there, still out there, doing the same, evil things to someone else," I said. "And it's because of *me*, Jo."

"Whoa, whoa, hold up," Jo said, taken aback by my words. "It is *not* because of you," she then met my eyes. "The only person in the *world* that it's because of or whose fault it is, is Campbell's. That's it. Not you, not anyone else. Campbell."

No matter what you do, no one will ever believe you.

"Jo," I sighed, "if I told someone, he would have gone to jail or at the bare minimum, been kicked out of the program. Do you know how awful I feel to not have done that and now he can go about his life to do the same thing to other girls?" I questioned passionately. "I mean, how many people has he already done this too and how many will he *keep* doing this to?"

"Iris," Jo said seriously, "just because you tell someone, doesn't mean they *always* go to jail. And I know you know that. But even if they do, the court process is hell. Having to tell everyone everything a million times, then going to court and sitting up there, seeing the person who hurt you, listening to the defense try to prove doubt or flaws in the prosecution, it's hard, and it sucks, Iris. Whether you do or don't tell someone what happens to you, it's hard. And it *hurts* either way. Either way, you're sad, either way you're angry, either way you're humiliated, ashamed, *guilty*. Either way, you're *all* those emotions. Telling someone doesn't change that. And *not* telling someone doesn't make you guilty or at fault for the things those people continue to choose to do. Iris, don't be so hard on yourself… promise me you won't blame yourself, for any of the bullshit with Campbell?" she then stuck out her pinky to me to "pinky-promise" her. "Please?"

I smiled but it was sad, "Alright, I promise," I said as I locked my pinky with hers.

As our pinkies were locked, she kissed her thumb and waited for me to do the same. I did and then she spoke.

"Now lock it," she said as she put her thumb towards mine, all the while our pinkies are still interlocked.

I smiled genuinely this time and "locked it" by pressing my thumb against hers.

She smiled then gave me a hug, "I love you, Iris. None of this is your fault, ever."

I smiled, closed my eyes, and squeezed Jo tighter, "I love you too, Jo. Thank you."

"And we can't feel guilty about stealing, okay?" Jo asked as we pulled away from our hug. "We're doing what we have to do. I don't want it to lead to you feeling guilty about something you shouldn't."

I nodded my head, "Okay."

"Okay?" Jo asked as she looked at me deeper to see if I was lying.

I nodded my head again, "Yeah, okay."

"Alright," Jo then hugged me again. Then in my ear she said, "Everything's going to be okay."

I squeezed Jo tighter and closed my eyes. Maybe, just maybe, she could be right.

Chapter 72

I woke up that Christmas morning to the room looking brighter than it typically did. Once my eyes were adjusted to the light, I got out of bed, walked over to the window, and pulled back the curtain. I looked out of our bedroom window and saw the entire driveway, lawn, street, trees, and everything else in sight, was covered in white snow. I smiled to myself as it once again made me feel more at home.

I turned around, saw Jo was still sleeping, and figured this was the perfect time to call my family and wish them a Merry Christmas. It was nine o'clock in Boston, which meant it was eight in Chicago, so I knew they'd be up. My mom was probably at work though.

I slipped on my slipper boats, grabbed my phone and headed downstairs. I first stopped in the kitchen to make coffee where I saw Christina and Megan.

"Merry Christmas, Iris," they both said with a smile.

"Merry Christmas, guys."

I made my coffee and the two girls continued talking and hanging out with one another. Once I was done, I went to the lounge and called my family.

"Merry Christmas!" they—including my mom—exclaimed over the phone.

I smiled, "Merry Christmas! Mom, you don't have to work?"

"Nope," my mom said. "Thanks to you, I don't have to this year."

My mom worked every holiday for as long as I can remember. Growing up, we needed the money and over the course of her several jobs she's had, most of them would pay time and a half on holidays. So, she always took advantage of that. But this year, since I was in The Stay program which allowed my family to have more money, she didn't have to. And it made me really happy.

"Really?" I smiled ear to ear. "That's awesome, Mom. I'm really glad to hear that."

"All thanks to you, buttercup."

We carried on talking. Leannah told me she planned to make a pie while Colton and Mom cooked dinner. She also told me Mom got her some clothes and makeup while Colton got her flowers, some candy, and a cookbook with various types of dessert recipes. I had a hunch that Colton got that so he could partake in the baking too. You know, the part where you eat it. He laughed at this and claimed that was not at all his motive, but I beg to differ. Colton said Mom got him a new pair of sneakers, which trust me, he *desperately* needed and Leannah got him a gift card to his favorite fast food joint. Mom was given flowers as well and a heart pendant necklace from Colton and breakfast in bed from Leannah. That's when they told me that something would be coming for me later in the day. I didn't want them to get me anything. But I knew nothing would have stopped them. It just sucked not being able to get them anything back.

"You and Jo still okay with food and all?" Colton then asked. In a previous phone call, I told him how Kalista left again but I lied about the part when I said we were fine.

"Hmm hm," I said, lying again.

"You sure?" he asked.

"Yeah no, we're good…thanks."

"Alright, just making sure."

"How is Jo anyway?" Leannah asked. "Is she all better from the food poisoning?"

Again, in a previous phone call, like a day or so after Jo got sick, I was catching them up on things, and Jo was one of them.

"Oh, yeah, she's basically back to normal."

"Oh, great," my mom said.

I sipped my coffee.

"Yeah, that's awesome," Leannah said. "Glad she's okay."

"Yeah, me too," I added.

"Food poisoning is no joke. I'm really glad she didn't have a case like I did that one time," my brother said. "That shit was awful."

"Oh God, that was really, really, bad," my mom said in a disturbed tone.

When Colton was sixteen, he had a super bad case of food poisoning. My mom was working that night, so Colton walked down to a food truck not too far from our house to get the three of us dinner. We had eaten from that food truck a couple times before and nothing was ever wrong with it. Well, that night, while Colton was on his way there, I was watching Leannah at home. She was eleven at the time and asked me if she could have Mac and Cheese instead. I figured that sounded good to me and it would be free since we already had a box of it in the cabinet. I felt bad that Colton already went out though, so I called him and asked if he would rather have that. He told me he didn't mind that he already left and that he would still get something from the food truck, but we could go ahead and make the Mac and Cheese. So, that's exactly what we did. Leannah and I began to boil the water and soon enough, Colton came home. He got a cheesesteak and began to eat it while Leannah and I started stirring in the cheese, milk, and butter, into the pasta. When it was ready, we sat down with Colton, and all ate together, like we typically did. After we all finished dinner and cleaned up, we started to watch TV together. About forty-five minutes to an hour after we all finished eating, I saw Colton had sat up and was holding his stomach. I asked him if he was okay, but he said no and that his stomach hurt really, really, bad. It was minutes later that he got up and darted for the bathroom. The rest of the night, he spent his time there throwing up his guts. Leannah cried and cried, she didn't understand what was happening and it scared badly. I calmed her down and explained that Colton just ate some bad food and his body was trying to get rid of it. I called my mom, but she couldn't leave work. She had also only been clean for about a year at that point, so she was trying to not fuck up her job, for lack of better words. I took care of Colton until my mom got home around midnight. And for the next couple of days, Colton stayed glued to the bathroom. It was pretty bad. I went to the store and got him basically the same stuff as I did for Jo, but he definitely needed more. I'm sure if we took him to the doctor or the hospital, he would have been a little better, but my mom couldn't afford it. She still feels terrible that she couldn't help him more. But, nevertheless, within a week and a half he was doing much, much better.

"That scared the living shit outta me," Leannah said.

"Yeah, I remember that," Colton said. "I felt so bad that you were so upset."

"I know, I did too," I added.

"Iris tried to explain to me what was going on, but my little eleven-year-old mind didn't get it," Leannah said. "I thought you were, like, dying.

"I felt like I was," Colton said, adding a chuckle to the end of it.

I snickered.

"Well, I'm just glad she's okay and everything's all good," Colton said, talking about Jo.

"Yeah, thanks, me too," I said with conviction.

"Just in time for Christmas too!" Leannah then said pleasantly.

I smiled, "Right."

The four of us talked some more. Mostly about their plans for the day and my lack thereof. Soon, my mom said she was going to start cleaning, leaving just Leannah, Colton, and me on the line. We talked about old Christmas memories (the few good or funny ones we had), how school was and when winter break ended, and anything else that came to mind. The three of us talked for a while actually and it was just what I needed. Being able to laugh with my brother and sister—two of the most important people in my life—brought me feelings of bliss that I'd been so desperately lacking. Listening to Colton's horrible jokes followed by Leannah's snort-laugh, stretched a smile across my face that silenced all the demons in my mind.

Hanging up the phone, I smiled as I sipped my coffee and watched the little white snowflakes kiss the ground.

"Merry Christmas!' Jo said as I walked back into our bedroom.

"Merry Christmas," I smiled, giving Jo a hug.

"How are you?" she asked as we pulled apart.

I exhaled, "I'm good," I said truthfully . "I was just talking with my family."

"Oh, yeah?" Jo asked as she picked her coffee up from the nightstand and took a sip. "How are they?"

"They're really good," I sat down on my bed. "My mom didn't have to work this Christmas—which has, like, never ever—happened before."

"That's great," Jo smiled. "I just got off the phone with my dad as well."

"How's he?"

"He's good," she smiled.

"What's his plans for today?"

"He said pretty much nothing," Jo replied. "But he's okay with it. He said he's just going to relax and watch football."

"Well, that sounds nice to me…Not the football part though. I don't understand that game."

Jo chuckled, "Me either. He'd always be like, 'Jo-Jo, do you want to watch the game with me?' and I'd sit and hang out with him, but I *never* understood it."

I laughed, "I don't know what it is about that sport, but my mind just can't grasp it!"

"Seriously! Me too," Jo laughed. "He would explain it to me a million times and it would just go in one ear, out the other."

"Maybe we're just stupid or something," I joked.

Jo, still laughing, said, "You know? That must be it."

The two of us then got our breakfast and began to eat while we decided our plan for the day. After finding out—courtesy of Google—that there would be a walk-through light show, food trucks, music, and other fun activities downtown, we decided on that. It started at five p.m. and there wasn't any kind of admission fee, so we were set.

After finishing eating and getting dressed, the two of us began to do our makeup. There was then a knock at our bedroom door. We looked at one another in a confused manner as *nobody* ever did that.

"Who could that be?" Jo asked as she set her eyeshadow brush down and walked to the door.

I shrugged.

"Hey, Merry Christmas," Christina said with a smile as Jo opened our door. She was holding a vase that had beautiful blue roses, irises, hydrangea, and lilies in them.

"Merry Christmas," Jo smiled. "Wow, those are gorgeous."

"Aren't they?!" Christina exclaimed. "They're for Iris."

"They're for me?" I asked in a shocked manner.

"Yeah!" Christina exclaimed.

"Aww, that's so sweet!" Jo said.

I set my eyebrow pencil down and walked over towards them. I then took the vase from Christina.

"Who are they from?!" Christina asked impatiently.

I opened the small, attached card and read it in my head.

Merry Christmas to the best daughter and sister anyone in this entire world could ever ask for. We miss you so much and can't thank you enough for your bravery, courage, and compassion. We love you more than anything, Iris. See you soon! Love Mom, Leannah, and Colton.

Warmth and happiness hit me like I injected it into my veins. The card and flowers meant so much to me.

"They're from my mom and siblings," I said with a smile from ear to ear.

"Aww, that's so sweet," Christina said.

"Did they really?" Jo asked with a smile. "That's so thoughtful."

I smiled and folded the note back to how it was.

Christina then chuckled, "That's so cute they gave your irises, and your name is Iris."

I chuckled, "Yeah, that's my brother—Colton. Every time he gets me flowers, he always gets me irises and blue roses. The lilies must be my mom and sister's touch."

"Why the blue roses? Any reason?" Jo asked as she examined the bouquet.

"When I was five, my grandma died. At her funeral, they handed out blue roses to put on her casket. Like I said, I was only five, so I don't have a ton of memories with her but the ones I do, are special. She was a really great woman. Colton gets me them to be reminded of her."

Jo smiled, "That's really, really thoughtful."

"Seriously," Christina added. "Talk about world's best brother?!"

I smiled and looked down at my bouquet.

"Well, I just wanted to bring them up to you," Christina said. "I was making breakfast when the flower guy rang the doorbell. You can't trust many people here, so I wanted to make sure they got to you safely."

"Thank you, Christina. I appreciate that."

"Yeah, sure thing. Anytime," she smiled then exited our room.

"She's really nice," Jo said as she closed the door.

"Yeah, she is," I agreed.

"Your family's awesome. Those flowers are seriously gorgeous."

I walked over to Jo's dresser that we were sharing to do our makeup and set down the bouquet. "I'll share them with you," I teased playfully.

She laughed, rolled her eyes playfully, and walked over to the dresser.

"You mind if I call them really quick, just to thank them?"

"Not at all!"

I went over to my vanity where my phone was. I picked it up, unlocked it, and dialed my mom's number.

"Did somebody get her flowers?" my mom said through the phone.

"I diddddd," I said, drawn out with a large grin.

"It's a good thing she did, or you would've ruined it," I heard Colton chuckle in the background.

"Oh shit," my mom said.

I then heard Leannah laugh as well.

"You guys are too much," I chuckled and rolled my eyes playfully. "But no, I just got them, and they are seriously so gorgeous. Thank you," I said sincerely. "And I *loved* the note. That's my favorite part."

"Aww, good," my mom said. "That was our goal."

I smiled, "They better not have been that much. I've never seen flowers like this before."

"Don't you worry about the price," Colton said. "You deserve them."

I smiled.

"Iris, did you like the lilies I picked out?" Leannah asked.

"You know, I thought you did that," I said. "Yes, I do. I *love* them."

"Good," Leannah said, I could practically feel her beaming through the phone.

"I already know the roses and irises were you, Colton," I said smugly.

He laughed, "How'd you know?"

"I don't know, maybe 'cause that's like the only flowers you ever get me."

"Oh right, right. Good guess."

I rolled my eyes and laughed. Jo even laughed as well.

I walked towards her and clicked the button to change the call from a phone call to FaceTime. "Guys, say hi to Jo."

"Hey, everyone! Merry Christmas," Jo waved brightly as she put her mascara wand back into the tube.

"Hey!" the three of them waved back.

"Aren't you beautiful!" my mom said.

"Aw, thank you, Ms. Cooke!"

"Please," my mom said, batting her hand, "call me Blair, honey."

"Oh, alright," Jo smiled. "It's so nice to finally be able to talk to you guys. I've heard nothing but good things."

"Same here," Colton said. "Iris tells us nothing but good things about you too."

"Well, that's a relief!" Jo teased.

I rolled my eyes playfully. "We found a light show thing downtown tonight that we're gonna go to."

"Oh, yeah?" my mom asked. "That sounds like fun."

"Yeah, there's gonna be music and food, stuff like that," Jo said. "I don't know how much of the food I'll eat, but—" she chuckled.

"Yeah, we were just talking about food poisoning this morning," Leannah said. "Are you okay?"

"Yeah, thank you, I'm much better now. Thank God."

"I know how you feel," Colton then added. "I had a really bad case of it a couple years ago."

"Yeah, Iris told me you did. That really sucks. Mine was pretty mild so I can only imagine how you felt."

"Oh, it was terrible," Colton stated. "Iris is the smart one not eating meat. I should be more like her," he joked.

Jo laughed.

"Well, my chances are definitely lower," I said lightheartedly.

We all talked for a beat more, then all said goodbye. It was really cool that Jo was able to meet my family.

"Your family's awesome," Jo said as I put my phone in my pocket. "They're so welcoming."

I smiled, "Thanks. It was cool you got to meet them. I'll have to meet you dad."

"For sure! He doesn't have an iPhone so we couldn't FaceTime him, but we surely can call him sometime."

"That'd be great."

Jo smiled and the two of us went back to applying our makeup and getting ready for the day.

We didn't do much the rest of the day. We simply waited until nighttime to have ourselves a fun, eventful, Christmas.

73

Chapter 73

We rounded the corner onto Pearl Street, which was blocked off for the event. It was *covered* with people. The road was lit up and decorated so beautifully. Sparkling bows, wreaths, reindeer, and Santa's were hanging off store fronts, while string lights were wrapped around light poles and bare trees. Christmas music played out loud along with the chatter and laughter of people and children.

We reached an open area in between a parking entrance and a cafe. In this area, there was a huge sleigh with several glittery and shiny packages that sat around it.

"This must have been where people could take their children to get pictures with Santa," I said as we approached it.

"Oh, yeah," Jo said. After a beat, "I always liked to tell Santa what I wanted when I was little," Jo chuckled.

"Really?"

"You didn't?" she asked.

"I didn't go much," I shrugged. "The entire period I believed in Santa, my mom was drinking and then on pills. The four of us went once, maybe twice, once she was clean for Leannah, but other than that, no, not really."

"Colton never took you?" she asked.

"He did…sometimes," I responded. "But he was always skeptical of the guys dressed as Santa. He would walk Leannah and I down to this place by our house, and a Santa would be all set up in front of one of the stores. It was pretty, uh, unofficial and tacky now that I look back on it."

"Well, I don't blame Colton then."

"Yeah, neither do I."

We kept walking, admiring all the decorations and soon made it to where a lot of food trucks, games, and a giant Christmas tree were set up. The Christmas tree was set up outside of a beautiful glass high-rise. The tree was huge. I mean, *gigantic*. It reminded me of the one from *The Nutcracker*; you know the one that grew to forty-one feet tall? This tree *had* to be just as tall. It was decorated with hundreds of ornaments, covered in tinsel garland, and strung with lights that twinkle. It truly was incredible.

Mesmerized by the tree, we both took out our phones and snapped some pictures. We tried taking a picture of ourselves with the tree in the background but a stranger—seeing us struggle—offered to take one for us.

"That's a good one," Jo said as she looked at the photo of us on my phone. "Send that to me!"

While I did so, we heard a man shout.

"Guess how many ornaments are in the jar! Step right up and take a guess!" He was standing across the street next to a large container with ornament balls. Being intrigued, the two of us wandered over.

"Merry Christmas, ladies! How you doing?" he asked in a cheerful tone.

"Merry Christmas," Jo and I both said, followed by, "Good."

"Do you want to take a guess? It's free! And if you win, you get a brand-new Samsung flatscreen TV!"

We shrugged, "Sure."

I knew we probably wouldn't win but A, it was still fun to guess and B, we could always sell the TV.

The man handed us two tickets. One that said "Keep this coupon" and one that we were supposed to write our names and guesses on. He told us that the winners would be announced over the speaker at eight p.m.

"Hhmmmm," Jo said aloud. "There's gotta be at least seven hundred."

"Nooo," I said, thinking she was way under. "*At least* twelve hundred."

"Twelve hundred?!" she asked in a shocked manner, thinking *I* was way over.

"Yeah*, at least*," I reiterated. "Look how big the jar is and how small the balls are."

Jo studied it with a thinking face as she teetered her head back and forth, "Yeah, true. I'm actually pretty bad with this shit."

I chuckled, "I am too."

The two of us continued staring at the container. We both ended up writing down random numbers as neither of us couldn't come to a logical conclusion as to how many balls could be inside. We laughed about it then walked off and headed to where more games were set up.

We came to a man that had a big booth set up. He was about fifty-years-old. In the booth, there was a wall of red and green small balloons and small Christmas themed stuffed animals. On the table that the man stood behind, were a bunch of red and green darts.

"Want to try your luck in a game of darts?" the man asked. "Five darts for a dollar."

Jo and I looked at one another.

"Sorry, we don't have any money," Jo said.

"Aw," the man said, "well, how about I give you both five darts for free? Consider it a Christmas gift."

Jo and I looked at one another once again. "Alright," we shrugged in unison.

He picked up two piles of darts, distributing five red ones to Jo and five green ones to me.

"Now, this game of balloon darts is a little different than your typical game," the man stated. "Young lady, you have all the red darts," he said to Jo. "And, miss, you have all the green," he then said to me. "Not only do you have to pop the balloons, but you also have to pop the balloons that match the color of your dart. If you pop a balloon that is *not* the color of your dart, your opponent gets the point," the man said. "Whoever gets the most points, gets to choose between Rudolph, Santa, or this here, adorable snowflake," he said as he gestured towards a small disfigured white plush with a smile on it that screamed serial killer.

I raised my eyebrow at Jo and she snickered, thinking the same thing about the toy.

"Alright, get ready," the man said. "Go!" He rang a bell, signaling the start of the game.

Jo and I began throwing our darts, hitting nothing but somehow everything. We laughed at this as it was clear we both were terrible at the game.

"I got one!" Jo shouted.

I threw another one of my darts, only it hit a red balloon, "Now you got two," I laughed.

"Hey, thanks," she chuckled, then threw her last dart.

I threw my second to last dart and hit one of my balloons, a green balloon, "Oh, finally!" My last dart struck the cork board.

"Alright, ladies," the man said, counting the darks, "It looks like you won, miss red! What stuffed animal would you like?" the man asked.

"The snowflake?" he teased with a smile as he knew we thought it looked weird.

"No," Jo laughed. "I'll take Rudolph, please."

The man unclipped the stuffed animal and handed it to her.

"Here you go."

She smiled, "Thank you."

"You're welcome, y'all ladies have a great rest of your Christmas."

We thanked him and told him to do the same.

The night continued, and Jo and I had a lot of fun. We played a couple more, free games, took pictures, watched the light show, and did other random fun stuff.

Around seven forty-five, we sat down outside of the Boston Luxe Hotel. It was a gorgeous, high-rise hotel made of mostly glass. There were little tables set up outside of the hotel which was where Jo and I were sitting.

"They should be announcing the winner of the raffle soon," I said

"Oh yeah, that's right," Jo said as she clicked the button on her phone to look at the time. "It's seven forty-eight."

"Do you want to stay after they announce the winners or leave?" I asked.

"Uh," Jo sighed. "If you want to stay, we can, but I'm fine with leaving."

"I'm fine with that too. I'm getting cold," I said.

"Yeah, same," Jo added. "But you know we have to at least stay to hear the raffle winner. You know, in case we win," Jo teased, knowing with the method we chose—the "first numbers that came to our minds" method—we wouldn't be winning anything.

I chuckled, "Yeah, you never know."

Soon, two clean cut, White men came out of the hotel. They were older than us by about a decade as they appeared to be in their late-twenties, early-thirties. They both were dressed super nice, like they were rich or something. The one man had on a tan, high-quality-looking scarf, a long navy peacoat, nice dark pants, and expensive looking black boots. The other man had on a plaid shirt, a thick, also high-quality-looking, black scarf, a gray peacoat, expensive jeans, and tan leather boots. Both men had on huge gold and diamond watches and leather gloves. Their hair and beards were sharp and cut to perfection, with not a hair out of line. As they now stood somewhat next to us on their phones, we were greeted with the smell of their seductive and expensive cologne.

"Alright everybody, it's time to announce the winner of the two thousand thirteen Winter Boston Ornament Contest!" a man's voice boomed over the intercom.

"Let's see if we're gonna get that TV," Jo teased, pulling her ticket out of her jeans back pocket.

I chuckled and took mine out as well, "Yeah, let's see."

"Take out those tickets because one lucky person is going to be going home with a brand-new Samsung Flatscreen TV!" the same voice exclaimed.

There was a slight pause then the voice spoke again, "Okay, inside the six-and-a-half-foot container, there are…six thousand, nine hundred and twenty-two ornaments. The contestant with the closest guess was Hannah, ticket number nine zero seven, nine zero, one zero. Hannah guessed six thousand four hundred and fifty, way to go Hannah! Come on down to the raffle stand to claim your prize!"

Jo and I burst into laughter as soon as the man said that the amount was in the six thousands; we guessed in the two thousands.

"Okay, so our method was *not* a good one," I laughed as I tossed my ticket onto the table.

Jo tossed hers up as well, "Yeah, not at all," she laughed.

"No luck with the raffle, huh?" the man wearing the navy peacoat asked with a smile. His teeth were whiter than the snow around us and straighter than a steel board.

We both turned and looked at the two men.

"No, not really," Jo said politely.

"What were your guys' guesses?" the man wearing the gray peacoat then asked.

"Two thousand, one hundred, and fifty-four," Jo said.

"And you?" he then asked me.

"Two thousand, one hundred, and ninety-seven," I said.

The man shook his head, "I was never good at those things."

"Same," the man in the navy peacoat chuckled.

I looked down.

"I'm Ethan," he put out his hand to shake mine.

I looked up, meeting his eyes. After a beat, I shook it and then he shook Jo's.

"And I'm Nolan," the other man smiled, which was picture perfect as well. He then shook our hands too.

"I'm Jolene, I go by Jo."

"I'm Iris."

"Wow, you guys have some pretty cool names," Nolan said.

"Thanks," Jo said.

"Yeah, thank you," I added.

"Well, do you guys' mind if we join you two?" Ethan asked.

Jo and I looked at one another.

Ping.

Breathe, Iris, breathe.

"No, that's fine," Jo said once I nodded my head at her that it was okay.

The two men pulled out the two unoccupied chairs next to the both of us. Nolan sat next to me, and Ethan sat next to Jo.

"Well, I guess I should have said Merry Christmas," Nolan said to the both of us with a slight chuckle.

"Oh, yeah," Ethan remarked, "Merry Christmas," he smiled. "Sorry about that, sometimes you forget what day it is."

Jo chuckled, "It's alright."

"So, what did you guys do today for Christmas?" Ethan asked.

"This," Jo motioned around us.

The men looked around at the fair goers.

"*This* is all you've done?" Ethan asked in a confused manner.

"Yeah," I added, forcing myself to speak.

"You guys didn't do anything with your family?" Nolan asked.

Jo and I looked at each other, we exchanged the same thought.

"Do you know about The Stay program?" Jo asked them.

They shook their heads which led Jo to explaining what it was and that we're in it.

"Oh shit," Ethan said, sitting back in his chair in somewhat shock.

"I've never heard of anything like that," Nolan said.

"So, you guys aren't from here?" Ethan asked.

"No," I shook my head.

"We're from Illinois," Jo said.

"Are you two sisters?" Nolan asked.

"No," Jo said. "We met a couple months ago at our new house."

"Oh, okay. So, where are some places you've been too?" Nolan asked.

"Uh," Jo said through a sigh as she tried to think, "West Virginia, Iowa, Maryland, and Georgia."

"Just Washington and Wyoming," I said, looking down.

"Wyoming, wow," Nolan said. I then looked over at him. "How was that?"

I looked at Jo, whose face changed to a blank expression. I then looked down at my fingers.

"It was fine," I said, fiddling with my bracelet.

"So," Jo jumped in, picking up on my discomfort, "what do you guys do for work?"

"Business; stocks, entrepreneurship, real estate," Ethan said. "Stuff like that."

Jo nodded her head, "That's cool. Are you guys on a trip now or something?" Jo asked. "You guys staying at this hotel?"

"Nah," Nolan said, waving his hand. "We have a Condo about ten minutes down the road from here."

"Oh," Jo said somewhat confused, "So, what were you doing here then?"

"We're the co-owners of this hotel," Ethan said humbly.

That smacked me out of my thoughts.

"Holy shit, really?" I asked.

Jo's face was covered in bewilderment too.

The men chuckled. Then Nolan said, "Yeah, but we've worked hard for what we have, so we don't like to brag."

"Are you two brothers then?" Jo asked.

"Yep, brothers and business partners," Ethan said.

"Nice," Jo said. "Pretty cool to get to do all you guys do with your own brother."

Nolan smiled, "For the most part," he teased.

Ethan then playfully swatted at his brother, and we all laughed.

The conversation continued and found its way to our ages. We told them and then learned that Ethan was thirty-three and Nolan was twenty-eight. I became quiet, trying to process how I felt about that. Before I could, Nolan asked if we wanted to go into the lobby as we must be cold. I was on autopilot as I followed everyone inside. Jo and I sat down on an expensive black leather couch while the men took a seat across from us on leather chairs. The place was incredible. There was a huge chandelier in the lobby, beautiful exotic-looking plants, a water fountain, and expensive-looking decor. The entire place was absolutely stunning.

Conversation ensued, with Jo and the men doing the most of it. She told them how she just got over food poisoning and how our host has been gone, which was why she ate the tainted food to begin with. They seemed concerned regarding Kalista's absence, and it seemed genuine. Even though I was on guard, I can't lie and say Nolan and Ethan weren't totally polite, respectful, funny, and…handsome. Because they were.

Around nine-forty though, we stood up and told them we better start making it back home. They offered us a ride so that we didn't have to walk.

Ping.

The machine inside me fired up. I could tell Jo felt the same way as she looked over at me, unsure what to say.

There were two options: Number one, walk home and avoid the chances of Nolan and Ethan doing something to us or number two, walk home in the twenty-degree snowy weather and risk a stranger doing something to us. The way I saw it, was choosing the lesser of two evils. Also, I figured since Nolan and Ethan seemed to be decent guys, it was the better option. Although, didn't they say that about Ted Bundy too?

Minutes later, we stepped onto the sidewalk in the cold Boston air, Jo and I were met with a brand-new, all black, tinted windows, Lamborghini Estoque. I had *never* in my life seen a car like that. I had only ever seen them in movies or commercials, but *never* in person. I was stunned, absolutely shocked. Now, I was NOT by any means a girl that was interested in cars or impressed by them, but the constant things that were proving these two men richer and richer, was absolutely blowing my mind.

"*This* is your guys' car?!" Jo asked, not hiding her astonishment. The valet just dropped it off.

The men chuckled.

"Yeah," Nolan said. "One of them."

"*One* of them?!" I repeated in shock.

Ethan chuckled, "Come on."

The four of us walked over to the car. Jo and I crawled into the back seat. Once we were in, Ethan and Nolan reset their seats and sat down.

"Your guys' car is incredible," Jo said several minutes into the ride as she looked around. "I've never been in a car nearly this nice."

"No?" Ethan asked rhetorically. "Well, I guess most people haven't. I'm glad to be able to give you guys this experience."

"Is this your car, Ethan or yours?" Jo asked as she looked at Nolan.

"Well, technically it's *my* car," Ethan said, "but we share all of our cars, so."

"Yeah, like, I own a Mercedes and a McLaren, and he owns this and a BMW," Nolan said.

I made a stunned face, "Wow. Those are some pretty expensive cars."

"When you work hard, you can have anything," Ethan said.

I looked at him, not completely agreeing but also not stating my opinion. I think, most of the time, yes, this was true. But, sometimes, it wasn't. I think the world was set up to not really help people that needed it most. At least, I saw this a lot in my life. It was part of the reason my mom couldn't get clean a lot of times—well, aside from the fact that she didn't *truly* want to until she finally did. Different Suboxone treatments and rehab programs were always way too expensive or complex. As a child, I always wondered how do they expect people who are dirt poor, who have nothing, to get clean and get their life together, when they make it so incredibly hard to do so? I guess I still wonder about that today.

"Wow, this is a beautiful house you guys get to stay at," Ethan said as he pulled up the cobblestone driveway of Kalista's home.

"Seriously, it's incredible," Nolan said.

"Yeah, it's pretty nice," Jo said.

Ethan parked the car and the two of them got out, folding the seats down so we could exit as well.

"Well, it was really great meeting you guys," Jo said. "And thank you so much for the ride, you really saved us there."

"Yeah seriously, thank you for that," I said.

"No problem," Ethan smiled. "It was really great to meet you guys too."

Jo and I smiled. Just then there was a pause and I noticed the two look at each other, non-verbally confirming something.

"Hey, were you guys doing anything for New Year's Eve?" Nolan asked as he looked at us.

Jo and I looked at one another.

"Uh, no, probably not. Why?" Jo asked.

The two looked at each other once more.

"Well, if you guys are interested," Ethan proceeded to say, "we'd love to have you over our condo to hang out and you know…stuff."

I glanced at Jo.

"We'd be willing to pay you guys five thousand dollars each," Nolan added.

Wait *what?*

Jo and I were absolutely stunned. Our faces instantly fell into expression of shock, surprise, bewilderment, and awe.

"Five thousand dollars?!" I blurted out. "Why the hell would you do that?!"

The men smiled and chuckled at our disbelief.

"Well, we had a really great time tonight. You both are really beautiful girls and have awesome personalities," Nolan said.

"Okay, but why would you offer to pay us?" Jo asked.

"We didn't think you'd do it for free?" Ethan asked in a confused tone. "And anyway, we know you guys are hurting for money right now with your host being gone and all. We figured we could all benefit."

Jo and I looked at one another with wide eyes. We didn't know about this. This was extreme, *very* extreme. Five thousand dollars to just hang out with them?! There had to be a catch, and I felt like it wasn't a good one.

"Oh, I don't know—" I began to say.

"There's no rush," Nolan said. "We'll give you guys our numbers and if you decide you want to take us up on the offer, then just text us. If not, no harm, no foul," he smiled.

Jo and I looked at each other once more. She nodded and shrugged.

"Okay," I said cautiously.

"Cool," Ethan smiled.

We gave them our phones and they put their numbers into them. After they gave us our phones back, they hugged us goodbye, and we thanked them again for the ride.

"Iris?" Jo said as we walked to the front door.

"Yeah?" I said, not taking my eyes off the door.

"What the fuck was that?"

"I don't know, Jo. I really don't know."

74

Chapter 74

"Alright, what the fuck was that?" Jo asked passionately as she closed our bedroom door.

I took my purse and coat off and put them on my bed, "I have no idea," I said in utter shock. "Five thousand dollars?"

"Why would *anyone* pay someone five grand just to hang out with them?" Jo asked in disbelief as she put her phone on her nightstand and her purse on the floor.

"Do you think they're even serious?" I asked. "Do you think they'd *really* pay us five grand to just hang out with them for one night?"

Jo shrugged, "I have no idea…something's off."

"That's what I'm saying."

"But then on the other hand," Jo began, "they are super rich. Five grand is probably nothing to them."

"But still, if they truly just want to hang out, why would they offer us money?" I asked. "Why wouldn't they just ask us…without a payment?"

"Maybe they really do wanna help us out?" Jo questioned.

I shook my head, unable to get my thoughts straight, "I don't know."

There was then a slight pause as we both tried to wrap our heads around this.

"So…" Jo said. "What should we do?"

I sighed, sitting down on my bed. "I have no idea…Is it wrong to say although I'm terrified, I'm tempted?"

Jo sat down on her bed and faced me, "No, that's not wrong at all. I mean, who wouldn't be?"

I scrubbed my face, running my hand through my hair, "I don't know."

Another pause.

"What if they're being legit though and it's not some kind of trap." Jo asked gingerly. "We can't pass up that kind of money."

"I know," I said softly. "I mean, there's the possibility that what they said is true," I looked up at Jo. "That they want to pay us to hang out so we both benefit from it."

"Yeah…there is," Jo said. After a beat, "Well, let's not think about it anymore tonight. Let's just get ready for bed."

"Alright," I said, and we both began to do just that before going to sleep.

I think subconsciously, Jo and I wanted what Nolan and Ethan said to be true. Actually, I *know* we did; who wouldn't? Who wouldn't want to spend a few hours with someone for five thousand dollars each? Especially people like us, people like Jo and me. People that had nothing and were at a point so desperate for the very minimum—for food, for no worries. Maybe the men saw this and used it to their advantage. Lure two young, pretty-but-desperate-for-money girls, to their home with the promise of a cash reward and then they follow out whatever evil plan they had in mind. That thought made me shiver. But then there was the other part—the desperate, wanting it to be true, part. And that part? That part was pretty fucking strong.

The next morning, Jo and I woke up around nine. I blinked several times to adjust my eyes to our very bright room due to the snow outside.

"Good morning," Jo said as she rubbed her eyes.

"Morning," I said back as I rolled onto my side to face her. "How'd you sleep?"

"Like a rock," Jo chuckled, rolling over on her side to face me as well. "All of this walking around has got me exhausted."

I chuckled, "Yeah me too," I said as I grabbed my phone from my nightstand. I then snickered, "Leannah texted me asking how the light show and all went."

Jo rolled onto her back and snickered as well, "Tell her, good and that we were offered ten grand to hang out with strangers a decade older than us for a night."

I put my phone down and rolled my eyes playfully, "I would never."

Jo then rolled back on her side and faced me, "Are you going to tell them about that?"

I sighed and rolled on my back, "I don't know, Jo," I answered. "Probably not. Depends on what we even do with it. If I tell anyone, it'll be Colton."

Jo looked at me for a moment, "You wouldn't want Leannah to know?"

I rolled onto my side to face her. "I don't know. I wouldn't want her thinking certain things are okay or right to do because *I* did it."

Jo nodded her head, "I get that. Like you wanna be a good role model for her."

"Exactly," I said. "If I tell her, 'Oh, Jo and I got offered five thousand dollars each to hang out with two men that we just met, and are a hell of a lot older than us, and we're gonna take it,' she might think that that's okay. And I wouldn't want her to do that. Not saying she would, but…I don't know."

Jo looked at me pensively, "I get it."

I scoffed lightly, "I say all that, yet here I am, not really wanting to turn it down."

"Well, it's hard to say no to ten grand when we literally have thirteen dollars, Iris," Jo said. "Don't be so hard on yourself. It would be a hard decision for anybody, regardless of their money situation."

I rolled over onto my back and shook my head, "I know. I guess I just never thought it'd be a hard decision for *me*."

Jo looked at me slightly perplexed, "Why's that?"

"Because I always thought of myself as a morally grounded person."

Jo smiled and readjusted herself, "I think you contemplating this offer says that you still are."

I let the words settle into me. I never thought of it that way. I guess the new Iris—the dismal, scared, hard on herself, Iris—didn't allow me to.

I looked over at her, meeting her eyes, "Thanks, Jo. That means a lot."

She smiled, "Good, 'cause I mean it."

75

Chapter 75

"I think you two ladies have something that doesn't belong to you."

I currently stood in front of a huge—tall and muscular, Black man wearing a shirt that said "Security" on the chest. Jo and I have just been busted for shoplifting at Shaw's.

We know, it was a terrible plan. We debated stealing from Shaw's as it was stupid to steal from a place you previously filled out paperwork that told them everything about you, save for your blood type. But, it was really the only grocery store within walking distance and we couldn't keep eating Cheez-Its and Seven-Eleven frozen burritos forever.

So that is how we ended up in this position, in front of a wall of a human, telling us to give him back the stuff we took or he'd call the police. We tried to lie at first; say we didn't have anything but that only made Lamon—the security man—angry. Then we tried to reason; ask if we could just buy some of the things we took. That was a no too. We were only making him grow more impatient. So with not wanting to be arrested and having no other options, Jo and I reluctantly took the food out from our purses, and handed them over.

"Well, that could have gone really fucking bad," Jo said.

We were now back home. After we got kicked out of Shaw's, we walked over to the Burger King to put *something* in our stomachs.

"I know," I looked down. "We got really lucky."

"Yeah…we probably shouldn't steal anymore," Jo said. "But I don't know what other option there is."

I didn't either. I thought for a long minute, racking my brain for anything. That's when the idea came to me albeit not one I was proud of.

"Wait," Jo looked at me. "What about Kalista's room?"

Jo looked up at me, "What about it?"

"Look at this house," I said as I looked around our incredibly gorgeous bedroom. "This place has to be at least like fifty million, at *least*," I stressed. "She has to have either money stashed in there somewhere or some shit that we could sell."

Jo's face lit up, "Wait, Iris, that's actually a great idea. If she ever does return, she'd never know who took it out of everyone here."

"Right," I said. "If she even notices it to begin with."

"Exactly," Jo smirked.

We exited our room and headed up a level to the third floor. We didn't see anybody in the hall as we walked down the long corridor and made it to the large wooden double doors. I looked behind me to make sure no one was around. I then looked back at the door and tried the knob. It was unlocked and the door crept open.

Jo and I both walked in, closed the door behind us, and turned on the light. The room was still as gorgeous as we remembered from the first time we were in here. Although, it had that abandoned and vacant vibe to it. The chandeliers still hung, but no longer sparkled. The hot tub was still there but no water was in it. The chocolate foundation still sat in the middle of the room but was empty. The huge bed had covers that were wrinkle-free and pulled to a crisp, like no one had slept there in a while. And the amazing walk-in closet was partially empty, missing half of its clothes, like someone packed them all up and left.

"There's gotta be something in here we could pawn," Jo said as she began to look around.

"For sure," I said as I also began to walk over to her nightstands. "Just look for anything of value…or cash, of course."

"Right," Jo then wandered into the bathroom.

I opened her nightstand and didn't find much. There was a blue raspberry lip balm, an inhaler, a bottle of Advil, and a pair of jumbled up earbuds. I closed the drawer and opened the larger drawer below to which I found about the same thing. There were a couple random CDs by various artists, Victoria Secret body lotion, two unlit Bath and Body Works candles, and a Bic Multi-Purpose Lighter. I closed that drawer and walked around the bed to the other nightstand. In here, I found random books in both drawers and a pair of glasses. I sighed at my negative results. I then began to look under her bed, in between the mattress, in the couch cushions, in the drawer of her coffee table by her couch, and other little areas. All of them produced the same result—junk.

I sighed and headed towards her closet. Just then, Jo came out of the bathroom with a disgusting look on her face.

"I don't know why I thought to look in the trash," she said.

"Why? What did you find?"

"Used condoms," she said with repulsion.

"Ew, Jo," I said, sucking my teeth in a vile manner.

Jo shook her whole body with disgust, "I know."

I shook my head, "Let's just look in the closet, there gotta be something there."

We then walked into her huge walk-in closet. The room was just like those expensive walk-in closets you see on TV. There were cubbies for clothes and shoes and a large table with several drawers in the middle of the room. There were plenty of shoes, clothes, and accessories. Our focus was jewelry though—something of value.

Finding it in the one foot by four-foot, white leather ottoman bench, there were tens of medium-sized, felt lined, jewelry boxes that beautifully store all her shiny and sparkly jewelry.

"Holy shit," Jo said as we both gawked down at all the boxes.

"Hopefully there's something of value in here," I said, still staring into the ottoman.

"Well, there's only one way to find out," Jo said as she began taking boxes out of the ottoman.

I followed her lead and did the same thing. We pulled out box after box, checking each one to see if anything looked to be real diamond, gold, or silver. We found mostly gaudy, costume jewelry that we *knew* was straight from Walmart, Target, or Burlington. However, after about twenty minutes of digging through Kalista's jewelry, our luck turned around.

"Hey, hey, hey, Iris, look at this," Jo said, tapping me on my upper arm with the back of her hand.

"What?" I asked as I gazed down at the open box.

Inside was a gold chain necklace with a tear drop shaped emerald stone surrounded with what looked to be diamonds.

"Whoa, holy shit," I said as I took the box from her and examined the necklace further.

Jo smirked, nodding her head as she felt like we were on to something.

"This has got to be real," I said. "Look how it glistens."

"I know!" Jo exclaimed. "It's definitely got some value behind it."

I smiled as I continued twisting the box, watching how the light caught the stones and sparkled. After a moment, guilt flooded into me.

"And we're just gonna take this? To pawn?" I asked. "What if it's important to Kalista or something?"

"No, no, no, no, no," Jo said, shaking her head and taking the box from me. "We can't do that, Iris."

"What?" I asked in a confused tone as it appeared she was not talking about the same thing I was.

"We can't feel guilty. We can't set ourselves back," Jo said as she set the box down beside her.

"Jo—"

"Iris, I know it's wrong, I do. But her leaving us is wrong, too. We have to do something, Iris. We have no money and are running out of options," Jo said. "If we sit here and contemplate all of the rights and wrongs, we're never gonna get anywhere."

I sighed, knowing she was right, although guilt was a powerful emotion to shake off.

"She's pushed us to do this," Jo said. "We would have *never* done this if she didn't leave. We aren't thieves or addicts or anything like that. We don't have a malicious motive. Our motive is survival, and don't you have to do whatever it takes to survive?"

Jo looked at me with complete seriousness. I looked at her back, as I once again, knew she was right.

"Yeah," I said quietly, nodding my head. "You do."

We spent another twenty, thirty minutes carefully looking over all the jewelry to see if it would be of any value. Once we were done, around one-fifteen-ish, we had four boxes set aside of what we wanted—well, *needed* to take. They included the necklace we initially found, a gold chain bracelet, a pair of diamond hoops, and two ruby rings. They all looked real enough and expensive enough for Jo and me to at least get *something* out of. We then put all the felt lined jewelry boxes back into the ottoman, put the lid on, put the stolen jewelry into my purse, and straightened up anything else we had to, before we left.

Once back in our room, we Googled nearby pawn shops and found that Easy Money Pawns was a ten-minute walk from Kalista's. We wasted no time putting on our coats and heading there. We got outside, into the cold on yet another mission to help ourselves. It seemed the more plans we concocted, the more wrong, reprehensible, and crooked they became. I mean, we were at a point that was so desperate, that we stole *jewelry* from someone we didn't really even know. And it didn't stop here.

Jo and I made it to Easy Money Pawns right before two. We pushed open the glass doors and entered the shop.

"Hey, ladies. How you two doing today?" an overweight White man asked us.

"Good," Jo said. "How are you?"

"Not too bad, not too bad," the man said. "What brings you two in today?"

"We have some jewelry we want to pawn," Jo said.

"Alright, let's see what you got," he said as he stood at the glass case.

Jo and I approached the counter, and I gingerly pulled the boxes out of my purse. I put them on the counter and the man turned around and grabbed his diamond tester and magnifying glass.

Jo and I began to open the lids and set all the jewelry out for him to look at.

"Alright, alright," he said as he picked up the gold bracelet and looked at it in the light.

The man began to inspect it. He then held the magnifying glass up to it. He started examining the bracelet.

"So, this is gold plated copper," the man said as he continued examining it.

Jo and I looked at one another.

"Okay, would you still buy that?" I asked.

"I'm afraid not, no, I'm sorry. But let's see what else you got."

The man was friendly towards us. He put the chain back into the box and Jo closed the lid and moved it aside.

"Earrings are nice," the man said. "Let's see if they're real," He placed the tip of his diamond tester on the stones.

We all waited—Jo and I nervously—to see if the tester would start to beep. However, it didn't. All we heard was silence as the tester flashed a red light, meaning the stones—or crystals, weren't diamonds.

Disappointment grew onto our faces as the man apologized and handed Jo back the earrings. She boxed them back up and put them with the bracelet.

"Let's try this emerald necklace you guys got," the man said as he carefully picked the necklace up out of the box.

He began to examine it all over, starting with the chain. After several minutes of looking at it through the magnifying glass, he spoke.

"Well, the chain is once again gold-plated copper but let's check the pendant out."

The man laid the necklace down on the glass counter and placed the tester on the stones that surrounded the emerald. Once again, silence. He tried each stone and there was nothing but crickets. He then placed his tester on the emerald. Just then, the greatest sound Jo and I thought we could ever possibly hear, filled our ears.

Buzzz!

The diamond tester buzzed and lit up green, indicating it was real. Jo and I lit up as well but with excitement.

"Ayyyeee, there you go," he smiled. "But don't get too excited yet. I still have to check out a few things."

Jo and I sobered up but were still excited.

"So, there's a thing jewelers and pawn brokers, well *some* pawn brokers, use to determine a gemstones value," the man said. "It's called the four C's; cut, color, clarity, and carat. This all determines the value of the stone."

He then began studying the stone again.

"The cut is nice," he said. "See how it catches the light nicely?" the man asked as he showed Jo and I how the light reflected off it.

"Yeah," I nodded my head.

Jo nodded her head as well.

The man then turned it back to himself, "Now, the darker the color, the more it's worth. You guys see how this is a very light green?" he asked.

We both looked and nodded our heads.

"That makes it less expensive," the man said. "Now, it's still real, so it's worth *something*. The lighter color just decreases its value."

"Alright," I nodded my head. I could deal with that. I mean, after all, we were just looking to buy some *groceries*.

"Clarity has to do with how clear the stone is," the man explained. "Are there scratches on it? Are there heavy abrasions? Stuff like that. As you guys can see, this stone is kinda in bad shape," he said reluctantly.

Jo and I looked at each other disappointedly.

"You see all these scratches and scuff marks on it?" he asked as he turned the stone towards us.

"Yeah," Jo said.

"Mhm hmm," I added as I looked closely.

"This decreases a gem's value too," the man said. "It can be buffed up and re-faced but if the scratches and marks are too deep into the stone then sometimes it can't be removed."

"Oh, alright," Jo said.

"You guys know about carats, right?" he then asked.

Jo and I both shook our heads.

"Not unless you're talking about the vegetable," I said.

The man laughed, "No, no, I'm not. Carats, when dealing with gems, are the weight and size of a stone. Typically, the larger the stone, the more expensive it is. But it's important to keep in mind that it's better to have a smaller stone with great cut, color, and clarity, than a large stone with poor cut, color, and clarity."

"Right. So, what's the…carat of our emerald?" I asked, still not sure what a carat really was or why it was called that.

"Well, I gotta see," the man said, then set the necklace down. He turned around and retrieved a small scale from behind him.

"Now, everything besides the emerald is worthless to me," the man said. "Can I take the stone out of the necklace?"

Jo and I looked at one another, unsure of what to say.

"Uh, yeah," Jo muttered. "That's fine."

"You sure?" the man asked as he looked at Jo, feeling her uncertainty. "You don't seem too confident about that," he added with a slight chuckle.

"Yeah, no, we're sure," she said with more confidence this time.

"Alright," the man said as he once again turned around, and grabbed a couple of tools. The man then turned back around with the tools and laid them next to the necklace. He had a tweezer looking thing and a pair of pliers.

"So, this stone is a prong set," he said, showing Jo and me.

I nodded my head with confusion while making an equally confused face. I didn't know what this meant.

"You see these little things holding the stone in?" the man asked as he showed us the gem closer.

"Yeah," Jo said as we both nodded our heads.

"That's called a prong," he said. "There're a couple different ways stones are set into the jewelry. This one has a prong setting."

"Okay," Jo said in a somewhat confused manner. "Is that good or?"

"Oh, yeah, yeah," the man jumped to say. "Prong set gems are really easy to get out," he added as he picked up his pliers.

The man began to bend the prong backwards, which naturally loosed the gem. After a few more seconds, all three of the prongs on the teardrop shaped emerald were loose and the man took the gem out.

"*Voilà*" the man said as he held the stone and looked at it.

Jo and I smiled as we looked up at the stone as well.

"I'll give you guys this back," he said as he handed us the chain.

Jo took it and we both had shameful looks on our faces. I couldn't believe we stole Kalista's jewelry and were now tearing it apart for money. But like Jo said, we would have *never* done this if she didn't leave. At least we reminded ourselves of this to suffocate the guilt.

He then weighed the gem and did some math. Apparently, it was a point thirty carat. After seeing our *Okay and what does that mean* faces, the man explained that it was the size of an accent stone and he could give us forty dollars for it.

"Forty bucks?!" Jo exclaimed.

My jaw hung open. We were both shocked that forty dollars was *all* he could give us. Although I'd take *anything*.

"I thought you said it was *real?!*" I stressed.

"It is, but, girls, it's all scuffed up, it's not even half a carat, the color isn't amazing, I mean—" the man said. "Most pawn brokers only give like seventy-five percent of what the stone or item is actually worth."

Jo and I sighed.

"But I still gotta check out those rings," the man said. "If you have a real emerald, maybe you have real rubies too."

"Alright," Jo said as she took the rings out of the box and handed them to the man.

He once again picked up his tester and placed the tip on the ruby. Jo and I watched, hoping it would make a noise, but, of course, it never did.

"I'm sorry, girls," the man said. "I'd be happy to give you forty for the emerald though."

Jo and I shrugged, not going to turn down any amount of cash. The man then cashed us out while he told us a story about the time he bought jewelry from a man that he didn't know was stolen. He told us the guy ended up getting caught and was sentenced to like six years in prison.

"Well, that went fucking south quickly," I said as pushed the doors open and scurried outside.

Jo scoffed, following behind me, "Yeah, seriously."

"You don't think he was on to us, do you?" I asked as we walked down in the direction we came from.

Jo shook her head, "I don't think so…do you?"

I shook my head, "No, I don't think so."

"Alright, good," Jo said. "Let's just get back home, put Kalista's jewelry away, and figure out where we're gonna get groceries from."

"Good plan," I said.

Once we got to Kalista's, we put back the jewelry we couldn't sell, just how we found it, and sat down on our beds, trying to now figure out where we'd get food for cheap, that wouldn't kill us.

76

Chapter 76

We decided we'd take the bus to the Target just outside of Boston. This was our best option as we figured we'd just end up spending more money on overpriced food at mini marts, if they didn't get us sick first.

As I waited for Jo to finish using the bathroom, I looked down. I pushed the cuff of my coat up and looked at my scar. I ran my fingers over it as the night it happened, once again replayed in my mind.

The door slammed shut.

The yelling started.

He picked up the coffee mug that sat on his nightstand and he launched it.

Smash!

It hit the wall and coffee sprayed like blood spatter.

Covering the walls.

The mirror.

The door.

The dresser.

The ceramic lay in shards on the floor by the door.

Challenging me to leave.

Letting me know they'd cut me if I did.

Flick.

I looked and saw the flame.

Then the cigarette.

Then the smoke.

More yelling.

Then the shove.

Thwack.

I hit the wall.

I bet you'll think of this the next time you want to be a whore.

The scream. *My* scream.

The tears. *My* tears.

No matter what you do, no one will ever believe you.

"Iris?"

Jo's voice broke through my thoughts and I looked up at her, staring at me with concern.

"Are you okay?"

I looked away then down at my sleeve that was still pushed up, fingers still laying across the burn.

"Yeah," I pushed my cuff down. "Yeah, I'm fine."

We boarded the bus which was half full, but Jo and I were able to find some seats in the back. I looked at the sky that was quickly turning gray when Jo's phone rang.

"It's my dad," she said. "Oh, you'll finally be able to…meet him?" she said, unsure of her word choice.

I smiled, "For sure."

"Hey, Dad," she said, answering the phone. "I'm good, how are you? Oh good. Yeah—yeah, can you tell me in a sec? I want you to meet Iris!" she exclaimed. "Okay," she then smiled. "One sec."

Jo began searching through her purse and within a few seconds, she pulled out her earbuds. Jo then plugged them into the phone and handed me one of the earbuds. We simultaneously put them into our opposite ears.

"Okay, you're good," she said to her dad.

"Hi, Iris," her dad said with warmth in his voice.

"Hi, Mr. Mulvoy," I gleamed. "How are you?"

"I'm doing good, sweetheart. How are you?"

"I'm good, thank you. I've heard so many good things about you."

"What? My Jo-Jo was talking good about me?" he joked.

Jo and I both laughed.

"Yes, she was!" I chuckled.

"Aww, ain't she sweet," he laughed.

Jo rolled her eyes playfully.

"But she's said the same about you," Jo's dad said. "Nothing but good."

I smiled at Jo and nudged her playfully. "Well, that makes me happy to hear," I said.

"So what are you two up to today?"

"We're on the bus right now going to Target," Jo said.

"Oh, yeah?" he asked. "What are you two getting there?"

"Just some groceries," Jo said.

"You have enough money, Jo-Jo?" he asked.

Jo and I unsurely looked at one another

"Yeah," Jo said, "we do."

"Alright, good," he said.

Jo's dad, David, who he preferred I called him, then asked how Colton and Leannah were doing. I told him good, and that Colton will be graduating come June, and Leannah just started her first year of high school. He was happy to hear that and asked how my mom was doing as well.

"So, Dad, what did you need to tell me?" Jo asked. "Or do you want to talk about it later?"

"Well—"

"I can take my earbud out if you guys want to talk," I interjected.

"Oh, no, no, no, it's not like that at all," Jo's dad explained. "Actually, it might be good for you to hear, Iris."

Jo and I looked at one another with confusion. I couldn't possibly think why what he had to tell Jo, would be good for me to hear.

"So, Jo-Jo, you know how I was looking for a new job? Right before you left?" he asked.

"Yeah, course," Jo answered.

"Well, I found one," he said, happiness ringing through his voice.

Jo's face lit up, "You did?! Where?!"

"Sterlings Auto Body in Chicago," he said. I could practically feel his grin through the phone.

Jo and I looked at one another with wide eyes.

"Chicago?!" Jo exclaimed.

"Yup, like the place Iris lives?" he snickered.

"We're moving to Chicago?!" Jo asked.

"We are," David answered. "Already got us a place."

"Wait, so everything is all done?" Jo asked. "Like, what do you mean you got us a place?"

"The house is sold, the new home is bought, and I start after the new year," her dad said. "I didn't want to tell you before everything was set in stone and let you down if it all didn't go through. Plus, I knew this would only be good news to you."

"So, did you do that on purpose?" Jo questioned, still in disbelief. "Like get a job and us a home in Chicago?!"

Her dad laughed, "Well, yes and no. I wanted to get out of Springfield because there were really no employment opportunities for me. Chicago is in big demand for car mechanics right now and after I found that out, and seeing how close you two became, I figured it was a win-win."

Jo smiled from ear to ear, I could tell she was truly happy…and so was I. To be honest, I was happier than I expressed, I think I was simply in shock. Ever since I met Jo, and we became close, I was dreading the time we would both go to new homes, or just simply *back* home. I was terrified, actually. I know we only lived like three hours apart, but that wasn't as simple as it seemed. We didn't have our own cars to take whenever we wanted to see one another, we didn't have gas money to spend on hours of driving, we had other life obligations, it wasn't as nearly as simple as it was for other people. But…Jo was my *best* friend. I mean, we were *each other's* best friends. We both didn't really have friends growing up, we both didn't ever feel like we connected with people, and we both, we just…are lonely people. Jo was the only person, besides Colton and Leannah, that truly ever understood me. She was the only person that heard everything I never said. She was the only person that would care for me the same way I had been caring for people all my life, but never received, although desperately wanted. She was the only person I could trust, I could count on, I could rely on. She was the only person that ever showed me the true definition of a friend. She was the one and only person beside my siblings that I was scared to death to lose. So, to have someone like her but then also have that evil voice in the back of your mind telling you, it's going to get taken from you, was more than petrifying. Now that the little evil voice was destroyed, peace, joy, and true happiness flooded into me.

Jo put her new address into Google and the two of us took in all the online photos. It was the same skinny, two-story shape, like my house is. The house was brick with the right side of the face, protruding forward in a half hexagon shape. There were three windows on the first floor and three windows on the second floor on this side of the house. On the left side of the home's face, there were about ten steps leading up to the front door that had a porch. There was a small window to the left of the black door and a single window above the porch's roof. The small property was fenced in with a black gate that locked right before the steps to the door.

"It's not the most *glamorous* place in the world but—" her dad began to say.

"No, it's perfect, Dad, seriously," Jo interrupted.

"Oh, good, I'm so glad, baby," David said.

I could hear in his voice that the confirmation from his daughter made him feel better. The home may have been somewhat run down and in a not super great area, but it was all theirs. And that's what mattered. *They* made the house a home, nothing else.

We then Googled how far apart our houses were and found it was only an eight-minute walk. I smiled so hard my cheeks hurt. Happiness flooded me like a dam that broke loose. I wasn't going to lose her.

David then went on to say how the pay increase at Sterlings was five dollars. So, he'd be making twenty-one dollars an hour instead of seventeen; about forty thousand a year instead of thirty-six. He said he planned to work more than forty-hours a week too so he should be making even more than that. He told us how excited he was for a fresh start and heard a lot of good things about the company; how they have retirement benefits, paid vacation time, and some other stuff. I was really happy for him.

"You'll probably be able to come home soon if you want, once I get started and paychecks start to come in," David said to Jo. "I mean, you know you can leave anytime, but you know what I mean."

"Well, I'm in no rush, so no pressure."

"Alright, baby," her dad said.

"Well, call me when you get to the new house and start to unpack and all."

"Will do, baby girl. I'll let you two go and enjoy the rest of your day. Iris, it was so nice to finally meet you—well, talk to you," he chuckled.

I laughed, "It was so nice to talk to you too, David. You really did an incredible thing, thank you. Above all though, I'm really happy you got such a good employment opportunity, that's really amazing."

"Thank you," he said with happiness in his voice. "I'm really glad I was able to get something that could work out for the three of us."

"Me too," I smiled as I hugged Jo.

Jo squeezed me back, "I love you, Dad. Talk to you soon."

"I love you more, Jo-Jo," he said. "I'll talk to you, baby."

"Bye," Jo smiled then clicked the red button, ending the call. She then leaned her head on my shoulder.

"This is fucking amazing," Jo said with purse bliss.

"Yeah, it is," I said as I leaned my head onto her head. I wore a smile larger than I ever had before. "It really, *really* is."

77

Chapter 77

It was now the last day of 2013. I guess, all better known as New Year's Eve. Jo and I had gotten as much food as we could at Target. Although, forty dollars-worth of food is like nothing. We got two frozen pizzas, four Healthy Choice bowls, three loaves of bread, ham and turkey lunchmeat, and two boxes of cereal. Our plan was to make it last as long as we possibly could, but that morning, the universe had other ideas in mind.

It was around eight-thirty, nine o'clock-ish, when I woke to the sound of Jo yelling.

"What the fuck!" I heard from the bathroom.

I got up from my bed and hurried in.

"What's going on?" I exclaimed.

Jo was sitting on her knees with the mini fridge's door open, looking into it. Our basically brand-new ham and turkey, and two Healthy Choice bowls were sitting on the floor, outside of the fridge.

"The fridge isn't working," Jo said, agitation dripping from her voice.

"What?" I exclaimed.

"Yeah, it's like sixty degrees in there," Jo said.

"Fuck," I knelt beside her. "Is our food okay?" but the moment I grabbed it, I knew it wasn't.

"I can't believe this," Jo rose to her knees, inspecting the back of the fridge.

"What happened?" I asked.

"I don't know, I came in here to get some cereal, opened the fridge because for some reason I thought we had milk, but we don't. I could feel it wasn't cold inside and that's when I saw the thermometer."

"Oh my God," I still said in disbelief. "What could have gone wrong?"

"I have no idea. Maybe it shorted out or something, but I can't find anything wrong with it. I mean, I don't know what I'm doing or looking for but," Jo said as she looked all around the fridge.

I stood up and began to examine it with her.

"Is there, like, a manual or something?" I asked.

Jo exhaled, "I don't know, probably not. I wouldn't know where I'd be either."

There was a slight pause.

"We just bought this shit," Jo said, gesturing towards the now bad food on the floor. "Now all we have is a box of cereal and two and a half loaves of fucking bread," she slumped down on the floor and leaned against the vanity.

I sat down next to her, leaning against the vanity as well.

"Now what, Iris?" Jo questioned. "Now what do we do? Not only is our fridge broken so we can't keep anything cold, but we also have three dollars and a box of cereal to our name."

I stayed silent for a moment while I pondered on the very few options we had. The only feasible one came to mind, and it wasn't one I wanted to admit at all…or accept. But what other choice did we *really* have at that point?

"We could go to Nolan and Ethan's place tonight," I said, looking at the floor.

"What?" Jo asked as she quickly turned her head to look at me.

I met her gaze.

"Are you serious?" she asked. "Iris—"

"Jo, what other choice do we have?" I asked with utter seriousness. "What other choice do we *seriously* have?"

Jo slumped against the vanity again, thinking, knowing I was right.

"Well…there's got to be another solution, I mean—"

"Jo, there's not," I said. "There's not. Okay, we tried, okay. We tried. We tried to make our money last, and we tried to do the right thing and get a job, and when no one would hire us, we tried to steal, and that didn't work, and we did something even worse and stole jewelry, and we thought we could pawn it and be set, but we weren't, and now our fridge is broken and were back at the bottom of the same pit we started in. We tried, Jo. We tried. And we have two dudes asking us to just come over and hang with them for five grand each. I mean? Are we really going to pass this up? Now? At this point?"

Jo looked defeated but like she knew I was right.

She sighed, "I mean, what if it's dangerous?"

"It can't be any worse than this," I said coldly. "Jo," I said seriously. "We have a box of cereal, some bread, and three dollars to our name. You just said it yourself. Even if we come up with some way to get "food-food" how are we gonna keep it cold? 'Cause we damn sure don't have money or resources to fix the fridge."

Jo looked at me with the same look as before.

"All we have to do is hang out with these dudes for a night," I said hopelessly. "That's all."

There was a slight pause.

"It *is* an opportunity we'll never see again," Jo said, coming around.

I looked down.

"Alright…I'll call them," Jo faltered.

I nodded my head and pursed my lips, "Alright."

Jo took out her phone from her back pocket, found Ethan's contact, and put it on speaker. As we listened to the ring, we both exhaled through unease.

"Hello?" Ethan said.

"Hey, Ethan," Jo said unconfidently. "It's Jo, remember me?"

"Jo! Hey!" he gleamed. "Of course! How are you?"

"Uh, I'm okay. How are you?"

"I'm doing pretty good."

"Good...so uh, so listen. Iris and I are interested in that offer you and Nolan gave us...if you guys are still down."

"Oh—oh, yeah, we are," he said in a shocked tone. "That'd be awesome."

"Five grand each right?" she asked.

"That's right, five grand."

"And how long would we have to stay?" Jo asked.

"Oh, I guess it depends on everything. But a couple hours?" he stated unsurely. "It's up to you guys."

Jo and I looked at each other and frowned. We thought that was a weird answer but didn't give it much thought.

"Alright, what time should we come over? We'll probably have to walk, so we'll need some time in advance."

"Oh no, no, we'll send a cab to you guys," Ethan said. "How does eight sound?"

Jo and I looked at one another again, we thought this was generous of him.

"Yeah, sure that's fine. Thank you," she said.

"Of course, and when you guys are ready to go home and the night's over, we'll have a cab take you back as well, not deducted from your five grand, of course," he chuckled.

Jo forced a laugh. I felt weird and uncomfortable. I felt like an item being bought.

"Thank you," Jo said.

"Iris is coming too, right?" he asked.

"Yeah, she's coming," Jo said blandly.

"Cool. Yeah, don't worry about anything, we'll have a cab there at eight just wear something nice," he said.

Jo and I looked at one another and frowned. We were confused as to why.

"Okay," Jo said, even more dry than her last words.

I knew she felt as weird as I did and as confused as I did, but we were getting five grand, we weren't going to dispute clothes.

"Alright, well awesome," he said with excitement in his voice. "I'll see you two tonight then."

"Alright, I'll see you. Thanks again," Jo said uncomfortably.

"Thank *you*," he said, I'm assuming with a grin.

Jo forced another chuckle, "See you."

"Bye," he said.

Jo then pressed the red end button and tossed her phone on the floor, sighing.

"It's gonna be okay," I said as I rubbed her back.

"Why do we have to wear something nice?" Jo asked. "We don't even have anything."

I looked away, knowing I had something.

"We, uh, we, actually do," I said as I looked back down in front of me at the floor.

Jo frowned, "What do you mean?"

I sighed deeply, "Remember that story I told you about with Nate on Halloween and how Campbell made me dress up as a black cat?"

"Of course," Jo said with conviction.

"Well, that"—I rolled my eyes and shook my head—"slutty black dress I wore, I had from a party I went to back in Seattle—well,

Steilacoom really. My roommate, Bianca, you know the one I told you about?"

"Yeah?"

"Well, Bianca was set on going to a party on the Fourth of July. She found two guys at the mall who were going to a party and made Melanie and I get new outfits for it. She said the stuff Melanie and I had were ugly—basically. So, after a dispute about how I didn't have the money," I snickered, "go figure, and how Melanie and I both didn't care, or want one, Bianca told us she'd buy them for us. And she did. She bought all our dresses. Well," I sighed, "that night didn't go as planned…at all. It was actually really bad, terrifying even."

Jo looked intrigued at what was to come next.

"The two guys that Bianca met from the mall—Theo and Mason—put drugs in a bottle of Blue Curaçao that they made Bianca and Melanie drinks for."

Jo's eyes widened as she was shocked.

"Luckily, I was able to get to them in time before anything happened, but, after everything, Bianca didn't want her dress or shoes anymore. She told me I could have them. So…I have that black dress and the dress she wore, along with two sets of heels," I said reluctantly as I knew once again, I was going to have to wear that God awful black dress.

"Well—well, what's it look like?" she asked curiously.

I made a painful expression, "It's bad, Jo. It's bad. But…it's all we got."

There was a slight pause.

"Well…can I see it?" she asked.

I stood up, "Come on."

I let the way out of the bathroom and into our walk-in closet where my suitcase was being stored. I sat down with the suitcase and Jo sat next to me. I unzipped it, dug around, and pulled out the black dress and Bianca's sparkly red dress. I held up Bianca's dress so Jo could see it.

Her eyes widened, "*That's* the dress?" she asked. I could tell she did not like it at all.

I pursed my lips," I told you it was bad."

Jo took the dress from me and held it up, continuing to look at it. "What does yours look like?" she asked, having no more words for the red dress. "I know it's black but."

I exhaled then held it up, "This is it."

Jo looked at me with a blank but also shocked expression, "You wore that?"

"Yup," I said dully. Jo then took the dress from me. "Twice," I added.

"Well," Jo looked at me sympathetically, "the second time wasn't really your choice."

I looked down, "Yeah."

"Or really the first I guess," Jo then added. "Wait, so did you pick out this dress?"

I scoffed, "Yeah right. No, it was the only dress in the store that was my size."

"What store?" Jo asked with a confused frown.

"Charlotte Russe," I said. "We were gonna try Forever Twenty-One, but some lady told us they were closed. They had a leak or some shit."

"Oh, damn," Jo said as she continued gawking at my dress.

"Yeah, so, this is all I have that's "nice,"" I said with finger quotes.

"Well, it'll have to do," Jo exhaled as she spoke. After a beat, Jo asked, "Do you want to wear the red one?" I knew Jo asked me this because of the Nate and Campbell situation.

"I don't think it'll fit," I said. "She was a size bigger than me."

"Oh, okay…are you okay with wearing the black one though?"

I shrugged, "It's becoming a routine at this point."

Jo flashed a saddened smile.

"Where are the shoes?" she asked, changing the topic.

"Right here," I said as I pulled them out from under some jumbled up short sleeve shirts.

"These are the ones Bianca wore," I handed her the heels. "Are you a size seven?"

"Yeah, that'll work," she said as she took the matching glittery red heels from me and began to examine them. "Wow, very Dorothy-ish."

I snickered lightly, "That girl loved anything bold and blinge-y."

"I can tell," Jo chuckled. She kicked her legs around to the side to try them on. "They fit though."

"Good," I said.

I looked down gloomily at the black dress and thought about having to wear it again. Jo must have noticed this because she said, "It's all over tonight, Iris. After we get this ten-grand, it's over."

I looked up at her and met her eyes, "I know."

She then smiled, "I love you," she said as she reached for a hug.

"I love you too, Jo," I said as I hugged her back.

We hugged for a moment then she pulled away.

"I'm gonna go call my dad, see how he's doing with unpacking and everything," Jo said, rising to her feet.

"Alright," I said.

"You promise you're okay?" she asked.

"Yeah, I'm fine," I forced a smile.

"Alright," she stood up and walked out of the closet.

I called my family around three and let them know that Jo said her dad was settling into the new home and unpacking. The day after Jo and I found out they were moving to Chicago, I of course called and told my family. They were so happy for me—and Jo and her dad. I told them I would let them know when Jo's dad was all settled in, so that day, I did that. But now it was seven-thirty and Jo and I just got done eating some cereal and toast for dinner. It was now time to get ready for Ethan and Nolan's house.

"Oh my God," Jo said as she looked at herself in the mirror.

I turned to look at her.

"This is fucking ridiculous," she then turned towards me.

It was skintight, ended *just* under her butt, and exposed almost all her boobs.

My eyes widened, "Oh, Jo."

"This is ridiculous," she said. "I feel like a hooker."

I pursed my lips and raised my eyebrows," Well, Bianca was a prostitute, so…"

Jo exhaled, shaking her head, "Whatever, I guess. I mean, I don't want to show up wearing something casual when they said to look nice and we don't get all the money, or it in general."

"Yeah, I feel that," I said dully.

Jo began to touch up her makeup and I looked at the black dress hanging over my vanity's chair. Morose spread through my veins.

Damn, baby, you look sexy as hell. Can't wait to take it off of you though.

I closed my eyes, forcing the thoughts to stop before they started. *Breathe, Iris, breathe.*

I took a breath and stood up. I quietly got dressed then turned around to meet Jo at the double vanity to fix my makeup as well. I forced myself to focus on that and not look at myself. Jo looked at me with sympathy as I came towards her. She knew better than anyone how wearing that dress again was dreadful. I silently picked up my makeup brush and my highlighting powder and began to touch up that portion of my makeup. I could tell Jo didn't know what to say. I *also* could tell she was just as uncomfortable with her outfit. The two of us continued fixing our makeup in silence. We brushed our hair, sprayed on some perfume, applied some lip gloss, and finalized ourselves by putting on our heels.

"Where should we leave this?" Jo asked as she held a piece of paper out to me.

"What is it?" I asked, taking it from her. "Is that their address?"

"Yeah…just in case," Jo said.

I looked up at Jo pensively and met her eyes, "Uh, on my bed. Someplace it won't be missed." I handed her back the paper.

Jo set it down on the center of my bed then sat down. She paused for a moment then spoke. "I figured you weren't telling your family what we were doing, and I obviously wasn't telling my dad, so, that's why I thought leaving the address would be a good idea…In case something were to happen."

I sat down next to Jo, "It's a good idea."

Jo smiled and just then we heard the sound of a car's horn coming from outside.

"That must be the cab," Jo said as she stood up and walked to the window, looking out of it. "Yeah, it is."

"Alright," I said as I stood up, grabbing my purse and phone. "You ready?"

Jo inhaled deeply then exhaled as she walked back towards me, "As I'll ever be."

I looked down, "Alright then, let's go,"

78

Chapter 78

The taxicab pulled up to the condo complex around eight-twenty. Jo and I grabbed our purses, thanked the man, and got out. He drove away and Jo and I headed towards the gold-colored doors. As soon as we entered, Ethan and Nolan were standing there waiting for us.

"Jo! Iris! Great to see you guys," Ethan exclaimed, as he gave each of us a hug.

Jo and I awkwardly hugged them back.

"You two look incredible," Nolan said as he hugged me, then hugged Jo.

"Thanks," I forced a smile. "Just something we had lying around."

I was trying to push down my awkwardness and uncomfortableness because I felt like if they didn't have a good time, we might not get the money. It was becoming important to me to make sure they had a great night.

"Well, it looks great," Nolan said with a smile.

"Thanks," I looked down.

"Shall we head up?" Ethan asked.

"Yeah," Jo smiled.

Nolan then extended out his hand for me to hold it. I looked at it for a moment, swallowed, then took it.

Breathe, Iris, breathe.

As we walked to the elevator, Ethan took Jo's hand as well. We went up to the twelfth floor, soon enough standing outside of Nolan and Ethan's apartment. When we walked in, we were immediately blown away. The place was absolutely stunning. As soon as you walked in and entered the living room, you were greeted by a beautiful back wall made completely of glass. The skyline of the dark Boston sky lit up by all the city life, illuminated through. There was a gorgeous white marble fireplace that was burning, a very expensive looking gray couch, two matching chairs, and a very abstract and elegant coffee table. As you rounded the corner, further into the living room, we were met with the back of another set of couches and a huge flat screen TV. I'm talking like *at least* seventy-five or eighty inches, *at least*. The place had cream colored walls, beautiful exotic plants, and abstract paintings hung on the walls that weren't made of glass. It was incredible. If it wasn't obvious before by the way these men dressed, the car's they had, and the businesses they owned, that they were filthy rich, this place *definitely* confirmed it.

"Oh my God, your home is incredible!" Jo exclaimed.

"Yeah, seriously, it's *gorgeous*," I added in awe. "I've *never* been anywhere this nice."

The two men humbly chuckled.

"Did you guys want a drink?" Ethan asked as he walked over to the kitchen area that sat next to the living area with the flat screen TV.

"Uh, I'll have some water," Jo said.

"Yeah, me too, please," I added.

Jo and I then walked towards the kitchen area, which was incredible as well. There was an island bar with a marble counter which matched the rest of the counters in the kitchen. Next to the island was a wall, separating the bar from the rest of the kitchen, but creating a walkway to the other part of the kitchen in front of the island. This wall also had a section that had glass shelves attached to it. These shelves held expensive looking drinking glasses. The cabinets were all plain, shiny white with no handles, creating a very elegant, sleek look.

Ethan took two glasses down from the shelves and set them next to the sink. He then walked through the archway to the fridge and returned with a Britta container.

"Aren't we special," Jo joked as she sat down at the island, "we get *Britta* water."

We all chuckled as I sat down next to her.

"Yes, you are," Ethan smiled as he poured both glasses. He soon turned around with both glasses, handing one to each of us.

"Thank you," Jo and I both said.

"No problem," Ethan smiled.

"Are you guys hungry?" Nolan asked. "We could order a pizza, or we could make you guys something."

I shook my head as I swallowed my water and set my glass down, "I'm good, thank you."

"Yeah, me too," Jo said. "We ate back at home."

"What did you guys have?" Nolan asked.

Jo and I laughed, embarrassed to tell them our meal, "Cereal and toast," Jo said.

"Cereal and toast?" Ethan asked with confusion.

"Why did you guys have that?" Nolan asked.

"Well, our fridge broke this morning and the couple things we bought the other day went bad. Cereal and bread are all we have," Jo said.

Ethan and Nolan frowned.

"Is your host still not back?" Ethan asked.

We both shook our heads.

"Nope, and nobody's heard from her," Jo said.

"Do you think she's okay?" Nolan asked.

"We think she's on a bender. She was the last time," I said.

"Damn, that's a shame," Nolan said.

I took another sip of my water.

"Well, why don't we all sit down on the couch?" Ethan suggested.

"Yeah, where would you guys rather hang out? In front of the TV or the fireplace?" Nolan asked.

I chuckled as I stood up, "I've never had to choose which *living room* I want to relax in."

Jo laughed as she then stood up, "Yeah same."

Ethan and Nolan both laughed.

"Well, the choice is yours," Nolan said as he looked at me.

After Ethan poured himself and Nolan a glass of scotch— Macallan scotch to be exact, which is twenty-eight hundred dollars a bottle, we settled on the living room with the fireplace. We all took a seat on the couches. I sat on the far-left couch and Nolan sat next to me. Jo sat down on the far-right couch, next to Ethan. The couches were small, only big enough for two people really. There was another couch the same size as the ones Jo and I were sitting on, in between us. The three couches were placed in a way that resembled almost a half-circle, so the four of us still faced one another.

"So, how have you guys been since we saw you last?" Nolan asked.

"We've been okay. How about you two?" Jo asked.

"Oh, you know, same old same old. Business as usual," Nolan replied.

"How's that going?" I asked as I sipped my water.

"It's going good," he said. "Stock market is doing good and the hotel is booming right now due to the holidays."

"That's great," Jo smiled.

"Yeah, glad to hear that," I said.

He looked at me and smiled flirtatiously. Discomfort rose inside of me, but I forced it down and smiled.

Breathe, Iris, breathe.

Somehow, the topic of Jo's dad getting a new job and them moving to Chicago came about.

"I'm sure you guys are excited, you seem pretty close," Ethan said as he sipped his drink then put his arm around Jo.

I could see this made Jo uncomfortable, but like me, unfortunately, she pushed this down to not jeopardize our money.

"Uh, yeah, we are. Super excited," she tried to act normal.

"Good," Ethan said. "And your mom? What is she going to do for work?"

I looked at Jo and she looked down.

"Oh, uh, my mom died when I was a child," she answered.

"Oh, I'm so sorry," Ethan began. "I had no idea."

"No, no, it's okay," she smiled ruefully. "You couldn't have known."

Ethan smiled, but I could tell he felt bad. There was a slight moment of silence, I felt sorry for her.

"Yeah, she, uh, she died in Nine-Eleven," Jo said, looking at the floor.

Nolan and Ethan both looked at Jo, shocked.

"Oh my gosh," Ethan said. "That's horrible, I'm so sorry."

"Yeah, that's awful," Nolan added. "I'm really sorry to hear that."

"It's okay," Jo said. "I have my dad, and we're really close."

"Well, I'm glad to hear that," Nolan said.

"Yeah, me too," Ethan smiled as he rubbed Jo's shoulder.

Jo forced a smile through a slightly crinkled nose.

"So, Iris," Nolan began as he picked up his drink, sipped it, then set it back down, "you said before you have a brother and a sister? What do they do?"

"Well, my brother works at a gas station by our house and my sister just started high school," I said.

"Nice, how old's your brother?" he asked.

"He's nineteen, he graduates this year."

"Oh, awesome!" he exclaimed. "I'm sure he's excited."

"Yeah," I smiled. "He is."

"Is he going to college or anything like that?" Ethan then asked.

"No, he's not," I replied. "We don't have money for that."

"I get it," Ethan said.

"He'll probably get into a trade job. You know, like carpentry or construction."

"Oh, cool," Nolan said.

Just then, Nolan put his arm around me and smiled at me. I forced a smile onto my face, making it as believable as possible.

The four of us carried on talking for hours. It actually was kind of enjoyable. Ethan and Nolan were genuine guys, especially for being as rich and as "high-life" as they were. They didn't do or say anything weird or set off any alarm bells to either of us. They were actually really sweet and kind. It was a nice night, *and* we were getting ten grand for it, which is something I still couldn't believe. But…I guess I shouldn't have. It wasn't until right after the ball dropped that the entire night took a turn, a turn Jo and I *never* thought it would take. I should have known this was *all* too good to be true.

79

Chapter 79

"FIVE, FOUR, THREE, TWO, ONE! HAPPY NEW YEAR!" we all yelled as we watched the ball drop and big *Two thousand and fourteen* numbers play across the TV.

We all hugged one another and popped those little confetti poppers. Ethan and Nolan even popped a bottle of champagne. After we had our little celebration, we sat back down, now in the living room with the TV.

We all began making small talk for a few minutes until the conversation died down. When there was a moment of silence, I noticed Ethan gave Nolan a look. One like *You want to ask now?* Nolan then gave a confirming look back. I frowned and looked at Jo, wondering if she saw this, which it appeared she did as she was slightly frowning, too.

"So did you guys want to get to it now?" Ethan then asked aloud.

Jo and I looked at each other very confused.

"Get to what?" I asked unsurely.

Ethan and Nolan looked at each other, twice as confused.

"What you guys are here for?" Ethan asked in a very confused tone.

"Yeah?" Nolan said in the same tone. "Sex?"

Jo and I snapped our heads towards one another.

Ping, ping, ping, ping.

"Whoa, whoa, whoa," Jo said, standing up from the couch, "you guys said come here to *hang out*. You *never* said anything about sex."

I stood up next to Jo, fear and confusion seeping into me.

Nolan and Ethan then stood up as well, also very confused.

"We said *And stuff*," Nolan stated.

"Yeah, why do you think we asked you guys to dress nice?" Ethan chimed in.

"Right, I mean, did you guys think we'd pay you five thousand dollars each to *just* hang out with us?" Nolan said in an absurd tone, but still being nice.

"Well," Jo said in a *I guess not* tone, "I don't know. But you *never* made it clear about having sex. You could have clarified that part."

"Look," Ethan said with his hands up, "if you guys don't want to, you don't have to. No one is making you guys. But we're not giving you ten grand to just hang out."

"Yeah, you guys are more than welcome to leave or to just hang out for as long as you want but, the plan was five grand each in exchange for sex," Nolan added.

Jo crossed her arms, "That was *never* said."

The men shrugged.

"Look, I'm sorry, we should have been clearer then," Ethan said after a beat. "But we honestly thought you guys figured that's what we meant."

"Not at all," Jo said.

While at first I was quiet from fear, now, I stayed quiet as I was thinking to myself.

"I'm sorry," Nolan said.

There was a moment of silence.

"Well, it was nice meeting you guys, but I guess we'll head out—"

Jo began to say.

"Jo, can I talk to you for a second?" I asked, interrupting her.

Jo looked at me blankly.

"Alone?" I added.

Jo continued to look at me with a blank expression, "Sure."

I proceeded to the front door and Jo followed. I opened the door, stepping into the hallway and then closed the door behind us.

"What? What are you thinking?" Jo asked.

I looked at her for a moment then sighed, looking down I said, "Jo, we should just do it."

"What?!"

"Look, if you don't want to, we won't. We'll leave. But, Jo, what else are we gonna do?" I asked, defeated and absolutely over this struggle.

Jo looked at me without an expression or emotion.

"We tried, Jo. We tried everything," I said. "And every single time we think we have a good plan behind us, it gets ruined and I'm tired, okay? I'm tired of being hungry and worried and desperate. I'm tired of not having any ounce of control over my life, I'm tired of struggling just to get through the day, I'm tired of getting looked at like dirt or a thief or worthless—"

"There's gotta be another choice, Iris," Jo said, shaking her head.

"There's not, Jo," I said sternly. "There's not. No one's gonna hire us, we're out of money, we have no food—there's no other choice," I looked at her and paused. "We don't just have the luxury of deciding we won't steal or pawn other people's stuff, or lie, or do half of the things we have. We're forced to do it. You know why? because we've been back into this corner and the walls only got closer and closer until we ended up here."

"Yeah, but we have the option to not sleep with them," Jo said sternly. "You heard them, they said we can leave. They aren't making us."

"But do we really have the option to not sleep with them, Jo?" I asked pensively.

Jo seemed confused, "Yeah?"

I shook my head, "Look," I said seriously, meeting her eyes, "I'm not making you…at all. If you don't want to, we'll leave. I get it, I do. We'll get our things, and we'll go," I then took a slight pause. "But all I'm saying, Jo, is we're losing. We have no money, no food, no more options. What are we really supposed to do, truly? Huh? We have *three* dollars," I said. "We tried, this whole month we've been trying, and trying, and trying. It comes to a point where there's nothing left to try. We're forced to do this, Jo. Whether you think those two men are in there making us or not, it's not about them and what they say, and it's not about us and what we feel. It's about how we have no more choices anymore." After a beat, I said, "Desperation is a disease, Jo. It crawls onto your skin, buries itself into your flesh, infects you, and makes you do things you never thought you would. It's a disease."

Jo stared at me with sadness, hopelessness, and desperation in her eyes. Even though it was obviously due to her not really wanting to sleep with Ethan, it was also because she knew I was right… unfortunately. She *knew* in order to end this, this is what we had to do. And that was the saddest part. The saddest and *worst* part. That our desperation—our disease—forced us to this. That this *sick* infection poisoned us so violently that we were alright with giving our bodies away for money—to stay alive.

Jo looked at me blankly.

"Jo," I sighed, "if you don't want to do it, we won't. I don't want to force you or make you feel like—"

"No," she interjected. "You're right, we have to."

I stepped back and waited for her to speak.

"You're right, Iris. What other choice do we have?" she asked with bitterness as she looked at me with her cold, blue eyes. "We're just gonna go home and be in the same spot we were earlier, and the day before, and the day before that, and the day before that. It's just going to keep getting worse. You're right. We don't get to choose. If we want to eat, to take care of ourselves, then we have to do this."

I looked at Jo with a mixture of sadness, numbness, and desperation. I knew she felt broken. She didn't want to do this; I didn't want to do this. I didn't know if I *could* do this. But like we both said, what other choice did we really have? Go back to Kalista's and starve? Continue to steal and get arrested? End up selling ourselves to a random man? At least Nolan and Ethan had a lot of money and weren't douchebags—from what we knew so far. This was it. This was unfortunately how the game would end. And there was *nothing* that was going to change that.

"Alright," I said monotonously in a low voice. "You're sure?"

Jo met my eyes then nodded her head, "We have to."

I gave a disappointed face and hugged her, "I love you, Jo. It's all over after this."

Jo squeezed me back and we embraced for a second. Jo then pulled away and looked at me, "I know," she said, forcing a smile. "I love you too."

I could tell she was trying to be strong, we both were.

I forced a smile, "Cough twice—loud, if something isn't right, promise?"

"Promise," she said.

I stuck my pinky finger out to her to which she smiled and stuck hers out to me. We interlocked them, kissed our thumbs, and touched our thumbs together.

We both exhaled, and I opened the door. The two of us walked in and approached Ethan and Nolan who were sitting on the couches in the living room with the fireplace. They both stood up when they saw us.

Jo and I looked at each other, confirming one final time that we were in fact going to do this.

I exhaled, "Five thousand each, right?"

"Yeah, that's right," Nolan said, taking a step closer to me.

"Let's see the cash before anything," Jo said.

"Alright," Ethan said as he walked towards the kitchen. "That's fair."

We followed him with our eyes as we saw him go into a bottom pantry drawer and pull out a quintessential steel case. He then walked back into the living room, sat down on the couch, and set the steel briefcase on the coffee table. We continued to watch as Nolan took a seat in one of the single chairs and watched his brother. Ethan began to unbuckle the briefcase and lifted its lid.

"Want to look?" he asked.

Jo and I looked at one another, not saying anything, then approached him. As we did, he turned the case towards us. In it were several one-hundred-dollar bills. The briefcase was pretty much filled with money.

"You guys can count it if you like?" Nolan stated as he sat up.

"Yeah, for sure," Ethan said as he sat back. "Go ahead."

Jo and I looked at one another, nonverbally agreeing that counting the money was a good idea. So, we sat down on the couch and began to count.

Several minutes passed and eventually, we finished counting. And it was in fact, ten thousand dollars in the case.

"Alright," Ethan smiled, "all good?"

We looked at each other again.

"Yeah...yeah, all good," Jo said.

"Alright cool," Nolan said as he stood up and walked towards me.

He extended his hand out for me to take. I swallowed then did. I then saw Ethan grab Jo's hand and smiled at her as well.

Nolan began leading me down the hallway towards the back of the condo. Ethan and Jo followed. Nolan stopped at a door on the left side of the hallway and Ethan led Jo several feet further down the hallway towards another door on the right.

Jo and I's desperate and emotionless eyes met. Nolan then opened the door and led me in. At the same time, Ethan opened his door and led Jo into the room, forcing Jo and I to break contact.

Nolan closed the door behind him and turned on the light. He began to make small talk before he began kissing me, but truthfully, I didn't hear a word he said. Not a single word. My mind was too distracted by the emptiness that was taking over again. The same emptiness I felt with Campbell. The same distant, numb, emotionless, emptiness. And while I laid there, forcing myself to kiss him back, forcing myself to rub on his body, and forcing myself to seem like I enjoyed having sex with him, I felt those emotions slip inside my veins, seep into my bones, wrap around my neck, finally suffocating me. It was almost like I was back in Campbell's arms all over again.

Desperation truly is a fucking disease.

80

Chapter 80

It was a little after one when Nolan and I came out of our room simultaneously as Ethan and Jo came out of theirs. Jo and I immediately made contact and I could tell she felt just as worthless, self-pitying, numb, and broken as myself. We both looked down to the floor and the four of us made our way back into the living room with the fireplace.

"Well, here you guys go," Ethan said as he picked up the briefcase and handed it to Jo. "It was a great time."

She took it without changing her facial expression or saying anything.

"If you guys ever want to hang out again or something, we'd be down," Nolan said.

I looked at him blankly, "Alright, thanks," I said monotonously, knowing we would *never* return.

"Sure thing," he smiled.

The two called us a cab and after hugging them goodbye, stepped out into the hallway. Nolan closed the door behind us, and Jo and I walked towards the elevator. We got on, pushed the button labeled "L" for Lobby, and sighed.

"Are you okay?" Jo asked.

I stared off into the distance then looked at her and shrugged, "I'm mostly disgusted with myself more than anything, but I'll get over that. Are you okay?"

"I feel the same way," she said monotonously.

I looked back down to the floor.

The two of us rode the elevator the rest of the way in silence. We got off at the same lobby we entered from and exited outside. We sat down on the building's ledge and waited for our taxi to pull up out front.

"But you know, it's all over now," Jo said, looking up at me from the briefcase, trying to be optimistic like she always did.

I met her gaze, smiling ruefully, "Yeah, it is," I said. "It truly and really is."

81

Chapter 81

In the morning, January 1, 2014, I woke up around nine. I stretched and looked down, realizing I was still in my black dress and that what occurred last night—well, I guess this morning—was in fact, not a dream. I sighed and that split second of joy I had from when I woke up, you know the kind when for a minute you forget about all your worries and problems from the day before, vanished. I pushed off my covers, stood up, and made my way to the bathroom. Once inside, I peeled off that black dress that I hated so much and stood in the mirror in my bra and underwear. I began to stare at myself. I could feel it. The slip-under. The way it felt right before all the thoughts came. The way it felt to drown.

You're a fucking whore.

I bet you liked it. Did he fuck you better than me?

You're a dirty fucking bitch.

You're a fucking slut.

My eyes welled up with tears as my thoughts persecuted me.

Don't cry, you fucking whore.

Stop. Please just stop.

Breathe, Iris, breathe.

I love you, Sis.

Please don't whittle away.

Meeting my gaze in the mirror, tears cascading down my cheeks, I forced myself to speak, "You didn't have a choice, Iris. You didn't have a choice. You had to do it. You aren't dirty, and you aren't gross."

You're a dirty fucking bitch.

I pushed the tears off my cheek.

"You're strong."

You're a fucking slut.

"And you're brave."

You're a fucking whore.

"And you're beautiful."

I kept going, suffocating his words.

"You're kind to people and you care about them—"

I love you, Sis.

"You're perfect just the way you are."

I love you, Sis.

"You're not your thoughts or his words, Iris."

Breathe, Iris, breathe.

"You will not whittle me away."

82

Chapter 82

Life passed on and day by day, things got better. Mentally, physically, emotionally. They got better. It really was true; time would heal all. And that was something I will always believe in. Jo and I were able to buy real food, or "food-food" as Jo would say. We were able to stop worrying and stressing over how we would eat, and we began to stop judging and hating ourselves for what we did to get the money. Kalista was still nowhere to be found but things were only getting better and going back to normal. Except for one thing. There was one thing that was bothering me the entire week and a half that passed by. And it was that Colton didn't know about what we did. I felt, in a strange way, guilty. Maybe I just felt like I needed to get it off my chest to him, but I almost felt like I was hiding something. Whatever it *truly* was, I didn't like it and I was beginning to not be able to stand it.

"Hey," I said to Jo as I entered our room.

Jo was sitting on her bed reading a book.

"Hey," she smiled.

I took in a deep breath, then exhaled.

"Iris, what's wrong?" She could see my anxiety and nervousness.

"I need to tell Colton what we did," I said.

She looked at me slightly confused as she closed her book and turned towards me, "Why do you say that?"

"I don't know," I said. "I've just had this bad feeling all week. And it's like, I feel like, if I just tell him, it'll go away."

"Well, Iris, if you want to tell him, you can."

I looked at her.

"He's not going to be mad at you, Iris," Jo said. "He knows what it's like to be desperate and to struggle. He'll understand."

I plopped down next to her on her bed and scoffed, "I'm not sure he'll understand why his sixteen-year-old sister slept with a twenty-eight-year-old man for money."

"If he knows all the other things you tried before that, I think he will," Jo said.

I met her eyes.

"You shouldn't have to feel guilty, Iris. If you think telling him will make you feel better, then call him and tell him."

I paused for a moment.

"Could I call him now, with you?" I asked.

"Of course," Jo said genuinely as she moved her book aside, and sat up, directly next to me.

I took out my phone from my hoodie pocket and dialed his number. It rang twice then he picked up.

"Hey, Iris."

"Hey, Colton."

"What's up?" he asked.

"Uh, nothing," I said as I looked at Jo.

"No?" he asked.

"No, not really. Jo is here. She's on speaker phone."

"Hi," Jo said with a smile.

"Oh, hey, Jo," Colton said. "How are you?"

"I'm good, thanks. You?"

"I'm good, no complaints."

"Good," Jo smiled.

There was a beat of silence.

"So, what's up, Iris?" Colton asked again. "Everything okay?"

I looked at Jo, she nodded her head, motioning that I could do it.

"Colton," I sighed, "I have to tell you something."

"Yeah? What's up?" I could hear he sounded slightly concerned.

"I lied, okay?" I stated. "I lied. Jo and I *have* been struggling."

"What?" he asked in a confused tone. "Iris, what are you talking about?"

"When you asked if I had money for food when Kalista left. I said I did, but the truth, Colton, is that I didn't. *We* didn't. We had money and food at first, but we began to run out and we tried to stretch the little bit of money we had, but of course that only lasted so long. We tried to get a job, but nobody hired us, and then Jo got sick, so I went to the store and stole stuff for her, which started the cycle of us stealing, but then we got caught. So, we stole Kalista's jewelry and tried to pawn it, but we only got forty bucks for one stupid emerald. So, we decided to go hang out with these guys that said they'd pay us five grand each to hang out with them on New Year's Eve, but it turned out they meant they'd pay us to have sex with them, and so we did," I blurted out, finally take a gasp of air.

There was a moment of silence, I knew Colton was taken aback, trying to process what I just threw at him.

"Wait, wait, slow down," he said. "You two slept with someone for money?"

"It wasn't like a group thing," I said. "It was separate. We met them on Christmas. We were outside of this hotel and they came out and started talking to us. Little did we know, they owned the hotel and were super fucking rich. So, they offered us a ride home and we took it because it was really cold and late. Well, they took us home in this incredible Lamborghini and when we got back to Kalista's, that's when they offered us to hang out with them for five grand each. We weren't going to do it at first, but our desperation pushed us. We had run out of food, our fridge broke, and we had three dollars left. We had *no* idea that they meant we'd come over for sex, they *never* clarified that. But we figured we had no other choice. We had no food, no money, we were out of options, we had to do it. So, we did. And we got the ten-grand."

"Iris," Colton sounded defeated and heartbroken. "Why didn't you ask us for money?"

"You guys don't have any to give me," I said. "You guys are just now not having to deal with the struggles we typically do, I couldn't burden you all."

"Iris, we're a family, we'd figure it out. You know I'd do anything I can to prevent you guys from doing something like that. How could you do that?" he asked in a very sad tone.

"Desperation, Colton. Desperation," I said. "We tried so much hard before it got to this point."

"Why would nobody hire you?" he asked. "Where did you guys try?"

"Everywhere!" I exclaimed. "Nobody wanted us because we either didn't have the right identification documents or because we're in this program."

"Because you're in this program?" he asked in a confused tone. "How do they know that?"

"It pops up on our license," I said defeatedly.

"What? Does it really?" he asked, taken aback.

"Yup," I said.

"And what's their reasoning for not hiring you since you're in The

Stay program?"

"That they've hired people in the program before and it wasn't good," I answered.

"And you told them you guys weren't like that?" he asked.

"Yes, Colton! We practically begged everyone. We told them we'd do *anything,* but they still didn't want to hear it."

Colton sighed, "That's fucked up."

"I know. So, we tried," I said, looking down.

"And then you stole you said?" Colton asked.

I sighed, "Remember Jo got sick with food poisoning?"

"Yeah," he answered.

"I stole stuff for her, which led us to stealing food. We didn't have any bad intentions, Colton. We were fucking hungry."

"I know, Sis. I know," he said. "And then you got caught?"

"Yeah, so stealing was out of our options because clearly, we don't *really* want to go to jail."

"Uh, yeah," Colton said in an obvious tone.

"From there, we figured, Kalista isn't home, and her house is gorgeous, she must have some nice stuff for us to pawn. Well, she didn't. A bunch of JCPenney clothes and Burlington jewelry. She had one necklace that ended up having a real emerald in it. The guy gave us forty dollars for it, and we took a bus to Target to buy food. It was enough for probably a week but a couple days later our fridge broke, and all our cold stuff went bad. Leaving us with a box of cereal and two loaves of bread."

"That's awful, Iris," I Colton said. "I *wish* you would have told me what was going on."

"I didn't want to stress you out, Colton," I pleaded. "We figured, we'd go hang out with those guys and get the money. We didn't know they meant to have sex with them."

"And so you guys did?" he asked, not really wanting to hear me confirm the truth.

I paused slightly.

"Yeah," I said quietly.

Colton didn't say anything, but I heard him exhale.

"We didn't want to, Colton. We were desperate."

"I know," Colton said. I could tell he was upset but didn't want to make me feel worse than I already did.

There was a slight moment of silence.

"Are you mad?" I asked.

"No," he answered genuinely. "No, Iris, no. I'm not mad. I'm fucking heartbroken you guys did that when you didn't want to because you were struggling so bad. I just *wish* it didn't come to that and you came to me the minute you needed help."

"You know I've always had problems doing that," I said.

He scoffed, "Yeah, I know."

I looked at Jo then looked down. I felt my eyes fill up with tears and soon enough, one struck my shirt.

"I'm sorry," I said through a broken voice. "I just wanted to handle it on my own so that you guys wouldn't worry."

Jo put her arm around my shoulder and rubbed it.

"Iris, I'm not mad at you or upset," he said. "So, there's nothing to be sorry about. I know you guys were desperate. I know how that feels, trust me. It's just hard to hear your little sister fought so hard on her own to do the right thing to stay afloat, but it didn't matter in the end because you were forced to sell yourself. It's even harder to hear when you know I would have done *anything* to help you," he said sternly.

"I know," I said despairingly as I continued to look at the floor. "I want to try to let you help me more, it's just hard."

"I know," he said. "You've always been really independent. I remember when you were like five or six years old and wanted to play with sidewalk chalk, you would carry both big ass tubs of it by yourself. You would drag that shit through the house, outside, and onto the sidewalk and you wouldn't let *anybody* help you. Even if it did take you triple the time to get it outside than it would if someone helped," he chuckled lightheartedly.

I somewhat chuckled and brushed the tear from my cheek. Jo smiled. "Yeah, I remember that."

"The thing is, I've only ever wanted to help, and you've only ever wanted to do stuff alone. And it's great that you're so independent, I *never* want you to lose that. But…I also don't want it to be the death of you. It's okay to ask for help sometimes, Iris. You know, whatever it is, you can come to me. I'll *always* be there for you."

"I know," I smiled. "Thanks, Colton. I'll try to in the future."

"And even if you don't necessarily *need* my help, you can still just let me know what's going on, so, it doesn't have to get to an extreme point," Colton added.

"Alright, thank you," I said. "And thank you for not being mad."

"Iris," Colton sighed, "I wouldn't be mad at you. I told you, I'm just sad you guys had to do that. I told you, I'm trying to change that part of me."

I smiled, "And you are."

I knew Colton smiled at that.

"Thank, Sis, I love you."

"I love you more."

Jo smiled and squeezed me as she still had her arm around my shoulder. I hugged her back with a smile.

"So," Colton said moments later, "you guys *really* got the ten grand?"

We looked at one another and somewhat smiled, happy that our rollercoaster of a month was finally over.

"Yeah, we did," I smiled.

There was a beat of silence.

"So, Sis?" Colton said.

"Yeah?"

"If you guys now have ten grand, why don't you just come home?"

Jo and I looked at one another.

"Kalista isn't coming back, you two live eight minutes from one another now, you've got plenty of money, Mom, Leannah, and I, and I'm sure your dad, Jo, are all doing fine financially. Why don't you two just come back home to where it's safer and stop all of this?"

Jo and I looked at one another in deep thought, not having thought of that before.

"I mean, what are you guys gonna do? Sit around all day with ten grand in your room? What if someone steals it?"

"Well, we've been locking our door because our food already got stolen about a month ago," I said. Carter and Sebastian.

"Wait, your *food* got stolen and you think it's a good idea to have *ten grand* laying around in there?" Colton asked.

"Well, the people that stole our food were these two jerks that don't like us because I rejected the one," I said. "They knew we were hungry, that's why they did it…to be spiteful."

"If they are going to spite you over some food, they're going to spite you over ten grand. You can believe that," Colton said.

Jo and I didn't really say anything to Colton's comment because we knew he was right.

"Besides that, guys. It's not safe, especially when there's no host," Colton said. "Look, this program was really *never* safe, but it was more so a necessity. Now that we have some benefits, and you guys have five grand, what's the point in staying?"

Jo and I looked at each other again, unsure of what to say.

"Well," I began, "to get more benefits for you guys."

"Look, hear me out. Let's say you two never got the five grand, okay? You were in the program and Mom, Leannah, and I, and Jo's dad, were all getting benefits, right?"

"Right," we both said.

"So, now, in the situation we are in, you have the five grand, but no Stay program. It's a wash, it's basically the same," Colton said. "If you guys come home with five grand each and "take care of yourselves" it would be the same thing as the government cutting you guys out of our expenses. Either way, we wouldn't be paying for you guys, so it doesn't affect us directly. Do you see what I mean?" Colton asked.

"Yeah," we said. "We see."

"Not that we wouldn't take care of you, I'm just saying," Colton added. "And look, you guys earned that money. You do *whatever* you want with it. I'm just saying, if you're concerned with us not getting benefits if you come home, well, with you having that five grand, you would be able to "support" yourselves. It's the same thing."

Jo and I looked pensively at one another. We knew Colton was on to something and that everything he said made perfect sense.

"Okay, so let's say we want to do that then," I began, "come home that is. How are we going to get out of this program? Jo and I couldn't even find a phone number to call when Kalista left us the second time."

"Iris," Colton said, "it's always easier to get out of government help than it is to get into it or assistance with it. There's a way."

"Well, if you find it, let us know because we couldn't find anything," I said.

Colton didn't say anything as I knew he was Googling something.

"And what would I tell my dad if I left?" Jo asked. "I kinda can't tell him I slept with a man fifteen years older than me for money..."

"Yeah, true," I said.

"You could always tell him you won like a scratch off or something like that?" Colton suggested.

"Oh, yeah, that's a good idea," I said.

"Yeah, it is actually," Jo said as she thought about it.

There was another slight moment of silence, I knew Colton was still Googling around.

"I'll look around more," Colton said. "I know there's gotta be a number or something to unenroll you guys. Take some time to think about it, and in the meantime, I'll find something in case you guys want to...okay?"

"Yeah, alright," I said. "Thanks, Colton."

"Yeah, thank you," Jo said.

"Anytime, guys. I love you, Sis."

"Love you too."

We ended the call and my hand dropped into my lap.

"Do you really wanna leave?" I asked Jo.

Jo looked at me, then back down to the ground and sighed, "I mean, my dad *did* say I could come home after he started his new job and all. And since I have this five grand, I'd be fine until his new pay comes in and everything."

I nodded my head, knowing her plan was sound.

"Would *you* want to leave?" Jo then asked me.

"I mean," I began, "I wouldn't be opposed. Only because of the five grand, if I didn't have that, I'd say no—"

"Yeah, no, same," Jo added.

"And because our homes are so close now," I added.

Jo looked at me and smiled. I smiled back.

"But, since I *do* have the money, and we *are* so close to one another... maybe it's not a bad idea after all," I said. "I mean, like Colton said, what are we gonna do here? Sit around, guarding our money like watch dogs?"

"I mean, I think he's right," Jo said. "It's gonna get stolen here. I don't think it's safe."

"It's not, or we'll have to spend it all on food," I added. "It'll just be a waste."

"And you know what?" Jo said, bulking up her voice with confidence. "We had *sex* with those guys. We *should* be able to spend it on what *we* want. Not be once again forced to use it only on food. Like, I know when we go home, we will use it to support ourselves but not entirely."

"Yeah, right," I said. "*Exactly.*"

"So, I mean…if Colton can find a way to disenroll us, I'm fine with going home."

"I think I am too," I said. "Even though I never thought I'd say that."

"Well, things are just different now," Jo said.

"Better-different," I smiled.

I smiled back, "Better-different ."

Chapter 83

Around five p.m., we heard from Colton. He told us he found out how to disenroll us by emailing with this woman named Jennifer. She said all we had to do was call her and provide our birthdate and other information. Apparently, they don't give out their phone number anymore because too many guests were calling about irrelevant things, something like that anyway. Nevertheless, we called Jennifer and she was super nice. She said as long as we had transportation back home, she would disenroll us. Before we got off the phone with Colton, we settled on him picking Jo and me up about halfway in Pittsburgh. He wanted to come all the way out to Boston to get us, but I wouldn't let him. So, with that, we confirmed with Jennifer we wanted to disenroll, hung up, and booked a Greyhound Wednesday the fifteenth. And just like that, it was all over.

"We're going home!" Jo exclaimed as she hugged me.

I hugged her back, "Yes we are!" a huge smile grew onto my face.

"I did *not* think this was happening today," she said as she pulled away.

I chuckled, "I know right, I didn't think so either."

"This literally came out of nowhere," Jo said.

"Yeah, you can thank my brother for that one," I said jokingly.

"Yeah, I can," Jo laughed. "No, it's a good thing. I miss my dad and I'm dying to see my new house. I think it's a good thing we are."

"Yeah, it is for sure. I miss my mom too and my siblings, so I'm excited."

Jo smiled, "Well, I guess I gotta call my dad now."

"Oh, yeah," I said, "I guess you do."

"I'll call my family while you do that," I said as I stood up.

I went downstairs and took a seat on the couch and called Colton first, just to make sure Thursday worked for him, as we wouldn't arrive in Pittsburgh until early Thursday morning. He already told me any day or time he would make himself available, but still. As figured, it was fine, and he was more than thrilled I was coming home. My mom and sister then got on the phone.

"Hi, guys," I smiled.

"Hey, Sis!" Leannah gleamed.

"Hey, baby," my mom said.

"I have some good news," I smiled. "I'm coming home Wednesday!"

"Shut up," Leannah said.

"You're kidding," my mom added.

"I'm not," I smiled.

"Honey, that's amazing!" my mom gleamed.

"Oh my God!" Leannah squealed. "I'm so happy you're coming home! I miss you so much, Sis!"

I chuckled, "I miss you too!"

"Why are you coming home?" my mom asked.

"Uh," I didn't have anything planned to say, "uh, well Kalista isn't coming back, and Jo and I won five grand off a scratch off. So, we figure now is the perfect time. Especially with her new home being so close."

"Wait, wait, you guys won five grand *each* off of a scratch off?" my mom asked in shock.

"Yeah, wait what?" Leannah asked. "Colton, did you know about this?"

Colton chuckled, "Yeah, I did. It was a surprise."

I smiled. Colton always had my back. Through a lie or through a truth, he had it.

"You little—" I heard Leannah playfully hit him as they both laughed.

"What?!" he joked. "It was a *surprise.*"

We all laughed.

"Well, I can't *wait* for you to come home," my mom said.

"I can't wait either," I said. "I miss you all."

"We miss you more," Leannah said.

"So, I'll be picking her and Jo up from Pittsburgh Thursday morning," Colton said.

"Oh, okay," my mom said. "And how are you getting there, Iris? The bus?"

"Yeah, the bus."

"I want to come pick up Iris!" Leannah said.

"Noooo, you have school," Colton said.

"It's only one day," Leannah pleaded.

"Doesn't matter," my mom said. "You gotta go."

"Well, don't *you* have school too?" Leannah asked Colton.

"No, I have study halls on Thursday. And anyway, even if I did have school, I'd miss it to get her."

"Oh, yeah, that's right, you do have study hall. I know, I know, I just wanted to come too," Leannah said.

"It's all good, Le," I said. "The car's not that big and Jo and I will have a lot of stuff. There won't be a lot of room."

"Yeah, yeah, yeah," Leannah teased.

"And anyway, why would you want to spend seven hours in a car with *Colton?*"

Leannah laughed.

"Hey, hey, hey, I won't come get you!" he teased.

"I'll take the bus!" I teased back.

"Fine," Colton said.

"Fine," I said.

We all then laughed at ourselves.

"What am I gonna do when y'all three crazy kids are back together in my house?!" my mom said.

"I don't know, Leannah and Iris seem to be the problem," Colton said.

Leannah scoffed playfully, "Says the *king* of trouble."

"Me? Never."

We all laughed some more.

"Well, I'll let you all go. I'm gonna eat some dinner and begin to pack. I'll see you all Thursday!"

"Alright, I'll see you, baby!" my mom said. "I love you."

"I love you too."

"I love you, Sis. I can't wait to see you!" Leannah said.

"Neither can I," I added with a smile. "And I love you too."

"I'll text you, Sis," Colton said. "Don't forget to send me the Pittsburgh bus station address."

"I won't, I'll do that right now."

"Alright, good. I love you."

"I love you too, bye guys."

"Bye," they all said.

I hung up, smiled, and exhaled. It truly was all over.

84

Chapter 84

It was now Wednesday the fifteenth and I woke to the sound of my alarm blaring at four a.m. Jo and I spent all yesterday packing and getting our things ready to leave. I opened my eyes, looked up at the ceiling, and smiled. It was a kind of smile I hadn't used in a very long time. Maybe not even at all while I was away. But that morning, that January fifteenth, *cold*, Wednesday morning, I used a smile I had missed for quite some time. It was over, it was all over. I was going to see my family again, my best friend was living less than a ten-minute walk away, I was escaping this program, there were so many things that allowed that smile onto my face. And I appreciated every, single, one of them.

"Today's the day," Jo said with a huge grin on her face as she looked over at me from her bed.

I smiled even bigger and pushed the covers off me, "I know, I can't believe it."

"Same, neither can I. I didn't think I'd be seeing this day for a *long* time."

"A *very* long time," I added.

Jo got out of bed and began stripping it, "It's crazy how fast things can change."

"I know right," I said as I got up and began to undress the pillows. "Either in a good way or a bad way."

"At least we got lucky this time and it changed in a good way," Jo said lightheartedly.

I chuckled, "Yeah seriously."

We kept taking the covers off the bed and once that was done, we gathered up the rest of our things that we couldn't pack before. Just little things like our makeup, toothbrushes, hairbrushes, phone chargers, the last minute stuff.

While doing so, I came across my black dress bundled up in the corner of the room. I picked it up and looked at it for a moment as I thought about how that dress really only ever brought trouble. In Steilacoom, in New Haven, and here in Boston, that dress only ever caused issues. I looked at it and thought about carrying Melanie's practically lifeless body down the stairs as well as Bianca's. I thought about Nate's mutilated face and how the image of it will *never* leave my mind. I thought about Nolan taking it off me and how he tossed it on the floor. I looked at it and only felt disgusted. True and utter disgust. I never knew it was possible to feel such hate for an inanimate object.

"I don't think I'll be taking this back home with me," I said as I balled it up and tossed it in the trash can.

"Yeah, that reminds me,"—she walked over to her vanity and picked up the neatly folded dress—"I don't want mine either. Do you want it back?" she held it out to me.

"Not one bit," I said emotionlessly.

Jo then balled up her dress as well and threw it in the trash, "You won't be missed," she said as she stared into the can.

I stared down at the dresses in the can as well, "Not at all. Not at fucking all."

It was around four forty-five a.m. when we were completely done packing and stood in the middle of our enormous room, one final time.

"So, this is it," I said as we looked around. "This is the last time we'll stand in this room."

"Or *any* room in this program that is," Jo said.

"*Any*, that's right," I looked at her and smiled.

We looked apart and continued looking around the room.

"No more shitty hosts to leave us to fend for ourselves," I said.

"Or people who won't hire us because we're in this program," Jo added.

"Or will bitch at us because we don't have—"

"'Documentation from list B and C,'" we simultaneously mocked.

We both laughed, shaking our heads, and rolling our eyes playfully.

"Yeah, this place won't be missed," Jo said.

"Or the people in it," I said.

"Yeah, *definitely* not," Jo said.

There was a slight pause.

"Well, I'm ready if you are," I said.

"I'm ready," Jo smiled.

I smiled back and extended the handle on my suitcase. Jo did the same and the two of us walked out of room twelve. We made our way downstairs quietly as everyone was still asleep. I don't think we *really* cared about waking anyone up, but we were still quiet. We hadn't told anybody that we were leaving. Why should've we? No one in that house was our friend. And frankly, I don't think anyone would even realize or care that we were gone.

We walked out of that mansion one last time, not looking back.

Jo looked at me and smiled as we got onto the sidewalk from the cobblestone driveway. I looked at her, smiled, and threw my arm around her, squeezing her. She squeezed me back and the two of us walked blissfully down Miller Street in the pitch-black darkness to the bus station. *Nothing* could have made me happier.

85

Chapter 85

Our Greyhound pulled up at exactly five-fifty. There were several people that waited in line for the bus with us and as soon as it pulled up, we all boarded one by one and found seats. Jo and I found two empty seats in the middle of the bus. We loaded our luggage then took a seat. We watched as about twenty-five to thirty people filled the bus, taking in all the new faces that we would be sitting with for the next thirteen hours. At exactly six a.m., the Black bus driver stood up and spoke.

"Good morning, ladies and gentlemen. My name is Douglas, I'll be your Greyhound driver from Boston, Massachusetts to Pittsburgh, Pennsylvania. I ask everyone to stay seated while the bus is moving unless you are making your way to the bathroom which is located at the far end of the bus. There are two, one on either side. We will be stopping at the Port Authority Bus Terminal in Manhattan, New York, in approximately four hours and thirty minutes. The Port Authority Bus Terminal is located about twenty minutes north of the World Trade Center—"

I glanced over at Jo. I saw she was looking at the bus driver, listening to him, with a slight smile. I could tell her smile was a bittersweet one.

"Alright? Everybody ready to go?" Douglas asked. I had missed the end of his speech.

Everyone said they were and Douglas sat back down, put the bus in drive, and pulled off.

Jo sat back and exhaled a sigh of relief. She had a smile on her face.

I smiled at her and rested my head as well, "We're going home."

Jo looked at me, still with the smile on her face, "I can't wait to see my new place."

"I know, I can't either!" I exclaimed.

"You're gonna have to help me pick out a few decorations for my room, you know that right?" Jo asked.

"Duh, who else would?"

"Well definitely not my dad," Jo joked. "He has *no* decoration skills."

I laughed.

"I'm serious," Jo chuckled. "Our blinds broke once so he took them down and hung up an old bed sheet."

"What?" I laughed as it was ridiculous. "No way."

"Honest to God!" Jo said.

"Damn, that's pretty bad. And I thought *my* mom was tacky for putting tin foil on the windows in the summer to keep the heat out."

"Oh, my dad does that too," Jo joked nonchalantly.

"No way."

"Yes," she began to laugh. "It must be an Illinois thing."

"No, try a crazy parent thing," I laughed.

"Or that," she laughed.

The two of us continued laughing. With our spirits being so high and moods being so great, we made it to New York in what felt like only an hour. When in reality, it actually took us the entire four and a half hours. It was a little after ten-thirty when Douglas put the bus into park and stood up.

"Alright, everybody," Douglas said, "we're here at the Port Authority. We'll be here for an hour. The bus will leave with or without you at exactly eleven forty-five. I don't care what you do in the meantime, but don't be late. Y'all can leave you stuff too; I'll be locking the doors."

Everyone stood up and began filing off the bus. Jo and I eventually got off and stepped onto eighth street. It was *bustling*. Taxis and cars were flying by, the sound of vehicle's horns filled our ears, people pushed by us, colorful billboards decorated the sky, and skyscraper buildings enclosed us and touched the heavens. It was honestly invigorating. I had never been to New York City, and I was fascinated. I looked over at Jo with excitement, but she was doing something on her phone.

"It's incredible here!" I exclaimed.

Jo looked up at me and chuckled, "It is pretty cool, isn't it?"

"For sure! It's a lot different from Chicago. I mean, Chicago is busy but, I don't know, this feels different."

Jo smiled, "It has that kind of effect."

She then took a slight pause. "I haven't been here in forever," she said as she looked up and around.

"When was the last time?" I asked.

"When my mom died," she said.

My face fell into a surprised expression. I had no idea she hadn't been back since her mom passed.

"What? Really?" I asked. "You and your dad haven't come to see the World Trade Center or anything like that?"

Jo shook her head, "No, we haven't had the money to travel out here."

I nodded my head, understanding, but feeling sorry for her. There was then a slight pause.

"Hey, but we're only a twenty-five-minute ride from there...could we go?"

I turned and looked at Jo as I had been watching the cars blaze by, "Of course," I said with conviction. "I'd love to."

Jo smiled but I knew she felt sadness inside.

I offered to pay for the taxi as it felt like it was the least I could do. We hailed an orange taxicab and climbed in. Soon enough, he dropped us off on Greenwich Street right out in front of the two pools. We stood on the sidewalk and looked out at the wide-open space in front of us. It was gorgeous in the same way it was eerie. I looked over at Jo who was looking out at the pools with a smile on her face. This made me smile too.

"Come on," I said blissfully as I grabbed her arm and headed towards the pools.

We walked towards the memorial and within seconds were met with two *huge* square holes in the ground that had smaller square holes inside of them. The border of the squares had all the names of the victims engraved on them. From these borders, water poured out and down like a waterfall into the abysses. Like before, it was gorgeous, but in the darkest, saddest way.

"How will I be able to find my mom's name?" Jo asked. "There were like three thousand people that died."

"Uh," I said as I looked around.

"Well, I guess I could try Google," Jo said.

"Oh, yeah, they know everything," I said lightheartedly.

Jo somewhat chuckled as she began typing away on her phone.

"Okay, here we go. Names dot Nine-Eleven memorial dot com," Jo said as she read from her phone.

I looked over her shoulder and read with her.

"She was in the south tower so it says her name would be on the south pool," Jo said.

"Alright, that makes sense," I said.

Jo clicked on *Find a Name* on the memorial tab. This led her to a search box to which Jo typed in her mom's name; Savannah Isabel Mulvoy. This brought up her panel number, a map of where her name was exactly on the pool, her birth date, and a little bit more of other information.

Jo scrolled down and was met with a photo of her mom. I saw Jo's eyes light up. Her mom was *beautiful*. She had shoulder length blonde hair and blue eyes, just like Jo. Her mom also had freckles and wore a big, bright, happy smile.

I watched Jo stare at the photo as tears welled up in her eyes. She was smiling but it was a painful smile. I couldn't lie, I was emotional too. My eyes filled with tears, but I forced them down. To know the sadness she felt, and the desperation to just have her mom here, even though she *never* could, tore me apart.

I put my arm around her and hugged her.

She chuckled at herself when I did this to keep from getting emotional. As she did, a tear fell off her cheek and struck her phone.

I rubbed her arm and leaned my head on her shoulder. After a moment, I wiped the teardrop off her phone and scrolled back up the screen to see where her mom's name was engraved.

"It says she's on panel S twenty-one. You want to go find her?" I asked gently.

Jo let go from our hug and wiped her eyes, "Yeah, let's go."

The two of us began walking around the pool as we were already at the south one. We walked around the entire square and eventually found panel S twenty-one. It faced Liberty Street. From here, we looked for Jo's mom's name and eventually we saw it. Engraved on the pool's border read, *Savannah Isabel Mulvoy*.

Jo ran her fingers over her mom's name as she stared down at it. I could see the tears fill back up into her eyes.

I put my arm around her shoulder once again as I looked down at

Ms. Mulvoy's name.

"I finally made it, Mom," Jo said with a smile. A beat later, she spoke, now sounding sad, "I love you, Mom…And I miss you." I could hear her getting choked up. "And I wish you were here. I always do."

I rubbed Jo's arm, "It's nice to finally meet you, Ms. Mulvoy."

Jo looked at me and smiled.

"Jo has been the greatest friend I could ever ask for. I know you're proud of her."

Jo smiled and hugged me back, "Iris has been the greatest friend too, Mom. I'd think you'd be happy I finally found one," she slightly chuckled.

I chuckled as well.

"But I'm glad I got to finally come here," Jo said as she still looked down at her mom's name. "I wish dad could too, but I know one day he'll be able to."

I smiled a bittersweet smile.

"I hope you're watching over me and thinking I'm making the right decisions in life," she added. "I know I don't always do, but I try. I know if you were here, I would have made better ones," Jo said, I could see she was getting emotional again.

"I just wish you could have been here to help. I just wish you were there. I wish you were there for my first day of middle school, and I wish you were there for my first day of high school. I wish you were there for all the times I was let down by people and the guys that stood me up. I wish you were there when Dad was falling apart because you weren't around, I wish you were there for me after what happened with Ian. I wish you were there to stop me from drowning myself in Tylenol and alcohol because I *know* you would have. I wish you were there to help me through everything that has happened in this program—if I even would've been in this program if you were still alive…I doubt it. I just wish you were here. Every day, every night. I wish you were here. For me, for dad…I-I-I don't know—" Jo shook her head as tears ran down her face.

I squeezed Jo tighter. I fought my emotions and swallowed them.

"I just miss you, Mom," Jo said. "I really, really do. You didn't deserve this. Dad didn't deserve this. *I* didn't deserve this. None of the people on these panels or their family and friends deserved this…I think about what life would've been like with you here. I think about it a lot actually. I know, maybe I shouldn't because nothing will bring you back, even though I'd trade anything in this entire world for it to. I think about how different my life would have been if you were here for it. I think about all the things you missed out on because your life was taken from you too soon. I think about it all, maybe more than I should. Well, I *know* more than I should. But I can't help it."

Another tear rolled down Jo's cheek.

"Dad tells me that I'm just like you," she smiled as she wiped her tears away. "He said that I'm outgoing and bubbly like you. He said that I've always been positive and that I have this way of seeing the good in every situation like you did."

Jo then half chuckled, half scoffed, "I wish I could do that in this situation…but it seems impossible. I wish I got more time with you, Mom," Jo squeezed her eyebrows together to keep from crying harder. "I wish I got to see for myself how I'm just like you. I wish I had more time to hear your laugh, to see your smile, to hear your voice. I wish I got more hugs and kisses, more *I love you's.* I wish I got to hear all your advice…I definitely needed it, especially now. There's just so many things I wish I could have, but I can't, and I never will."

Jo tried to hold it together, but tears fell from her eyes, striking her jacket as she began to lightly cry.

I squeezed her, rested my head on her shoulder, and rubbed her arm, "I love you, Jo."

After a moment she responded. "I love you too, Iris," she said as she pulled away and forced a smile at me.

I smiled at her as she wiped her eyes. She then turned back towards the pool and looked out into the huge waterfall. There was a long moment of silence. For several minutes, Jo and I just looked out at the beautiful chaos.

After some time, Jo exhaled and looked back down at her mom's name. She touched the words and traced her fingers around them.

"I miss you, Mom. I wish things were different. I would do anything to make them different, but I can't."

A tear rolled down Jo's cheek, but she ignored it as she stayed fixated on the words.

"So, until we meet again, watch over me, okay? Watch over Dad, Iris, and her family too. Guide me in all the ways you would if you were here, because I need it. I need you, Mom."

A tear now escaped from my left eye and ran down my cheek.

"I miss you when I close my eyes, and I miss you when I open them again," Jo said, fighting back her emotions. "And I always will…I'll see you when I see you, Mom. I love you, more than anything, always."

Tears ran from both of Jo's eyes as she kissed her three fingers and touched her mom's name.

"Thank you for giving me life, even if you can't have the one that you so desperately deserved. I'm forever grateful," she said then took her hand away.

Another tear rolled down my cheek.

"I'll see you later, Ms. Mulvoy," I said with my fingers on her name. "It was an honor."

I took my fingers off her name and Jo turned towards me. She latched onto me and began to silently cry. I held onto her tightly. I held her the same way she held me when I told her about Campbell; sympathetically, genuinely, caringly, and compassionately. A way most people *never* did…or could.

We stood in front of panel S twenty-one for about two minutes just embracing. I couldn't imagine the pain Jo felt. And I *never* wanted to.

"Thank you for coming here with me," Jo said as she pulled away and wiped her eyes.

"Of course, Jo. There's no place I'd rather be," I smiled gently.

Smiled softly at me as well. She then pulled out her phone, took a picture of her mom's engraving, and touched it one last time.

"I guess we should get back to the bus, we don't want to miss it," she said softly as she put her phone back into her bag.

"Yeah, that wouldn't be good…come on," I said as I put my arm around her shoulder.

We began to walk towards Liberty Street but as we did, Jo glanced back. We paused and I looked at her. She was looking at where her mom's name was. She smiled a melancholic smile then looked back towards the street, continuing our walk. I looked at her and rubbed her arm. She swung her arm around my shoulder and the two of us walked towards the street filled with bittersweetness, heartache, and peace. A true beautiful disaster.

86

Chapter 86

We got back onto the bus and settled at exactly eleven forty: five minutes before the bus was set to leave. Jo sat back down in the window seat, and I sat in my aisle seat. She rested her head against the glass and just stayed quiet to herself while everyone boarded the bus and stored their luggage. I wanted to say or do something, but there was nothing I could do. Sure, I could give her all the hugs and encouraging, comforting words in the world, but it wasn't what she wanted. She wanted what I couldn't give her, no one could. She wanted her mom. And that was the worst kind of pain. That kind of pain when you see someone you love and care about, sad, in distress, and broken and you can't do anything to make it right. *That* was the worst pain one could feel…at least to me.

So, I did the only thing I could. I curled up beside her, rested my head on her arm, and closed my eyes. I know it didn't take away all the pain, not even close. But, if it could take away some, even just the smallest amount, absorb it like she did mine, then I was okay.

I felt the bus pull away minutes later and began to travel down the road. I must have been tied, or emotionally drained, or maybe even both, because I woke up almost four hours later around three-thirty.

I opened my eyes and sat up as I came back to my senses. As I did this, Jo opened her eyes and sat up too.

"Did you fall asleep too?" I asked.

"I guess so," Jo said.

I laughed, "You have an imprint on your face from the window frame."

Jo chuckled as she took out her phone and used the reflection of the black screen to look at herself.

She laughed again, shaking her head, "Oh my God,"

I chuckled, "That means you slept good."

"Well, I did, so you must be right," she joked.

I laughed and shook my head.

"Where are we?" Jo asked as she looked outside.

"No clue," I said.

"Harrisburg," a man, about sixty years old said. He sat in the seat directly over the aisle next to me.

"Where's that?" Jo asked in a confused tone. "Is that in Pennsylvania?"

"Yeah, we're about halfway there," the man replied.

"Oh, okay, thank you," Jo said.

He nodded his head and went back to doing his crossword puzzle. I turned back towards Jo and saw her unlocking her phone and going to her photo gallery. She clicked on the picture she took of her mom's name and began to stare at it.

"Your mom was gorgeous," I said.

Jo looked up at me, smiled, then looked back down.

"Thank you…everyone says that," she chuckled.

"Because it's true."

Jo smiled at me, and I smiled back.

"I could see a lot of you in her too," I said.

Jo locked her phone, "Everyone says that also," she laughed.

I chuckled, "Well, I'm sure you love hearing it."

"I do," she smiled. "It's one of my favorite compliments."

I smiled then thought to myself. "I think it'd be my biggest *insult* if someone said I was just like my dad."

Jo chuckled, "From how you've described him, I'd say so too."

"Yeah, I wouldn't ever want to hear that."

Jo looked at me pensively, "Who *would* you want to be told you remind them of in your family?"

I thought for a moment, "Definitely Colton. He has a good heart, and he always means well. He's not afraid to take a punch or two if it means sticking up for someone he loves or protecting them. He'll do anything for you, and he can keep a secret like no other."

Jo smiled at me.

"He knows how to make people feel better and just what to say when you're feeling down. He's always had his priorities straight and he's the most loyal person I know. He's strong and insightful and deep"—I smiled to myself as I thought about him—"Yeah, Colton. I'd like people to think I remind them of him."

"You know, I think you just described yourself," Jo said genuinely.

I met her eyes, "Thanks, Jo." Her comment meant more to me than she knew.

She smiled back, "You're welcome."

"Well, in about four hours you'll get to meet him and *truly* decide for yourself," I said, making the mood lighthearted.

"I know, I can't wait!" she exclaimed. "We're so close."

I leaned my head back on the seat. I felt true and pure bliss. "I know."

Time went on and Jo and I continued talking about any and everything. We talked about our families, past stories, things we saw out the window on the highway, people in the program, we talked about it all. We talked about deep things, sad things, happy things, and funny things. We learned even more about one another and the more we did, the more truly and eternally grateful I was to have her in my life.

87

Chapter 87

The moment we had been waiting for, was finally here. We arrived at the bus station in Pittsburgh around eight p.m. Jo and I anxiously waited for people to clear out of the bus's aisle so that we could get our luggage down and exit. Soon enough, however, we did, and after making our way through the bus station, we stepped out onto the sidewalk on the corner of Franklin Avenue and East Monroe Street.

"We're finally here!" Jo smiled as she looked around.

"Thirteen hours later and we made it!"

"Right?" Jo laughed.

"Let me call Colton to see when he'll be here and where he wants to meet," I said as I dug around in my purse for my phone.

"Alright, cool," Jo said. "I'll text my dad and let him know we're here too."

"Good idea," I said as I found my phone and pulled it out of my bag.

Jo began to text, and I began to call Colton.

"Hey, Sis!" he exclaimed. "I'm about ten minutes away. "Are you there yet?"

"Oh shit, you're that close?" I asked, surprised.

"Hell yeah," he said playfully. "Not gonna have y'all waiting for me."

I laughed, "Thanks. But yeah, we're here. We just exited the bus station. Uh, there's not really anywhere to park here," I said as I looked around. "There's a parking lot across the street we could walk to?"

"Yeah, that would be good," he said.

"Okay, cool."

"See you in a few, love you," he said.

"Love you too," I said then hung up the phone.

I told Jo and the two of us crossed the street, continuing down Franklin Avenue to the entrance of the parking lot. Within another minute, we entered, parked out suitcases, and sat down on the curb.

"So, this is gonna be weird not living together," Jo said. "That's all we've ever known."

I thought to myself about how she was right, "Yeah, that's true. I guess we only ever *have* lived together."

"See?"

"Well, at least we know we can because most people can't live with their friends," I said lightheartedly.

"That's true. Yeah, at least we know we won't rip one another's heads off if we have to stay together."

I laughed, "I don't know, you might get on my nerves at some point," I teased.

Jo looked at me with a playful, offended face and scoffed, "Well, I could say the same for you."

"Oh, could you?"

"Hell yeah."

I shook my head playfully and chuckled as did Jo.

"No, but for real, thank you," I said a moment later, being serious. "You've been a really great friend to me."

Jo smiled, "You have been too."

"Thanks but, I mean like, with everything with Campbell…you really helped me with that."

Jo looked at me, "Of course. I know what it's like. I didn't want you to feel alone like I did."

I smiled then looked down at my sneakers. "I really appreciate it, Jo," I looked back at her. "I wouldn't be where I am without you."

Jo smiled, put her arm around me, and leaned her head on my shoulder, "You're welcome, Iris. I love you."

I smiled and leaned my head on hers, "I love you too."

Just then, I saw a black Honda come out from under the bridge and turn into the parking lot. Jo and I ended our embrace, and my eyes lit up when I realized it was Colton.

"Colton!" I yelled. I jumped up from the curb and ran towards the car. Colton flung the driver's door open and came running towards me. I jumped into his arms, holding him tight as he swung me around.

"I missed you so much," I said as we embraced.

"I missed you more!" he said.

When he set me down and we pulled apart, Jo appeared next to us.

"It's so great to meet you!" Colton exclaimed, pulling Jo in for a hug.

"You too!" she gleamed.

"You guys ready to go?" he asked as he pulled away. "Long way back to Chicago!"

Our eyes widened as we were *fully* aware of this.

"Oh, yeah, we're ready," I said, nodding my head.

Jo smiled.

"Alright, you guys get in, I'll grab your bags," Colton said as he jogged to where we abandoned our luggage.

"You sure?" Jo asked.

"Yeah, no worries. I got it," he said as he grabbed my suitcase.

"Thank you," Jo said, then opened the back seat door.

I climbed into the passenger seat and smiled ever wider.

"I missed this car," I said as I looked around. "You see that stain?" I asked Jo as I pointed at a reddish stain on the back of the driver's seat.

"Yeah?" Jo chuckled.

Colton was learning how to drive, and I was in the backseat with an open bottle of fruit punch. He took a turn too fast and I jolted. Well, when I did, the drink came out of my hands and poured *all* over the seat.

Jo put her hand to her mouth.

"My mom was *pissssedddddd*" I said, drawn out for emphasis.

"Oh my God, I bet," Jo said.

"She had just gotten the car too," I said.

"That sucks," Jo said with a crinkled nose. "Did you get in trouble?"

"Well, she yelled at me and then had me clean it. Nothing crazy but yeah, she was pissed."

"Who was?" Colton asked as he got into the car.

"Mom when I spilled the fruit punch on her seat."

Colton laughed, "Oh yeah, she was really heated."

Jo laughed as she shook her head from left to right.

"How about the time you and Leannah were messing around in the back seat, and you made mom back into that pole?" Colton asked.

"Iris!" Jo exclaimed through a chuckle.

"Hey!" I said with my hands up, "In my defense, Mom is a terrible driver."

They both laughed.

"That's true, she is," Colton said.

"That's too funny," Jo said.

"I'm pretty sure *you* have made her a better driver than *she's* made you," I said to Colton.

"I think you might be right on that one," he said.

We all chuckled.

"Alright, well do you guys wanna stop anywhere to get something to eat or drink? Use the bathroom before we head back?" Colton asked.

I shook my head then looked at Jo, "I'm good unless you want to."

"No, I'm good too," she said.

"Alright cool, then Chicago it is," he said as he clicked the start button on his phone's GPS.

He put the car in drive, turned around in the empty parking lot, and headed back the way he came.

We all continued talking and Colton and Jo got to know one another more. Somehow, in a way I don't even know, the conversation landed on when a fire hydrant broke in front of our home in 2007. Colton was twelve, I was ten, and Leannah was eight. Everyone's little, tiny yards were getting flooded, and the street was drowning. Neighbors came outside on their stoops and porches, cursing and screaming up a storm about how mad they were, and how everything was getting messed up. Well, Colton, Leannah, and I were outside when it happened. It didn't take long for our small yard to turn into a mud pit, and it didn't take long for the three of us to roll around in it like pigs. We created all *kinds* of crazy games and ways to have fun in that mud. We held onto the metal chain link fence that bordered our property and skated around in it. We hung off the big tree in the front yard and splashed into it. We even had a huge, huge mud fight. We caused a gigantic mess, but we had the best time doing it.

"And I'm swinging from the tree yelling, 'Iris, catch me!'" Colton laughed uncontrollably as he told the story.

Jo and I laughed hard as well.

"Well, clearly, she can't catch me," Colton laughed at himself. "I fall and she moves out of the way, and I splash up so much mud"—Colton began to laugh harder—"that little Leannah got *covered* head to toe, drenched."

We all laughed and laughed as Colton and I recounted the memories from that day.

"I'm pretty sure *she* was the one that started the mud fight!" I exclaimed as I dried my eyes from laughing so hard.

"She was!" Colton exclaimed.

"Wait, *eight*-year-old Leannah started the mud fight?!" Jo asked in disbelief through a laugh.

"Yes," I laughed. "She got up with this sour look on her face, scooped as much mud up as she could with both her tiny hands, raised them over her shoulder, and launched it at Colton."

"Oh my God!" Jo laughed.

"It hit me right in the gut too! That kid had a mean throw," he laughed.

I kept on laughing as well, "Then you threw some back at her and I threw some at you."

"So, you teamed up on him," Jo instigated.

"That's right you did! You little rat," he nudged me playfully.

We all laughed and carried on. I watched as Jo and Colton laughed with one another like they had known each other for *years*. I smiled and a true sense of bliss, joy, and peace filled inside of me, there to stay. I leaned my head back on the seat and smiled as I looked out the window into the dark Ohio sky.

My name is Iris Dallas Cooke and no, I haven't had the most glamourous life. I don't live in a multi-million-dollar mansion or own a Lamborghini. I don't understand stocks that will lead me to wealth, and I definitely don't own a hotel or know the first thing about doing so. I don't live in the suburbs with a picket white fence or have neighbors like Susan. My family has always struggled with money, and I've known nothing other than the low-income class. I live in a terrible area in Chicago in a house that is held together by the pressure of life's struggles. I don't have a dad, and never have. My mom's struggled with addiction my whole life. I've witnessed and dealt with things no one my age, or, maybe even in general, should have. And because of all this, I had to go into a government program that mostly caused turmoil in my life. So no, I haven't had the newest iPhone or the nicest clothes, I haven't gone to the best schools, and I haven't had the luxury of buying things I wanted "just because." But, if I don't have any of that, or anything else, I do have one thing. And that's my family. I have a mom that got herself clean for my siblings and I, and has been the best mom since, I have a brother that would do *anything* for his loved ones at *any* time of the day, and I have a sister that looks at life through rose-colored glasses and I pray to *God* she never loses that. And I have Jo. The truest, greatest, most genuine friend I could *ever* ask for. So, no, I don't have a house with a cared for lawn or a car that's free from interior stains and body damage. But…thousands of people have that stuff. I have what all those people don't, my family. My small, little family and I wouldn't trade them for *anything* in this entire world.

Acknowledgment

There are many people I'd like to thank who helped me along not only this journey but in life.

I'd like to thank my mom who has never stopped encouraging me to publish this. Mom, you have been my best friend and rock my entire life and I wouldn't be the person I am today without you.

I'd like to thank my talented brother, Chris, for designing the cover. I couldn't have brought my vision to life without you!

I'd like to thank my boyfriend, Jakob. There are many words in the English language, but still not enough to convey my feelings for you. So, thank you for being you and the greatest man I know.

I'd also like to thank my three best friends, Bridgette, Ashley, and Alexa, who have stayed by my side even after I gave them a 700 page version of *The Stay.* Sorry!

Bridgette, for being someone I could count on no matter what and the kindest soul I know, thank you.

Ashley, for being the only one I shared my short-stories with as kids and the best advice giver, thank you.

Alexa, a future sister-in-law, for all your love and support when I didn't deserve it, thank you.

And to the readers who have made it this far, thank you. This is nothing without you.

Resources

If you or a loved one are struggling, please reach out. There is always help and someone who understands.
RAINN National Sexual Assault Hotline - 1-800-656-4673
National Domestic Violence Hotline - 1-800-799-7233
SAMHSA - Substance Abuse and Mental Health Services
Administration - 1-800-662-4357
Suicide & Crisis Lifeline - 988

About the Author

Carly Rifon is a twenty-four-year old writer, reader, and cat lover. Carly received a Bachelor's Degree in Criminal Justice at Wilmington University in 2022. She currently resides in Delaware, where she was born and raised. This is her first novel.